INTRIGUE

Seek thrills. Solve crimes. Justice served.

Innocent Witness
Julie Anne Lindsey

Shadow Survivors
Julie Miller

MILLS & BOON

INNOCENT WITNESS
© 2024 by Julie Anne Lindsey
Philippine Copyright 2024
Australian Copyright 2024
New Zealand Copyright 2024

First Published 2024
First Australian Paperback Edition 2024
ISBN 978 1 038 90765 3

SHADOW SURVIVORS
© 2024 by Julie Miller
Philippine Copyright 2024
Australian Copyright 2024
New Zealand Copyright 2024

First Published 2024
First Australian Paperback Edition 2024
ISBN 978 1 038 90765 3

MIX
Paper | Supporting
responsible forestry
FSC® C001695

Published by
Harlequin Mills & Boon
An imprint of Harlequin Enterprises (Australia) Pty Limited
(ABN 47 001 180 918), a subsidiary of HarperCollins
Publishers Australia Pty Limited
(ABN 36 009 913 517)
Level 19, 201 Elizabeth Street
SYDNEY NSW 2000 AUSTRALIA

Cover art used by arrangement with Harlequin Books S.A.. All rights reserved.

Printed and bound in Australia by McPherson's Printing Group

Innocent Witness

Julie Anne Lindsey

MILLS & BOON

Julie Anne Lindsey is an obsessive reader who was once torn between the love of her two favorite genres: toe-curling romance and chew-your-nails suspense. Now she gets to write both for Harlequin Intrigue. When she's not creating new worlds, Julie can be found carpooling her three kids around northeastern Ohio and plotting with her shamelessly enabling friends. Winner of the Daphne du Maurier Award for Excellence in Mystery/Suspense, Julie is a member of International Thriller Writers, Romance Writers of America and Sisters in Crime. Learn more about Julie and her books at julieannelindsey.com.

Visit the Author Profile page
at millsandboon.com.au.

CAST OF CHARACTERS

Hayley Campbell—A Marshal's Bluff, North Carolina, social worker, formerly in love with Finn Beaumont, now in search of a missing teen.

Finn Beaumont—A Marshal's Bluff detective investigating the death of a local philanthropist. Still in love with his ex, Hayley Campbell, he'll stop at nothing to protect her, return the teen to safety and bring a killer into custody.

Dean Beaumont—A private investigator and brother to Finn, working hard to assist local law enforcement in locating the missing teen and arresting a killer.

Gage Myers—New to the foster care system following the untimely death of his parents, he's become an unintentional witness to a high-profile murder and is currently on the run.

Katherine Everett—A local philanthropist with a community center and homeless shelter project in development.

Chip Everett—Katherine's widower, who stands to inherit the empire, is a prime suspect in her death.

Chapter One

Hayley Campbell settled onto the bench at her usual picnic table and unpacked her lunch. The small park, nestled between the public library and social-services department, was her private oasis from 11:00 a.m. to noon, every Monday through Friday. The cooler of sandwiches and drinks at her side was a personal offering to anyone in need.

For Hayley, becoming a social worker had felt more like a calling than a choice, and she couldn't imagine doing anything else. Though at twenty-four, she still looked more like the average high schooler than a legitimate representative of the county. Occasionally, judges, lawyers and local law-enforcement officials tried to overlook her or not take her opinions as seriously as those of her older coworkers. It was an inclination she understood, but never indulged. She did her best to be a voice for the youth of Marshal's Bluff, North Carolina, and anyone else who needed to be heard.

Within a few minutes, a number of familiar

faces began to arrive. She opened the large cooler at her side and continued her meal. Folks young and old made their way to her table, selected a drink and sandwich, then waved their goodbyes. She ate and read and watched closely for the one face she always hoped to see. Then, finally, he appeared.

"Hey, you," she said, brightening. She closed her book and set it aside as fourteen-year-old Gage Myers approached.

Composed of gangly limbs and one big heart, he took the seat across from her with a small grin. "Hey."

Gage had lost both his parents in a car accident the year before, and Hayley was assigned his case. Her heart had split wide open for him when she placed him into foster care. His parents had both been only children, and their parents were already deceased. Gage was one of many cases she'd never forget—she was sure of it. But he was something more too.

His olive skin was unusually ruddy as he watched her. His wide brown eyes, heavy-lidded. He looked as if he hadn't slept, but also as if he wanted to run.

Hayley shifted, suddenly nervous and hoping not to seem that way. A gust of wind tossed strands of stick-straight blond hair into her eyes. She tucked the locks behind her ear with care, using the small distraction to further evaluate her friend.

Gage's fingers and T-shirt were spattered with spray paint, a sign something had been on his mind. He used street art to work through the emotions too big to process with words. He'd been in trouble for defacing property more than once, but she'd never found it in her to be angry. His paintings were powerful, and it was a necessary outlet for the teen.

"You okay?" she asked finally, reaching to press the back of her hand against his forehead. "Are you getting sick?"

He rolled those big appreciative eyes up at her, the way he always did when she offered him comfort. "I think I saw something I shouldn't have," he said. "I don't really want to talk about it."

"Okay." She handed him a sandwich, a napkin and a drink. "You want to talk about something else?"

He shrugged and ate quickly, as if he hadn't in a while.

A growth spurt? She wondered. *Or hadn't he eaten breakfast? And if not, why?*

"How're the Michaelsons?" she asked, feigning casual as she fished for information. Gage's foster parents had never struck her as a good fit for the system. But they'd been housing children in need for more than a decade, caring for dozens of youths in that time, and they were one of the rare couples willing to host teenagers. Still, something always felt off when Hayley visited. Maybe Gage had witnessed something questionable there.

He shook his head, as if reading her mind. "It's not them this time." He sighed and glanced away.

She hated his clarification of "this time," but held her tongue, sensing there was more he wanted to say. But she intended to circle back. If there had been other times the Michaelsons were a problem, she needed to know.

Gage's lips parted, but he didn't speak. Something was stopping him.

"You know you can trust me, right?" she asked. "I will always have your best interests at heart, and I'd never take any action without keeping you in the loop. I'm here to be your advocate. Whatever you need."

She wished for the dozenth time that she could foster him, instead of the Michaelsons. Instead of anyone else. She'd try to adopt him if she thought the courts would consider it, but the system liked to see kids placed with couples, preferably married and stable ones. Ones who'd been out of college and in the workforce more than eighteen months, unlike Hayley.

His gaze lifted to something over her shoulder, and his expression changed. He gathered the empty sandwich baggie and napkin from his vanquished lunch and stood. "I'd better go. Thank

you for this." He wiggled the trash in his hands.
"I needed it, and it was great."

"Wait." Hayley rose and removed another sandwich from the cooler. "Take this. And come back
at five when I get off work," she said. "We can
talk. If something's wrong at your foster home,
you can stay with me while we straighten it out.
Let me help you."

He nodded, eyes flicking to the distance again.
"Yeah, all right."

She retook her seat. "All right," she echoed,
swallowing the lump in her throat. She glanced
over her shoulder, in the direction Gage had
looked, but saw nothing of interest, then turned
back to watch him go. Every fiber in her body
urged her to chase after him, but she had no
grounds to make him stay. "See you at five,"
she called, needing the confirmation.

He waved and nodded, then picked up the pace
as he strode away.

THE AFTERNOON DRAGGED for Hayley as she attended a court hearing and made several home
visits, checking on the other children in her caseload. At the office, she rushed through the paperwork, one eye on the clock and eager to take
Gage somewhere safe so they could talk.

She was out the door at five-o'clock sharp,
blinking against the bright southern summer
sun. The air was thick and balmy, eighty-nine

degrees with extreme humidity. The soft scents of sunblock and charcoal grills drifted by. Life in coastal North Carolina was beautiful at any time, but August was Hayley's favorite. She loved the extreme heat and the way everything was in bloom, lush and alive. Laughter carried on the wind, from parks and beaches, ice-cream parlors and outdoor cafés. She couldn't imagine living anywhere else, but she'd be a lot happier in the moment, once she knew Gage was okay.

At five thirty, she gave up the wait and began a slow walk to her car.

The social-services staff parked their cars in a series of spaces along the perimeter of a nearby church's lot. It was a protective measure against potentially unhappy clients, or family members of clients, who lashed out when court appointments didn't go the way they'd wanted. And it was an added level of privacy for workers.

In Hayley's experience, the people willing to destroy private property over a particular outcome probably weren't the ones who should have children in their care. But she also knew the system sometimes failed, and anyone could reach a breaking point when someone they loved was taken from them. She hoped to become part of the solution and a support for those in times of trouble.

She waited outside her car until six, then she called Mrs. Michaelson.

Gage's foster mom claimed she hadn't seen him since the night before, and she accused him of being on drugs before Hayley could get any useful information.

She rubbed her forehead as they disconnected. Gage was not on drugs. His eyes had been clear, if worry-filled, this morning. He'd been alert and on edge, not hung over.

Something else was wrong.

She climbed into her car and started the engine. She had a few ideas of where Gage could be. She'd had to search for him before, in the early days following his parents' deaths, when grief and despair had made him reckless and hostile. She hated to think of him feeling those ways again. Hated to think of him upset and alone.

The drive from Social Services, on the periphery of downtown Marshal's Bluff, to the fringe areas along the warehouse and shipping district was shockingly quick. The landscape changed in a matter of blocks, trading community parks and tree-lined streets for abandoned housing and condemned buildings.

To Gage's eyes, a neighborhood full of blank canvases for his art.

She slowed as small groups of people came into view, scanning each of their faces for Gage. Hayley noticed evidence of his artwork here and there, all older pieces she'd seen last fall.

After a trip around the block, she decided to go

on foot, talk to folks, ask for help. She parked her sedan at the curb and climbed out, hyperaware that her pencil skirt and blouse stood out in ways that were unlikely to help her blend. She could thank her appearance in court for that. Typically, she wore jeans and a nice top. Outfits that made her more approachable to the people she helped. Less authoritarian.

Old Downtown was filled with buildings that blocked the bay views. Most were crumbling from age and in need of repair. Windows and doors were barred and boarded. No Trespassing signs were posted everywhere, so property owners wouldn't be sued if someone became injured while inside.

Hayley approached a group of young men on the stoop attached to a former barbershop and offered a small, hip-high wave. "I'm looking for a friend named Gage," she said. "Do you know him?"

The nearest kid, wearing baggy jeans and a long-sleeved flannel shirt, despite the heat, shot her a disbelieving look. "Who are you? His mom?"

Hayley shook her head, saddened by the thought. She'd give just about anything to bring Gage's mom back to him, or to have the honor of caring for him herself, but those things weren't options right now. And all that mattered was finding him and bringing him home safely. "I'm just a friend," she said. "He's about your age. He's an artist. He painted these." She lifted a finger to indicate a small black silhouette on one of the boarded windows.

Gage regularly used the image to depict children like himself, the ones he felt went unseen. Untethered numbers in case files. Kids nobody really knew.

"You know him?" the boy asked.

She bit her tongue against the obvious response. She'd made that clear, hadn't she? "Have you seen him?"

"Nah."

"Thanks." Hayley sighed and moved along.

"Hey," one of the other kids called to her, making her turn around. "Lady, I ain't trying to get in your business, but you shouldn't be down here. Nothing good is gonna find someone like you on this street."

"Noted," she said. "But I'm worried about my friend, and I need to know he's okay. If you see him, I hope you'll tell him I was here."

Dusk was settling, but she walked the neighborhood for nearly an hour as the sun lowered in the sky, eventually blunted by the buildings. She talked to knots and clusters of people along the way. Most were less friendly than the first group she'd encountered. Eventually, she was forced to call it a night, so she started back to her car.

The street was quieter on her return trip— the people she'd spoken to earlier were already gone. Her nerves coiled tightly at the realization she was alone. Wind off the water stirred loose sheets of newspaper and scooted empty plastic bags over broken asphalt, causing her to start and jump. Each sound and movement increased her already hurried pace.

When the breeze settled and silence returned, the echoing clicks of her high heels were offset by a softer, more distant sound of footfalls.

She beeped the locks open on her sedan and wrenched the door wide, tossing her purse onto the passenger seat. She slid behind the wheel with a sigh of relief.

In her rearview mirror, a shadow grew from the space between two buildings, stretching and morphing into the silhouette of a man. He moved pointedly across the street in her direction, barely ten yards away.

She waited, wondering if someone she'd spoken to earlier had something they wanted to tell her now.

Then he raised a gun.

Hayley started the car's engine and jerked the shifter into Drive as the first bullet ripped through the evening air, eliciting a scream from her core.

She peeled away as the second and third shots exploded behind her.

Chapter Two

Marshal's Bluff Detective Finn Beaumont collapsed onto his office chair and kicked his legs out in front of him. His head fell back, and he hooked one bent arm across his eyes. He was tired to his core, exhausted in ways he hadn't been in ages. And it was hot as blazes outside, where he'd spent most of his day, in a dress shirt and slacks, questioning socialites in swimming pools and executives on golf courses.

It'd been one of those days when he'd wondered if he really knew his town at all.

Katherine Everett, a local philanthropist known widely throughout the community simply as Kate, was officially missing. Kate's grandfather had established the largest shipping company in the area and grown it into a national conglomerate. Today, Everett Industries transported goods along both coasts and the gulf, as well as to countless inlet towns. Kate managed the family's estate and funneled her heart and soul into Marshal's Bluff rehabilitation efforts.

Everyone loved her, but she was gone. And after ten hours of interviewing her neighbors, family and friends, Finn was no closer to guessing her whereabouts than the moment he'd received the call this morning announcing her disappearance.

His appreciation for her work and love of his job were just two of the many reasons he needed to find her fast. At twenty-five, he was both the newest and youngest detective on the force, and he had a lot to prove. When people with money went missing, and a ransom note didn't follow, foul play was a scary possibility. According to everyone he'd interviewed, Kate wasn't the sort to take off without letting someone know, and the calendars at her home and office showed a number of appointments happening all week. None had been canceled.

More bad signs.

The phone on Finn's desk rang, and he forced his head up, then stretched to lift the receiver. "Beaumont."

"Detective Beaumont," the desk clerk responded. "I have a social worker here who'd like to see you immediately. Possible missing child and gunshots fired in Old Downtown."

Finn rubbed his forehead. "Anyone hurt?"

"No, sir. Units are en route for follow-up."

He exhaled a long breath. He'd been on the clock nearly twelve hours, but sure. He'd see the social worker. "I guess there's always time for one more crisis, right?"

"That's the job," the clerk said, then disconnected the call.

A moment later, Finn heard the steady click-clack of high heels in the hallway.

He'd gotten nowhere while looking for Kate today, but maybe he could end the shift on a positive note by helping the social worker. He sat taller and straightened the files he'd slung onto his desk earlier, in a hurry to make his next set of interviews on time.

"Finn?"

His limbs froze, and his gaze snapped to his open office door. He'd know that voice anywhere, though he hadn't heard it in more than a year. "Hayley?"

Hayley Campbell had crashed into his life like a freight train during her first few weeks as a social worker. She'd faced off with some pretty rough-looking folks outside the courthouse when they didn't like the verdict about losing their children. He'd intervened before things escalated too far. And he'd asked her out the minute she'd stopped insisting she'd had the situation covered. Shockingly, she'd agreed.

The story of the whirlwind romance that followed was one he thought they'd tell their grandkids. But when he'd proposed a few months later, she said no. And she'd proceeded to ghost him until he stopped trying to reach her or make sense of her reaction.

He'd eventually let it go, but he wasn't over it. He doubted he ever would be. Life was like that sometimes, he supposed. People had to take the good with the bad. And the months he'd spent with Hayley were some of the best of his life.

Now, she stood before him in a pencil skirt and blouse that emphasized every dang curve on her petite little frame. Straight blond hair tucked behind her ears, she had a look on her face he knew all too well. Determination.

"Come in," he said, hoping to sound calmer than he felt. "Have a seat." The desk clerk's words rushed back to him with a slap. "You saw a shooter?"

He pulled a bottle of water from the nearby mini fridge and reassessed her expression when she didn't answer. Now, he could see she was doing all she could to hold herself together. "Talk to me, Hayley."

The sound of his voice seemed to pull her back to him, and she wet her lips. Unshed tears filled her blue eyes as she accepted the water and drank greedily.

Was she in shock?

He scanned her body more carefully, searching for signs of injury or physical trauma.

"I know it's not fair of me to come here like this," she said, voice shaky, "but I need help, and

I don't want him to become another case ignored because he's been in trouble before. He hasn't run away. Either something happened to him, or he's hiding because he thinks something will happen."

Finn crossed his arms and sat on the edge of his desk before her. "Okay. I'm missing a lot of pieces, so let's start at the beginning. Who are you worried about? And when did you first know something was wrong? Take your time and be as specific as possible. Especially about this shooter."

She inhaled slowly, then released the breath and began talking about her lunch hour.

Finn took mental notes as she spoke, and a few literal ones on a pad of paper he scooped up, sticking with her as she carefully laid out the details of her day.

"When the first shot went off, I thought, maybe it was because I look like a person with money," she said, glancing at her modest skirt and sensible heels. "In that area, any amount of money is enough, you know?"

He nodded, tongue-tied as he imagined getting his hands on the person who'd taken a shot at his— Finn's brain halted and misfired. His what? Hayley wasn't his anything anymore. She hadn't been in a very long time. He cleared his throat and pushed ahead. "How many shots were fired?"

"Three. But by the second one, I was driving

away. I don't think a robber would have persisted like that. I think this has something to do with Gage's disappearance. I called 911 on my way here, but I wasn't going to wait around for them. I needed to talk to you."

Finn's chest tightened at her final words. She'd avoided him for a year, but when she needed help, she still looked to him. That had to count for something.

"All right." He pushed onto his feet and rounded the desk to his chair. "I need to get your official written statement and make a report. You can tell me all you know about... Gage, is it?"

She nodded. "Yes."

"I'll share his description and relevant information with Dispatch and let officers know he's missing, possibly in danger."

"Thank you." She released a long, steady breath. "What happens then?"

"Then I'll follow you home," he said. "It's unlikely the shooter will show up at your place, but an escort might make you feel better. It'll certainly help me."

HAYLEY SMILED, relieved and exhausted. Finn hadn't changed at all in the time they'd been apart. He was still kind and accepting. Still listened and didn't interrupt. And he still had her best interest at heart, even after she'd walked out on his proposal without an explanation. Then she'd hid from him, like a coward, for more than a year. "I'd appreciate it."

An hour later, she pulled into the driveway outside her cottage, several blocks from the bay, with Finn behind her.

Her neighborhood was a series of older homes packed closely together. The tiny yards spilled into one another all the way to the end of each block. It was a blue-collar, working-class section of town, established at the turn of the last century, when most of the male citizens worked on the docks or on ships in some capacity, hence its proximity to the sea. These days, however, her block had more retirees than worker bees. That fact had been a selling point on this property over all the others in her price range. The way Hayley saw it, a block full of retirees likely meant someone was home all the time, which would keep crime low. Witnesses tended to ruin a criminal's day.

She grabbed her things from the passenger seat and climbed out, then met Finn on the porch. Hopefully, she hadn't left anything she'd regret Finn seeing in plain sight inside. She was tidy, but it'd been a while since she'd had company. An errant bra on the couch or coffee table wasn't unheard of at her place, mostly because removing the torture device was her go-to move after a long day at the office.

Hayley turned on the porch light as they entered. "I didn't expect to get back so late," she said, mostly out of nerves and habit. Finn used to worry about her returning to a dark home.

Her heart rate rose as they stood in the entryway between her living room and staircase to the second floor. The cottage suddenly felt smaller and warmer than she remembered.

She'd furnished the space in hand-me-downs and thrift-store finds, full of colors and textures that made her happy. Mismatched throw rugs and tables she'd saved from the curb on trash day, sanded and given new life with fresh paint.

"Can I get you a glass of sweet tea or a cup of coffee?" she asked.

He looked tired and a little anxious, but the second part couldn't be true. He was Finn Beaumont, a full six feet of handsomeness, with lean muscles, broad shoulders and two perfect, extra large hands.

She resisted the urge to pluck the fabric of her shirt away from her chest.

Her female coworkers always took an extra minute to check their hair and refresh their lipstick before going to the police station or courthouse, just in case they'd see him.

"Sweet tea sounds nice," he said. "Thank you."

Hayley hustled into the kitchen, glad for the moment alone to collect her marbles. She poured a glass of tea from the pitcher she kept in her fridge, then straightened her skirt, took a deep breath and hurried back to the living room.

Finn stood at the fireplace, examining framed photographs on her mantel. She'd replaced the images of her and Finn with snapshots of children from her caseload, their artwork, or pics of her at community events and charity drives. The first photo he'd taken of her on the Beaumont ranch stood at the center of her collection.

The old wooden floorboards creaked as she moved in his direction.

"How's your mom?" he asked, casting a glance over his shoulder.

"She's fine," she said, passing him the glass.

Hayley didn't keep pictures of her mom, or talk about her, for a number of reasons. Her mother didn't bring her joy, peace or any of the other things Hayley needed her home to provide. And most of her memories involving the older woman upset her.

Finn scanned her briefly, then took a small sip of his tea. "You look nice. Were you in court today?"

"Yeah." She moved to the couch and Finn followed. "You look as if you've had a big day too."

He raised his eyebrows then laughed. "I have. But no one shot at me, so there's that."

She smiled.

"And even the worst days have bright spots," he added.

She sat and pulled a throw pillow onto her lap, hugging it to her chest. "How's your family doing? I recommend their ranch for rehabilitation every chance I get. I think some folks take me up on it."

Finn sipped the tea again before setting his glass on the coffee table. "I know my folks appreciate that." He rested his hands on his lap and grinned. "It's been a big year for the Beaumonts. Have you heard?"

She swiveled in his direction, curiosity piqued. "No. Do tell."

"Dean got back with his ex, Nicole. They're engaged now."

Hayley's heart swelled. She loved Dean, and knew he wasn't over his ex, but she'd expected him to move on, not find his way back to her. Did things like that really happen? "That's wonderful," she said, meaning it to her core. "Nicole has the younger sister who stayed at the ranch, right?"

"That's the one." Finn hooked one ankle over the opposite knee. "Nicole came to him for help when her sister went missing. They worked out their troubles, saved the sister and fell in love all over again. They're getting married in the spring."

Hayley pressed her lips together and felt her cheeks heat. The parallels between her situation with Finn and his brother's situation with his ex were hard to ignore. But she wasn't naive enough to think there'd be a way back to him for her. Not after what she'd done. Finn was kind and forgiving, but she'd gone too far.

"And then there's Austin," he began, a dimple sinking into his cheek at the appearance of his mischievous grin.

"What did Austin do?" She'd always liked Austin. He was the oldest of the biological Beaumont boys, third in line of the five, which actually made him a bit of a middle child and a goofball. Dean and Jake had been adopted as young boys, around the same time Austin and Lincoln were born only sixteen months apart. As a result, the brothers were close in every way and inseparable friends.

"He's currently engaged to a local real-estate agent," he said.

She shook her head in awe. "You're kidding?"

"Nope. He took her case when she thought someone was following her. She was right, and we handled that. Now Austin and Scarlet are planning a big Christmas wedding."

Hayley laughed. "I can't believe the Beaumont boys are getting married. Your mama must be elated. She's obsessed with seeing your family grow."

Finn's smile fell a bit, and reality knocked the awe from Hayley's tone.

"Oh—" She winced. "I didn't mean to—"

Finn had proposed long before Dean or Austin, but Hayley had said no.

He lifted a palm. "You had your reasons."

She had, but she also owed him an explanation. The words piled on her tongue, but wouldn't quite fall from her lips.

Silence stretched as he searched her eyes. "I suppose I should get going and let you rest," he said, the words low and thick. "I'll get a neighborhood patrol on your block tonight for good measure, and I'll keep you posted with any updates we have on Gage. You'll do the same?"

"Of course." She rose and walked Finn to the door.

"You still have my number?" he asked, pausing on her front porch.

She nodded.

His gaze flicked over her face once more. "For what it's worth, I'm glad you came to me," he said. "You can always ask me for help. Tomorrow or ten years from now. Won't matter."

She leaned against the doorjamb as her knees went a little weak.

"I mean it, Hayley. If you ever need anything, you can call me. Whether you're having a hard time and just want someone to listen, or you need a background check on your date. Maybe help opening a jar or reaching a high shelf."

She laughed. "Let me guess. You're my man?"

"I will always be your man," he said. Then he turned with a wink and jogged away.

Chapter Three

Hayley arrived at Social Services early the next morning. She hadn't slept well and decided to use the extra time to get ahead on paperwork. But the moment she'd taken a seat behind her desk, her mind was back on Gage.

A call to Mrs. Michaelson had confirmed his continued absence, which meant he was still missing and in trouble. He was a kid alone and on foot. And whatever he'd gotten into possibly involved a gunman.

She shivered at the memory of the silhouette as it had grown from the shadows. She wasn't sure she'd have survived if not for her car.

Gage didn't even have a cell phone.

By the time her coworkers began showing up, Hayley had already moved her laptop outside and set up a hot spot on her phone. If she worked at the picnic table where she ate lunch, it would reduce her chances of missing Gage if he stopped by to see her. Thankfully, her day's schedule was light. No court appearances, and only two home visits. She could keep a lookout from the park most of the day.

Sweat gathered on her brow and across the back of her neck as hours passed and the sun rose in the sky. She'd worn a blue silk sleeveless blouse with tan capri pants and flats. All in all, better suited for running than the prior day's pencil skirt and heels.

She'd struggled to choose between tops this morning and was mildly distressed by the outcome. She'd initially leaned toward a more figure-flattering cream blouse, but ultimately selected the blue because it matched her eyes. And Finn always used to comment when she wore blue.

The resulting internal cringe was nearly painful. She shouldn't be thinking about Finn Beaumont right now, or which color he'd liked on her a year ago. She should be focused on Gage and the gunman.

But since her mind had opened the Finn rabbit hole, she let herself tumble back down for another moment or two.

Two of his brothers were planning weddings. That was unexpected news. Dean never dated after Nicole broke his heart and Austin just never dated. Or, Hayley had never seen him with the same girl more than twice while she was with Finn anyway. Now, Dean had reunited with the woman he loved, and Austin had committed to a local real-estate agent. Whoever she was, she must be special. The Beaumonts certainly were.

Hayley loved the whole family and wanted them to be happy. She wished she could meet the women who'd stolen Austin and Dean's hearts. She wished she could attend the wedding ceremonies and celebrate with them. They were the brothers she'd never had. And now, she never would.

If only she'd been less broken and more understanding of her own damage at the time of Finn's proposal, she'd be part of his family now too. Instead, she'd done what she always did. She'd panicked and she'd run. She hadn't even seen the pattern until it was pointed out to her in therapy. She was working hard on correcting that kind of behavior these days. But until the proposal, she hadn't understood all the ways her emotional damage had shaped her entire life.

A cool breeze picked up, pulling her back to the moment. She glanced around, wondering how long she'd been lost in thought. Then she opened her cooler and unpacked her lunch. The day was slipping away without any good news.

An hour later, she collected her things, ready for her two afternoon appointments.

A large black SUV pulled away from the curb across the street and moved slowly past the social-services building. The fine hairs along Hayley's arms and the back of her neck stood at attention as she watched it disappear around the corner. The vehicle was high-end and new, a familiar make and model, but she'd missed the license plate.

Thankfully, she didn't see the vehicle again all afternoon.

She returned to the picnic table at five o'clock and waited until six before leaving. She traded texts with Finn about the fact neither of them had news on Gage's whereabouts. And she fought the urge to go back to Old Downtown and overturn every brick until she found him.

At six, she began the slow trek to her car.

Intuition prickled across her skin as she scanned the world around her, feeling someone's gaze on her as she moved. She hoped it belonged to Gage.

Kids played in the park and coworkers chatted in the lot, but none paid any attention to her as she passed.

The dark SUV from lunch appeared at the curb across the street, and Hayley's steps faltered. This time, a man in a black T-shirt, jeans and a ball cap leaned against the hood, mirrored sunglasses covering his eyes.

She picked up the pace, wondering, belatedly, if she should've turned back to talk with her coworkers until the man left. But it was too late. Now, he'd know what she drove.

He crossed his arms and widened his stance, appearing to watch her as she unlocked her car door.

She pulled a flyer wedged beneath one windshield wiper into the car with her and locked the door. She raised her phone in the man's direction to snap a photo, but he turned away, then climbed behind the wheel of his SUV and merged smoothly into evening traffic.

A gush of relief rushed over her lips a moment before the three words scrawled across the paper came into view.

Leave This Alone

FINN PACED THE sidewalk outside the pub near the precinct. Hayley's message had been brief but pointed. She was leaving work and on her way to meet him. He'd suggested they chat over dinner, and she'd named the pub they used to frequent.

He'd walked straight out of his office and jogged the block and a half to wait for her.

Her navy blue sedan swung into the narrow parking area beside the pub a moment later, and she climbed out looking on edge.

He tried not to notice the way her pants clung to her narrow hips and trim thighs. Or how the blue of her blouse perfectly matched her eyes. But he couldn't stop the smile that formed at the sight of her sleek blond hair, pulled into the world's tiniest ponytail.

"You okay?" he asked as she reached his side.

"No."

Alarm shot through Finn's limbs as he opened the pub's door and waited while she stepped inside. A million reasons for her answer raced through his mind. None of them were good.

The hostess smiled. "Two?"

"Yeah. A booth if you have one," Finn said.

The young woman's gaze slid over Hayley. "Sure. Right this way."

She led them to a table in the corner and left them with a pair of menus.

Hayley sat near the window, leaving Finn the seat with a clear view of the door and room at large, which he appreciated. She frowned as she watched the hostess walk away. "I forgot what it was like to go anywhere with you."

"What do you mean?" He glanced around the busy pub, then back at her. Nothing seemed amiss. They'd passed several available tables on their way to this one, but his request had been strategic. "I thought a booth would give us more privacy."

She sighed and pulled a folded piece of paper from her purse, then passed it to him. "This was on my windshield when I left work, and I park at the church a block away from Social Services. That means whoever left it knew which car was mine. I'm afraid it might've been the same person who saw me drive away last night after they shot at me."

Finn raised his eyebrows. "You think the shooter wrote this?"

"I don't know," she said. "But a man was standing outside an SUV, watching me, when I found it. And I think I saw the same vehicle near the park at lunchtime. The guy left when I tried to take a picture of him."

"Did he look like the shooter?" Finn asked, blood pressure rising.

This wasn't the way he'd expected their exchange to go. Hayley hadn't mentioned any of this in her text. She'd just wanted to meet, and he'd assumed, at worst, she was still worried about Gage's absence. At best, he'd thought she might just want to see him again.

Hayley raised her narrow shoulders in an exaggerated shrug. "I didn't get a good look at the person who followed me last night. All I know is Gage never went back to his foster home, and he didn't reach out to me today. I'm doing everything I can to find him, which for the record feels like nothing, and everything about my day was absurdly unremarkable until that appeared."

Finn read the note again. "You think this is a reference to Gage's situation?"

"What else could it be?" she asked. "Searching for him is the only thing I'm doing differently, and Gage said he thought he saw something he shouldn't. I'm guessing whoever is responsible for whatever he saw left this note."

Finn rested against the seat back, telling himself to remain calm and collected. He couldn't let his attachment to Hayley interfere with his ability to do his best work for her. "I'm going to need another formal statement," he said. "I'll put the note into evidence after we eat."

A waitress arrived with a notepad and a smile. "Are y'all ready to order?"

Finn watched Hayley for the answer, allowing her to decide. She hadn't even looked at the menu.

She slid her attention from the woman to Finn and pursed her lips. "Just a soda for me."

"And what can I get you?" the waitress asked, shifting one hip against the table and angling toward him as she spoke.

"You're not hungry?" Finn asked Hayley, confused. "Have you already eaten?"

"No. I'm just shaken."

"You have to eat." He looked at the waitress, who was smiling.

He frowned. "Can we get a basket of chicken tenders to split? Honey for dip. And I'll have black coffee."

"Sure thing, sugar. Anything else?"

"No."

The waitress left, and Hayley rolled her eyes.

"Did you want something different?" he asked.

She used to love chicken strips with honey. Had that changed this year?

She shook her head. "The order was good. Thank you. I'm just— What am I going to do?"

He waited, unsure how to answer without more specifics.

"I know this is bad," she said, pointing to the note he'd refolded and set aside. "I need to know how bad and what to do next."

"Well," Finn began, rubbing a hand along his jaw, "we'll need more information to answer the first part. Should we wait until you've had something to eat before we tackle the second? You look like you're ready to drop."

"No," she said. "And I am." She let her eyes close briefly and tipped her head over one shoulder.

Finn willed his gaze away from the exposed length of her neck.

Her lids opened and she straightened, fixing her attention on him. "I'm being followed by a man in an SUV who knows where I work and what I drive. Gage is still missing, and the man with the SUV doesn't want me looking for him, but I can't stop doing that. Gage's life could be in danger. Meanwhile there's a possibility this guy is the same person who shot at me. I feel sick."

Finn rested his forearms on the table between them and clasped his hands. Apparently they were going to talk about the tough stuff before eating. "You're right to be concerned about all that. I'm doing everything I can on my end to figure out what happened in Old Downtown last night. Officers walked the area you described but didn't find any evidence of the shooting. They're looking for the shell casings from the shots fired. If we find them, we can use ballistics to try to match the gun to other crimes and possibly get a lead on the shooter. I was running on the theory the shooting was a separate issue from the kid's disappearance, but the note makes this personal, and given the big picture, it's smart to proceed as if these things are related."

"Okay," she said softly, sounding frightened but in agreement. "Now what?"

"Now, I think it would be wise if someone looked after you for the next few days while we figure out what's going on here."

Her nose wrinkled. "Like a bodyguard?"

"More like a personal protection detail," he said. "I'll put a cruiser in your neighborhood and assign one to you at work. I'll fill in whenever I can so you're as comfortable as possible while being followed around."

Hayley blinked. "You're going to follow me around?"

"Just until we're sure you're safe."

The waitress returned with a tray and bent low to set it on the table, temporarily blocking his view of Hayley. "Chicken fingers with honey, black coffee and a soda," she said. "Is there anything else I can do for you?" She stood and cocked her hip again.

Finn followed Hayley's droll, heavy-lidded gaze to the smiling young woman. "No. This is everything. Thank you."

She left.

Hayley raised a chicken finger and pointed it at him. "That waitress is hitting on you. Just like the hostess. It's blatant and rude. We could be here together."

He furrowed his brow. "What?"

"You're an actual detective, Finn. You're literally paid to notice details, yet you are oblivious. How is that possible?"

Finn leaned forward, shamelessly enjoying her undivided attention and hint of possessiveness in her tone. "Probably because all I see right now is you."

A blush stole across her beautiful face, and she lowered the chicken. "Fine. You can follow me around, but you have to help me look for Gage too."

"Deal." He was already doing the latter, and he wanted the extra time with her.

She slid her hand over the table, fingers outstretched for a shake.

Finn curled his palm around hers and held tight, letting the intoxicating buzz of her touch course through him. "I will protect you," he promised. "And we'll find Gage. Together."

Chapter Four

Hayley rose with the sun the next morning. Unable to find sleep in more than small bits and patches during the night, she was glad to give up and get moving. She checked her phone with hope for missed news, preferably a message that Gage had been found, or a text directly from the teen saying he was safe. The only waiting notifications were social-media updates from coworkers and a few junk emails she marked as spam.

Disappointment washed over her, but not surprise. Nothing had ever come easily. At least, she supposed, this was familiar territory. Time to set a plan and get to work.

She hurried through her morning routine, dressing for the day and sending good thoughts into the universe, hoping the energy would find its way to Gage. Something to keep his chin up until she found him. And she would find him. Whatever it took. She wasn't sure she'd recover if something happened to the teen. He'd already experienced too much tragedy. He deserved a home filled with love and a safe place to exist while he grieved the loss of his parents. A place he could become the man he wanted to be without all the noise. Somewhere he could focus on his art and express himself freely.

Not on the run. Not alone and afraid.

She willed away the budding tears and pressed the brew button on her single-cup coffee maker. Then she packed a cooler of sandwiches, baggies of pretzels and cold water bottles while she finished her first cup. She returned the empty mug to the machine and brewed a refill.

Someone knew where Gage was. If she couldn't find him, she could at least find someone to point her in the right direction. All she needed was a lead.

Her thoughts circled back to the SUV outside her office and the note left on her windshield, then to the man with the gun. None of those things were clues to Gage's whereabouts, but they were all clues. She just had to figure out what they meant.

"What did you see, Gage?" she whispered, remembering his worried words to her at lunch, and hating that she hadn't been able to stop this, whatever it was, from happening.

Memories of the gunman sent a shiver down her spine, and she crept toward her front window for a careful peek outside. He knew her car and license-plate number, and her place of employment, so why not her address?

A familiar black pickup truck sat at the curb across the street. Finn was behind the wheel, a laptop balanced on something inside his cab as he typed away, stealing occasional glances into his mirrors and at her front door.

"Of course, you're already outside," she murmured, smiling as she rolled her eyes. "The Beaumont brothers and their big, dumb, hero hearts." She slipped onto her porch when he turned his attention back to his computer, then marched down her walkway in his direction.

As she drew nearer, it became clear he wasn't just starting work a little early. He'd been outside her place all night. He was wearing the same shirt from last night, and his usually clean-shaven face was dark with stubble. His hair pointed in all directions from one too many finger combs, and there was a level of fatigue in his eyes that only came from pulling an all-nighter.

He turned to face her before she reached the center of the street.

"Still got those heightened senses, I see."

He grinned, hooking one elbow through the open window. "Keeps me alive."

"Handy." She stopped at his door and lifted her chin to indicate the mess of empty snack wrappers at his side. "You want to come in for coffee, or are you full of jerky and candy?"

He climbed out and closed his door with a grin. "Coffee sounds amazing."

Hayley inhaled, steadying herself against his intoxicating nearness. Even after a night in his truck, his trademark mix of cologne and sea air seemed to cling to his clothes and skin. The inviting scent of his spearmint gum beckoned her closer. Heat from his body seemed to grip and pull her, as did his sleepy eyes and disheveled hair. Up close, Finn Beaumont was mesmerizing.

Memories of sleepless nights they'd once shared slid into mind, unbidden, raising her body temperature and heating her cheeks. She forced away the images and willed her heart and head to get a grip. Nothing about her bone-deep attraction and attachment to him would help her find Gage, and that sweet missing boy was all that mattered.

"Penny for your thoughts?" Finn asked, voice low and careful.

She shrugged, feigning confidence. "You could've stayed inside, you know. There wasn't any reason to sleep in your truck. I have a spare room."

He rubbed a hand against his stubbled cheek, looking suddenly boyish and shy. "I'll keep that in mind. For now, I think all I need is a little coffee, and I'll be good to go."

She nodded and turned back to her home, leading the way across the street. "I'm asking a coworker to take some tasks off my plate today and tomorrow. I want to double down on my efforts to locate Gage before much more time passes. I'd hoped to get news during the night, but I haven't."

He nodded as she held open her front door for him. "If we don't make solid progress fast, I'll reach out to Dean and Austin, see if they can help."

Hayley's heart swelled. The duo owned a private-investigations office together, and they were very good. "Thank you."

"Of course. How much of your work were you able to off-load?"

"Most of it. I figure the less time I spend at the office, the less likely I'll be to draw a criminal stalker there. It's a building full of folks trying to make the world a little better for local kids and families. I can't be the reason something bad potentially comes into their lives."

"Always troubleshooting for others," he said with a small smile.

"That's the job."

"That's your heart," he corrected.

Hayley scanned his dark brown eyes. "Kind of like the way you insist on seeing the best in people."

She felt like a failure for not getting the whole story from Gage while he'd been right there at the picnic table with her. She'd failed when she let him walk away. Yet Finn managed to see her in the best light. As if she wasn't at least partially at fault.

"I can reach out to your supervisor," Finn suggested. "Let them know you're part of an ongoing investigation and that you'll be working with Marshal's Bluff PD outside the office for a few days."

"Not yet," she said. "I'm holding out hope that Gage will turn up soon and fill us in on what's happening. Then, I can take care of him while you arrest whoever is behind the gunshots."

She selected a mug from the cupboard and brewed him a cup of coffee, then passed it his way.

"Thanks." Finn accepted and blew over the steamy surface before taking a greedy gulp.

"You're welcome. Thank you for keeping an eye on me last night. Are you headed home to rest now, or are you on the clock for a bit longer?"

He lowered the cup slightly, eyebrows raised. "I've been off the clock since last night. Today's supposed to be my day off, but I'm in the middle of another case, so that was never happening. Why? What do you need?"

"I thought you might come with me to ask around about Gage, but I don't want to add more work for you on your day off." The people who roamed Old Downtown were unlikely to talk to a lawman, but at least some of the folks in Gage's world were likely to be motivated by a badge.

His foster parents and siblings, for example. And Hayley could use all the help she could get.

Finn finished his coffee and set the mug on the counter. "Helping you will never be work, Hayley."

She blinked. Something in his tone suggested he might not be as angry with her for running away from his proposal as she'd imagined. That maybe he was over it. And not necessarily over her.

"Where do you want to start?" he asked, moving the mug to her sink for a rinse and allowing her to take the lead, despite a shiny detective badge on the leather bifold perpetually clipped to his pocket.

I'd like to start with a deeply apologetic kiss, she thought, but she pushed the silly notion aside.

"I was thinking I should go back to Old Downtown." Where she'd been shot at. Where her gut said Gage had been likely last seen.

"I'll drive."

FINN PARKED HIS pickup along the crumbling curb of Front Street in Old Downtown. The area was dreary, even by morning light. There would be more people around as the day commenced, but the danger increased with the population in this neighborhood, and Finn intended to keep Hayley as far away from trouble as possible. Meanwhile, they'd have to settle for questioning the early risers, typically an older, less hostile group.

Hayley swung open her door and climbed down, pulling a large black tote behind her. "Ready?" She closed the door without waiting for his response.

He met her at his back bumper and gave her a curious look. "What's with the luggage?"

He'd assumed it was her work or laptop bag when she'd carried it to his truck. Maybe she thought it would be stolen if she left it behind? "I've got a lockbox behind my seat, if you'd feel better leaving your things in there."

She smiled. "No thanks. I plan to give this away."

Finn frowned. "What?"

"I usually bring sandwiches and water to the office and distribute them at lunch. Folks know they can help themselves. Since I won't be there today, I thought I'd do what I can down here."

Finn opened his mouth to speak, but words failed. He'd grown up in a family that made sure as many folks as possible had something to eat every day. His parents, particularly his mama, were still dedicated to the task. Since becoming a detective, he'd taken a much smaller role in the family's daily efforts, but seeing Hayley's considerate and giving nature in action melted him a little. He'd held out hope of getting over her one day, but clearly that wouldn't be today. Spending time with her on this case would set him back months in his quest to move on, but some sadistic part of him would enjoy the pain.

A woman wearing too many layers of clothing for the increasing heat and humidity appeared on the corner. She eyed him skeptically before taking note of Hayley at his side.

Hayley unzipped her bag and liberated a small bottle of water. She extended it in the woman's direction. "Going to be another hot one today."

The woman froze, but Hayley continued moving toward her.

"You can have this if you want it."

Finn slowed, hanging back to allow the women to interact.

"I have food too. If you're hungry," Hayley offered.

"What do you want for it?"

"Nothing." Hayley passed the water and a small pack of pretzels to the other woman.

"What are you doing down here?"

"I'm looking for the boy who makes those." She tipped her head to indicate a dark patch of graffiti, the silhouette of a child at the end of a long shadow. "He's my friend, and I haven't seen him in a couple days. I'm worried." She dug a sandwich from her sack and passed that to the woman as well. "If you need a place to stay tonight, somewhere cool and safe," she added, "the mission on Second Avenue has openings for women and children."

The woman's expression softened. "You're her, aren't you?"

"Who?" Hayley asked.

"The angel."

Hayley's eyes widened for a moment, but she rearranged her features quickly. Anyone who wasn't staring at her, like Finn was, probably wouldn't have noticed. "Pardon?"

The woman finished the water without answering. She tucked the sandwich into the pocket of her baggy cardigan. "I've got a place around the corner. I don't like the mission. It's too crowded, and there's a curfew."

"If you run into anyone who might need somewhere, will you let them know?" Hayley asked.

"Sure." The woman's gaze flickered back to the graffiti. "He's a nice kid," she said. "Seems right that he'd have someone like you." She lifted her eyes briefly to Finn, then moved away.

Hayley's expression fell with the woman's parting words, and Finn moved quickly to her side. "You all right?"

"Fine." She forced a tight smile. "Worried about Gage. That's all."

He wasn't convinced that was the whole story, but Finn knew better than to push her past her comfort zone. The last time he did that, she'd avoided him for a year.

They moved onward, searching for pedestrians to ask about Gage. Block by block, until her bag was empty. Everyone seemed to know the boy who painted the shadows of children. They were kind and concerned, but no one knew where he'd gone.

Finn's presence could easily have deterred folks from talking to her, but Hayley was just so genuine. Everyone could see it. The tough things she'd been through had somehow strengthened her instead of breaking her. She'd become stronger without becoming hardened. In truth, she was probably softer and more gentle-hearted as a result. People seemed to sense and respect that.

He set a hand on her back when they turned around at the waterfront.

Her narrow shoulders curved in defeat.

Regardless of how many people were willing to talk, Gage was still missing. Just like the heiress, Kate. And that was incredibly frustrating.

"Hey." The deep bass of a male voice turned them on their heels. A large man approached slowly from a nearby dock. He was tall and broad-shouldered with thickly muscled arms and deep-set brown eyes. He lifted his chin to Finn, then refocused on Hayley.

"Timothy!" Hayley moved quickly in the man's direction, meeting him halfway and smiling widely. "How are you? How's Sonia?"

Timothy's lips twitched as he seemed to be

fighting a smile and he nodded. "All good, thanks to you. I heard you're looking for the little tagger."

"I am," she said, jerking her attention to Finn, then back to her friend. "He's missing, and I think he's in trouble. Have you seen him around here in the last day or two?"

"I try not to spend too much time out this way these days, but I heard you were here yesterday, and a friend told me why. I asked around for you." He balled one hand into a fist at his side, then stretched his fingers before letting them hang loose once more. "I encouraged folks to talk. I was just headed your way, to be honest. You shouldn't be down here. This place just ain't for you."

"You heard something?" she asked, ignoring his sage advice.

Finn glanced at Timothy's hand again and imagined it wouldn't take much effort on the mammoth's part to encourage anyone to do anything.

The man's steely gaze flicked to Finn. "What kind of law are you?"

"I'm with the Marshal's Bluff PD," Finn answered.

Hayley declared, "He's a friend."

Timothy rolled his shoulders and refocused on Hayley. "Some folks saw your boy at the rave a couple of nights ago. They noticed, because he was new, and he was running."

Hayley took a half step back, and Finn leaned forward to steady her.

"Running from who?" Finn asked.

"Don't know," the man said. "But more than one person saw him, so he was there."

"Where?"

"Winthrop's—you know it?"

"Yeah." The old warehouse had nearly burned down several years back. The owners couldn't afford the repairs, and their insurance had lapsed, so the city had condemned it. "That place isn't structurally sound. No one should be in there, especially not a crowd. The whole thing could've collapsed."

The guy made a painfully bland expression. "Not my business."

"Do you know when the next rave will be?" Finn asked.

If ravers recognized Gage because he wasn't a regular, then maybe Finn and another detective could drop in and talk to attendees. Get firsthand information.

"Nah, man. It's a pop-up. Place changes. Day changes. Time changes. You know that, Detective." The last few words were said in a pointed tone, and Finn bristled. He hadn't told Timothy he was a detective, but he was right on both counts. Finn knew all about the raves. They were a thorn in the side of Marshal's Bluff PD. The department tried to bust up the parties anytime they could, but getting wind of one ahead of time had proven impossible, and hearing about a rave while it was in motion was rare. Lots of drugs and money exchanged hands on those nights, along with plenty of other illegal activities, he was sure. "Why'd you ask if I was a detective if you already knew?"

"That wasn't what I asked." Timothy turned dark eyes back to Hayley. "I asked what kind of law you are. She knew the answer."

Finn considered the words. Timothy had wanted to know if he could be trusted.

With that, the man turned and walked away.

Chapter Five

Hayley chewed her lip as she walked at Finn's side. She'd spoken to a lot of people in a short amount of time. No one had known where Gage was, but several women with children now planned to sleep at the mission, and more than a dozen souls weren't hungry at the moment, thanks to her trip to Old Downtown. Despite feelings of defeat, she couldn't be wholly disappointed in the morning's outcome.

She was especially thankful for Timothy's efforts to acquire information on the missing teen, though she hoped no one had been harmed in the process. Timothy's rage was legendary and the reason he'd lost his little girl to the system last year. The only thing bigger than his temper was his love for Sonia. So he'd taken the required anger-management courses, started working out and joined a local basketball league to burn off the excess stress of his job and being a single parent. He'd gotten Sonia back in only a few months. He did the work and set a good example for his daughter. Hayley had endless respect for that. And sincere appreciation for the lead he'd provided on Gage, thin as it was.

"I know the rave has been over for days," she said, stealing a look at Finn. "But Winthrop's is only two blocks from here."

He slid his eyes to her without missing a step. "You want to go there?"

She nodded. "I know Gage isn't there, and likely no one else will be either, but it's all we've got to go on right now. If we leave without stopping by, I'll wonder if we missed a huge clue, and it will eat at me."

Finn inhaled deeply and released the breath on a slow exhale. "I'd rather send a couple of uniforms to follow up on that, but I don't suppose that'll satisfy you?"

Hayley stopped walking. "It's the only place I know he's been in the last couple of days, aside from visiting me at lunch. I need to see it."

She was certain every protective fiber in Finn's body wanted to get her away from Old Downtown as quickly as possible, but he knew her well enough to understand she wasn't asking his permission. Letting her go alone was more dangerous than going with her, so he'd agree eventually. "Come with me?"

A long, quiet moment elapsed between them. A muscle in his jaw flexed and tightened. Then, he cracked. First his expression, then his stance.

"Fine, but I go in first, and you stay with me. Not just where I can see you, but within arm's reach. That place was condemned for a reason. It's unsafe. And it's known to attract trouble."

"Agreed." Hayley turned and headed in the direction of the old warehouse that overlooked the harbor. She concentrated to keep her steps even, though she wanted to break into a run. As if Gage might be there if she hurried. Instead, she slowed her breathing, reminding herself to be vigilant and focused. She had no idea what she might find if she really looked.

Finn increased his pace casually when they got closer to the building, his long strides forcing her to speed up. He placed himself a half step ahead on the sidewalk outside the door, then raised one arm in front of her like a gate.

Hayley stilled, surveying the crumbling, neglected exterior. Winthrop's was a stout, vacant space that had once held boats and shipping containers for the fishing company. The property, formerly home to a thriving enterprise, was now a heinous eyesore. Its charred bricks and cracked windows rotted darkly beneath a scorched metal roof. All evidence of the fire that had bankrupted the owners.

Finn opened the door with little effort, and she followed him inside—they were as silent as two ghosts.

The air was hot and dry, laced with salt from

the nearby ocean and ash from the singed interior beams. Litter covered the floor—empty liquor bottles and beer cans, fast-food wrappers and cigarette butts. Ironic, she thought, to smoke in a building that'd nearly burned to the ground.

Finn moved methodically through the space, examining the open areas, then clearing the sections blocked from view by partial walls and pallets of materials from an abandoned reconstruction effort.

Distant sounds of the ocean, bleating tugboats and screaming gulls, traveled in through a large portion of missing wall at the back. Hayley moved to the floor's edge and peered over the steep plummet to the water. Intense sunlight reflected off the crystal surface, while small white wave breaks rolled steadily toward the shore. The drop from the warehouse was survivable, if the unfortunate person landed far enough away to hit the water, or close enough to begin an early roll down the hillside, instead of a midpoint smack against the narrow, rocky shoreline below.

Thankfully there wasn't any sign of Gage, hurt, suffering, or worse, in view.

She imagined him running through the warehouse packed with people and music raging into the rafters, then leaping to his escape.

"You okay?" Finn asked, moving to her side.

"Yeah." She pulled her gaze away from the

water, blinking to refocus on him in the shadow of the building. "Notice anything useful?"

He shook his head. "You want to walk the perimeter?"

She led the way back through the front door and around the side of the building. Her skin heated with the late morning sun as they moved over broken asphalt. Humidity tugged at her hair and added beads of sweat to her temples.

When they'd finished the circuit, Finn turned to her, hands on hips. His frown suggested he was as frustrated as she was. "I'm sorry this didn't go better."

"It's not your fault," she said, feeling the pressure of defeat on her chest once more. "At least everyone around here knows I'm looking for him. Someone will deliver the message."

Finn nodded, his keen gaze and trained eyes dragging over everything in sight, probably seeing a lot more than she did in the dirty streets and dilapidated landscape. "I'm in the middle of a missing-persons case too," he said, surprising her with the unexpected disclosure. "I was looking for her all day yesterday and hoping for a win today. I'm not used to striking out twice in a row."

Hayley had no doubt that was true, but she kept the thought to herself. Beaumont men rarely failed at anything they were determined to achieve. "Who were you looking for?" she asked. "I'm sure they'll turn up with you on the case."

She offered a small smile he didn't return.

"Katherine Everett."

"The philanthropist?" she asked, officially stunned.

"Yep."

Hayley raised her eyebrows. "Any chance she'll turn up at a spa retreat in the mountains?"

"So far, she doesn't seem to be anywhere."

"Did you know she's building a shelter and community center down here?" Hayley asked. "She wants to make better use of all these blocks of crime and waste."

"I've heard," he said. "My family's ranch donated to the effort. It's long overdue. People experiencing homelessness should have somewhere safe to stay while getting on their feet."

Hayley's heart swelled at his words. It was easy to forget how steeped in this community Finn and his family were, and that his parents dedicated themselves to the betterment of life for Marshal's Bluff youths. "It's hard enough for people to find themselves in need of shelter. Harder still when the only placement available is in the basement of an old church—not that staying at the mission isn't better than being on the street," she clarified.

"There's a lot to be said for dignity," Finn agreed. "The entire project will add hope to an area that's been without it too long. This town has too many people in need. Kate's project will be an incredible boon."

"It will," she agreed. "The number of kids in our local foster system is beginning to outweigh the number of available families. I don't suppose you've thought of adopting?" Hayley asked.

When she'd dated Finn, he'd talked about wanting children of his own, but he'd make a great role model for any child. He was tough but fair, strong-willed but willing to compromise and loving but never a pushover. All things that struggling youths needed in their lives. For their emotional security and as an example of what a leader and high-quality human should be. "Or maybe becoming a foster parent?"

Finn pursed his lips. "I work too many hours. Kids need routine and reliability, not an adult running off at all hours, or one who's never home for dinner." He dragged emotion-filled eyes back to her. "If I had someone to care for, I'd want them to know they could count on me to be there."

Hayley tucked a swath of windblown hair behind her ear, his searing gaze burning a hole in her heart.

"How about you?" he asked. "Have you considered fostering or adoption?"

"I wanted to foster Gage," she confessed. "I knew the moment I met him. I could be there for him, helping in any way he needed. I could make him feel seen and loved. Support him through his grief. But I also know the system prefers couples and people twice my age for foster families, so I didn't bother throwing my hat in the ring."

Finn frowned. "What happened with him? How'd he end up on your caseload?"

"He lost his parents last year. A drunk driver. Before that, the three of them were a run-of-the-mill, happy family."

Breath left Finn in an audible whoosh. "Oh, man. To go from that to the system—"

"Yeah."

"No relatives?"

"None." Though Hayley certainly felt as if Gage was her family, and she wished she would've asked to foster him when she had the chance. She should've pleaded her case. But at the time, she'd felt the way Finn had described, unsure she had time to be all the things Gage needed. She was gone ten hours a day and often brought her work home. Plus, she'd never been a parent. She had no experience raising a teen, and she'd been a teen not so long ago in the court's eyes. She wasn't sure she'd ever actually been a kid, though. She'd been taking care of herself and her alcoholic mother since she could reach the doorknob to let herself in and out for school and trips to buy bread and eggs. "I didn't try to get him placed into my care, because I knew there'd be a fight in court. I'd have to prove myself, and I didn't want him drawn into all that when he'd just been orphaned. It wasn't fair."

"Most things aren't," Finn replied. "But you're the one out here looking for him now. What about the family he was placed with, what are they doing?"

Hayley bit back a barrage of unkind thoughts about the Michaelsons. "They have several kids at their place. I'm sure they're doing their best."

Finn narrowed his eyes. "Yeah?"

She looked away. The Michaelsons weren't her favorite foster family, but they seemed to do what they could, and that was more than she could say for some.

"I'm just learning Gage's story, and so far I know you're the one feeding him lunch every day. You're the one he came to see when something was wrong. You know about his art, and there's pride in your eyes when you look at it. Even though you know defacing public property is a crime. I'd say the two of you have chosen one another, regardless of the court's decision. You should see what you can do about that after we find him."

Hayley blinked back tears at the perfection of his words and the sincerity in the delivery. "He's a good kid. He shouldn't be painting the buildings, but he's not hurting anything down here, and he's working through his stuff." She scanned their surroundings in search of Gage's work and spotted an example several buildings away. Finn was right. She was proud of the kid's talent, and his outlet of choice. Plenty of other young adults in his situation would lash out with violence or fall into drug use. Gage chose to send messages to others who felt unseen, and to the system that made them feel that way.

She moved toward the painting in slow motion, drawn by something she couldn't put a finger on.

"What do you see?" Finn asked, falling into step at her side.

"It's unfinished." She lifted a finger to the silhouette when she noticed the missing section. "Why would he leave it like that?"

Finn examined the place where the image ended abruptly. "Out of paint?" he mused.

Hayley spotted a can on the ground across the street and went to pick it up. She gave the cylinder a shake then pointed the nozzle at the ground and pressed. A thick stream of black emerged.

Finn grunted. "We're not far from the rave location. He said he saw something he shouldn't?"

She turned slowly, following his train of thought. "He could've been standing across the street, painting, when something went wrong. Then he ran."

"Raves are nice and loud," Finn said. "Plenty of people and chaos. Easy place to disappear."

And Winthrop's warehouse had a giant escape hatch in back.

A spike of adrenaline shot through her. She was likely standing where Gage had been when he'd seen the thing that scared him. If she was right, then she knew what he'd been doing and where he'd run to hide. "What did he see?"

She scanned the area with new eyes, searching all the places and things visible from her standpoint. An apparition of heat rolled like fog above the street. The rising sun baked her fair skin.

Finn rubbed the back of his neck. "With a rave going on nearby, there would've been a lot of witnesses if something happened on the street. I'd guess he saw something done discreetly, through a window or in an alley."

"It's not uncommon for people to keep their mouths shut about crime," Hayley said. "No one wants to get involved or become a snitch."

"But Gage ran," Finn countered. "He'd had a safe and normal life last year. So the question becomes, did he run explicitly out of fear, or because he was being chased?"

"Chased," Hayley said, suddenly confident in her answer. "Why run through the rave if not? And why was the can over here, when he was painting across the street, and the rave was down there?"

Finn looked from Hayley to the incomplete artwork, then down the block to Winthrop's warehouse. "The can could've been kicked or blown over—" Finn's words stopped short, and his gaze fixed on something.

"What is it?" Hayley asked, moving closer to watch and listen.

"My gut," he said. "See the big orange *Xs* painted on those doors?"

She followed his line of sight to the set of buildings in question. All were in rough shape, but none appeared any worse than the other structures around them. "It means they're marked for demolition."

"They're being razed for Kate's project," Finn added. "She purchased a large section of adjoining properties. Construction won't begin until next year, but removal of everything in the work zone starts in a few weeks. I read up on all the details after she went missing." He turned to Hayley, eyes wary. "Kate disappeared two nights ago."

"The same night Gage saw something." Hayley considered the unlikely possibility that her friend's disappearance could have anything to do with a wealthy philanthropist. "Kate wouldn't have any reason to visit this place at night, would she?" Or at all? Didn't investors only show up when their projects were complete? To cut a ribbon with giant scissors and make a public speech?

Finn took a step toward the nearest building with a big, orange *X*. He bumped her as he passed. "We might as well take a look around while we're here."

"You don't think the two are connected?"

He tipped his head noncommittally, left then right. "Probably not, but I like to cover my bases."

Hayley stepped aside when they reached the door, allowing Finn to try the knob.

Her heart rate climbed as the barrier creaked open. A wall of heat and sour air sent them back a step.

Finn covered his mouth and nose with the collar of his shirt, while she fought the urge to gag. "Stay here."

Hayley easily complied, angling her face away, desperate for the fresher air.

A low guttural moan and series of cuss words rose from the detective inside. He crouched over a still form covered in newspapers and raised a cell phone to his ear. "We've got a crime scene," he said.

"Is that...?" Hayley asked.

He glanced remorsefully in her direction. "Yeah." He stretched upright and returned to the doorway. "This is Detective Finn Beaumont," he told the person on the other end of his call. "I need the coroner and a CSI team with complete discretion. No lights or sirens. Unmarked vehicles. I've just found the body of Katherine Everett."

Chapter Six

Hayley leaned against a telephone pole on the sidewalk near Gage's unfinished painting while men and women swarmed the street, working the crime scene. The first responders on-site wore plain clothes, as Finn had requested. Those who came later had on ball caps and T-shirts with the Marshal's Bluff PD logo, or the simple black polos of the coroner's office. A handful, presently taking photographs, setting up small, numbered teepees, or swabbing the building for trace evidence, wore lanyards and carried toolboxes with *CSI* emblazoned on them.

Hayley used the massive wooden pole at her back for support and concentrated on her breathing. She didn't need a criminal-justice degree to know what Gage had seen that night. And how much trouble he was in now. There'd be a large bounty on the head of the person who killed Katherine Everett, beloved community member and philanthropist. She and her family's money single-handedly funded two seasonal soup kitchens, kept the lights on at the mission's shelter for women and children and made sure no Marshal's Bluff student left school on weekends, holidays or summer breaks without food. Her family had the means to hunt down anyone with information about her murder. Making Gage a major liability to the killer.

Understanding why anyone would want to harm her was another story.

The coroner had declared the cause of death as blunt-force trauma. The weapon, a broken two-by-four, had done irreparable damage to her skull and brain. The bullet in her chest was unnecessary excess.

A commotion at the opposite curb drew Hayley's attention to a news van, the first of what would undoubtedly be many within the hour. Thankfully, Kate's body was long gone, removed from the crime scene by the coroner as quickly as possible following his arrival. There'd been a brief exam, preliminary findings were recorded, then she was loaded into the van and taken away. The media wouldn't get the salacious photos they hoped for today.

Officers met the crew as they climbed out, directing them to relocate behind the barricades a block away.

Yep, Hayley thought. *Chaos is coming.*

An unmistakable thrumming drew her eyes to

the sky, where a helicopter appeared, bearing the local television station's call number in bright red.

Word was definitely out now.

A sharp whistle turned her around and raised an unexpected smile on her lips.

Austin and Dean Beaumont appeared. They strode in her direction, long legs eating up the distance to her side.

Austin lifted her off the ground in a hug, and Dean embraced her the moment his little brother set her free. They smiled broadly, offering warm greetings and reminding her of another reason she'd loved being in Finn's life. His brothers were the very best.

"We just heard about this," Dean said, blue eyes flashing with interest. "We were hired to take the missing-persons case this morning."

"Barely started our research before the call came," Austin added. "This is messed up."

"Agreed," Hayley said.

Dean scanned the bustling scene, then shot the chopper a death stare. "She was a huge proponent of good things here. I can't understand who'd do this."

"That makes two of us," Hayley said.

"Three," Austin countered. "How much do you know?"

Hayley exchanged information with the brothers, falling easily into the familiar rapport. Austin was a Beaumont by blood. Dean and his younger brother, Jake, an ATF agent, had been adopted as kids, not that it mattered, or anyone ever talked about it. Still, in her line of work, and with her heart set on gaining custody of Gage, it warmed her to know families could blend and heal into one perfect unit when enough love and dedication was involved. She had both in spades.

Austin folded his arms, taking in the scene. "You think your missing kid saw what happened?"

She nodded and pointed to the unfinished painting. "I think he was painting when he saw her murder, or the killer leaving the scene, and ran."

Dean scrubbed a hand through thick, dark hair and swore. "That'd put a target on his back. Whoever killed Kate will know her family has the money and connections necessary to find them."

Austin's gaze traveled thoughtfully over the silhouette painted on the nearby building. "Your kid painted this?"

Hayley nodded, pride filling her chest.

"He's good."

"He is," she agreed.

Gage's potential to heal from his unthinkable losses and become a man who made a difference in the world was outstanding. Even if he felt lost sometimes, Hayley could see the warm, bright future out there waiting for him. And she'd stick by him until he saw it too.

"I've noticed these shadow people popping up around here for a few months," Austin said. "I wondered who was responsible." He turned an appreciative look her way. "I'm impressed the artist is just a kid."

Hayley swallowed the lump in her throat. "He's a good kid who's had a bad year, and he doesn't deserve any of this."

Dean gave Hayley a pat on her back, then headed across the street toward Finn.

Austin watched him go, then squinted appraisingly at Hayley.

Goose bumps rose on her skin. It was already unfair that Beaumont men were so disarmingly attractive, but the fact they also seemed to share some kind of mind-reading ability was just too much. She rolled her eyes. "What?"

"Long time no see. Where ya been hiding, Campbell?"

She looked away, in no kind of headspace for the conversation he wanted.

"Okay," he relented, breaking into a ridiculously breathtaking smile. "I get it. We can talk about what happened between you and my brother another time."

"I'm literally never talking to you about that," she said sweetly. "Ever."

"Wrong."

Hayley laughed despite herself. "Goof."

Finn's pain had no doubt affected everyone

who loved him. She was sorry about that, but
there was only one person she'd discuss her failed
relationship with, and it was Finn, not Austin.

"I know some people out this way," he said,
changing the subject. "I'll put out some feelers
and see what I can learn about your boy. One
thing that's always true in this business is that
nothing goes completely unseen. If my informants can't dig him up, or won't tell me where
he is, I can at least ask them to keep him safe
until we find whoever's responsible for this." He
tipped his head toward the building where Kate's
body had been found.

Unexpected emotion stung her eyes and blurred
her vision. The idea strangers might look out for
Gage until she could do the job herself pulled
her heartstrings. Renegade tears rolled over her
cheeks, and she swiped them away.

"Hey now." Austin stepped forward, pulling
her against his chest and wrapping her in a hug.
He rubbed her back in small, awkward strokes.
"We'll find him and bring him back to you safely.
That's a promise."

Hayley returned his embrace, holding on tight
to her would-have-been brother-in-law and to a
thousand silent prayers that he was right.

FINN'S GAZE DRIFTED past Dean's shoulder, drawn
to Hayley yet again. He couldn't quite believe
she'd dropped back into his life after a year of

silence, or that she was really standing across the street right now. Had they actually spent the day together? And how was she so wholly un-affected by their split, when it had broken him completely?

They'd been in love. He'd proposed, and she'd vanished.

The memory still gutted him, but he was glad to see she was doing well. Even at his worst, he'd hated the possibility she was sad or alone. He'd had a horde of family members to comfort and annoy him during the tough times. Hayley didn't have that.

Across the street, Austin's smile faded and he embraced her. Hayley held him tight.

"What do you suppose that's about?" Dean asked.

"It's been a day," Finn answered honestly. And it was barely afternoon. "I'm sure she needed it."

"We all miss her, ya know?" Dean asked.

"I know."

Hayley fit with his family in ways he never dreamed someone could. She belonged with them, if not with him. And he hoped that maybe, after this case was closed, she'd come around more often. She didn't have to be lonely when there was an army of Beaumonts who loved her. If she wanted them, he'd even keep himself in check so she wouldn't feel as if their presence in her life required his.

"You ever find out what happened with her?" Dean asked.

"Why she loved me one minute and disappeared on me the next?" Finn squinted against the southern summer sun. "Nope. And I don't plan on it. If she wants me to know, she'll tell me."

"Funny she didn't call the police about the gunman or her missing kid," Dean said, his tone painfully casual.

Finn frowned. "She came directly to the station."

Dean nodded, keen gaze darting back across the street to Hayley and Finn. "Most people get shot at, they call 911."

"And?"

"She drove straight to you."

Finn widened his stance and crossed his arms over his chest. "Because she's smart."

Dean grinned.

"I plan to find her missing kid as soon as possible," Finn said. "Likely before we figure out who's after him. I'd like to set him up at the ranch until I'm sure he'll be safe elsewhere. I can't promise he won't run again if we take him back to the foster home, and Hayley will want to keep him with her if he doesn't stay there."

"That'd put her in danger," Dean said.

"Exactly. Any idea how many beds are open at the ranch right now?"

"No, but there's always room for one more," Dean said, quoting their mama. "I'll let her know he's coming when I drop in for dinner."

Finn nodded his gratitude. "He paints those."

Dean followed his raised finger to the painting behind Hayley and Finn. "She mentioned that. Kid's got talent."

"And a heart for people. Probably one of the reasons Hayley bonded with him so quickly."

"He'll be a good fit at the ranch," Dean said. "Lincoln can show him the ropes. Redirect his energies. Give him another outlet while this is sorted."

"Good idea. Lincoln could use a project involving people." Their brother, a recent veteran and current stable hand, spent too much time alone, brooding, with the animals. "He'd be feral by now, if not for Josi."

Dean puffed air through his nose. "I don't know how she puts up with him, but they make it work."

Finn couldn't help wondering how long they'd continue to make it work after Lincoln realized he was in love with the young stable manager, but that answer would come in time.

"Heads up," Dean said, pulling Finn's attention to Hayley and Austin.

The pair headed across the street.

Hayley appeared unsure, as if she might be asked to vacate the crime scene, even with the three of them at her side. Austin looked as he always did, entitled to be anywhere he pleased.

"Hey there, brother," Austin said, offering Finn the quick two-step handshake they'd adopted in high school. "Your girl caught me up on things. Now, what's our move?"

Finn ignored the pinch in his chest at Austin's word choice, then turned to the beauty at his side. "I think it's time to let your office know you'll be out for a few more days. Until we identify Katherine Everett's killer, we'll need a revised plan for your safety."

Hayley nodded. "Okay."

And Finn would start by accepting that spare bedroom she'd mentioned this morning.

Chapter Seven

Hayley curled on her couch that night with a bottle of water and take-out tacos. She and Finn had left the crime scene shortly after his brothers' arrival, and she'd tagged along when Finn was called to the station. A few hours later, they'd picked up dinner. Nothing about her day seemed real. In fact, she'd spent the past twenty-four hours feeling as if she was trapped in a terrible dream. Gage's fear. His disappearance. The gunman. Now a dead socialite. None of it made any sense.

Still, the truth sat two cushions away, unwrapping his third El Guaco Taco. The urge to poke Finn with a finger, just to make sure she wasn't dreaming, circled in her thoughts. Her one true love, and almost-fiancé, was at her home after a year of silence between them, and planning to sleep over. For her protection. Was any of this even real?

"Ow." Finn turned amused eyes on her. "What was that for?"

She bent the finger she'd poked him with and returned the hand to her lap. "Making sure I'm awake," she admitted. "This day has me questioning everything."

"Well, I appreciate the offer to stay in the spare room," he said, running a paper napkin over his lips. "The truck isn't as comfortable as it looks."

Hayley laughed, surprising herself and earning a grin from Finn.

He gathered their discarded wrappers when they finished, then headed for her kitchen.

"You don't have to clean up," she called, twisting to watch him over the back of the couch as he walked away.

"And you didn't have to let me stay here, but you did." He retook his seat a moment later, a little closer to her this time.

"Do you really think someone might show up here?" she asked, images of the man outside the black SUV flashing through her mind.

Finn offered a small, encouraging smile. "I don't want you to worry, so consider this a favor to me. I always assume the worst where criminals are concerned, and in a worst-case scenario, I can do a much better job protecting you from in here than from outside. Plus, this gives me peace of mind, which means I might get some sleep. I need the rest if I'm going to find Gage and capture Kate's killer as soon as possible."

Hayley relaxed by a fraction. "Have I thanked

you for helping me? Because it's all I can think about. I needed someone, and you were the only name in my head. After everything that happened between us, you never hesitated."

"Did you think I might?" he asked, a note of concern in his tone.

"No," she said instantly, and honestly. "But it still feels unbelievable. I owe you—"

"Ten bucks for tacos?" he asked, shifting forward and taking his gaze with him. "Don't worry about it."

Finn might not want to hear it, but she had things she needed to say.

"An apology."

"We don't need to talk about that right now."

"Finn." Hayley swiveled on her seat to face him fully. "We should've talked about this a year ago, but I was a coward."

He shook his head, still not meeting her eye. "It's fine. It's in the past. What matters most now is that you knew you could come to me. I will find Gage, and Dean's talked to our folks. Gage can stay at the ranch until we know he's safe. They're already making room. You and I can visit as often as you want while we find the person who's been following you and hunting him."

Hayley's heart swelled at Finn's casual use of the word *we*. He wasn't pulling the detective card or shoving her away. He certainly had every right, especially when he hadn't let her apologize or explain why she'd vanished on him last year. He deserved so much better.

Finn's phone rang and his lips twitched with the hint of a smile as he looked at the display. He lifted a finger to Hayley, indicating he needed a moment before he answered.

An immediate and nonsensical stroke of displeasure coursed through her. Was he seeing someone? Did she care? She certainly had no right.

"Hey, Mama," he said. "Everything okay?"

Hayley grabbed her water bottle for a long drink, then worked to get her head on straight. She wasn't the jealous type, and she had no claim to Finn. Clearly, all the turmoil from a wild day had scrambled her brain.

"Which channel?" he asked, pulling Hayley's attention to him once more.

She grabbed the television remote and passed it his way.

"Thanks, Mama. Love you." He disconnected the call and navigated to the local news. "They're covering Kate's case on Channel Three."

"I saw the chopper this morning."

"Yeah," he said. "I guess they sent a crew later."

Finn leaned forward, resting his elbows on his thighs as he waited.

Two overly charismatic anchors announced the next segment, and Finn pumped up the volume.

Soon the streets of Old Downtown appeared.

Words scrolled across the bottom of the screen announcing "Death of a Philanthropist: Body of Katherine Everett located among trash in abandoned building."

"She was covered in newspapers," Finn complained. "It was meant to disguise the body as a sleeping squatter. They make it sound as if she was tossed beside a pile of garbage bags, or worse. The media always has to sensationalize everything." He kneaded together his hands, visibly annoyed. "They do this junk intentionally for views, and it gets the public all wound up. Then the phone lines at the station are bombarded for a week with citizens worried about a million nonemergency, nonthreatening things."

Hayley tucked her feet beneath her and focused on the television. She knew exactly what he meant. Anytime something bad happened in town, the local news blew it up as big as they could and anxiety rose across the board. Social workers, counselors and medical professionals all saw corresponding rises in their workload for as long as the secondary situation continued being covered.

On the TV screen, a reporter stood outside the building where Kate's body had been found. The sun was low in the sky, the CSI team gone, as she gave the most generic of comments about the day's events.

"This is good," Finn said. "Sounds as if we've

kept a lid on the details." The relief in his features touched Hayley's heart.

Finn gave his all in everything he did.

He'd done a lot of very nice things with her once.

She shook away the sudden rush of heat and memories as the camera angle changed, widening to reveal a familiar face at the reporter's side. "A local private detective, Austin Beaumont, has been at the scene all day."

Finn groaned. "This explains why Mama was watching the news. He must've told her he'd be on."

"Why didn't he tell you?" Hayley asked.

The look on Finn's face suggested he could think of a number of reasons his brother hadn't mentioned the on-screen interview, and none of them were great.

"Can you tell us what brought you to Old Downtown today?" the reporter asked. "Were you hired to assist in the investigation of Katherine Everett's murder? Was it Marshal's Bluff PD who reached out to you, or was it a private party?"

Austin sucked his teeth and stared at the camera. "At Beaumont Investigations, we take privacy seriously, and we don't answer questions." He tipped two fingers to the brim of his hat and walked away.

Hayley burst into laughter.

Finn smiled as he watched her. "I thought that

was going to go much more poorly. He hates reporters."

"Well, he's smart," she said. "He parlayed that annoyance into excellent business exposure."

Finn lifted the remote, whether to turn the television off or the volume down, she wasn't sure, but her breath caught as a familiar figure and dark SUV appeared on-screen. "What's wrong?" he asked.

Hayley blinked, afraid the man might disappear if she looked away. "I think that's the guy I saw outside the parking lot when I found the note."

Finn paused the television before the scene could change. Then he lifted his phone once more.

A mass of chills ran down Hayley's spine, and a slight tremor began in her hands.

"Ball cap. Sunglasses. Black T-shirt," Finn said to someone on the phone. He pointed the remote toward her television again and the SUV rolled off-screen.

"Dammit," Finn said. "They didn't catch the plate." He wrapped up his call and turned to her. "How do you feel about staying at my place?"

"Not great," she said honestly. "I'm hoping Gage will realize he needs help and come here to find me."

Finn leveled her with his trademark no-nonsense stare. "I understand that, but I can protect you better there."

She dithered, frozen by an impossible choice. How could she risk missing Gage? But how could she know he'd come? If he didn't seek her, and she or Finn were injured as a result of waiting for him, it would be her fault. If she left and Gage was injured after arriving and not finding the help he needed, it would be her fault.

"I can assign someone to keep an eye on the house," Finn said gently. "If Gage comes here, they'll intercept him."

Her heart dropped at the possibility Gage would come to her home for help, and she wouldn't be there.

"I have a guest room too," he reminded her. "It's not the same as sleeping in your own bed, but at least you'll know you aren't in danger."

"I'm not sure I'll be able to rest anywhere tonight," she admitted.

Not with Finn under the same roof.

"What if I remind you that the minute my mama knows you're there she'll be on her way with casseroles and hugs? All shameless ploys to keep you."

Hayley thought of Mrs. Beaumont's warm hugs and casseroles, then pushed onto her feet. Everyone would be safer if she agreed to Finn's terms, and that was all that mattered. "Who can say no to your mama's casseroles?"

"No one yet."

"I guess I'd better get dressed and pack a bag," she said, heading swiftly toward the stairs.

"Mama wins again."

FINN DROVE SLOWLY to his place, watching carefully for signs of a tail. He'd been concerned twice in town, but as the traffic and bustle of Marshal's Bluff gave way to rural back roads lined with farms and livestock, his truck quickly became the only vehicle in sight.

Dean and Austin were already in place. They'd swept the property and posted up as additional eyes to verify Finn and Hayley arrived safely.

The home had been purchased under the name of a limited-liability corporation to increase anonymity. And he'd spent several long weekends outfitting the place with abundant security measures.

Still, an influx of misplaced dread tightened his gut as they drew nearer. The last time Hayley had visited Finn's home, he'd proposed. He'd spent hours preparing that day, lining the driveway and drenching the sprawling trees in twinkle lights. Even longer practicing what he would say. The weight of the engagement ring in his pocket had felt life-affirming. He'd known without a doubt that the woman at his side was meant for him, and he would've done everything in his power to make her happy. Forever.

An hour later, she'd been gone. And his phone

hadn't stopped ringing for days as the news swept through his family.

"I forgot how beautiful this place is," Hayley said, pulling him back to the moment.

Security lighting illuminated his home and perimeter landscaping now. Hidden cameras tracked and reported everything to a system inside. Silhouettes of his brothers' parked vehicles came into view at the back of the home as the driveway snaked around an incline.

Two familiar figures moved into view, hands raised in greeting as Finn drove the final few yards.

"Looks like we're all clear," he said, glancing her way.

Hayley's smile was radiant. "I'm always amazed by how intimidating this couple of goof-balls can appear."

Finn shifted the truck into Park and considered his approaching brothers once more, trying to see them from someone else's perspective.

They were tall and broad, moving in near sync with long, determined strides. Their expressions were hidden beneath the shadows of plain black ball caps. He supposed, at first glance, or if he squinted a little, he could imagine them as dangerous. But anytime he saw Austin and Dean working together like this, he could only think of the time they'd attempted to build a tree house, only to wind up in a fight over the design that rolled them both off the platform.

Finn climbed out to thank their personal protection detail. They exchanged greetings and farewells, then Finn grabbed Hayley's bags and led her into his home.

He watched from the window as his brothers' taillights shrank in the distance—but he knew they wouldn't go far. Dean and Austin would likely split up and take shifts. One keeping watch on Finn's home, the other running leads on Gage's whereabouts. Like Finn, the PIs wouldn't get much sleep until this was over.

"I'll take your things to the guest room," Finn said, turning back to Hayley. "Make yourself at home. Consider this place yours until it's safe for you to go home."

"Thank you."

Finn moved through the open-concept living space and kitchen to a hallway with three bedrooms and a shared bath. His throat tightened as he fought a wave of unexpected and unpleasant emotions. Now wasn't the time to get nostalgic or wish things had gone differently. They hadn't. And that was life.

"Wow," Hayley said, her voice carrying to his ears. "You've completely remodeled."

He opened the guest-room door and set her bags on the bed, allowing himself one long breath before squaring his shoulders and heading back. "Yeah."

He'd taken his excess energy out on his home following their breakup, starting with refaced cabinets, new countertops and a farmhouse sink in the kitchen. Refinished floors, new paint and light fixtures everywhere else. He'd barely had a day off in the last year that hadn't involved at least one trip to the local hardware store.

"It's great," she said. "I love it."

"Thanks." Finn emerged from the hallway to find her admiring the kitchen. "Can I get you something to drink?"

She shook her head and her cheeks darkened.

He told himself she wasn't thinking of the things they'd done on his old countertop, and he pushed the thoughts from his mind as well.

"I should probably try to sleep," she said.

"Of course. I've got some work to do so…" He let his eyes fall shut when she passed him, making the trip to her room, not his.

THE SOUND OF the doorbell shot Finn onto his feet the next morning. He stumbled back, knocking his calves against the couch and blinking away the remnants of sleep he hadn't meant to get. A bevy of curses ran through his thoughts as he moved forward, wiping his eyes and hoping to stop the bell from chiming again.

A rush of breath left his chest as he passed

the front window. A familiar truck was parked beyond the porch. He checked his watch, then opened the door.

His parents waited outside, smiling brightly as the barrier swung wide.

"Morning, Mama," he said, planting a kiss on her head as she hustled past.

"Morning, baby boy," she cooed, already half-way to the kitchen. She'd tied her salt-and-pepper hair away from her face in a low ponytail and wore jeans with boots and a T-shirt. Oven mitts covered her hands, a foil-covered casserole in her grip.

Finn was still wearing the sweatpants and T-shirt he'd changed into before beginning his on-line research the night before.

"Dad." He drew the older man into a quick hug, then followed him to the new granite-topped island.

"Morning."

Finn dragged a hand through sleep-mussed hair and rubbed fatigue from his eyes. "Can't say I'm surprised to see y'all, but you could've waited until at least eight."

"We've been up since five thirty," his dad said, adjusting the cowboy hat on his head. His black T-shirt was new and emblazoned with the ranch insignia. His jeans and boots were probably from the year he'd gotten married. "Your mama's been trying to get me out the door since six."

Mrs. Beaumont tucked the casserole into Finn's

oven and set the timer. "He came up with every chore under the sun to do before we could leave."

"That's the life of a farmer," his dad said, setting additional dishes and bags onto the counter. "Can't be helped."

"We have farm hands," she countered. "You were stalling."

"You were rushing."

Mama shrugged and turned her eyes to Finn. "Where is Hayley? Can we see her?"

"She's not a puppy," his father said. "And she's probably still in bed. It's barely seven a.m."

"Nonsense. Who's sleeping at this hour?"

Finn raised a hand. "I was sleeping until you rang the bell."

"Silly." His mama fixed him with a no-nonsense stare. "It's time to start your day. We've heard all about what's going on. It was smart of you to bring Hayley here. She's much safer in our hands than alone at her place."

Finn traded a look with their father. His mother's use of the word *our* implied that she planned to stay involved. Probably not the best idea, but there was little to be done about it. No one talked her out of anything. Ever.

"We fixed up the storage cabin for the missing boy. Gage, is it?" she asked. "He'll like it. Tell me about him."

Soft footfalls turned all their heads to the hallway, where Hayley appeared. Her pink cotton sleep shorts and white tank top were slightly askew. As if she'd hurried out of bed without thought of straightening them. Emotion crumpled her features. "Morning, Mama," she said, voice cracking.

"Sweet girl," his mama said, a moment before engulfing her in a hug.

A lump formed in Finn's throat as his father welcomed her back too.

Working this case without getting his heart broken again in the process was quickly disappearing as an option.

Chapter Eight

Hayley sank into the Beaumonts' welcoming arms. Though she prided herself on her fierce independence, there was something about a group hug from good parents, even if they weren't hers, that made everything better. Mr. and Mrs. Beaumont treated the entire world like family. They'd cared for her emotionally since the day they'd met, celebrating her victories, asking about her troubles and supporting her silently when she just needed to be in the presence of someone who truly saw her. She'd missed them horribly for the past year, but the weight of their absence hadn't fully hit until now.

She wiped her eyes discreetly as the couple pulled away. Then she smiled through tears of joy. "It's so nice to see you again."

"We brought food," Mrs. Beaumont said, batting away a few renegade tears. "There's a casserole warming in the oven, and I prepared some sandwiches, potato salad, fruit salad and a cheese-and-cracker assortment for later. There's a lasagna in the freezer, and a pie in the fridge."

A bubble of laughter broke on Hayley's lips. She looked to Finn, and found him smiling as well. The expression sent a jolt of warmth through her core.

Mr. Beaumont carried a pile of plates to the island, arranging one before each stool. Finn poured coffee into four mugs, and their fearless matriarch bustled cheerfully, preparing for the meal.

This could have been Hayley's life.

Every day.

But she'd let fear and unhealed trauma take that from her, and it was too late to get it back.

Hayley shoved aside past regrets and focused on the present. "Did I hear you say you've made room for Gage at the ranch?"

Mr. and Mrs. Beaumont turned to her, pride in their nearly matching expressions.

"We did," Mr. Beaumont said. "We turned one of the small storage cabins into a private space for him. He'll have plenty of room for independence and privacy while still being a stone's throw from us." He turned a thumb back and forth between his wife and himself. "Lincoln will work with him until he finds his rhythm."

Mrs. Beaumont's expression melted into concern. "Is that okay? We haven't overstepped?"

Hayley refreshed her smile, realizing it had begun to droop. "No. Of course not. The cabin sounds perfect. Thank you."

Finn moved in her direction and set a hand between her shoulder blades. "Gage is very important to Hayley," he said, giving voice to her thoughts when her tongue became wholly tied.

She dropped her gaze to the floor. "I should've fought for the ability to foster him the moment we met. I should be the one caring for him."

"You are." Finn spread his fingers and pressed gently against her back, offering the reassurance she craved.

When she raised her eyes to his, electricity crackled in the air.

Mr. Beaumont cleared his throat, breaking the strange spell. He exchanged a look with his wife. "We know quite a few people in positions to help you when the time comes. You can count on that."

Hayley's bottom lip quivered, and she nodded, unable to speak once more.

The Beaumonts had strong ties to everyone in the courthouse and offices related to child and family services. Their ranch was a major player in the rehabilitation and healing of youths. If anyone had the ability to influence related outcomes, it was them.

"Here, sweet girl," Mrs. Beaumont said, approaching and separating Hayley from Finn. "Let me feed you. Then you can tell us all about the boy who stole your heart."

Hayley's traitorous gaze moved to Finn and back to his mother, who'd caught the slip.

Mrs. Beaumont added scoops of casserole and warm, sliced bread to their plates. His father served fruit salad, and Finn delivered the caffeine.

Together, they took their seats and dug in.

Hayley told the Beaumonts all she knew and loved about Gage. Then she shared the little she'd learned about his disappearance. The older couple listened carefully. When the plates were mostly empty, Hayley's heart and stomach full, Mrs. Beaumont turned serious eyes on her son.

"Tell me what you know about Kate's death," she directed Finn.

He caught her up quickly, then refilled everyone's mugs.

"It's a real shame," his mother said. "Kate was a special woman. Her heart for this town and its citizens was huge. She was smart in business and driven by her compassion. I can't imagine who'd want to stop her."

"Was it a robbery?" his dad asked.

Finn shook his head. "Unlikely. She didn't have a purse or identification on her, which could point to a mugging, except that she was still wearing a watch and necklace with a combined value higher than my annual salary. And someone covered her in newspapers. Could've been a sign of regret as much as an attempt to disguise the body. The missing purse was possibly a failed attempt to misdirect the police or hide her identity."

"Any suspects?" Mrs. Beaumont asked.

"None that stand out for now," Finn said, taking a long pull on his coffee. "Finding our young witness will be a major help."

Hayley chewed her lip, reminded again that Gage was in hiding, alone and scared.

"I've got plans to interview the husband and some workers from the charity," Finn said. "We'll visit Gage's foster family while we're out, see if we can make some progress on that end as well."

"I doubt they know anything," Hayley said. "If he'd gone back there, someone would've called me."

"Speaking to the other foster kids could be useful," Finn said. "When I was young, I told my brothers everything."

"Still do," his mother said, looking slightly affronted. "Luckily, I've got a sixth sense for when something is going on with my kids, and I can usually press the weak link for information."

"For the record, I was never the weak link," Finn declared, one palm against his chest.

Hayley smiled, falling easily into rhythm with the family she'd always wanted. The family she could've had.

If she hadn't panicked and blown it.

FINN PILOTED HIS truck into the Michaelsons' driveway an hour later. His parents had hurried away after breakfast to handle business on the ranch, and Hayley had gotten ready quickly for a new day of investigation.

Despite the heat, she'd chosen jeans that stopped midcalf, sneakers and a blue silk tank top that accentuated her eyes and her curves.

"Here we go," she said, climbing down from the cab.

Finn met her at the front of his truck and reached for her hand. She accepted easily, and he squeezed her fingers before releasing her to lead the way to the door.

The old clapboard home was gray from age and weather. The red front door was battered with dents and dings. An array of toys and children's bikes cluttered the overgrown front lawn and walkway. All in all, it wasn't an idyllic scene, but Finn tried not to judge.

"How many kids are living here?" he asked, scrutinizing the postage-stamp yard and modest home.

"Five," Hayley said. "There are three bedrooms. Three middle-schoolers in one. Gage and a younger boy in another. Mr. and Mrs. Michaelson in the last."

Finn stared into the overflowing trash receptacle as Hayley rang the bell. Beer bottles were visible inside the bags. He had no problem with enjoying a drink or two, but there were more than a few visible bottles.

The door swept open before Finn could point out his concerns.

A woman in her late forties blinked against the sun. Her wide brown eyes were tired, her frame thin and shoulders curved. "Miss Campbell?" the woman asked, clearly stunned to see Hayley, though the disappearance of a child in her care should've made this meeting obvious and inevitable.

"Hello, Stacy," Hayley said. "May we come in?"

The woman stepped onto the porch, pulling her door shut behind her. "Sorry. Everyone is still sleeping. Can we talk here?"

Hayley's eyes darted to the closed door and back. She forced a tight smile. "Of course. This is my friend, Detective Beaumont. We're here to talk to you about Gage."

The woman looked at Finn, skin paling. "I'm not sure what you mean."

Finn flashed his badge, blank cop expression in place. "Can you tell us anything more about his disappearance? Have you heard from him? Any idea where he might've gone?"

She wrapped her arms around her middle, thin dark hair floating above her shoulders in the wind. A T-shirt and jeans hung from her gaunt frame, and heavy makeup circled her eyes. "Gage hasn't been home in a while now. I've asked everyone and searched everywhere but no one has seen him. Teenagers are like that. Always running off and disappearing. Probably one of the reasons it's so hard to find families who will take kids his age."

Hayley's jaw dropped, and Finn pressed a palm discreetly against her back.

"Ma'am, I'm quite familiar with teens and young people who struggle," he said. "I grew up at the Beaumont ranch, have you heard of it?"

She worked her jaw. "Sure."

"I've spent a lifetime in this arena, and in my experience, kids come home when they can. Assuming this is a safe place offering food, shelter and welcoming arms."

"Of course, it is." She tutted and slid her eyes to Hayley. "We offer all those things here."

Finn straightened to his full height, drawing the other woman's attention once more. "In that case, we have to ask what's stopped him from being here these past couple of nights. And every answer I can think of is reason for your concern, not contempt."

"Couple of nights?" Mrs. Michaelson raised an eyebrow. "That kid has barely bothered to spend more than a few hours at a time here in weeks."

"Weeks!" Hayley yipped. "What do you mean? How is that even possible?"

Mrs. Michaelson shrugged. "I told you—teens like their space. I can hardly help it if Gage won't stick around."

Finn opened his mouth to speak, but Hayley beat him to it.

"Why haven't you reported him missing?" Hayley demanded. "Or as a runaway?"

"He's a teen," Mrs. Michaelson said dryly. "They come and go. Besides, he always comes back eventually."

A little gasping sound leaped from Hayley's mouth. Her pointer finger flew up, and Finn grabbed it, covering her entire tiny fist with his.

He gave a small shake of his head when she struggled. "Ms. Campbell has lunch regularly with Gage and had no prior knowledge that there was a problem here."

"Guess he had you fooled too," the woman sneered.

Finn released Hayley and widened his stance, catching Mrs. Michaelson with his most pointed gaze. "You've continued to receive and deposit payments from the state for his full-time care, though you've only seen him a few hours at a time?"

The smug expression slowly bled from her face.

Hayley stiffened. "If you can't be bothered to report one of the children in your care as missing, it's clearly time for a thorough review of your status as a foster family. I'm guessing no children should be staying here."

"Well, good luck finding anyone to take in these teens. Besides, it sounds as if you're the one who dropped the ball on Gage. Not us." She ducked back inside and pulled the door shut hard behind her.

Hayley made a deep sound low in her throat. She turned and stormed up the walkway toward Finn's truck, towing him along by the hand.

Finn spun Hayley to face him when they reached the passenger-side door. The tears in her eyes tore through his heart like talons. "Hey," he whispered, stealing a look at the home before pulling Hayley against his chest with ease. "This isn't your fault. She's in the wrong and trying to project that back on you. Her anger and accusations were redirects. Nothing more." He ran the backs of his fingers gently along her cheek, then tucked a swath of hair behind her ear. "We'll figure this out. Together. Okay?"

She nodded and wiped away a stream of falling teardrops. "Okay."

A red playground ball rolled into view from behind a patch of hedges, and a dirty-faced kid crept out to grab it. He startled when he saw Finn and Hayley watching. "My ball," he said in explanation, moving slowly to retrieve the toy. "I'm not supposed to play out front."

Finn's gaze jerked to the home and back to the boy. "You live with the Michaelsons?"

He nodded.

So much for everyone being asleep, as Mrs. Michaelson had said.

"I'm Finn. What's your name?"

"Parker."

Hayley crouched before him, immediately bringing herself to the child's height. "Hi, Parker. I'm Hayley. Do you remember me?"

Another nod.

"Have you seen Gage lately?" she asked.

"No." The boy wet his lips and dared a look over one shoulder to the home at his back. "But he always comes back for me."

Finn's muscles tightened as he imagined all the reasons a teenage boy would come back for a kid who was no older than eight. "He took care of you when he was here?"

"Yes, sir."

Hayley glanced at Finn in alarm. "How did Gage take care of you?"

The kid hugged his ball but didn't speak.

"You can tell me anything," Hayley promised. "I won't tell the Michaelsons, and if you're unhappy here, I can help you with that."

Something Finn suspected was hope flashed in the boy's eyes.

"Gage shared his food when we got some, and he gave me water when we had to play outside all day. It gets hot. Sometimes we aren't allowed to go in, and I get a headache."

Hayley raised a hand to her mouth, but dropped it quickly away. "Gage is a great kid. So are you. I'm not surprised you're such good friends. Did he help you with anything else?"

"He told us all stories when the grown-ups fought."

"Do they fight a lot?" she asked.

Parker looked at his ball.

Finn considered that a big yes.

"Do you have any idea where Gage is now?" Hayley asked. "We're trying to find him and make sure he's okay."

"I think he went home," Parker whispered.

"Where's—" Finn's words were cut short when Parker suddenly stiffened, turned and ran away.

He darted into the trees along the lawn's edge as the front door opened, and Mrs. Michaelson stepped outside.

"What are you still doing here?" she yelled. "You can't just hang around on my property!"

Finn felt the anger vibrating from Hayley's small frame and opened the passenger door to usher her inside. "We'll sort this out with the courts," he said quietly. "Meanwhile, let's go before we stir up a bees' nest and possibly make things tougher for the kids."

He closed her door and rounded the hood, keeping one eye on the angry woman in the distance. When he climbed into the cab, Hayley was on her cell phone.

"We need a wellness check at 1318 Sandpiper Lane," she told whoever was on the other end of the line. "I'd also like to request a full and comprehensive review of the Michaelsons."

Finn shifted into gear and pulled onto the street with a grin. It sounded as if smug Mrs. Michaelson was the one to open that can of worms, and Hayley Campbell was going to make her eat them.

The cell phone in his pocket began to ring as Hayley finished her call. Austin's number appeared on the dashboard console.

Finn tapped the screen to answer. "Hey, I've got you on speaker. I'm in the truck with Hayley."

"I'm glad you're together," Austin said. "I swung by Hayley's place, and it looks as if someone's inside. Since it's not you, I'm assuming it's a break-in. Things look secure from the front. They must've used a back door or a side window to enter."

Hayley dropped her cell phone to her lap. "Someone's inside my house?"

"Yep," Austin said. "I saw a light go on behind the curtain."

Finn took the next right, setting a course to Hayley's home. "Have you called it in?"

"Kind of what I'm doing now, Detective," Austin drawled.

Finn cast a look at Hayley's worried face, then returned his attention to the road. "Keep watch. We're on our way."

Chapter Nine

Hayley's muscles tensed as she processed the situation. She shifted and slid on the bench seat as Finn took a final wild turn into her neighborhood. "How long has Austin been watching my house?"

"Since last night. He and Dean have been taking shifts since they left my place."

Panic warred with appreciation in her chest as the truck roared onto her street, then entered her driveway.

Austin's truck stood empty at the end of the block.

Finn unlatched his seat belt and set a hand on the butt of his gun.

"What are you doing?" she whispered, curling nervous fingers around Finn's wrist before he attempted to leave her behind. "Shouldn't you text Austin to see where he is? Or call for backup?"

Finn gave her a pointed stare, and she released him. "I need you to wait here. Lock the doors. Keep your phone at the ready. I'll check the house and report back."

Hayley reached for her door's handle, then she climbed out of the cab.

Finn hurried after her. "What are you doing?" he hissed, speeding around the hood to meet her.

"I'm not waiting alone out here like a sitting duck," she said. "I'll take my chances with whatever is going on in there. Right beside a trained lawman with a gun."

Finn pursed his lips but didn't argue. He tipped his head toward the front door, and she nodded.

Hayley moved along behind him, attempting to mimic his strides and posture, hoping not to alert the intruder to their presence. She crept up her front steps, then followed his example as he pressed his back to the wall near her door. On the opposite side of her porch, the front window curtain shifted.

Finn raised a closed fist, indicating she should wait.

This time she didn't protest.

The distinct clattering of dishes in the kitchen set her heart to a sprint as Finn reached for the front doorknob.

The door swung open before his fingers made contact.

Hayley's breaths stopped as she sent up a flurry of silent prayers.

Finn cussed and holstered his weapon. "What are you doing?"

"Eating, man." Austin poked his head and

shoulders over the threshold, looking both ways before grinning at her. "Hey, Hayley. Come on in."

She nearly collapsed in relief as Finn ushered her through the door. She made a mental note to pinch Austin for scaring her.

His sandy hair was messy, void of his typically present ball cap, and he looked utterly at ease in a T-shirt, jeans and sneakers. He scooped a spoonful of ice cream from a bowl. "Welcome to your lovely home."

"Thanks," she answered, stepping aside so Finn could close the door.

"Ow!" Austin pressed a palm to his biceps. "You pinched me."

"You scared the daylights out of me."

Finn snorted behind her.

"And that's my ice cream," she continued, infinitely thankful to see Austin instead of a dangerous criminal. "Why didn't you call or text to let us know you were okay?" The rich, salty scent of warm grilled cheese reached her nose and she stiffened. "Are you cooking?"

Austin's wide smile returned. "Yeah. You should join us."

She followed his gaze to a narrow figure in the archway beyond. "Gage!"

The teen leaned against the jamb, long, narrow arms wrapped around his middle. His clothes and hair were dirty, and his cheeks were red with exposure from the sun. "I'm sorry—"

Hayley launched herself through the room, cutting off his unnecessary apology. "You're okay! I was so scared. I worried that you were hurt or abducted." *Or worse*, she thought, biting back the tears. She pulled him against her and rose onto tiptoes to tuck his head against her shoulder.

He hugged her back, instantly accepting the embrace. Then his thin body began to shake with stifled sobs.

"You're going to be okay now," she whispered. "I won't let anything bad happen to you. Neither will these guys. Or their family. Or the local police. And you're absolutely not going back to the Michaelsons."

He sucked in a ragged breath, regaining his composure and straightening with effort. He forced a tight smile through the tears. "I didn't mean to scare you."

"I was terrified," she said. "We think we know what you saw, and whoever is responsible for Kate's death might be following me too. Probably looking for you."

His eyes widened. "That's the reason I didn't come here sooner. I was trying to make sure I didn't accidentally bring him here. I've been hiding and waiting until it was safe."

"I'm just glad you're here," she said, sliding

her arm around his back and pulling him to her side. "How'd you get in?"

He frowned. "I came through your doggy door."

Austin moseyed in their direction, pulling an empty spoon from his mouth. "You really need to close that up or get a dog. Are you hungry?" He slid past them and headed for her stove.

The doggy door was tiny compared to the boy before her, but she supposed, if he managed to work his way inside, so could someone else. "Noted," she said. "And, yes. Something smells delicious."

Sounds of sizzling butter turned her to the stove, where Austin was loading another grilled cheese. "Good. We can talk over food."

Hayley searched the refrigerator for side dishes. "You are your mother."

Austin winked.

A few sliced apples and washed grapes later, the foursome settled around her small kitchen table. She nibbled on apples, too emotionally jarred to work up an appetite, but deeply satisfied with the turn of events.

Gage had come to her, just as she'd hoped. He trusted her to help him, which meant the world. More, Austin had been there to welcome and feed him. And the Beaumonts had prepared a place for him to stay safely on their ranch. Emotion stung her eyes and clogged her throat as she scanned the trio of men before her.

"Do you mind if I shower?" Gage asked. "I don't have anything else to wear, but I'd really like to wash up. Shampoo my hair. Maybe brush my teeth?"

Hayley nodded and stood, glad to be useful, when it seemed everyone else was doing things for her these days. "Of course. Come on. I have everything you need." She kept an assortment of travel-size toiletries for youths taken into emergency care without time to gather their things. Or others who simply didn't have anything of their own.

"I keep a change of clothes in my gym bag," Finn said. "You're welcome to wear that while I toss your outfit into the wash. It'll be a little big, but it's clean, and I'm guessing it'll fit better than anything in Hayley's closet."

Gage smiled, and the expression spread to the others.

The Beaumonts were broader, their bodies honed and matured, but Gage wasn't much shorter, and he'd likely be their height in the next year or two. He looked down the six-inch gap in height between himself and Hayley. "You're probably right about that."

Finn made a trip outside and returned with the bag.

Hayley walked Gage to the bathroom, then waited for him to toss his dirty clothes into the hallway.

"HE FIT THROUGH the doggy door?" Finn asked, eyeballing the small rubber flap across the room.

"Yep." Austin grinned. "You remember life at that age. He's a rack of growing bones. And I've got to be honest, I don't think he's eaten in a while."

Finn's jaw locked as he thought of Hayley feeding Gage and so many others lunch each workday. After meeting Mrs. Michaelson, he wasn't sure the kids in her care were getting much else, and he hoped the system moved quickly to review the family and extract the youths in their care.

"How was he otherwise?" Finn asked, knowing Austin would be a good judge. His brother had been around as many troubled teens as he had and would have insight. There was a lot to infer from a kid's general disposition and unspoken vibe. Even Gage's mannerisms were likely to say more than the teen himself. Frequently, a combination of those things would reveal whether or not the individual might be willing to make healthy changes. Or if he was already determined to resist.

"I like him," Austin said, resting his backside against the sink and crossing his arms over his chest. "He was terrified when he saw me let myself inside, but once I mentioned Hayley's name and yours, he relaxed."

"Mine?" Finn worked the concept around his

mind, unable to make sense of it. "How did he know my name?"

"Apparently the love of your life still talks about you too."

Finn frowned to stop his lips from smiling. He didn't have to ask how his brother had gotten inside. Austin was quite proud of his lock-picking skills. "Okay. What else?"

Austin held Finn's eye contact for a long beat before moving on. "He's polite, apologetic for his disappearance and the break-in. He stands tall, looks folks in the eyes and he washed his hands before eating. I'd say he was being raised right before whatever happened to his family."

"Car accident," Finn said. "Drunk driver on their weekly date night."

His brother's face paled, and he scrubbed a heavy hand over his hair. "That's horrible. He was where? Home with a sitter? Got a call from the hospital?"

Finn shook his head, feeling heat course through his chest. He'd looked into the case last night when he couldn't sleep, and what he'd found still haunted him. "The sitter fell through, and the kid begged them to go anyway. He was thirteen and convinced he could manage a couple of hours on his own while they had dinner. Mom reluctantly agreed. They ate at a restaurant two miles from home and died just outside their neighborhood. He heard the commotion but didn't think much of it until a sheriff came to the door. Apparently Mom's last words were about her son being home alone."

Austin's eyes shone with emotion, and he cussed.

"Yeah."

"What'd I miss?" Hayley asked, reappearing in the room like a ninja.

Austin spun away, and Finn cleared his throat. "We're just talking through our next steps."

"Good," she said. "We need a plan."

"I'll take his statement after he finishes in the shower," Finn said. "We'll have time while his clothes finish washing and drying. We can sit in the living room together. Someplace comfortable." He watched Hayley carefully, trying to determine her mood and mindset. "You should stick with him—he's clearly attached to you. He trusts you. We don't want him to hold back on anything or get scared."

She nodded, and her lips curled into a small prideful smile. "Agreed."

Austin pulled the dish towel from his shoulder and hung it over the sink's edge. "I'll tell him about the ranch and ask if he'd be willing to check it out. Then we can explain why it's the safest place for him right now and let him decide if he's willing to give it a chance. We don't want him running again."

"What if he says no?" Hayley asked, uncertainty in her eyes.

Finn lifted an arm toward the living room. Gage would likely finish showering soon, and finding all the adults holed up in the kitchen could give the wrong impression. They were definitely talking about him, but they weren't attempting to hide it from him. Better to get comfortable in the next room. In Finn's experience, transparency bred trust, and this kid needed to know they could all be trusted, not just Hayley. "Can we?"

She nodded, and they moved to the next room.

"If he doesn't like the ranch, he can stay at my place," Austin said, dropping onto the overstuffed armchair beside the couch. "It's cozy and well-protected. Food's not as good, but there are fewer kids and livestock to hassle him."

Finn rolled his eyes.

"And if you want him to stay someplace completely unconnected to the family," Austin added, "Scarlet can probably get us access to an empty home for a few nights. We can talk to the owners about paying rent for a few days."

Finn didn't hate that idea. Having a real-estate agent in the family had been surprisingly beneficial to the Beaumonts. "I like that."

The stairs creaked, and their heads turned collectively to see Gage.

His hair was mussed and damp. Finn's clothes

hung from his narrow hips and shoulders, as expected, but something strange twisted in Finn's chest at the sight of him. He'd only met this kid an hour ago, but it was easy to understand why Hayley had become so attached. He was kind and vulnerable, but smart enough to make it on his own when he'd thought he was protecting Hayley. The intention alone was priceless.

"Come on down," Hayley said. "We were just talking about our next steps, and we need your input."

Gage's concerned expression morphed into surprise. He followed her request and settled on the couch between her and Finn. "What's up?"

Hayley told Gage about the ranch, and he listened, glancing to Austin and Finn a few times while she spoke.

"Is that where you want me to go?" he asked when she finished.

"I wish I could keep you with me, but I think the ranch is the best option for now," she said. "Until the killer is found, and you're safe again."

His skin paled at the word *killer*.

Finn accessed the recording feature on his phone. "I need to get an official statement from you about what you saw in Old Downtown the other night and anything before or after that you feel is relevant."

Gage took a deep breath and exhaled with a

shudder. He rubbed his palms up and down his thighs, then wet his lips and nodded.

"Whenever you're ready," Finn said, pressing the button to begin the recording, then setting the device between them.

Gage set the stage, then spoke about his art, the thrumming bass of the nearby rave and the draw of people to the sound, like moths to the light. "I didn't see anyone go inside the other building, but I heard yelling in the pause between songs down the street. It sounded like a fight. Then the music came back, and I didn't hear the voices anymore, so I went across the street to see if I'd imagined them. I hadn't. There were two silhouettes inside the building marked for demolition. One was Kate. I'd talked to her earlier when a few of us were playing ball in the intersection. She'd explained how she was planning to fix up that part of Old Downtown, and she asked us what we thought was most important in a new shelter or community center. We all had things to say, and she listened. It seemed like she really wanted to get things right. She even said there would be part-time jobs for older teens to work with younger kids, packing lunches and getting them onto their buses for school when it starts again. At first it made sense to me that she'd be there, checking out the area, but it was kind of weird to see she was still there at night. And it was also hard to understand why anyone would argue with her. She was so kind. Still, I saw something move toward her, like a bat, maybe." His skin paled as he spoke. "Then she fell. A few seconds later, I heard a gunshot."

"Were you able to get a look at the person she was with?" Finn asked.

"No. They were behind the wall. I only had a glimpse at her through the broken window."

"Could you tell by the voice if it was a man or woman?" Finn asked.

Gage kneaded his hands together, brow furrowed in concentration. "Not for sure. I heard a woman's voice in that moment between the MC's voice and the next song, but I've been thinking about it, and I'm not sure if it was Kate's voice or not. It could've been a second woman, or it might've been her, and the other person could've been a man."

"Was she alone when she spoke to you earlier, when you were playing ball?" Finn asked.

"As far as I could see, yeah."

Hayley set a hand on his shoulder. "A man took a shot at me in that area, and a man stood outside the parking lot where I park for work."

Austin leaned forward. "Gage, when you ran, did you see who chased you?"

Finn considered the question. It was a good one. Typically, male criminals were more likely to give chase, and women tended to regroup and strategize, but there were exceptions to even the strongest rules. And he couldn't rely wholly on past scenarios to predict the future. Any murderer would have motivation to stop a witness before they reported what they'd seen.

Gage took another long beat to consider before he spoke. "I think it was a man. They seemed big, with heavy footfalls on the street. And they were close when I reached the rave. I thought I was caught, but the crowd was thick, and that building has a hole in the back wall. I ran to the opening, then ducked and doubled back instead of going out. I hid in the crowd until I thought it was safe to leave. I think whoever it was assumed I left."

Hayley swelled with pride. "That was smart. If they nearly caught you in a footrace to the rave, they might've gotten ahold of you if you'd tried your luck outside again."

He twisted on the cushion to look at her. "I was going to tell you everything the next day, but I kept thinking that maybe no one knew it was me. And maybe if I didn't say anything it would go away. Her body would be found, and the police would handle it. I didn't want to bring you into it or put myself in the spotlight."

She rubbed his back, and Finn's heart gave another heavy thud. Hayley was a natural at comforting hurting people. She had a heart for their pain, an internal drive to comfort. She'd make a perfect foster mom, and he was sure the court would give her a fair shot when this was over.

From what he knows about the system between his connections and his family's, he was sure a judge would consider giving Hayley a chance at fostering Gage. The kid clearly accepted her as a mentor and confidante, and she would never let him down.

"Sorry I worried you," he whispered.

"Thank you for coming to me," Hayley responded.

Finn stopped the recording app and stood. They'd been at her home long enough for anyone watching to take notice. It was time to get moving, if they wanted to stay safe. "Who wants to see some livestock?"

Chapter Ten

Hayley leaned forward on her seat as Finn turned onto the long, familiar gravel lane. Returning to the Beaumont ranch for the first time in more than a year was nearly as breathtaking an experience as seeing it for the first time. She wished Gage had ridden with her so she could see his face as they arrived. Instead, he'd gone with Austin, who'd taken the lead in their little two-truck caravan.

She felt Finn's gaze on her cheek as her eyes widened in pleasure. Thick green grass rolled all the way to the horizon, split down the center by a dark ribbon of driveway and interspersed with fencing and livestock in their respective fields. The occasional human in a straw cowboy hat or colorful baseball cap waved an arm overhead as they rolled past.

Outbuildings, a large, impressive stable and several cabins dotted the land, each lovely, but none compared to the sprawling farmhouse before them. The Beaumont home spoke of generations of farmers and the decades of love bestowed upon it by this family.

Mr. and Mrs. Beaumont appeared on the porch as Finn parked his truck beside Austin's.

Hayley had to stop herself from running to greet them again. She hoped Gage would soon feel the same way. She wanted the family who meant so much to her to be important to him as well.

"Ready?" Finn asked, unfastening his seat belt.

"Always." She climbed down from the cab, taking a long beat to enjoy the view. Thick, dark mulch overflowed with bright blooms all around the farmhouse, and the arching cloudless blue sky stretched like a dome overhead.

Gage moved in her direction, nervous energy pouring off him in waves. The tension in his youthful face and posture set her slightly on edge.

"Give it a chance, okay?" She slid her arm beneath his and pulled him close, tipping her head back slightly to look up at his face. "I love this place and these people," she whispered, the words meant only for him. "They're not like anyone else I've ever known, and they're the very best of us. I'm sure of it."

His expression was grim, but he nodded. He was probably thinking of the last time Hayley had taken him to stay with a family. Look at how that had turned out. She needed to ask him more about the Michaelsons, and let him know what she thought of him not going back there for weeks, according to his foster mother, but this wasn't the right time. In this moment, she needed to give him the sense of peace and security he greatly deserved.

"Trust me," she urged, tugging his arm when he didn't look at her. She waited for those concerned brown eyes to fall on hers. Then she smiled. "If you aren't completely comfortable here before I leave, I will take you with me. That's a promise."

Gage pressed his lips together. "Austin said staying with you could put you in danger."

Hayley shook her head. "Staying at my house could put us in danger, but I'm not staying there right now, and I won't ask you to stay anywhere you aren't comfortable ever again."

He scrutinized her for a long moment before turning to the silent crowd on the Beaumonts' porch.

Finn and Austin had joined their parents, along with another brother, Lincoln, and the stable manager, Josi. All watched intently as she spoke to Gage.

"Look at them," she whispered again. "What's not to love?"

They all smiled brightly, eagerly, except Lincoln, who seemed to be sizing up Gage. He was probably already thinking of chores to keep the teen mentally engaged and physically exhausted.

Josi looked at the brooding man beside her then elbowed his ribs.

Lincoln grunted and a partial smile bloomed on his face before he shut it down.

Hayley glanced at Finn, wondering if he'd caught the exchange, but his eyes were focused tightly on her. Fresh heat spread over her cheeks in response.

Gage straightened as if prepared for battle. "All right. I can do this. I don't want to put you in danger or cause you any more trouble."

"Hey." She stopped him as he tried to move forward. "You are not a burden to me. Understand? I'm only asking you to give them and this place a try. There's no wrong answer."

He nodded, not speaking.

"You are not a burden to me," she repeated, more slowly this time. "You are my friend, and I'm going to take care of you. These guys are going to help me. By the time I leave today, they'll all be your friends too. If they aren't, I meant what I said. Got it?"

"Yeah."

"Well?" Mrs. Beaumont asked from the bottom of the porch steps, nearly vibrating with excitement. "Will you stay?" she asked. "At least for the tour?"

"Sure," Gage agreed, and the older woman rushed to greet him.

"Can I hug you? I'm a hugger," she explained. "Isn't that right?"

The crowd murmured in confirmation, and Gage lifted his arms.

She wrapped him in a tight embrace, and within seconds, he hugged her back.

Hayley's eyes burned with appreciation. This was the safe place Gage needed, and she would be eternally grateful.

"It's lovely to meet you, Gage," Mrs. Beaumont said as she released him. "This is my family. You'll meet Dean soon, if you haven't already. I believe he's watching Hayley's place now. You know Finn and Austin. This is my husband, Garrett. I'm Mary. And this is Josi and Lincoln."

The family members took turns greeting him while Mrs. Beaumont fussed and Finn made his way to Hayley's side.

"I'm sure this isn't overwhelming at all," Finn teased, nudging her with his elbow.

She laughed, recalling the first time she'd been introduced to the family. The Beaumonts were wonderful, but they could be a lot. Especially upon introduction.

"Are you hungry?" Mrs. Beaumont asked, steering Gage up the porch steps toward the farmhouse door. "I always keep food and snacks on hand. Help yourself anytime. We have meals at..." The sound of her voice trailed off as the group followed inside.

"Do you remember the first time I brought you here?" Finn asked.

"How could I forget?" Hayley turned a bright smile on him. "I thought you were all too good to be true. Gathering around that giant table for dinner, talking and laughing like friends. I was sure it was a show. I couldn't understand how you willingly spent so much time together and still liked one another."

Finn's eyebrows tented, then his expression slid into one of concern. "I sometimes forget my life isn't everyone else's normal. I wish it was."

"Me too."

He set a palm against her back and rubbed gently before pulling away.

Hayley felt the absence of his touch in her core, and maybe in her heart as well. She shook off the unwanted feeling and concentrated on the moment at hand. She needed to be sure Gage was at home on the ranch, then she needed to get back out there with Finn to see what they could learn about Kate's death. The sooner the killer was arrested, the sooner Gage wouldn't be in danger, and she could apply to be his guardian.

The farmhouse front door opened and Gage appeared, chatting with the young blond stable manager. Lincoln followed with his usual frown. All three members of the little group carried a bottle of water in one hand. The guys also held half of a sandwich.

"Not sure how Josi got away without being fed," Finn said. "Then again, she puts up with Lincoln all day every day, so we've suspected she was a magician for a while now."

Hayley laughed and raised her fingers in a wave as the trio passed.

Lincoln slowed. "We're giving the kid a tour."

Josi reached up to smack the brim of his hat. "His name is Gage."

Lincoln glared until she turned away, then grinned as he straightened his hat.

Finn shook his head, having clearly seen the exchange this time. "I don't get them."

Hayley fell into step behind the trio, giving them distance. Finn kept pace at her side.

"Do you have a dog?" Gage asked Lincoln.

"No."

"Really? Why not?" Gage frowned. "Don't they help with herding or something? You've got lots of room and the rescues are always full."

Lincoln looked past the teen to Josi, who grinned.

"He has a point," she said. "We've got miniature cows and donkeys, horses, goats and sheep. Chickens galore. No dog?"

Lincoln stopped suddenly and turned to pin Hayley with a curious stare. "Weren't you getting a dog last year?"

She'd wanted to badly but couldn't bring herself to take the plunge. "I decided I was gone too much to be the parent I wanted to be."

Josi looked to Gage. "Have you ever had a dog?"

The teen's cheeks paled and he nodded. "Larry."

"Where is he now?" Hayley asked, suddenly concerned he'd been forgotten in the chaos of losing Gage's parents. Had he been taken to the pound? Cast off somehow? Left to the streets?

"I got him when I was in preschool," Gage explained. "He died a few months before my parents. He was ten."

Josi's eyes shone with emotion and darted to Lincoln.

"Ten's a good long life for a dog," Lincoln said. "We've had a few over the years that only made it to eight or nine, but they were loved. They were happy."

Gage nodded. "Yeah."

Hayley's stomach tightened with the new knowledge. She'd had no idea he'd lost a lifelong friend and his parents in the same year. "I'm going to get a dog soon," she blurted, drawing the eyes of all three companions.

"Really?" Gage asked, his expression both stunned and hopeful.

"Mmm-hmm," she said, processing the possibility at warp speed. "I plan to work less overtime soon, so I'll be home for dinner every night, and the office is near enough for me to walk him at lunchtime." She could set up her cooler at the usual picnic table before she left. Maybe even bring the dog on some work-related visits.

"Let's go," Lincoln said, clapping Gage on the shoulder. "We'll check out the stable and your cabin while they talk." He lifted his chin to indicate something behind Hayley.

She turned to find Austin making his way across the field.

"Are you running from me?" he called as Lincoln led Gage and Josi through the open barn doors.

"Always," Lincoln hollered, then vanished inside.

Finn set his hands on his hips and turned to his approaching brother. "Any news?"

"Nope. One of my informants says he was at the rave that night. Saw a kid fitting Gage's description tear through the place. That was all he remembered. Most folks were high, so everyone he asked today had no idea what he was talking about."

Hayley groaned. "So there aren't any new leads on who was chasing him."

Or who'd killed Kate.

"So what's next?" she asked.

Finn rolled his shoulders and squinted against the sun. "I'll check in with the officers who stayed in Old Downtown to do interviews. Maybe something someone said will be a clue, even if it isn't a definitive ID of the killer."

Austin rubbed his palms. "I'll head back to the office and dig into Kate's social-media accounts. I'll look at everyone on her friends lists, check out her posts, read their posts, see who she interacted with on the days leading up to her death. The usual."

Familiar laughter turned Hayley back to the barn, where Gage was leading the pack in her direction.

"I like it here," he called. "You were right. I want to stay."

A long breath of relief rushed from her chest. "If that's what you want."

"I do." He smiled widely as he reached her, then wrapped her in a hug. "Thank you."

Lincoln's lips twitched, and Hayley felt her eyebrows raise. The fleeting expression looked a lot like a smile. Three in an hour had to be a new record for him. "In that case," he said, pulling a cell phone from his pocket, "this is for you. We set it up when we heard you were coming. It's got all our numbers in there and Hayley's."

"Seriously?" Gage asked, obviously flabbergasted.

"Yep."

Gage accepted the phone with an expression of pure joy. "This is sick!"

Hayley tamped down the rush of emotion, laughing outwardly at the roller coaster of feelings she'd been on today. "You can call me if you need anything. Even if you're just bored or lonely."

"Or if Lincoln gets on your nerves," Josi offered.

The group laughed, but Lincoln pinned her with his grumpiest of looks.

"I'll be his favorite in a day or two," Lincoln said. "Now let's check out your mini apartment." He turned and headed for the small cabins behind the stable.

Gage shot Hayley a stunned look. "Apartment?"

"Everyone staying on-site has their own space," she explained as they all followed Lincoln. "Those larger cabins belong to Lincoln and Josi. The smaller ones are used for teens staying here on a short-term basis."

"This one," Lincoln said, stopping at the door to a unit near his own, "is for you."

Finn crossed his arms and leaned toward Hayley as his brother unlocked the door. "This one is usually used for storage, so it's a work in progress."

"Ranch was full," Austin added, inserting himself into the exchange. "But there wasn't any stopping Mama when she heard about your situation."

Hayley watched as the group filed inside.

"Are you serious?" Gage's voice carried through

the open door to her heart. "Hayley! You've got to see this!"

She darted forward, slipping into the former storage unit before coming to an immediate halt. The Beaumonts had arranged a twin bed and small desk on one wall. A chest of drawers on another. The bed was covered in a navy blue blanket and topped with a puffy white pillow. An oval throw rug covered the floor. The desk doubled as a nightstand with a lamp positioned closest to the headboard. An open notebook contained a two-word message in bright blue letters.

Welcome, Gage!

Hayley looked first at Josi, then at each Beaumont with silent adoration. "Thank you."

Gage dragged his eyes from the notebook to Hayley. "This is where I get to stay while I'm here? In this cabin?"

"Yep," Austin answered, then reached beneath the desk to open the door to a pint-size refrigerator. "We stocked this with drinks and snacks. Kids your age keep ridiculous hours, and we thought you'd rather have some things at your place than go hungry or make the trek to our folks' house at two a.m."

"My place," Gage repeated, awestruck.

Finn shifted, reminding Hayley he was still right there at her side. "Only until we find the person who killed Kate and chased you. I don't plan to let that take long."

Gage's smile filled the room. "How old do you have to be to stay here?"

"At the ranch?" Josi asked.

He nodded. "Hayley said the other kids will be removed from the Michaelsons' home. I looked after them when I could, especially Parker. He's eight."

"You're probably the youngest," Josi said. "We typically host kids closer to high-school graduation. Some are even my age on occasion."

"We look at each applicant on a case-by-case basis," Lincoln said. "Eight is too young to be here, I think. Not everyone we host is in a good place emotionally. You're in danger, and you've been through a lot, but you seem like you've got a clear head. Not all our kids do."

Gage's expression fell, and his brow creased in concern. "Where will Parker go?"

"Someplace nice and safe," Hayley promised. "I'll personally interview each family to be sure they're up to par this time."

"When will he move?" he asked.

"Soon. I've requested a review of the home and one-on-one interviews for the kids. Without the Michaelsons listening or influencing them in any way. The children will have the freedom to speak candidly."

Something in Gage's expression said he didn't

think that was good enough, but Hayley didn't press the issue. She told herself to take his willingness to stay with the Beaumonts as a win and she'd let the social workers handling the Michaelsons do their jobs. She had a good team at the office and in front of her.

Finn's phone buzzed and he removed it from his pocket to look at the screen. "If you're set here, we should take off," he said, looking to Gage, then Hayley.

The sudden tension in his jawline set her feet in motion. She gave each of the individuals before her a hug, adding an extra squeeze to Gage before stepping back. "Call me if you need anything, and I'll be here in under thirty minutes."

"I'm good," he assured.

"If anything changes," she said, backing through the door and into the grass.

"Take care of him," she called, turning to follow Finn, who was already moving toward his truck.

He stopped to catch her hand and urge her into a jog.

"What happened?" she asked, on high alert as they launched into his cab and peeled out of the driveway.

Finn placed his portable emergency light on the roof and hit the gas "There was a break-in at your office."

Chapter Eleven

Finn piloted his truck into the lot outside the social-services office. A pair of Marshal's Bluff cruisers were already in place. A uniformed officer stood guard at the door. The building had closed for the day only a short while earlier, so whoever had broken in hadn't waited long to act.

Typically, break-ins were executed under cover of night and at a location with items of high resale potential. Whatever the criminal had been seeking was likely only valuable to one person, and Finn suspected that person was searching for Gage Myers. The timing, when factored in with Kate's murder and the witness who'd gotten away, was too coincidental. And Finn didn't believe in coincidences.

"I can't believe this is happening," Hayley whispered, releasing her safety belt as he pulled his key from the ignition.

He climbed out and met her on the sidewalk. "How do you feel about working the scene together?"

She raised her eyebrows. "You want my help in there?"

As a general rule, he did his best to keep civilians away from crime scenes, but Hayley was familiar with the case and location in ways no one else on-site was, making her invaluable. Not to mention, he preferred to keep her close. For her safety and his sanity. "I'll do the talking and interacting with staff and officers," he said. "You evaluate the office. This is your territory. You'll know better than anyone if something is missing or has been left behind. Take your time and concentrate. If there's a mess, it could be a distraction. If something new has appeared, I need to know that too. The item could be a camera or recording device. Make note of anything that feels off."

Her expression morphed from shock to resolve, and she nodded. "Got it."

Finn held her gaze one moment longer, then took the lead as they approached the officer at the door.

"Detective Beaumont," the older gentleman said, accepting Finn's outstretched hand for a quick shake.

Finn stepped aside, allowing Hayley to pass. "This is—"

"Hi, Don," she said sweetly, pausing inside the small vestibule. "How's Cora?"

"Better every day," the older officer said. "I'll let her know you asked about her."

"Thank you."

Finn matched Hayley's pace as they moved through the quiet hallway. "How do you know Don?"

"Through his wife. She had a pretty serious surgery last month. I brought dinner once or twice. They're good people. Do you know them well?"

"Barely at all." Even in a department as small as his, everyone had a job to do, and it was easy to stay busy. He rarely spent any real time with anyone outside his immediate team.

A pair of men in suits appeared at the open door to Social Services. They bent their heads together as they moved away, each carrying a stack of files and loose papers.

"They work in human resources," Hayley whispered, then waved. "Caleb, Frank."

The men stopped, looking curiously at their coworker.

Finn extended a hand to each man in turn. "Hello, I'm Detective Beaumont."

They both murmured quick hellos.

"What can you tell us about the break-in?" Finn asked.

Their collective attention swung back to Hayley, as they were probably wondering why she was there and was being accompanied by a detective.

The taller of the pair was first to respond. He cleared his throat and forced a tight smile in Finn's direction. "I'm Caleb Morrison, the management leader here. I organize and facilitate the teams. I also act as a liaison between all staff and administration." His gaze slid briefly to Hayley before returning to Finn. "The break-in appears to have been directed at Ms. Campbell or someone on her caseload. Beyond that, I'm not sure."

The heavier man at Caleb's side wiggled his blue-gloved fingers. "I'm Frank Riggs. These files were tossed out of the cabinets in our portion of the offices. We're supposed to see if anything's missing. We barely print anything these days, so unless someone was searching for something from years ago, all this mess was likely for show. Or the result of a hissy fit."

Hayley snorted lightly, then covered her nose with one hand. "Sorry."

Finn fought a smile.

"Someone is hot for one of your cases," Frank said, looking much more serious. "I'd stick with this guy as much as you can until this is sorted." He tipped his head at Finn and scanned him appreciatively. "Shouldn't be a hardship."

Hayley took Finn's elbow in her hand and tugged him away, waving goodbye to Frank and Caleb with her free hand.

"I like Frank," Finn said.

Hayley laughed, and the sound warmed his heart.

A second officer stood guard inside the social-services door and raised his chin in greeting.

Before Finn could ask the man for information, Hayley gasped. He followed her wide-eyed stare to a crime-scene photographer, snapping shots of an absolute disaster. Presumably Hayley's desk.

The rolling chair had been overturned on its mat. All the metal drawers were open. Trinkets, framed photos, toys and keepsakes littered the floor and desktop. Office supplies were fanned across the carpet.

It seemed Frank had been on the right track. This certainly looked like the site of a recent hissy fit. Not at all what Finn had anticipated.

The photographer stepped away, and Finn donned a pair of gloves, then passed a second set to Hayley. "I guess it's time to get to work. Tell me about the space."

The room was large and divided into sections by groups of desks, presumably the teams Caleb had mentioned.

Hayley tugged the gloves over her trembling hands. "This is my desk. These belong to my team members." She swung a pointed finger from desk to desk. "Those are the other teams, and that door leads to Human Resources and Administration." Her voice cracked, and she released a thin, shaky breath.

"You okay?"

"I can do this," she assured him quietly, then crouched to examine the mess.

Finn scanned the bigger picture first, then slowly pulled his attention inward to the single destroyed workstation.

Everything else appeared untouched and utterly ignored.

The office was in need of sprucing up. The carpet was threadbare, while the wall paint was chipping and faded.

"Recognize these desks?" she asked, rising to her feet once more. "They were handed down to us from the police station after your renovations last year."

Finn grimaced. He hadn't recognized them, but he'd certainly noticed they were old.

"They're a step up from what we had," she said, probably reading his expression. "We were glad to get them, and it's nice they didn't go straight to a landfill somewhere. Our desks went to other places in need. A church office and some homeschooling moms, I believe."

Finn made a mental note to circle back to the topic of funding for Social Services when he had more time. His family would surely have ideas on how to help the department who helped everyone else.

"What do you think?" she asked.

"I think someone knew what they were after and where to find it."

"The guy who's been following me," she mused.

Finn nodded, then raised his hand to a passing crime-scene technician. "Are you finished here?"

The young man gave the room a glance. "We're wrapping up now. We've got all we need."

"Anything you can share that might help me?"

"Afraid not," the man said. "No prints. No signs of a break-in. The alarm was triggered at the interior point of entry." He pointed to a keypad on the wall inside the social-services area.

Finn considered that a moment. "Someone accessed the building before closing and waited until the coast was clear to make his way in here."

"That's my guess," the tech said. "I'll get the photos over to you along with lab analysis on a couple small things. Hair. Mud. Probably left by workers or clients, but both were in the line of fire, so I'm taking a closer look." He tipped his head to the overturned chair.

"Appreciate it," Finn said.

"Can I clean up, Ryan?" Hayley asked.

"Okay by me," the tech said. "But Beaumont's the boss."

"Well, don't tell him that too often," she teased. "We'll all pay the price."

Hayley collected an armload of her things from the floor as the tech took his leave. "Ryan and I met a few months ago. His wife teaches second grade, and I had one of her students on my case-load. She introduced us."

Finn shook his head. Everyone who met Hayley was instantly charmed. Not because she was perfect, but because she was honest and real.

She narrowed her eyes, but before she could voice her thoughts, Caleb appeared with a frown.

"Detective?" he asked.

Finn snapped easily back to work mode. "Find something?"

"No. We've been through all the folders. Everything appears to be in order."

"Thank you." Finn set his hands on his hips and looked at the open door to Human Resources. What had made the burglar dig through the paper files? "You took your laptop home with you?" he asked Hayley.

"Yes. Why?"

It was possible that whoever had come for her computer might've tried the filing cabinets as the next most logical place to find information on a case.

"Just theorizing," he said. "The interior alarm was already triggered when they came in, so they had to hurry, then leave empty-handed. Explains the hissy fit."

She grinned.

Finn went to wrap things up with the officers on duty while Hayley rearranged and tidied her desk.

An image of her in his arms at a fundraiser

caught his eye upon return. A dozen bright, youthful faces filled the space at their sides. They'd made huge differences for the betterment of their community when they were together. He'd thought they'd grow old doing those same things.

What had gone so wrong? And how had he not seen it coming?

HAYLEY PACKED A few more of her things during a quick trip home, then rejoined Finn in his truck. "Thanks," she said, buckling up for the ride back to his place.

It hadn't occurred to her, until the break-in at her office, that there were a number of little things she'd like to protect in case there was a burglary. She would've been safe at Finn's place, but her precious photos, mementos and keepsakes were irreplaceable too. So she'd been thrilled when he hadn't objected to her picking up a little more of her stuff.

"Any chance you have a spare key on you?" he asked, dropping his cell phone into the truck's cupholder. "And would you mind if Dean or Austin replace your locks with a keypad version as soon as possible? Something we'll be able to monitor? Maybe one of those doorbells with a camera too."

"They can have mine," she said, lifting a key between them. "Whatever makes my home safer is perfect." Especially since she hoped to share the place with Gage when this was over.

Finn took the key and shifted into Drive.

It broke her heart to think of how close she'd come to spending her life with him, and how she'd ruined it by waiting far too long to face her demons.

Soon the familiar home appeared, situated atop a hill with mature trees and plenty of lush green grass. Enough room for chubby toddler legs to run and growing childhood bodies to play. The wide gravel swath outside an attached garage had ample space for guests, family and friends to park. Even enough for future teenage drivers she'd once believed would belong to her and Finn.

Never underestimate how much can change in a year, she thought.

Or the limits on how badly one person can mess up.

A few moments later, Finn unlocked the front door and waited for her in the kitchen while she delivered her things to the guest room. She returned to him with squared shoulders. Things between them couldn't go back to the way they were, but they could certainly be improved. And that started with an explanation for her behavior last year. Finn would never bring up something so painfully personal in the midst of a serious investigation. She, on the other hand, needed to say her piece. She owed him at least that much.

Finn clapped his hands as she emerged from the hallway. "Austin's on his way over to grab that house key, and I've made some sandwiches. Nothing fancy, but I'm hungry and thought you might be too. Also, I'm hoping we can brainstorm."

Hayley froze. The sudden change of mental direction nearly gave her whiplash.

He passed her a plate with a handful of kettle chips and a pickle spear beside a sandwich cut into two triangles.

"BLT," he said. "I microwaved the leftover bacon from breakfast."

She took a seat at the island, unsure she could eat until she got a few secrets off her chest. Her attention caught on a large whiteboard with wheels in the living area.

"For the brainstorming," he said around a mouthful of sandwich.

She blinked. "Right."

Finn wiped his mouth, looking ten years younger at home than he did on the job. He'd turned a baseball hat around on his head and visibly relaxed down to his toes. It was easy to remember he was twenty-five when he was on duty. At home, like this, it was hard to believe he wasn't late for class somewhere. "Now that Gage is safe, we can redirect our attention. Uniformed officers have done preliminary interviews with Kate's family and staff. I'll go over the official transcripts before we start knocking on doors."

He rose and crossed the room to grab his satchel and a laptop. He set the latter beside her plate, then freed a second laptop from his bag. "Are you still a magician when it comes to social-media stalking?"

Hayley reluctantly set aside her need for confession and willed herself to refocus. Finn wanted her help now. The rest could wait.

"Hayley?" he coaxed. "You okay?"

She refreshed her smile. "I believe stalking is illegal, Detective, but I'm still quite good at research."

"Excellent." Finn opened the lid on his laptop. "I was hoping you'd say that. I'm looking for details on all the latest posts and interactions from Kate. Austin usually helps with this, but he's spread thin. If you find something you want him to dig into, he can. Otherwise, let's see how much progress we can make tonight. I'll read all the interviews and anything else that's been added to the case file while you search, and we'll see what stands out."

"Deal." She raised her half sandwich to him in a toast.

Several hours later, her eyes stung, and her body ached from being hunched over the laptop. She stood and stretched.

"Anything?" he asked.

"Nothing's screaming *motive* to me," she admitted, "but I generally see the good in people so—"

He set aside his laptop and turned to face her. "What are your overall thoughts and insights?"

She considered his question and what she'd learned that could be relevant. "I hadn't realized Kate's husband had such a Cinderella story. His family was practically homeless when he met her. The fact his path ever crossed hers is a miracle. For them to fall in love, get married and make it eight years together is probably like winning the lottery. Literally and figuratively." Hayley wasn't sure how she felt about it. Happy for the couple, but also a little suspicious, because money was the number-one reason for divorce—she felt somewhat guilty for thinking the last part.

Finn rolled his shoulders and arched his back, apparently as stiff and uncomfortable as she'd been. "Paul was poor before they married?"

"Very much. He was working at a YMCA when she came to see how she could help. Then poof. Love."

Finn grunted. "I'll see if there's a prenup. If so, I'll need to know what he stood to lose if the marriage fell apart."

Hayley frowned. "Am I a sappy dope if I really don't want that to pan out? Not another man who vowed to love, honor and cherish his wife only to murder her for her money."

"No." The smile on Finn's face was brittle, and she flinched when her phone buzzed.

"It's my coworker," she said, lifting the device to read the message. "The kids are being removed from the Michaelsons' home tomorrow morning."

Finn's expression brightened a moment before he went into work mode. "That's good."

"Yeah," she said, feeling the first flutters of nerves return. "Finn?"

"Yeah?"

Hayley inhaled deeply, then spoke the words that had been on her heart for a year. "I'm sorry I ran away when you proposed."

He tensed and the air thickened...and all evidence of the carefree young man disappeared.

"It wasn't because I didn't love you, or because I didn't want to marry you, because I did. More than anything." She paused to let him process, then searched for the strength to go on.

His jaw tensed and flexed, but his body was otherwise motionless.

"I've told you my mom drinks," Hayley went on. "That she's unreliable, difficult and mean. I didn't tell you how bad it was growing up with her. It was awful." Hayley nearly choked on the words. Nothing she could say would make it better or believable. If she hadn't lived her life, seen it with her eyes, experienced it herself, she'd never have believed a mother could be like hers. The way she probably still was. "She was supposed to love and protect me. She did not. And she stood by while the men in her life hurt me too." Tears sprung to her eyes, and her chin jutted forward in defiance to everyone who'd tried to make her a terrible, hateful human. "I hadn't dealt with that pain or processed the trauma, and in a very twisted way, your profession of love and desire to protect me felt like betrayal. It triggered all these suppressed, ignored, bottled-up feelings and I just...ran."

The same way she'd run away from her mother's trailer. The way she'd run from almost everything good in her life before it could hurt her too. Only her job had ever given her joy without fear, and that was probably because she worked hard and faced her share of troubles, according to her therapist. She trusted that joy, because she'd felt she'd earned it. "I know now that I don't have to earn love and that I am deserving of it as well. But I didn't know that then."

Finn's Adam's apple bobbed. "You don't owe me an explanation."

"You're right. I owe you a whole lot more. You didn't deserve the pain I caused you. I want you to know I'm getting the help I need, and I'm doing better all the time. I shouldn't have waited so long to get myself together." She locked her eyes on Finn, desperate for him to understand what she couldn't say. She'd do anything to take back the moment she'd ran. Because she knew now, from a healed perspective, he'd have stayed with her through it all. "I didn't believe something as wonderful as you could be meant for someone as damaged as me."

Regret swelled her tongue and halted her words. Then the tears began to fall.

Finn stepped carefully forward and opened his arms as an offering.

Part of her longed to turn and leave.

Instead, she stepped into his embrace and let him cradle her protectively against his chest until the tears ran dry.

Chapter Twelve

The muffled sound of a ringing phone drew Hayley from a restless sleep. She groaned with the crash of memories. She'd confessed her soul to Finn, then she'd cried herself to sleep. He'd barely said a word.

The past few days' worth of tension and fear had poured out of her, along with a lifetime of heartache and pain. She'd only intended to tell Finn as much as necessary to clear the air, but instead a dam had burst. She wasn't able to stop her words or tears until she'd become completely deflated.

Like the man he was, Finn had held her, comforted her, then walked her to bed so she could rest and recover. Despite the fact she'd hurt him. Despite the fact she'd unleashed a torrent of emotion without warning. Despite the fact she'd basically ambushed him. He'd even brought her a cold, wet cloth for her eyes. A glass of water and a couple of Tylenol to prevent a headache.

Hayley rolled onto her side and pulled the pillow over her head in residual horror. Finn hadn't been angry that she'd kept so much of herself from him while they were together. He didn't tell her that none of it mattered now, because they were over. He'd just been there. Strong and silent. Giving her the emotional space to fall apart while he held her together.

Then he'd left her alone with her demons.

At least she wouldn't have to face him for a few more hours. The first rays of sunlight were barely visible on the horizon beyond her window. With a little luck, she'd be ready to face him by the time the day began.

Her ears pricked when the muffled voice in the next room said Gage's name. Instinct made her sit upright and tightened her nerves. She stared at her closed bedroom door, hyperfocused on each low warble as the words came faster, desperate to dissect the meanings.

"I'm waking her now," Finn said suddenly, right outside her room.

Panic pushed her onto her feet. "Come in."

The door opened, and Finn's eyes met hers with alarm.

"What happened?" she asked, fear swirling in her anxious heart and muddled mind.

"Gage is missing."

THIRTY MINUTES LATER, Hayley burst from Finn's pickup and onto the grass outside his family's farmhouse.

Mrs. Beaumont waited on the wide wraparound porch. "Come in. I made breakfast and put on the coffee." She opened her arms to embrace them, then ushered them inside.

Hayley's lip trembled at the warm reception. She was thankful for the love of a mother when she needed it most, even if the mother wasn't hers. "Thank you."

The oversize eat-in kitchen smelled of biscuits and gravy. Beaumont men sat at the nearby table and hovered around an island the size of a boat. Josi filled mugs with coffee at the counter.

The family quieted as they took note of Hayley's arrival.

She stroked flyaway hairs away from her puffy eyes and swollen cheeks. The haphazard ponytail she'd wrangled into place on the drive between homes was already falling over one shoulder. She could only imagine what she looked like. She hadn't been brave enough to meet her own eyes in the bathroom mirror while brushing her teeth and hair.

Josi passed her a steaming mug. "I'm so sorry."

Lincoln stepped forward, into the space behind the young blonde, before Hayley could form words. "We don't know what happened," he said, jaw tense and eyes hard. "Gage was happy when we left him to settle in for bed. This morning, he was gone. He took his phone, but he won't answer."

"Why would he do that?" Hayley whispered, posing the question to herself as much as to the others.

"That's what I keep saying," Lincoln grumbled. "Doesn't make any sense."

Josi passed Finn a mug when he joined them at the counter.

The warmth of his nearness added a small measure of comfort to Hayley's weary soul.

"Have you thoroughly checked his room?" Finn asked. "Notice signs of trouble? Maybe a note?"

The responding death glare from Lincoln raised the fine hairs on Hayley's neck. "Of course, I have," he said.

Josi shifted discreetly, angling her body by an inch until her shoulder brushed Lincoln's chest.

His gaze flickered to her before jerking back to his brother. "I'm well aware of what to look for when a kid goes missing," he added, only slightly less hostile. "This isn't my first rodeo, and you know it."

Finn raised a palm. "I'm just trying to ask what you found."

"Nothing. That's the problem," Lincoln stormed. "The place is spotless. Nothing's missing except him and his phone."

Hayley thought about Finn's advice to her at the office crime scene. "Did Gage happen to leave anything behind? Something you didn't provide?" Something to suggest he planned to come back?

"Yeah. These," Josi said, pulling a folded row of photo-booth pictures from her back pocket. "I brought them along to help the search party."

Hayley took the strip gingerly. "There's a search party?"

Josi nodded. "They went out about twenty minutes ago. Lincoln went over to wake him around five thirty on his way to the stables. He looked around for a few minutes, thinking he'd just gone out to walk or clear his head. As soon as we realized he was nowhere near, I reached out to some of the farm hands just starting their days, then headed over here to let the Beaumonts know. Lincoln called Finn, and the others fanned across the property. No word so far."

Finn leaned closer, peering at the strip of black-and-white images in her hand. "That's Parker."

Hayley nodded. The pair were closer than she'd realized.

"Who?" Lincoln asked.

"Another boy staying with the same foster family," Finn explained. "He said Gage took care of him whenever he was there."

Fresh alarm shot through Hayley as she dragged her gaze from the photos to Finn. "All the kids are being removed from the Michaelsons' care today. Including Parker."

Josi sucked in a small, audible breath. "He's

the boy Gage asked about. He wanted to know how old kids had to be to stay here."

Hayley felt herself begin to nod, recalling Gage's question. In all the chaos, she'd completely forgotten.

Josi had told him Parker was too young.

FINN MARCHED ONTO the Michaelsons' porch at just after eight. He knocked more forcefully than necessary, then waited impatiently with Hayley at his side.

She'd spoken by phone with the social worker who'd reviewed the Michaelsons at her request. The other woman had found the couple lacking and confirmed the children would only be there another few hours. She was on her way to begin the process now.

Finn knocked again.

The front door sucked open with force, and Mrs. Michaelson glared out. A cacophony of voices and noise filled the home behind her. "Ugh," she groaned. "You again. Haven't you done enough? Sending people out here to ask a bunch of questions, disrupt the kids' days and poke through my life. Go away."

"Mrs. Michaelson," Finn began calmly, raising a palm to indicate she would be wise to wait. "We're here to speak with Parker." With a little luck, the kid had spoken to Gage last night. If Gage had used his new phone to call the Michaelsons' residence, Parker might even know where to find the older boy.

The sound of approaching vehicles drew his attention over one shoulder. A cruiser and unmarked sedan pulled into the space behind his truck at the curb.

The sedan was expected, but a uniformed officer was not.

"Why are the police here?" Hayley asked, gaze jumping to Finn.

"Haven't you heard?" Mrs. Michaelson asked. "Parker's gone."

"What do you mean he's gone?" Hayley cried.

A woman in tan pants and a navy blouse jogged up the steps to join them. She frowned at Hayley. "I just got the call. I changed directions and came right over as soon as I heard. I haven't even been to the office."

"I don't understand," Hayley said, eyes pleading. "Are you saying Parker ran away too?"

The uniformed officers were next to reach the porch. Officer Young tipped his head in greeting. "Mrs. Michaelson called to report a missing child this morning. We're here to take the report and interview the family."

Finn pointed to the nearby trash bin, filled to the brim with beer cans and empty alcohol containers. "You'll want to make note of that. The contents have doubled since the last time I was here."

"Hey now," Mrs. Michaelson protested, opening the door to allow the officers to pass. "Why don't you mind your business," she suggested. "Maybe concentrate on finding Gage, because he's still not here."

Finn held the door when the woman stepped out of the officers' way. He waved for Hayley and her coworker to enter ahead of him, then paused to level Mrs. Michaelson with an icy look. "If you're exposing vulnerable children to parties serving that much alcohol, or worse, you and your husband are putting it away on your own, that is absolutely our business."

Three middle schoolers at the kitchen counter went silent.

"Where's Mr. Michaelson now?" Officer Young asked. "We're hoping to catch him before he leaves for work."

"Already gone," Mrs. Michaelson reported, shoving the door shut behind the crowd. "He's a fisherman. Boat leaves before dawn, and he's always on it."

Hayley and her coworker went into business mode, instructing the children to gather their things.

The officers walked Mrs. Michaelson to the kitchen table to take her statement.

Finn took a spin around the first floor, looking for additional signs of trouble. The rooms were relatively tidy, considering the number of kids under the roof. According to the coat hooks and cubbies on the kitchen wall, there were five children in total at the modest suburban home. Pieces of masking tape with neat black letters spelled the names Gage, Parker, Orion, Wesley and Trent. Hopefully, one of the latter would be cooperative and helpful in finding Gage and Parker.

He paused in the kitchen to listen while Mrs. Michaelson relayed her timeline of events, beginning last night and ending this morning. "Ms. Campbell and I spoke with Parker when we were here before," he said, interrupting. "He said Gage goes home when he takes off. Any idea what that means?"

The officers raised their eyebrows in interest.

Mrs. Michaelson crossed her arms. "No. This is his home. Or it was."

Officer Young pursed his lips, presumably in thought. "Whatever happened to his family's place?"

"I assume it sold," Finn said. "It's been a while."

Hayley reappeared with one of the boys, a pillow and his bag. "I can check the county auditor's site."

"I've got this," Finn said. Dean's fiancé was a Realtor. If they needed any additional information on the home or property, he'd give his brother a call. Hayley had her hands full with more important things.

"Okay." She led the boys and her coworker outside to help settle them in the sedan.

"Where are they going?" Mrs. Michaelson complained.

Finn left the officers to handle the angry woman, then joined Hayley in his truck.

She looked exhausted and disheveled as she climbed aboard once more. "Any chance we can trace the cell phone Lincoln gave Gage?" she asked. "Get a list of numbers he called or everyone who called the Michaelsons' landline since last night? Confirm whether or not Gage contacted Parker?"

"You're certain they're together?" Finn asked, feeling the truth of the words as he spoke. The boys' united disappearance was another coincidence too big to ignore.

She nodded. "I'm sure of it."

"Josi told Gage that Parker was too young for the ranch," Finn said, shifting into Drive and thinking aloud. "Gage thought Parker wasn't safe with the Michaelsons, and this is Gage's way of protecting him?"

"I think so," Hayley said. "Which is hard to get my head around considering the danger Gage is in. How can he possibly protect a little kid and himself while on the run? Parker would've been safe and happy if Gage would've given us time to place him in another home."

"But Gage is new to the system," Finn said,

suddenly more tired than he'd been in a very long time. "You and I know the Michaelsons are the exception to the rule, and that wherever Parker is placed next will likely be filled with love and compassion. But this was Gage's only experience in foster care. He has no idea how good things can be, only how bad they've been."

Hayley raised her cell phone. "I'm going to try Gage's number again." She turned away and left a pleading voice mail, begging him to return to the ranch. She assured him it was okay to take Parker with him, and she vowed to protect them both.

Finn focused on the road, willing the rest of their day to get significantly better than the start.

Chapter Thirteen

Hayley concentrated on her breaths as Finn drove along the bay toward Old Downtown. It seemed like the most reasonable place to start their search for Gage and Parker. Gage was known to spend time in the area, and there were plenty of places for two boys to hole up and hide out. She hated the thought of them being there, especially knowing how many things could go wrong, but she also hoped they were somewhere in those neglected blocks, so she and Finn could find them and bring them home.

Sunlight twinkled off cresting waves and brilliant blue water, creating a postcard-worthy view beyond her window. Warm southern sun heated her skin, the familiar humidity cocooning her through the open window as they slowed for a turn.

Hayley kneaded her hands.

"We'll start on the outskirts," Finn said. "Talk to everyone we see, just like we did that first day. Then we'll move inward, toward the heart of the area, and finally toward the waterfront properties where the rave was held and Kate's body was located."

Hayley crossed and uncrossed her legs, knee bobbing as they rolled toward their destination. "I'm glad it's still early. I'm willing to turn over every piece of trash and rubble down here if needed." And thanks to the long summer days, she'd have nearly twelve more hours of light to do it.

"I don't think it'll come to that," Finn said. "Gage is trying to protect Parker, so he'll be strategic about where he takes him."

She stared into the distance, where traffic vanished along with all signs of grass and trees, replaced with sprawling concrete and desolation, dark storefronts with painted windows and barred doors. "That's what bothers me about him coming here. Gage knows what safe means. He had it with his family. If he's here now, I don't think he plans to stay longer than necessary. Which makes finding them fast even more important."

Finn glanced Hayley's way, his eyes skimming her face, then his gaze dropped to her twisting hands and bouncing knee. "I got the feeling most people in Old Downtown knew Gage, or at least recognized him from his art. He's spent a lot of time down here. His shadow children are everywhere. Chances are he talked to someone long enough to make friends. Maybe he went to them for help with Parker. Maybe he shared something that will lead us to the place he's calling home."

Hayley inhaled deeply and shook her hands out at the wrists. "You're right. I need to stay positive and focused." No more letting her unbearably negative imagination run away.

The truck slowed along the curb near a highway overpass, and Finn's attention moved to his rearview mirror.

"What is it?" Hayley turned, noticing a black SUV behind them.

The other vehicle sat on the previous block, angled against the curb as if it had pulled over as suddenly as they had. The SUV stood out as badly as Finn's truck in this area. It was shiny and new, while the rides parked between them were old and rusted.

"That SUV's been following us," Finn said. "It's not the same make or model as the one from the news, but it's been back there since we turned off Bay View. If we're being tailed because they're also looking for the boys, I need to know. And if we're being tailed for some other reason, I should probably know that too."

Her stomach churned as he opened his door. "Where are you going?" she hissed, reaching for him as he climbed out.

"Stay here, please." Finn turned toward the SUV in question. "Lock the doors."

"Wait!" Hayley gasped as his door closed. She

hit the automatic locks, then dialed 911 on her cell phone. She hovered her thumb over the screen, ready to send the call, and twisted in her seat to watch Finn move confidently away. Every horrific possibility charged through her mind as she braced for the pending encounter. Most involved bullets and blood.

The SUV launched forward with a bark of the tires.

Finn lurched sideways, thrown between parked cars.

"No!" The word tore from her throat in a scream as the SUV rocketed past her.

Hayley was on the sidewalk in an instant, racing toward Finn as the SUV rounded a corner behind her. Her sharp, pounding strides ate up the space between the truck and the location where Finn had disappeared. "Finn!"

A low moan slowed her steps.

He rose slowly off the concrete, from the space between parked cars. Palms bloody and arms rubbed raw from wrist to elbow. "Guess they didn't want to talk."

Her grip on the phone relaxed, and she burst forward, wrapping herself around him. "Oh, my goodness!" The force of her attack hug knocked him back against a busted Toyota. "You could've been killed!"

"Just a few scratches," he said, straightening

to his full height, taking her with him. "I'm fine, but I'm getting blood on you."

She released him to better survey his physical damage. "I almost called 911."

"No need." He rolled his shoulders and tipped his head from side to side, stretching the muscles of his neck. "I don't suppose you got a look at the license plate?"

"I wasn't looking for a license plate." Her only thoughts had been of him. "I think you need to see a doctor. Maybe we should visit an urgent care before we keep going."

"I definitely don't need a doctor," he said, testing his fingers, wrists and elbows. Wincing with each move. "I couldn't see the driver. Too much sunlight reflecting on the windshield."

Hayley crossed her arms over her middle, hating that she'd thrown herself at him the way she had. Hating that whoever had tried to hit him would get away with it.

"Hey," he called, following her. "What's wrong?"

"You were nearly killed."

"I told you. I'm—"

She spun to glare at him. "Do not tell me you're fine."

Finn grinned. "Suit yourself."

She turned back to the truck, taking slow, deep breaths to regain her calm. She couldn't think about what would happen if she lost him. Even if she couldn't keep Finn in her life when this was over, the world was a better place with him in it.

Finn opened the driver's-side door and pulled a bottle of water from behind his seat. He unscrewed the lid and poured the contents over his hands and forearms, then used a towel from his gym bag to wipe away most of the blood. A few thin streams sprouted anew. "See? The rest of this will scab up by lunch. I don't even need stitches."

"Keep downplaying what just happened and you might need a few," Hayley warned. She rounded the truck's grill, reached the passenger's door and climbed aboard.

Finn slid behind the wheel and started the engine. He pumped up the air-conditioning and pointed the vents in her direction. "I'm going to call this in before we move on," he said. He tapped the vehicle's dashboard screen while she buckled up.

Hayley swallowed a sudden wave of panic as he calmly relayed the details of his near death to someone at Marshal's Bluff PD.

The voice on the other end of the line sounded distorted as heat climbed her neck and her ears began to ring. She leaned forward on her seat, fighting nausea and searching for oxygen.

Gage was missing. A killer wanted him dead. Parker was likely in tow.

And she thought she'd seen Finn mowed down

by a Range Rover. Had imagined him never getting up again.

Her vision tunneled and she closed her eyes against the dark spots encroaching on her vision.

"Hayley." Finn's steady voice echoed in her ears. "Hey. Are you okay? Can you hear me?"

Her seat belt gave way with a snap, and Finn's big hands curled around her biceps, dragging her toward him.

In the next moment she was across his lap, curled against his chest, face pressed to his neck. "Shh," he said softly. "I've got you, and we're both just fine. I promise."

Hayley held on to his words like a lifeline as he stroked her back and gripped her tight. She pressed her palms to his chest and counted the beats of his heart until she was calm once more.

"Better?" he asked, not missing the release of tension in her body.

She raised her face to his, embarrassed at her unexpected reaction to the stress, infinitely thankful for his reaction to her. "I thought I lost you again."

His eyes darkened, and his lips parted. His gaze lowered to her mouth. "I'm right here."

Suddenly, every moment with him seemed so much more important than it had an hour before. This was it for her and Finn. They'd find Gage. Finn would arrest the killer. And the man she loved would be out of her life all over again. She hated the future, but she still had this moment.

Before she could talk herself out of it, she burrowed her fingers into the soft hair at the back of his head and urged his mouth to hers. She kissed him tenderly, hoping to convey how truly precious he was to her. She was desperate to show him all the things she hadn't found the courage to say.

And for one terrifying moment, Finn grew stone-still.

She dropped her hand away, pulling back in humiliation. "I am so sorry," she said in a rush, horrified by her unsolicited actions. "I didn't mean to—"

"Hayley." The deep rumble of pleasure in his chest had barely registered before his mouth returned to hers. The gentle sweep of his tongue sent fire through her veins, and the heady mix of joy and desire overtook her. She adjusted her body to better align with his, their hearts pounding together in a staccato rhythm.

"Ms. Campbell?" a deep male voice called, somewhat muffled by the closed windows.

A round of whoops and catcalls followed, returning her rudely to reality.

Hayley scrambled back to her side of the truck as a group of laughing teens came into view outside the windshield. She smoothed her hair as they closed in on the truck.

Finn stared at her, breathing heavy, his lips

slightly swollen from her kisses. "Friends of yours?" Finn asked quietly, shifting his attention to the group.

"I only know the spokesman."

He powered down the window and set his bloody elbow across the frame.

"Ms. C?" A young man she recognized as Keith Shane, a former child from her caseload, frowned back. "What are you doing down here?" His attention flicked to Finn and his bloody arm, then back to her. "You okay?"

"Fine," she said, hoping to appear as if it was true and hating her word choice. She'd just yelled at Finn for saying the same thing. And like Finn, she was absolutely not fine. She'd just made out in the front seat of a truck in broad daylight. And been caught. She was supposed to be looking for two missing children. And behaving like a professional grown-up.

Keith crouched to stare boldly through the open window. "So what's going on in here?"

"This is Detective Beaumont," Hayley said, thankful her voice sounded natural and unbothered. "Detective, this is Keith."

The young man's brow rose briefly, then furrowed. His gaze hardened on the detective. "Did he bring you down here for a reason I need to know about?"

Her heart warmed at the kid's protective tone, and she smiled. "Actually, yes. We're looking for two boys. Parker and Gage, ages eight and four-teen. Gage is the artist who paints the shadow children on the buildings. Do you know him?"

The group behind Keith made a few comments in approval of the artwork. Keith took another long look at Finn before turning to confer with his friends.

"If you've seen either boy today," Finn said, voice thick with authority, "we need to know. We have reasons to believe both kids are in significant danger."

The group dragged their eyes from Finn to Hayley, apparently deciding what to do next.

"They aren't in any trouble," Hayley assured them. "I want to protect them, but first I need to find them."

A short, wiry guy in a plain white tank top and navy basketball shorts stepped forward. "I saw that kid at a rave." He glanced at Finn.

"We know about the rave," Finn said. "We know Gage was there. Someone was chasing him. Any chance you got a look at that person?"

The kid nodded. "Yeah, it was an old rich dude."

"How old?"

He shrugged. "I don't know. Thirty."

Hayley felt her breath catch. This was a new lead. "How did you know he was rich?"

"His clothes." The kid plucked the material of his tank top away from his chest. "He was bou-gie as hell. V-neck T-shirt. Three-hundred-dollar boat shoes. A watch I could hock to buy my ma a house."

"Ever seen him before that night?" she asked.

The kid shrugged. "Maybe. There's been a lot of folks like that around lately. Preparing for the community center, I guess. I figured your boy got caught taking something from him, or maybe he painted on the wrong building."

Finn straightened, giving up any final pretense of casual. "Anything else we should know?"

The teens commiserated. "Nah," Keith said, retaking his role as spokesman. "But I wouldn't worry. That guy never had a chance at catching him. Kids disappear down here for a lot of reasons. And if they don't want to be found, they won't be." The sad smile he offered Hayley implied that she could expect the same result.

She could only hope he was wrong. "Any idea where he calls home?" she asked.

The group traded looks then shook their heads.

Finn distributed his business cards. "If you see Gage or think of anything that can help us find and protect him, give me a call."

Hayley offered a composed smile. "I'm safe with the detective," she said, noting the lingering concern in Keith's eyes. "He's one of the good ones."

Keith nodded in acceptance, then led his friends away.

Finn powered up the window and set his hands on the wheel. "Well, that was—"

"Embarrassing? Humiliating? Awful?" Hayley offered, feeling latent heat rise over her cheeks.

"I was going to say lucky," Finn said. "Based on his description, we can assume I was right in theorizing that Kate's killer wasn't robbing her. People in expensive shoes don't come down here at night if they can avoid it. They certainly don't chase kids into raves without serious motivation."

"Like getting away with murder," she mused.

"Yep." He shifted the truck into gear and headed deeper into Old Downtown.

Chapter Fourteen

Hayley tried not to obsess over the kiss. She'd acted impulsively but didn't regret it. And he'd kissed her back. Good and right. Her toes curled inside her shoes at the memory. The timing, location and audience were severely unfortunate, but damn...

Had it been more than just heightened emotions that had caused Finn to return the affection? He'd yet to comment on her tearful confession the night before. Not that they'd had time to talk about anything other than Gage and Parker today.

Finn turned onto the street where the rave had taken place and Kate's body had been discovered. The hour was early, and they'd yet to see anyone other than Keith and his friends.

She wet her still tingling lips and pushed aside thoughts of personal problems. Something more important suddenly had her attention. "Do you see all these signs?" she asked. "I didn't notice them when we were here before."

Rectangles of sturdy white cardboard had been

affixed to multiple buildings in the area, each marked with the logo of an unfamiliar company.

"Is that an investment group?" he asked.

"Maybe. I've never heard of Lighthouse, Inc. Is it one of Kate's companies?"

"I'm not sure," he said, parking the truck once more. "What do you think about taking another look at the warehouse where the old rich guy was seen?" He smiled. "I want to be sure we didn't miss anything there."

Hayley agreed and followed him out of the truck, then into the site of the rave. Empty plastic bags and sheets of newspapers blew over the silent, empty street as they entered. Their footfalls echoed in the stillness.

"Stay close," he said, posture tense, clearly on high alert.

She easily complied.

Dust motes sparkled like silver confetti in shafts of sunlight through broken windows. Sounds of the distant sea rose through the missing rear wall to her ears. A Lighthouse, Inc. sign on the broken boards drew her eyes. "Look."

They moved to the back, approaching the sign for inspection.

"Condemned," Finn read. "Marked for demolition. Unsafe for inhabitants and industry." He snapped a photo of the large cardboard warning then tapped his phone screen. "Let's see what Dean can learn about the company."

"They seem to own everything nearby," Hayley said. That had to mean something. "Maybe Lighthouse, Inc. is involved in the community-center project somehow."

Finn stilled. He worked his jaw and slid his gaze over the space around them, posture stiffening incrementally.

Hayley followed his eyes, searching for what had gotten his attention, but seeing nothing unusual. "What is it?"

"I'm not sure." His phone rang, and she started. "Hey," he answered, raising the device to his ear. "We're at the warehouse now—"

The sounds of squealing tires and rapid gunfire erupted from the world outside.

Splinters of wood burst into the air around them, and a scream ripped from Hayley's throat. Finn's body collided with hers in the next heartbeat, jolting them forward.

"Run!" he hollered, thrusting her toward the missing back wall, where nothing stood between them and the sea far below.

"But—" Something bounced and rolled in her peripheral vision as the car roared away, and she recognized the urgency. "Is that dynamite?" she screeched.

Finn jerked her by the wrist, forcing her into a sprint. "Jump!" he yelled a moment before they launched into the air.

Her feet left the warehouse floorboards, bicycling high above the sea.

Their joint freefall began as the warehouse exploded.

Another scream ripped from Hayley. Her ears rang and her vision blurred with the intensity of the boom.

Debris blew into the sky around them. Bits of busted stone and chunks of roofing. Clods of earth and fractured beams. A thousand pieces of instant shrapnel. Some sliced her clothes and others bit her skin.

Then, it was all swallowed by harbor water.

The impact pushed the air from her lungs. Shock separated her mind and limbs, leaving her body to twist and roll helplessly in the dark silence of the sea. She searched for the surface, fighting the pitch and heave of undercurrents, burning with need for oxygen.

Would she survive an explosion only to drown in the waters below?

Demanding hands gripped her waist in the next moment, propelling her upward. She recognized Finn's touch before she saw him. Before she took her next breath.

Her mouth opened and her body gasped as they broke the surface—she pulled sweet salt air deep into her lungs.

"I've got you," he promised, between the raspy breaths and the rhythmic kicking of his legs. "Are you okay?" he asked, treading water as he caressed her cheek and scanned her face with worried eyes.

She opened her mouth to speak, but a fit of coughing erupted instead. Followed by a stomach full of salt water. How much had she swallowed?

Finn pulled her against his chest and began an awkward backstroke toward the shore.

Emergency sirens wailed in the distance, growing louder and more fervent with each inch of progress Finn made.

He towed her through a floating field of charred and busted planks, dodging the larger, most ragged pieces. "Only a little farther," he promised, his breaths coming rougher and shorter.

Slowly, Hayley's mind and body reunited, coordinating her limbs. She helped him paddle until his feet struck the ground below.

"Help is on the way," he panted, setting her gingerly on the rocky shore. "They'll be here soon."

She took a mental inventory of her faculties and scanned her body for injuries. All her parts were accounted for, and the cuts and bruises were shockingly few. Though she'd still have been dead, if not for Finn. "You saved my life."

He dipped his chin in acknowledgement, eyes scanning the top of the hill, where a cluster of onlookers had appeared. Blood lined his mouth, seeping from a split in his lip, and a large purple knot had formed beside his right eye.

"You're hurt." She reached for his hands, pulling him down, certain her shaking legs wouldn't hold her if she tried to stand. "Sit. It could be bad. Adrenaline can cover serious injuries."

He wobbled slightly, then fell to his knees, his body stiff as he winced. His shirt was torn and his arms were bleeding. Suddenly, the scrapes from the earlier road incident seemed like paper cuts in comparison.

Hayley's gaze shot to the warehouse on the hill, or what remained of it. The explosion had demolished the back half, reducing that portion of the structure to rubble. *Exactly what dynamite tended to do*, she thought. And they'd been inside moments before it blew. She sucked a ragged breath as something horrendous came to mind. "What if—" The words were lodged in her throat, unable to break free.

What if Gage and Parker had been there too?

"We were alone," Finn said, offering comfort and apparently reading her mind. He eased into the space beside her then reached for her trembling hands.

"Someone blew up a building to kill us," she said. The words were nonsensical. How could anything so outrageous be true?

Finn gave her fingers a squeeze. "I'm guessing they used C-4 from a nearby construction site, and the one who threw the explosive was probably the same person driving the SUV that nearly hit me." His normally tanned skin was unusually white, and his gaze slightly unfocused.

"I think you should lay back," Hayley said. "You're going to need stitches. I don't know how much blood you've lost. Or if you have other injuries. Did anything hit your head as we fell?" There had been a lot of large debris, and he'd used his body to protect her.

"I'm all right," he said. "Just wondering what's taking the ambulance so long."

"There they are!" someone called from the top of the hill, drawing Hayley's eyes back to the growing crowd. She waved a limp arm overhead.

"Help is coming!" a stranger called. "They're almost here!"

"I can't believe they're alive!" someone else yelled. "That place blew into splinters!"

Finn slumped against Hayley's side, and she wound an arm around him. Hopefully, the crowd was enough deterrent to keep their near-assassin from taking another shot. Neither she nor Finn were in any condition to run again. She wasn't convinced they were even ready to stand.

A collection of rocks and dirt slid over the hill in their direction, accompanied by a pair of EMTs. The men wore matching uniforms and expressions of disbelief while carrying backboards and medical kits.

Hayley knew exactly how they felt.

A long hour later, she and Finn were sequestered in side-by-side ambulances. Hayley's EMT had examined her swiftly, cleaned her wounds, then hooked her up to an IV to replenish lost fluids.

Outside the open bay doors, uniformed officers interviewed the crowd. From what she could piece together, several people had heard the squealing tires that preceded the dynamite delivery, but no one had seen the car causing all the noise or its driver.

Finn strode into view, scowling, with an EMT trailing behind.

"Detective," the medic pleaded. "I haven't finished." He swiped an alcohol pad over the back of Finn's arm as they moved.

"Yes," Finn corrected. "You have. I appreciated the IV and bandages. The rest of this will heal on its own."

Hayley smiled despite herself. "You should go to the hospital and let them check you more thoroughly," she said, watching as he climbed aboard with her.

"I'm fine. I wasn't hit by anything big, and I've cliff-dived from greater heights. I got a little dinged up, but it's been handled. What about you?"

"Oh, I'm super," she said, struggling to maintain her smile. Images of Finn cliff-diving helped.

She wished she could've been there to see him make a leap like that for fun.

He looked to the EMT for confirmation. "She's okay?"

"She's going to heal completely, with rest and fluids," the man said. "For the record, I don't think either of you are okay. That was quite an experience. You both need to take a few days and rest. Visible wounds or not."

"Noted," Finn said, though he didn't look convinced. He looked like a losing prizefighter. His split lip had swollen, and the knot on his head had grown. "If we're cleared to go, I think we're ready."

Hayley nodded in agreement when he turned her way.

The EMT sighed and removed Hayley's IV. "Fluids and rest," he repeated. "Something over-the-counter for pain."

"Thank you." Hayley waved. She let Finn help her down from the ambulance then along the sidewalk to his truck on the next block.

The day was insufferably hot, the air thick with stifling humidity. A secondary crowd had gathered outside the warehouse remains.

She recognized Dean on the outskirts surveying the scene.

Finn unlocked the pickup as they approached, and Hayley climbed inside.

Her previously soaked clothes were wrinkled

and dirty, and had been dried by the relentless heat. She peeled strands of tangled hair from her cheeks and neck. "Are you sure you're okay?" she asked.

"Physically, sure," he said. "But I've been wondering how long we were followed." He eased behind the wheel with a small wince. "Some of what we said after leaving the truck might've been overheard. Maybe even our chat with Keith and his friends."

Hayley tensed, thinking about all the things she'd spoken with Finn about in the time before the explosion. "Someone could know we're looking for the spot Gage called home. They'll be looking for it too."

Finn shifted into gear and piloted the vehicle back toward town, scanning pedestrians and passing traffic with care. "Gage's file mentioned active involvement at his middle school last year. Band. Soccer. Art camps. His parents led a few extracurriculars as well. Let's start there, and see if there's any place he could make a temporary home. Somewhere to relive the better days."

"He attended Virginia Dare middle school," Hayley said. She reached for her phone before remembering it was at the bottom of the bay. "He was part of the swim team too, and I think there's a pool on the property."

Finn stretched across the cab and opened the

glove box. He withdrew a handgun and cell phone. "Do you remember the address of his home?"

She searched her memory for the information but came up empty. "No. I'm sorry."

"Would you mind giving your office a call? Asking someone to look in the file?"

She took the device with trembling fingers, and Finn made the next turn toward the middle school. By the time they arrived, she'd gained the information they needed, and Finn had passed it on to his team.

"I'll ask Dispatch to send a cruiser to the house and talk to the new owners," he said. "We'll let them know there's a possibility a couple of kids might show up, try to sleep in the backyard playhouse or elsewhere on the grounds. If that happens, the owners can give the station a call."

Hayley wiped tears from her cheeks, unsure what had prompted them this time.

"You doing okay?" Finn asked.

She shook her head, unable to lie. "I thought I was tough, but this whole situation has been awful. How do you do this every day?"

Finn smiled kindly. "This isn't a typical workweek," he said. "I'm not usually in continual danger, and the good I do is always worth the trouble. I'm sorry you're in the line of fire this week. If I could change that, I would."

"Don't feel too badly," she said. "I brought the fire."

Finn chose a spot in the middle-school parking lot, then turned stormy eyes on her.

A cascade of goose bumps scattered over her skin in the quiet cab, and her lips parted of their own accord. "I kissed you," she whispered. Somehow, that had been the least dangerous yet most traumatic event to occur since breakfast.

Maybe the timing was wrong, but she'd bared her heart to him in words last night and in actions this morning. She needed to know where he stood on the matter. She needed to settle at least this one thing in a time when everything else was beyond her reach. She had no means of getting answers to Gage's whereabouts. Or Parker's. Had no way of knowing who'd killed Kate and wanted to kill her too. But she could ask Finn to be direct with her, and she could get this one issue solved.

"We should talk about that when this is over," he said, turning his attention to something beyond the truck's window. "Looks like the groundskeeper is headed our way."

She followed Finn's gaze to a man in jeans and a navy blue T-shirt with the school's logo.

Grass clippings stuck to the bottoms of his pant legs and a curious look crossed his heavily creased face. He grinned as he drew near. "Finn Beaumont. What brings you around here? How's your family doing?"

Finn climbed out and met the man on the passenger's side. He shook his hand.

Hayley powered down her window, hoping to hide her aching limbs and frazzled nerves by remaining inside the truck.

"Nice to see you again, Eric," Finn said. "The family's good. This is Hayley Campbell. She's a social worker, and we're looking for a former student. He's in foster care now, attending the high school this year. He's gone missing. Runaway, we believe. We're hoping you might be able to help."

The older man accepted the handshake then crossed his arms and listened intently as Finn covered the important details of Gage's story. Eric removed his hat when Finn finished. "I remember Gage. Remember the accident. Hell, I remember his folks. Nice, good people. What happened to them was unthinkable. Our whole community grieved. I hate to hear he's taken off, but his world must be in a shambles."

Hayley nearly choked at the painful understatement. Eric didn't know the half of it. She passed a business card through the open window and into his hand. "If you see him, will you reach out to the police or call me directly?"

"Will do." Eric raised two fingers to his forehead, saluting them as Finn retook his seat behind the wheel and shifted into Reverse.

Hayley sent out another round of prayers to the universe as they motored away.

Let us find those boys before the killer can.

Chapter Fifteen

Hayley tried and failed to rest all afternoon. Her body was sore and fatigued, but her mind was in overdrive. She'd nearly died today while under the protection of a lawman. What chance did Gage have at survival on his own while caring for a kid?

Finn's brothers and other detectives had visited the pool where Gage used to swim, along with a few other spots from the teen's past, but none had revealed any indication the boys had been there.

Meanwhile, Finn and Hayley had returned to his house. Mrs. Beaumont had delivered a delicious lunch, and Hayley had taken a lengthy, indulgent shower, but her tension only increased. She couldn't shake the sensation a giant clock was counting down, and the boys were running out of time.

She dragged Finn's laptop onto the couch with her while he took his turn in the shower. If she couldn't be on the streets searching for Gage and Parker, she could at least keep looking for clues online. She started with the name of the company that had plastered signs all over Old Downtown.

Her initial findings revealed Lighthouse, Inc. to be a small company located in Marshal's Bluff. Real-estate projects seemed to be the business's focus, but it was unclear if Lighthouse, Inc. was an investment group or something else. The website was static, and the accompanying social-media accounts were sorely lacking.

Sounds of the shower filtered to her ears, and Hayley did her best to ignore them. In the big scheme of her current problems, matters of the heart should've been less than irrelevant. But knowing Finn was naked and separated from her by one closed door made it unreasonably hard to concentrate.

She clicked the next link on her web search, and an image of Kate pulled her focus back to where it belonged. The article featured the philanthropist as the keynote speaker at a recent fundraising gala. The caption below the photo identified her and the men at her side. Her husband, Topper, and Conrad Forester, the CEO of Lighthouse, Inc.

Hayley swung her feet onto the floor and opened another browser window, starting a second search. She added Kate and her husband's names to the words *Lighthouse, Inc.* Several links appeared. Each time, the results also mentioned Conrad Forester. Apparently, the trio had golfed together, boated together and attended a number of other community events.

Did they simply run in the same circles, or were they friends outside their work? The three of them? Or only two? If the latter, then who was the third wheel? More importantly, was their connection relevant to the case?

The water shut off in the bathroom, and Hayley rose to her feet. She paced the carpeted space between the couch and hallway, waiting for Finn to appear. She wasn't a detective, but something inside her told her this new knowledge mattered. Finn would know for sure.

When the door opened and he emerged in a clingy T-shirt and cloud of Finn-scented steam, she allowed herself a moment to appreciate the view.

Her eyes met his a heartbeat later, and his mischievous grin suggested he'd noticed exactly how long it'd taken her to pull herself together. "What's up?" he asked, rubbing a towel over damp, tousled hair.

"I think I found something." She pointed over her shoulder, refusing to steal another glance at his nicely curved biceps as he draped the towel around his neck.

"What is it?"

She returned to the couch and passed him the laptop, recapping her concern.

"That is interesting," he agreed. "It makes sense a company involved in real estate would know her.

Their work probably brought them together from time to time. The frequent interactions could've made them friends."

"Do you think they were collaborating on the community-center project?"

Finn grinned. "I can think of one way to find out. How are you feeling?"

"Like I could sleep until retirement, but I'm too wound up to rest."

Finn checked his watch. "If we hurry, we might catch Mr. Forester at work before office hours end."

"Then we'd better get moving."

LIGHTHOUSE, INC. was housed in a single-story cottage in the shopping district. The former residential property was covered in gray-blue vinyl siding and trimmed in white. A small porch with two steps and a coordinating black handrail matched the roof and front door. According to the sign in the window, the office was open.

Finn held the door for Hayley. "After you."

Seashell wind chimes jangled overhead as she crossed the threshold.

"May I help you?" a young woman in a periwinkle-blue sundress asked. Her long brown hair hung in waves across her shoulders. The welcome desk where she sat was white and tidy, topped with a keyboard and monitor.

Finn raised his detective shield. "We're here to speak with Conrad Forester."

Her eyes widened in response. She looked from Finn to Hayley, then to a set of closed doors on the far wall before managing to recover. "Do you have an appointment?"

Finn wiggled the badge. "Yep."

She nodded shakily. "Right." She turned her focus to the monitor and typed something with her keyboard.

Hayley gave the office a more thorough look while they waited. A small sitting area beside the welcome desk held a couch, a set of armchairs and a coffee table covered in boating magazines. A placard on one of the closed doors across the room identified it as a restroom. The others, Hayley presumed, were offices.

"He'll be right out," the woman said.

Finn turned to stare at the closed doors, ignoring the comfortable-looking couch and armchairs. Hayley followed his lead.

Soon, one of the doors opened, and a tall, broad-shouldered man stepped out. "Detective."

"Mr. Forester," Finn said, approaching for a handshake. "This is Hayley Campbell."

"Good afternoon." Mr. Forester offered her a plaintive smile. His face was tan and his forehead lined with creases. A sprinkle of gray touched his otherwise sandy hair. He didn't invite them in. "What can I do for you?" he asked, swinging troubled brown eyes back to Finn.

"I'm looking into the murder of Katherine Everett," Finn said.

Mr. Forester nodded solemnly. "A true shame. She'll be greatly missed in this community."

"Couldn't agree more," Finn said. "I also couldn't help noticing signs for your company all over the area where her body was discovered."

The soft sounds of typing ceased, and Hayley fought the urge to look at the woman who'd welcomed them. Instead, she kept her eyes on the man before her, as he seemed to pale at the mention of his company signs in conjunction with Kate's murder.

"We're planning to improve the area near the bay," Forester said. "The changes will bring in local businesses, reduce crime, create condos along the waterfront and single-family homes along the fringe. Parks. Playgrounds. The whole deal." His smile grew as he spoke, and his demeanor became congenial. As if he was reciting a canned pitch for the media or as a marketing speech, not explaining himself to a detective investigating a homicide.

Hayley struggled to keep her expression blank and guarded.

"Condos," Finn repeated, the disbelief in the single word making it fall flat. "In Old Downtown."

She understood the skepticism. The area in

question was too raw and riddled with trouble. The criminal population alone would likely destroy or make off with any decent building materials before the things on Forester's list ever came to fruition.

Creating a community center and homeless shelter in an area was one thing. The people and the area were in desperate need of love and housing. Replacing everything with high-end housing and businesses was rubbing salt in a proverbial wound.

"Shopping too," Forester said. "Pubs, cafés, jobs. Whatever it takes to get families down that way."

Finn stared at him, silently scrutinizing. Hayley would've confessed to anything if she'd been on the other side of that look, but Forester kept up the unbothered grin. "How well did you know Katherine Everett?" Finn asked.

Forester rocked back on his heels. "Not well." He put his palms in front of him. "We weren't strangers, but we were friendly enough to say hello when we crossed paths."

"That happened a lot," Finn said. "I understand the two of you were friends. You did a number of things together. Boating. Golfing. Charity events and whatnot."

"Well." Forester chuckled. "That's what business owners do, isn't it? We lend a hand however we can. Golf outings, nautical events, dinners—they're all for a cause."

Finn sucked his teeth. "So you didn't have a personal relationship with Kate or her husband?"

Forester's smile slipped by a fraction. A ringing phone drew his attention through the open door behind him. "I'm sorry to do this, but I've been expecting that call. Would you mind?"

"Not at all," Finn said. "I'll be in touch if I need anything else."

Forester took his leave, pulling the door closed in his wake.

Hayley waved to the woman at the welcome desk on her way out, then they hurried back to Finn's truck. "Are you thinking what I'm thinking?" she asked.

"Depends." Finn opened the door and waited while she climbed inside. "Are you thinking he seemed extremely on edge beneath the forced smile?"

"Yeah, and I'm guessing Kate's plans would've put a big dent in the value of his condos."

FINN STRETCHED HIS aching limbs into cotton joggers and an old concert T-shirt later that evening, thankful for the rest of the night off. His team at Marshal's Bluff PD was working around the clock to find the missing boys and put the pieces of Kate's murder investigation together. Finn had no doubt they'd be in touch if anything significant came to light. Meanwhile, he needed to recuperate. He'd barely had the energy to visit with his mom and shower after the explosion. The trip to Lighthouse, Inc. had put him over the edge. But there was still one more thing he needed to do. Having a talk with Hayley about her confession the previous night, and their kiss earlier today, was already overdue.

He'd originally imagined her reason for confiding in him was simply to clear the air so they could move forward as friends. Especially since they'd become impromptu roommates. The kiss they'd shared, however, made him wonder if there was hope for more. It wasn't uncommon for people under extreme stress to find physical outlets, and all the things they'd been through certainly qualified as stressful, but he wanted to hear it from Hayley. Was her behavior a result of heightened emotions, or was there a chance they could find their way back to one another? He'd never forgive himself if the case ended, and she walked away because he hadn't taken the opportunity to set things straight while he had a chance.

Finn inhaled deeply, then released the breath slowly. He'd dreamed of being in Hayley's life again, and now she was living under his roof, sharing his meals and at his side in every moment of the day. He didn't want to screw that up or scare her away again. Whatever happened between them, he'd never stop protecting her in any way he could.

His eyes found her as he moved down the hall

toward the living room. She looked like his personal heaven curled on the couch in a messy bun, oversize shirt and sleep shorts. She was so much more than a beautiful woman, human and friend. She was the place he wanted to get lost in, but he didn't have that luxury. Not while two boys were missing and a killer was at large. Hell, he wasn't sure he had that option at all. But it was time he and Hayley figured that out.

"Hey." She smiled as he entered the room. "How are you feeling?"

"Like I was in an explosion." He stopped in the kitchen and pulled two bottles from the fridge, then lifted them in question.

"Yes, please." Her eyes traveled the length of his arms and neck, pausing briefly on every cut, scrape and bandage, then on his swollen eye. "You look terrible."

"I feel terrible. How about you? You doing okay?"

Hayley pulled her bottom lip between her teeth. "I'm still hoping you want to talk." The blush creeping over her lightly freckled cheeks said she'd been thinking about her confession and their recent kiss as well.

Finn carried the bottles of water to the coffee table and took a seat on the couch beside her. She moved closer, leaning in and fitting perfectly against his side. He released a contented sigh and let his arm curve around her. This could've been their life.

If he'd gone after her that night.

If she'd found her voice sooner.

If he'd seen the signs of her pain and asked about them.

If he'd had a clue.

"Finn?"

He shook away the what-ifs and angled his head toward her, resting his chin atop her crown. "Yeah?"

"I hate that all of this is happening, but I'm glad you're here. We're alive today because of you."

He stroked her soft hair and inhaled her sweet scent, unsure of what to say. His every action today, and every day since she'd shown up unexpectedly in his office, were born of instinct and a bone-deep need to protect her at any cost. "You will always be safe with me," he promised.

"I know." She pulled away to look into his eyes. "I'm sorry I lost it last night when I was explaining myself. I wanted you to know all those things, but I didn't expect to be flooded with emotion while I shared. I definitely didn't think I'd be so embarrassed by the outburst I'd cry myself to sleep."

"You never have to be embarrassed with me," he said softly, meaning it to his core. "You can always tell me anything."

She gave a sad laugh. "I left you without an

explanation last year. Then I dumped the whole story on you last night and left again. This is not who I'm trying to be."

Her words drew a small smile over his face.

"I know who you are, Hayley Campbell," he stated simply, stroking the backs of his fingers across her cheek. "I wish I'd known about your pain sooner, but I'm glad you told me. A lot of things make more sense now. And because I know, I can be more aware and sensitive to you."

"Do you have any questions?" she asked, gaze darting away then back. "I can try to fill in any blanks I left."

Finn opened his mouth to say he'd listen to anything she wanted to tell him, but he wouldn't pry. Instead, a different set of words rolled off his tongue. "Why'd you kiss me today?"

Hayley froze in his arms and pulled in a deep breath. "I thought you'd been hit by that car. The possibility I'd lost you again, forever and for real this time, was gutting. I never want to live in that reality. Even if you never speak to me again after this case ends, I need to know you're okay and happy somewhere. Nothing else makes any sense. You know?"

He pulled her against his chest and held her a little more tightly, because he knew exactly what she meant.

Chapter Sixteen

Hayley forced herself to push away from Finn's protective hold. She had more to say and needed to get it out before the phone rang or someone else tried to kill them. She tucked her feet beneath her and angled to face him on the cushions. "I want you to know I'm committed to healing. I don't want to hurt anymore, and I don't want to hurt anyone else like I hurt you. It's been a long road just getting this far, but I won't quit. I still meet with my therapist weekly to sort through the thoughts and feelings that make me feel unlovable. I have no intention of going back to where I was last year."

His kind eyes crinkled at the corners and he tipped his head slightly. Interest and something that looked a lot like pride flashed in his expression. "I believe you. Do you want to talk about it?"

She shifted, debating, but knew she needed to be brave and honest. "A little."

Finn nodded, holding her gaze. Then he waited

patiently while she gathered the right words to continue.

"So far my key takeaways have been that my mother is an alcoholic. She has been for the majority of my life, and she will always be. She doesn't accept this as truth, and she is nowhere near the point of seeking help. Her behavior isn't my fault, and there's nothing I could've done better that would've changed her choices or healed her illness. She has to do that herself. I tried talking to her about it over dinner last fall, but she accused me of making slanderous accusations to hurt her."

Hayley took another steadying breath and swallowed, determined not to cry again. "I've accepted that my childhood was a series of minor and major abuses, and that I've both survived and thrived as a human despite her. Those unfortunate experiences have shaped and burdened every relationship I've had, including what I had with you. I'm distrustful and needy. Desperate to help others while neglecting myself. And a whole slew of other opposing concepts that keep me unsettled. But I'm working on those too." She pressed her lips together. "I will not pretend everything is fine like my mother."

Finn set a hand over hers as he'd done so many times before, an offer of shared strength. "How often do you get to see or speak to your mother now?" Finn asked, cutting to the quick of Hayley's pain. Seeing the thing she hadn't been able to say.

"I don't. Not since that dinner last year." Because until Hayley fully healed, interacting with her mother would only destroy the progress she'd fought so hard to make. She waited for Finn to say more, then tensed with each passing breath in silence. "What are you thinking?"

"I'm thinking that you used self-sabotage to avoid happiness," he said.

"I did."

"That's not uncommon when you spent so long being miserable."

Hayley nodded, thankful for the millionth time that Finn understood but never judged. "I should've trusted you with all of this sooner." She'd known in her heart that he wasn't like the others who'd hurt her, but her instinct had still been to run.

Finn opened his arms and raised his chin, coaxing her closer. She fell against him, immediately cocooned in his embrace.

"I'm broken in so many ways," she whispered.

"You are healing in far more." He pulled her onto his lap and pressed a kiss to the top of her head. "I'm glad you're on this path," he said softly. "You deserve happiness, Hayley. You deserve the world."

She tipped her head away for a view of his sincere brown eyes. "What if the only thing I've wanted in a very long time is you, and I ruined it?"

Finn's gaze darkened, and he lifted a palm to cradle her jaw. One strong thumb stroked her cheek. "I'm right here, just like I always have been. Like I always will be."

Her gaze dropped to his lips, and he angled his mouth to hers in response. The delicious scent of him encompassed her. The heat of his skin and tantalizing pressure of his embrace was instant ecstasy. When the kiss deepened and their tongues met in that perfect, familiar, sensual slide, she knew she'd finally come home.

HAYLEY WOKE ON the couch in Finn's arms the next morning. A call from his team roused them both from a deep slumber. It was the first truly good night of rest Hayley had had since the mess with Gage first began. Finn appeared astonished at the sight of the clock. She assumed he was feeling the same way.

An hour later, like the days before, they were up and out the door. Hastily dressed in denim capris, black flats and a white silk tank, she sat beside him in his pickup as they approached Katherine Everett's home. They rolled along the winding paved driveway that stretched between a posh gated entrance and the massive brick estate. The experience was a little like traveling to another world. "I had no idea homes like this existed in Marshal's Bluff," Hayley said, leaning forward to drink in the views. Majestic oaks lined the path, their gnarled, moss-soaked limbs stretching overhead, the road before them dappled in golden light.

"There are a few," he said. "And there are usually lawyers waiting for me when I visit."

She wrinkled her nose. "Frustrating."

Finn piloted the truck around a stone fountain outside the sprawling estate and parked near a sleek Mercedes convertible. He inhaled deeply, perhaps preparing himself for those lawyers. Then he opened his door.

Hayley followed suit and met him at the fountain, where they exchanged small smiles.

"You should get one," she teased. "Your yard chickens would love it."

Finn snorted before schooling his features into detective mode and leading the way to the home's front doors. He rang the bell and scanned the structure while he waited.

Hayley tried not to gawk as she admired the detail work along the eaves, around the windows and in the stylized shrubbery. Katherine Everett had always appeared so casual and down-to-earth online and during her television interviews. No different than those she helped. Clearly, that had been a mask.

Finn pressed the bell a second time and shifted for a peek through the beveled glass.

"Are you sure he's home?" Hayley asked. They'd come without calling after all.

"I believe that's his car of choice," Finn said, nodding toward the convertible. "One of a dozen registered in his name. Plus, it's still fairly early, and given his recent loss, I'd expect a husband to be taking time off from whatever he does to grieve."

"What does he do?" Hayley asked, realizing she had no idea. Was being the spouse of Kate enough to keep a person busy?

Finn's eyebrows tented. "Not much as far as I can tell."

The door opened, sweeping her attention to a woman in black slacks and a crimson blouse. "May I help you?"

Finn flashed his badge and her lips turned down in distaste.

"The police have already been here to speak with Mr. Everett," she said, coolly. "I'm sure they have everything they need, and Mr. Everett's attorney's contact information for future inquiries."

Finn stepped toward her, causing her to step back. "I won't keep him long. I understand this is a sensitive time for Mr. Everett, but I'm sure he's as interested in finding his wife's killer as I am. Would you mind letting him know I'm here?"

The woman pulled her chin back and balked.

"My name is Detective Beaumont."

She turned with a huff. "I'll see if Mr. Everett is available." She left the front door open and stormed into the home.

Finn waited for Hayley to step into the foyer, then he followed the woman across acres of Italian marble and through sliding glass doors to a rear patio.

Hayley hurried along in their wake, devouring the delicious interior views. Each space she passed looked more like an image from a design magazine than the last. As if Pinterest had exploded and all the pieces landed in one magnificent array for the Everetts to enjoy.

She stole one last peek at the mind-bending gourmet kitchen before stepping back into the scorching summer heat.

It took a moment for her eyes to adjust as sunlight glinted off the water of an impressive inground pool. Gorgeous tropical-looking plants and landscaping ran the length of the space between home and cabana. An outdoor kitchen, bar, fireplace and rocky waterfall feature filled the area nearest a hot tub. Finn and the woman stopped short of the bubbling water, where a shirtless man was sitting chest-deep.

Mirrored sunglasses covered his eyes as he sipped from a tall glass. A few soft words were exchanged, and he rose, revealing orange board shorts and the physique of a significantly younger man. If not for the thinning gray hair, Mr. Everett might've been in his late thirties instead of his early fifties. Perhaps that answered the question of what he did all day as Kate's husband. Clearly, he worked out.

The woman presented him with a large striped beach towel, and he wrapped it around his waist.

"This way," she said, flipping her wrist as she passed Hayley near the patio doors. "You can wait in the study."

Finn slowed at her side and set a hand against the small of her back as they reentered the home. A few footsteps later, they arrived at a fancy office Hayley had noticed on her way through.

An executive desk the size of an elephant centered the room and mahogany bookshelves climbed from floor to ceiling along the back wall. Matching leather armchairs faced the perfectly clean desk. A single framed photo of Kate and the man from the hot tub adorned the glossy wooden surface. They appeared happy on a boat at sea.

"Wait here," the woman said, then pulled the tall double doors shut behind her.

Finn circled the room's periphery without speaking, and Hayley took a seat in an armchair. Something about the space made her think they might be on camera. The room was too pristine to be anyone's real office, too staged to be used as more than a prop.

This was most likely the enhanced, if not blatantly false, image Mr. Everett wanted people to believe of him, Hayley realized. A middle-aged man's push-up bra and French tips. The idea only made her more curious about who he truly was.

The doors reopened, and the man from the hot tub entered. The sunglasses were gone, as were the board shorts. Now, he had on navy dress shorts with boat shoes and a salmon-pink polo shirt with a designer insignia on the collar. She couldn't help wondering if his shoes were the same ones Keith's friend had seen on the man chasing Gage through the rave.

"Mr. Everett," Finn said, offering his hand. "Thank you for seeing me."

Kate's husband nodded, frowning. "Of course. Call me Topper. Please make yourself at home."

Finn took the seat beside Hayley's, clearly unimpressed. "This is Hayley Campbell, a local social worker interested in your wife's project."

She smiled. Mr. Everett did not.

"What can I do for you today, Detective?" he asked, moving to the seat behind the large desk. "You have news on my wife's case?"

"A bit, yes." Finn angled forward, pinning the other man with an inscrutable cop stare. "I was hoping you could tell me about Lighthouse, Inc."

Mr. Everett leaned away, causing the spring in his chair to squeak. His eyes narrowed, as if he was deep in thought. "I believe they've worked with my wife on various projects of the past."

"What about her community center in Old Downtown?" Finn asked.

"I couldn't say." Mr. Everett's gaze roamed to the grandfather clock beside his window, to the ceiling and then to Hayley, before returning to Finn. "Kate had a number of things in motion all the time. No one could keep up." He forced a pitiful smile. "She was a force."

"Agreed," Finn said. "What can you tell me about Lighthouse, Inc. in general?"

"It's a local business."

"Investors?" Finn asked.

"Land developers, I believe."

"How well do you know the owners of the company?"

Hayley let her attention bounce from Finn to Mr. Everett and back, nerves tightening.

"We're acquainted," Mr. Everett hedged, swaying forward once more. He anchored his forearms on the desk and laced his fingers.

"I see. How did you meet, initially?"

"Conrad is a member of Ardent Lakes."

"Conrad Forester," Finn clarified.

"Yes."

Hayley recognized Ardent Lakes as the name of a local country club. She'd driven past the gates a hundred times, but had never been inside. "Mr. Everett," she said, pulling both men's attention to her. "Sorry to interrupt, but I'm wondering about the community center." She'd been introduced as a social worker. She might as well play her role. "A great many people will benefit from the completed project. I hope it will continue. In your wife's honor, perhaps?"

Everett cleared his throat. "As I mentioned, I don't typically get involved in Kate's work, so I can't say what will happen now. I suppose that will be at the discretion of the board of trustees." His attention flickered to the clock again, then back to Finn. "I hate to rush you, but I have somewhere I need to be." He rose and pulled a set of car keys from his pocket as if in evidence.

"Of course." Finn pressed onto his feet and offered his hand once more in a farewell shake. "Thank you for your time. I'll be in touch if I need anything else."

Mr. Everett hurried ahead of them to the office door, then opened it and walked with them outside. He boarded the little blue car while she and Finn loaded into the truck.

She glanced in the rearview mirror as they motored down the lane, their pickup leading the way. Her eyes fixed on the strange man behind them. "That was weird, right?"

"Yup."

"Do you think he's hiding something?"

Everett's thinning brown hair lifted on the breeze, eyes hidden behind those darn sunglasses once more.

"Probably," Finn said.

"Do you think he killed her?"

"Statistically, the odds aren't in his favor," Finn

said. "Realistically, I don't know. Could be he's just glad to inherit the kingdom. Everybody's hiding something, but most of the things we get squirrelly about as individuals are irrelevant outside our heads."

She relaxed against the sun-warmed seat back, certainly able to relate. "Should we visit the country club next?" she asked. "Or maybe drive past a few parks and look for the boys?"

Finn slowed at the end of the driveway, checking both directions and signaling his turn for the man behind them. "We can do all of that if you're up to it. The day's still young."

The sound of squealing tires on pavement turned Hayley's eyes away from Finn. Her heart lurched into a sprint as the black SUV from Old Downtown raced along the street in their direction.

"Get down," Finn yelled, one arm swinging out to force her head toward her knees.

Rapid gunfire ripped across the truck in the next heartbeat, shattering the windshield and raining a storm of pebbled glass over her back as she screamed.

Chapter Seventeen

A few phone calls later, Finn walked the crime scene with Dean, a pair of officers and a detective from his team. His pickup would be towed to a local shop for repair after the bullet casings were located. Dean and Austin had come to the rescue with a company-owned SUV. Dean would ride back with Austin. Hayley and Finn would keep the vehicle owned by the PI firm as long as they needed.

Meanwhile, Hayley sat in Austin's pickup, watching safely from a short distance. Austin, for his part, played the role of shocked citizen, gaping at the chaos, only there to comfort a shaken friend. He would see everything from his vantage point that Finn and those walking the crime scene would miss.

"What do you think?" Dean asked, folding his arms and turning his attention to Finn. "Everett followed you down the drive because he had some place to be. Was the shooting about you and Hayley or him?"

Finn rubbed his stubbled chin and scanned the broader area. His gaze slid over the squat navy blue convertible still parked behind his truck. The car's owner rocked from foot to foot several feet away, speaking with officers again. He'd made multiple phone calls, likely to his lawyers, and retreated into his home twice, but he kept boomeranging back. "Any idea where he was headed?"

"He had a reservation at the country club's restaurant," Dean said.

"Standing day and time?" Finn asked.

If Mr. Everett was a creature of habit, and someone wanted him dead, knowing when and where to expect him would make the work easy. It was the main reason Finn continuously warned women in self-defense classes not to create obvious routines in their daily lives. They never knew who was watching, or what motive they might have. For a determined killer, catching Everett leaving his driveway on a low-traffic residential road was far better than at the busy club.

Still, Everett had been in the hot tub when they'd arrived.

"Nope." Dean arched an eyebrow. "This reservation was set today."

"Who called it in?"

Dean shrugged. "My contact at the club didn't say. Only that the reservation wasn't on the books when she got there this morning."

Finn grunted. It was possible whoever wanted

Everett dead had a contact at the club who'd tipped them off about his new reservation. Or maybe they'd simply been waiting outside the home for him to leave. Thankfully, Austin was keeping watch now. He would know if anyone on the street seemed suspicious and contact Finn as soon as he spotted them.

A rookie officer Finn recognized as Traci Landers moved in his direction, and the brothers parted slightly to make room for her in the small huddle.

"Learn anything good?" Finn asked, flicking his gaze in Mr. Everett's direction.

Officer Landers followed his attention, then turned back with a nod. "He thinks whoever killed his wife is targeting him now, and he's requested a patrol for his safety."

"I like that," Finn said. "Let's get him a babysitter. I want him safe if he's in danger, and if this is all some sort of ruse, I want to know that too. Get someone good to watch him. Someone who'll pick up on anything that doesn't seem right."

"Will do," Landers said. "We've collected several casings from the shots fired. I'm taking those to the lab. If the same weapon has been used in any other crimes on record, we'll know soon."

More importantly, they'd know whether or not these bullets matched the one the coroner pulled from Kate.

Officer Landers's brow furrowed as she looked

more closely at Finn. "You sure you don't want the medic to take a look at you?"

He forced his eyes to meet hers, determined not to look at the new cuts on his arms and cheek. Pebbles of broken windshield had nicked his skin, drawing fresh blood and staining his truck seat. "Nothing a little alcohol and peroxide won't heal." The windshield would be easy to replace. Bloodstained leather was another story. One he didn't want to think about. At least the cuts would take care of themselves.

Thankfully, Hayley had been physically unscathed. Emotionally, she'd been stunned silent, possibly in shock, though she'd also refused the medic.

Officer Landers tipped a finger to her hat and stepped away.

"How's Hayley holding up?" Dean asked, gaze drifting to Austin's truck. "I imagine social work isn't usually so brutal."

Finn gripped the back of his neck, hating that she'd been through any of the dangerous and heartbreaking things she'd experienced lately. "She's tougher than she looks." And he'd only recently learned the whole truth of that statement. Hayley had faced obstacles and had the odds stacked against her all her life. Yet here she was, a heart larger and warmer than the sun, proving that children weren't doomed to repeat the flawed lives of their parents and that sometimes those who'd had it the hardest learned to love the biggest.

Finn began to move in her direction before he'd made the conscious decision to do so. Hayley needed a safe place to recuperate, rest and heal. He wanted to be that for her. "I'm heading out," he told Dean. "Keep me posted."

"Where are you going?"

"I'm taking Hayley home."

No words had ever felt sweeter.

HAYLEY STOOD IN Finn's small bathroom, thankful for an incredible distraction from the sheer chaos of the last several days. Outside those walls, nothing seemed to be going her way. Inside, however, she couldn't complain.

Finn leaned against the counter, patiently allowing her to clean and rebandage a few of his deeper wounds. Some of the injuries he'd received during the explosion were out of his reach and in need of care following his shower. Hayley didn't need to be asked twice.

She swabbed each cut and puncture with an alcohol pad, then dabbed a fresh layer of ointment onto the angry, reddened skin before applying a new patch of gauze and medical tape. She tried not to steal unnecessary glances at his handsome face and bare chest in the still steamy bathroom mirror. And she refused the barrage of clear memories, reminding her of all the ways she'd touched and been touched by Finn Beaumont.

He winced slightly as she covered the worst of his cuts, and she paused before continuing her work. The kisses they'd recently shared, and the sweet words they'd exchanged, had meant a lot. But when the strongest man she knew humbled himself to ask for her help with something so personal, she knew she'd regained his trust. Trust was everything. And his willingness to be vulnerable spoke volumes.

Finn's strength and perseverance benefited everyone, but those same traits came at a price for him. Especially when accepting help with the little things. She'd seen him help his family build a pole barn in a week, but refused to get help tying his shoes after fracturing his wrist taking down a drunk-and-disorderly.

Her heart fluttered as their eyes met in the mirror's reflection. She set aside the tape. "Finished."

He swept his shirt off the countertop and threaded it over his head. "I appreciate it."

"Anytime. I appreciate all the things you do for me too."

Finn turned to face her, a smile playing on his lips. "I suppose I have to make you dinner?"

Hayley scoffed, eagerly playing along. "Of course, you do. Don't make me call your mama."

"Don't even joke about that." His strong arms

snaked out, gripping her waist and moving her close on a laugh.

She arched as goose bumps scattered over her skin. The thrill of possibility burst in her chest. Finn's guard was down. He'd left the serious parts of himself somewhere else in favor of this precious, carefree moment with her.

She melted against him, hanging on with delight.

He buried his face against her neck, holding her as if she was his life preserver and not the other way around. "I am so sorry you were in that truck with me today," he whispered. "Or at that warehouse. All I ever want to do is protect you, and I'm failing miserably."

"You're not."

Heat from his nearness, his tone, the scent of him was all around her, igniting fire in her veins. She moaned as his lips drew a path along the rim of her ear. "Finn?" she asked, sliding her hands beneath the hem of his shirt.

He pulled back, blinking unfocused eyes, visibly struggling for control. "Too much?" he rasped.

"More."

Strong fingers burrowed into her hair, cradling her head. Then his mouth took hers in a deep, tantalizing kiss.

She traced the ridges of his abs and planes of his broad chest with greedy fingers, pushing the fabric of his shirt upward, exposing miles of tanned skin.

Finn broke the kiss, eyes wild and searching. His lips tipped into a wolfish grin at whatever he saw in her expression. Then he reached over his head and freed the shirt he'd just put on.

Emboldened, she did the same. Her shirt landed in a discarded puddle beside his, earning a low, toe-curling growl from Finn.

She tipped her chin in challenge and ran a fingertip down his torso to the waistband of his pants.

Another cuss crossed his lips, followed by a cautious plea. "Are you sure?"

She rose onto her toes, pressing her body against his warm skin. "Take me to bed, Detective."

Finn didn't need to be asked twice.

He gripped her hips in his hands and hauled her off the ground in one burst of movement.

A delighted squeal erupted from her chest as he swept her off her feet, and strode easily to his room.

She pulled him down with her, onto his sheets, and enjoyed the view.

He held himself above her, palms planted beside each of her shoulders, elbows locked. An expression of awe and admiration graced his handsome face. "I've missed you," he said softly. "So damn much."

"I've missed you too." She rose to meet him, kissing him slowly and drawing him down to her. She savored each mind-bending sweep of his tongue and expert stroke of his hand, feeling more beautiful and cherished than she had in far too long. Since the last time she'd been with him.

When there was nothing more between them, and their bodies rocked together to a perfect end, there was no denying her love for Finn Beaumont. As strong and resilient as the man himself.

She could only hope he might feel the same way again one day.

FINN SLIPPED AWAY from Hayley when her breaths grew long and even, her body taken by sleep. They'd talked for hours, clinging to one another and making up for a year of lost time. But when Hayley had drifted off, Finn's mind had begun to race.

Moonlight streamed through the window onto her beautifully peaceful face, and he kissed her cheek before he rose. His heart broke anew at the thought of losing her again. He probably should've taken things more slowly, not been so greedy. Shouldn't have risked scaring her away. But her sweet kisses and tender urging had reduced his logic to rubble. And he'd taken her at her word. She wanted him. He needed her. Shamelessly, he regretted nothing.

He only hoped she'd feel the same in the morning.

Finn tugged on his T-shirt and sweatpants, then

padded into the living room, grabbing a bottle of water and his laptop from the kitchen on his way. He had files and transcripts to review. Lab reports and evidence photos to request. Maybe he'd even find a lead they could follow in the morning. Something that would bring them closer to locating Gage and Parker, or Kate's killer.

He took a seat on the couch and booted up his laptop, then waited for his usual browser windows to load. He logged in to his work email, forcing images of a climaxing Hayley from his mind.

He had a lot of work to do if he wanted to gain her love and trust again.

He'd have to be careful not to scare her away. He'd take his time and watch her for signs she was ready, because he couldn't lose her again.

The computer on his lap brought him back to the moment, to the awful reminder that he and Hayley had shared one too many near-death experiences this week. Until he found the culprit, it was only a matter of time before there was another drive-by shooting or explosion. And he needed to locate Gage and Parker before the killer found them instead.

Finn's inbox was full, as always, so he started at the top.

Several hours later, he'd worked through every message, reviewed every shared document, interview transcript and piece of evidence from crimes related to Kate's death. He'd replayed news footage and listened to audio files from interrogations until his heavy, scratchy eyes drifted shut.

He woke to the sound of his ringing phone and peeled his eyes open to blazing sunlight through the front window. His laptop rested on the floor beside the couch, where he'd accidentally fallen asleep.

Finn swiveled upright, planting his feet on the floor and searching the space around him for his phone. "Beaumont," he answered, catching the call before it went to voice mail.

"Are you sleeping?" Dean asked, his voice a tone of mock horror. "It's after seven."

Finn rubbed a hand over his tired eyes and mussed hair. "I had a late night."

"Oh, yeah?" His brother's tone implied the reason had been Hayley.

Finn supposed his brother was right on a number of counts.

A fresh bolt of panic lanced his gut. "Oh, no." He'd left her in bed so he could slip away and work. If she'd woken without him during the night, she was sure to think— "Hey, can I call you back," Finn asked abruptly, already moving toward the hallway. "Unless you've got news. Then let me have it, and I'll call you back after that."

"No," Dean said. "I was just calling to say Mama's on her way to your place with breakfast, and I'm hungry, so I'm coming too. I figured we can talk shop over cheesy grits and hash browns."

Finn spun back to face the front window. "How long ago did she leave?"

"I'm not sure. She was gone when I got there," Dean said. "Dad pointed me in your direction. Honestly, if I knew I'd have to drive all over town for my breakfast, I could've picked something up on my way to work."

"It's not too late for that," Finn said.

"I don't know," Dean said. "I'm committed to those grits."

"See you when you get here." Finn disconnected outside his partially closed bedroom door. "Hayley?" He rapped his knuckles gently on the frame. "Are you up?"

"Yeah."

Finn stepped cautiously into the room.

She sat on the edge of the bed, dressed in cut-off jean shorts and a faded blue T-shirt. She'd pulled her thick hair away from her face in a ponytail. Her expression was guarded and wary.

"Mom and Dean are on their ways over for breakfast." He smiled. "You sleep well?"

Hayley nodded and stood, her phone clutched in one hand.

"News?" he asked, looking pointedly at the little device, and hoping she planned to speak soon. He couldn't have ruined things for them already. Could he?

"Nothing yet," she said. "I was hoping, but—"

"Hey." Finn extended an arm as she approached, then wrapped it around her when she tried to pass him. "Can I make you some coffee while we wait for Mama?"

"That sounds nice. Thank you."

Finn sighed and let his head fall forward, tightening his grip a bit when she tried to get away. He raised his eyes to hers and waited for Hayley to meet his gaze. "I snuck away to work last night. I was trying to find a thread to pull on this case. I didn't mean to fall asleep out there. I was supposed to get back here after I finished reviewing files."

Her cheeks darkened, and she averted her gaze. "It's okay. I get it."

Finn raised his hands to cup her cheeks. "I mean it. I wanted to be right here with you."

She looked into his eyes, scanning, seeking.

The doorbell rang.

He held his ground for another long beat then pressed a tender kiss to her forehead before relenting. "Come on." He slid his hand over hers. "We'd better let Mama in before she jimmies the lock."

Hayley laughed softly, and a measure of weight rolled off his shoulders. "She wouldn't."

"Probably not," he admitted. "But she's fully capable, and I don't want to test her."

He led Hayley down the hall, and she broke away at the kitchen. He turned toward the front door. "Morning, Mama," he said, inviting her in a moment later with a hug.

"Morning, sweet boy." She patted his cheek and passed him a set of thermal casserole bags. "Breakfast is in there. Where's Hayley?"

"I'm here," Hayley called. "Making coffee. Would you like a cup?"

"Oh, yes, please!"

His brother's truck appeared at the end of Finn's driveway, so he left the door open and headed for the kitchen. "Dean just pulled up."

Finn unpacked his mom's casseroles while she pulled dishes from the cupboards and silverware from the drawer.

"Knock, knock," Dean said, stepping inside and closing the door behind him. "Something smells great." He greeted his mother and Hayley with hugs, then offered raised eyebrows to Finn. "You look beat."

"Sit," their mom ordered. "Let's talk over breakfast."

The meal became a business meeting, as expected, and Finn kept one hand on Hayley as often as possible.

She blushed and hid behind her mug when his mother looked in their direction a little too long, but she didn't make any effort to push him away. A good sign, he hoped.

"And now we're waiting for something else to come up," Dean said, concluding a lengthy list of places he and Austin had looked for Gage and Parker during the night.

"Do you have any other ideas?" his mother asked Hayley.

"No, ma'am. I wish I did."

Finn gathered her empty plate and cup, then pressed a kiss to her temple as he stood. "Can I get you anything else?"

His mother's eyes bulged and a smile wider than the Atlantic spread over her pink cheeks.

Dean shook his head.

"Well, I'm not worried," Finn said, setting their plates into the sink. The words were true enough, even if he wasn't sure what to do next. "Things always seem the worst right before a big break."

They still needed to visit the country club. See if anyone thought Mr. Everett and Mr. Forester were closer than they claimed. Or if there was anything else another member might want to share.

"True," Dean agreed, taking another swig from his mug. "It's some kind of phenomenon. Just when things start to look impossible in a case, they take off full-speed."

Hayley didn't look swayed. "What about all the cold cases out there?"

Dean frowned.

Finn tried not to smile. She had a point, but this case wasn't destined to go unfinished. Not if he could help it.

"Okay." She released an audible sigh. "Did anyone find out if Kate had a prenup? Her husband seemed squirrelly, and he had a lot to gain from her death."

"My team has confirmed the prenup," Finn said. "But not the specifics. According to a memo I read last night, they've put in a request with the Everett family lawyer and a local judge, hoping one of the two will comply. They've requested financial records as well."

Finn's phone vibrated, and he shifted to pull the device from his pocket. The name on the screen sent his attention to Hayley. "It's Eric."

She straightened. "The middle school's groundskeeper?"

"Yeah."

The room fell silent as he accepted the call using the speaker option. "Beaumont."

"Hey, kid, this might be a long shot," the older man said, bypassing a traditional greeting. "But Gage Myers has been on my mind since the moment you told me what's going on with him. And I recalled his father being an incredible artist."

That tracked, given the talent Gage had shown in his street art. "Go on," Finn said.

"Like I said, this might be nothing, but I remember the two of them spending a lot of time at a little art studio on the bay. His father used to lead classes there for students at the middle school. I'm not sure the place is used much anymore. He was the main volunteer, and the program was funded by an arts project that he organized."

Hayley covered her mouth, eyes springing wide. And just like that, they had a new lead.

Chapter Eighteen

The art studio Eric had mentioned was a small rectangular building overlooking the bay. The clapboard structure was schoolhouse-red and perched upon tall wooden pillars that had been darkened and worn from weather and age. An abundance of windows faced the water, and a broad wooden deck stretched into the gravel parking lot out back.

A dense thicket of leafy trees cast heavy shade over the structure, effectively hiding it from the road. Hayley walked toward the deck stairs slowly, immediately thankful for a break from the sweltering sun. Multicolored handprints adorned the glass beside floating images of paint palettes, brushes and smocks. Wooden easels had been permanently anchored to the railing, securing them from storms and assuring they'd be there for any artist in need. Sunny yellow letters stenciled on a blue door encouraged guests to enter.

She climbed the steps and tried the knob, but

it didn't turn. "Locked," she said, searching over her shoulder for Finn, who'd disappeared.

She moved to the window, scanning for signs of movement, then cupped her hands around her eyes to peer inside. A shadow outside a window on the opposite side of the quiet building peered back.

Finn's familiar face became clear, as clouds passed over the sun. He pointed to something in the space between them.

Hayley adjusted her hands and gaze to find a long table covered in a blanket, the tip of a pillow poking out on the floor beneath. She straightened and hurried to the door, then knocked. "Gage? Parker? It's me, Hayley. Are you in there?"

Her heart jolted and hammered at the possibility she'd finally found the boys. They were safe, and they'd been well hidden in the old art studio. Protected from the sun and weather. They might've had access to running water and they'd had at least one blanket and pillow. It was more than she'd dared to hope. Images of the kids huddled together in a filthy, crumbling structure in Old Downtown had haunted her dreams. "Gage? Are you okay? I've been so worried. Please answer."

The wooden stairs behind her creaked, and she spun on a sharp intake of breath.

Finn stilled, palms up. "It's just me."

She pressed a hand to her chest and rushed back to the window for another look. "The boys made that blanket fort. Right?"

"I'm hoping," Finn said.

She tried opening the window, but it was secure. "How did they get in?"

"I don't know. The windows on the other side are all locked too." Finn gave the old blue door a thorough inspection, then dragged his fingers along the wooden trim overhead.

"Maybe Gage knew where to find a key," she suggested, recognizing Finn's attempt to do the same.

"Maybe, but I don't," Finn said, extracting a credit card from his wallet. "So it looks like I have to break in."

She returned to him with a smile. "I hoped you'd say that."

He slid the plastic rectangle between the door and frame, then wiggled the knob while he worked the card. A moment later, the door opened.

"You're actual magic," Hayley said, slipping inside while he put away the credit card.

"More like a reformed troublemaker, but I like your take a little better."

She flipped the light switch beside the door. Nothing happened. "I guess no one paid the bill lately."

"Judging by the layer of dust on the windows

and countertops, I'd say it's been a while since the place was used as more than a hideout," Finn said.

The wide wooden floorboards were splattered with a rainbow of spilled paints. The walls were covered in murals of the sand and sea. Forgotten art projects hung from the hand drawn waves and surf. A countertop with a sink overlooked the rear deck. The rest of the building was an uninterrupted space, save for a room with an open door on their right.

Finn tapped his phone to life, and a moment later a beam of light illuminated the area. He headed toward the door.

Hayley wiped sweat from her forehead as she crouched to peek under the table covered by a blanket. Candy and snack wrappers littered the area inside the tiny fort. A second blanket covered the floor and empty water bottles had been flattened in the corner. A small notebook kept a tally of food and drinks, along with prices. On pages further back, a hangman game was in progress. Two words, four letters for the first, five for the second. The phrase *don't worry*, minus the two *o's*, had been revealed.

Her heart ached as she clutched the notebook to her chest and stood. "They were here," she said. "This is Gage's handwriting."

Finn returned to her, extinguishing the light.

"There's a supply closet and restroom back there. The shelves are mostly bare. What's that?"

Hayley passed the book to him.

He examined the pages before returning the item to her. Then he squatted for a look at the space beneath the table. "Was he budgeting?"

"Looks like it. Should we wait for them to come back?" she asked, hoping the answer was yes.

Finn stretched to his full height. "I'll ask Dean to keep watch from afar. They might avoid returning if they see anyone nearby. You're probably right about Gage knowing where to find a spare key to this place since his dad spent so much time here. He's smart. I don't know who'd think to look for him at this place."

"Where do you think they got the snacks and water?" Hayley said.

Finn anchored his hands on his hips and shook his head. "I don't know."

"We should visit the closest convenience stores. See if anyone remembers them."

"That sounds like a plan," Finn said. He opened his arm in the direction of the door they'd used to enter. "After you."

Hayley bent to return the notebook, but as she placed it under the table, a new idea came to mind. "Can I leave a note for the boys?"

Finn smiled. "Absolutely. Make sure they have

all our contact information. My folks' and brothers' numbers too."

She retrieved a pencil from atop the blanket, then began to write. She didn't stop until she was satisfied Gage understood the danger he was in and all the people who were on his side.

She sent up prayers for the boys' protection as she left the little studio, then climbed back into the borrowed SUV.

Finn navigated the scenic byway, the sound on one side, miles of marsh and natural sand dunes on the other. His attention bounced routinely from road to rearview mirror, likely watching for a tail.

Hayley kept her eyes glued to the coastline in search of a small shop or café. People were creatures of habit. If she and Finn found the place where the boys had gotten their snacks and water, they'd probably know where to expect them to shop again.

Less than a mile later, a small orange building appeared. The building's paint was faded and blistered by unhindered sunlight. An attached dock extending into the water was lined in stacks of brightly colored kayaks and paddleboards. The sign at the roadside declared the business to be Eco Exploration, Marshal's Bluff's premier nature-excursion-and-tour company.

"We have a tour company?" Hayley asked.

The SUV slowed.

"Three, believe it or not," Finn said, engaging the turn signal. "The others target fishermen and head out to sea. This place does dolphin-sighting boat tours and gets folks onto the water for exploring and appreciating the natural beauty here."

"Huh." She unbuckled when he parked, then joined him in the lot. "I forget to soak in the views sometimes. I need to make a point of it when this ends."

Finn slid mischievous eyes her way. "You still kayak?"

"Not as much as I should." She'd hidden behind her work since their breakup. But she was healing now, and all the near-death experiences were heavy reminders that she'd only live once. Her job helped a lot of people, but she needed to make time for herself. Take weekends and evenings to recuperate and soak up the beauty around her. "Any chance they sell snacks and water?" she asked.

"About one hundred percent." Finn stopped at the open shop door and motioned her inside ahead of him.

She crossed the threshold and plucked the fabric of her shirt away from her chest.

Box fans rattled in the open windows, and a pitiful cross breeze from one open door to the other stirred a dusting of sand on the floor.

"No tours today," a young woman at the counter called. Her cheeks were ruddy from the heat, and she fanned her face with a clipboard. "Storm's coming."

Hayley envied the woman's string-bikini top and cutoff shorts, but doubted they were small enough to prevent her inevitable heatstroke if she stayed inside much longer. "We don't need a tour," she said as kindly as possible. "I'm a social worker looking for two missing children. We thought you might've seen them."

The woman's expression turned from bored to alarmed. "Do you have a picture?"

"Of the older boy," Hayley said. She flipped through the images on her phone in search of a recent shot of Gage.

"Have you seen a lot of children this week?" Finn asked, pulling the woman's attention to him.

Her lips parted, and she blinked.

Hayley fought a smile. The Beaumont men had that effect on women. The best part was that none of them seemed to know.

"Yes," she answered belatedly. "It's our busy season. Tourists," she added.

"The boys we're looking for are eight and fourteen," Hayley said. "They're in danger, and it's imperative that we find them before they're harmed." She found a selfie of Gage with a surfboard and turned the phone to face the woman. "They might've bought some drinks and snacks."

Hayley had taken Gage to the beach once, because he said that was where he felt most at peace, and it was his first summer without his parents to take him.

The woman's eyebrows rose and she levered herself off her stool. "I've seen them," she said excitedly. "They didn't buy anything, but they were in here yesterday hanging around when a tour was about to leave. I asked where their mom was, and the older one said she was already on the boat. So I told them to hurry up or they'd miss it, and they left."

A spike of hope and joy shot through Hayley. Gage and Parker had been in the same store where she was standing, only a day before. And they'd been okay. She turned to look for Finn.

He tipped his head in the direction of a wire display stand near the open door to the dock. The same snacks she'd seen in the blanket fort were represented. A small refrigeration unit hummed beside the rack. Bottles of water were visible beyond the glass door.

This was where the boys had gotten their food-stuffs.

She smiled as she realized the list of snacks and prices Gage had made wasn't a result of him managing a budget. He'd tracked the things he'd taken to survive. As if he might've planned to pay later.

"Thank you," Hayley said, turning back to the

woman. "If you see them again, will you call me?" She extracted a business card from her bag and passed it to the woman. "Actually. Will you give them a note?"

The woman nodded, expression soft. "Of course."

Hayley wrote a similar letter to the one she'd left at the studio, then passed it to the clerk. "I appreciate this so much. And I'd like a bottle of water." She handed the woman enough money to cover the drink and the boys' snacks. "Keep the change."

She smiled brightly at Hayley. "I'm glad to help."

Outside, the breeze had picked up, and Hayley inhaled deeply, glad to be free of the stuffy building. Beads of sweat formed on her upper lip and brow as they moved toward their ride. The boys would need water soon. "We should wait here and see if they come back."

"I still want to visit the country club," Finn said, unlocking the SUV so they could climb inside. He started the engine and pumped up the air-conditioning, apparently not as impervious to the heat as he seemed.

Hayley wet her lips, anxiety rising in her chest at the thought of leaving this place. "We know the boys have been here and the art studio. I think we should split up and keep watch over both."

Finn frowned. "We're not splitting up. You've

been in just as much danger as they have. More, as far as I know. So you're staying with me. Dean will stake out the studio."

"Finn—" Her protest was cut short by the ringing of his phone.

He raised a finger, letting her know he needed to take the call. Then he raised the device to his ear. "Beaumont."

Hayley scanned the nearby road, trees and parking lot while she waited, willing the boys to appear. She was so close to finding them. Practically walking in their footsteps. Separated only by a day.

"When?" Finn asked, pulling her eyes back to him. He shifted the SUV into gear and pressed the phone between his ear and shoulder as he drew the safety belt across his torso. "I'm on my way." He disconnected the call and dropped the phone into the cupholder. A heartbeat later, the SUV tore away from the shack with a spray of dust and gravel.

Hayley grabbed her seat belt, snapping it into place as the tires hit asphalt and they rocketed forward. "What happened?"

"Police Chief Harmen called a press conference. The team got a hit on the SUV from the drive-by. A doorbell camera belonging to one of Everett's neighbors recorded the shooting, and Tech Services pulled a partial license-plate number. It's the same SUV that was seen near the explosion and caught on the news near Kate's death site. The vehicle is registered to Lance Stevens. He's being picked up and hauled in for questioning."

Chapter Nineteen

Finn ignored the speed limit on the way back to town. The scenic byway they traveled was meant to be taken slowly and enjoyed, but there wasn't anything he'd enjoy more today than meeting Lance Stevens. The name of the man being brought in for questioning, possibly the one responsible for repeatedly putting Hayley in danger, circled in his mind. Had the man worked alone? Or was this crime spree his own? And if so, why?

Finn would've requested to perform the interview himself if he thought he was the better choice for the job. Unfortunately, he wasn't convinced he'd stop himself from flattening the suspect given an opportunity. And he couldn't afford to damage any chance they had at building a case that would put Mr. Stevens away for a very long time.

News of today's press conference was nearly as intriguing as news of a suspect. Finn could only assume one was directly related to the other. Police Chief Harmen wasn't one to waste time unnecessarily, or interact with the media when he could avoid it. Given the widespread interest in Katherine Everett's death, he expected everyone in town would be tuned in, and anyone with a camera and microphone would be outside the precinct, hoping for a front-row seat.

Unfortunately for Finn, he and Hayley had been as far from the police station as possible without leaving Marshal's Bluff, and the return trip was infuriatingly long.

Traffic thickened as he reached the blocks nearest the station, slowing their progress further. News trucks clogged the streets and reporters hurried on foot toward the squat brick building in question. A row of cruisers stood guard inside the gate, looking authoritative and giving the impression of protection. The display of a formidable team. From the number of squad cars alone, he knew there were enough hands on deck to keep the conference orderly and peaceful.

"This is a lot of people," Hayley said, giving voice to his thought. "It's nice that so many folks care about what he wants to say, but I've never been a fan of crowds."

Finn completely understood. People were fine. People were smart. Crowds were often chaotic, thoughtless and emotional. A dangerous combination.

The station doors opened as Finn crept along behind a caravan of gawkers and rubberneckers.

The chief of police strode onto the concrete steps and into view.

Hayley tuned the SUV's radio to the call numbers of a station represented by a nearby news van.

A female announcer's voice broke through the speakers. "...here for you live from the Marshal's Bluff police station, where Chief Harmen has called a press conference on the case of Katherine Everett."

Finn grimaced. He could only imagine what the details on his case would sound like through the filtered lens of local media. After everything he and Hayley had been through this week, he wanted the information firsthand. "Hang on," he said, turning his eyes back to the road. He pressed the gas pedal and turned the wheel, causing cars to honk and onlookers to complain.

"What are you doing?" Hayley asked, pressing a palm against the dashboard to steady herself as he angled the vehicle onto the curb outside the station's open gate.

"Getting us a parking space." He unlocked the doors and climbed out, then waited for Hayley to join him. Dark clouds raced overhead as he took her hand and towed her past a set of uniformed officers.

Finn wasn't usually a superstitious man, but the sudden shadow cast upon this moment felt like a bad omen. He pulled Hayley closer in response. He flashed his detective's shield as he pushed his way to the front of the crowd, where an array of microphones on stands had been arranged.

Chief Harmen's eyes caught Finn's, and he gave a small shake of his head.

Finn straightened. Something had gone wrong.

"Hello," the chief said, effectively quieting the crowd. "I'm Police Chief Harmen, and this press conference has been called to update you on the investigation into Katherine Everett's murder. A male suspect has been identified in connection to that crime and several other crimes we believe to be related. We do not yet know if the suspect worked alone or in conjunction with others. Additionally, we are not releasing the name of the suspect at this time. However, you can be assured that despite his attorney's best attempts, we will not be swayed from finishing the work we've started. Katherine Everett, her family, friends and the community, will see justice served."

Frustration tightened Finn's muscles. He wouldn't be able to listen in on the interview of Lance Stevens today. Not because traffic had made him late, but because the criminal's attorney had likely already escorted him home. Either Stevens had money, or someone who did had interceded on his behalf. Kate's husband and Conrad Forester came instantly to mind.

"The investigation remains fluid and active at this time," Chief Harmen continued. "Anyone with information about the death of Katherine Everett, the warehouse explosion in Old Downtown or the recent shooting outside the Everett family estate should contact Marshal's Bluff PD. Thank you. Now, I'll take a few questions."

The crowd erupted in shouts, every member of the media vying to be heard and chosen.

Finn pressed the pads of his fingers to his closed eyelids.

"Hey." Hayley tugged his hands away from his face, meeting his tired eyes with her sincere gaze. "It's just a setback. Things always start moving fast when they seem to be at a standstill, right?"

His lips twitched, fighting a small smile as she returned the words of their earlier conversation to him. "I believe I've heard that somewhere."

Hayley held on to his hands as he let them drop. "I can't believe Stevens's attorney got here before we did," she said. "Summoning a public defender when I need one for a case can take forever."

He gave her fingers a gentle squeeze. "Money can't buy peace or happiness, but it can keep a lawyer on retainer."

Hayley frowned. "Who do you suppose paid for this one?"

"An excellent question." If the lawyer wasn't Stevens's, then whoever sent him over here likely had good reason. And that information would be priceless.

"Please!" Chief Harmen hollered into the mics, pumping his palms up and down in a failed attempt to regain control. "I'd appreciate your patience while I try to hear from a few more members of the media."

The rev of a motorcycle drew Finn's attention to the slow-moving traffic outside the gate. A driver in black leather with a matching helmet and mirrored visor slowed his ride to a crawl and set his feet on the ground to steady himself.

"Chief Harmen," a female voice called loudly, "can you comment on rumors that a fourteen-year-old boy is suspected in the shooting and bludgeoning death of Katherine Everett? Or that he is now considered a fugitive on the run?"

Hayley gasped, and Finn spun to face the crowd, attempting to identify the woman who'd spoken.

He needed to find that reporter and ask where she'd gotten that information. Someone had clearly fed her the lies to generate another narrative, or worse, to put the entire community on the lookout for Gage.

Sudden rapid gunfire blasted through the air, and Hayley dropped to the ground, pulling Finn down with her.

Screams and chaos erupted as he checked her for injuries.

"I'm okay," she said. "But they aren't."

He followed her trembling finger to several fallen crowd members. Honking horns and the sounds of multiple fender benders formed the backdrop to barking tires and the growl of a motorcycle engine.

The driver angled away, guiding his ride between stopped cars, seeking a path for escape.

"Stay here," Finn demanded, pushing Hayley toward the police station's steps. "Go inside. Tell them who you are and that I went after the shooter. He's on a black motorcycle stuck in traffic. Don't leave!" He freed his weapon and made a run for the waiting SUV.

The motorcycle jumped onto the sidewalk and rounded the corner, now out of sight.

Finn dove into his vehicle and gunned the engine to life. He squeezed the SUV between parked cars and a nearby shop, knocking off his passenger mirror in the process. On the next block, he had the motorcycle in his sights, and he lifted his cell phone to call for backup.

HAYLEY STARED AFTER FINN, stunned motionless as he climbed into the SUV and raced away.

Around her, people panicked, screaming and running around mindlessly. Some toward the building. Some into the street. Others rushed to help the injured, who were lying in puddles of blood on the ground.

Several uniformed officers climbed into waiting cruisers, eager to give chase, just as Finn had. Except the cruisers were blocked by traffic and throngs of frightened citizens.

In the distance, ambulance sirens wailed to life.

Hayley shoved herself upright, struggling to process the horror. An armed gunman was on the loose, and Finn had gone after him. The realization of what might happen next gripped her chest and squeezed. Her breaths were short, and her head lightened uncomfortably. What if the next person to take a bullet was Finn? Who would help him?

A set of strong hands curled over her biceps and turned her in a new direction. "Let's get you out of here."

Hayley pulled back, intuition flaring. "No. I'm okay, thank y—" Words froze on her tongue as she took in the man at her side.

Conrad Forester, the CEO of Lighthouse, Inc., glared back, and his grip on her tightened. He appeared presentable and calm in a sharp gray suit and red tie, as if he'd only been present for the press conference like everyone else. "Let me rephrase. Come with me now, and do not cause any trouble, or those boys will die."

FINN KEPT THE motorcycle in view as he radioed for backup. Dispatch assigned two cars, but neither were close, and the cruisers from the precinct were several minutes behind. The motorcycle zigzagged through traffic, keeping a steady pace and changing directions frequently, trying and failing to shake Finn.

The vehicle darted into the shadows of an overpass, and Finn plunged in behind.

He blinked, adjusting his eyes to the darkness a moment before readjusting them to the sun on the other side. "He's getting on the highway near Mill Street," Finn called, projecting his voice toward the phone in the cupholder, Dispatch on the other end of the line.

A dozen similar motorcycles appeared in the space of his next heartbeat, all joining the first and forming a pack. Instinct raised the hairs on his arms, and suddenly he wasn't so sure he'd been a top-tier tail and not a detective engaged in a trap.

He pressed the gas pedal to the floor, determined to keep his eye on the motorcycle carrying the shooter, but the bikes began to weave in and out of lanes. An 85-mile-per-hour game of cups.

Then the central interchange appeared. A mass of twinning highways with multiple on-and-off-ramps made it impossible to know which lane to stay in. Increasing traffic made it harder to maneuver quickly. But the pack of motorcycles split up, scattering in every direction, and Finn realized the whole truth. It didn't matter which lane he was in, because he couldn't follow them all.

He'd been tricked.

Chapter Twenty

Mr. Forester led Hayley through the chaos of a terrorized crowd to a waiting sedan. Her limbs felt numb, and all hope of rescue vanished as his threat settled into her heart and mind. He had Gage and Parker. And he'd hurt them if she drew attention to herself or tried to run away.

"Get in," he whispered. The words landed harshly against her hair. The heat and scent of his sour breath knotted her stomach, and she rolled her shoulders forward, wishing she could curl into a ball or hide.

She dropped onto the passenger seat as instructed, then flinched at the slamming of the door beside her. Outside the tinted glass, uniformed officers rushed to calm the crowd. They looked everywhere except in her direction, too distracted by the recent shots fired and a line of incoming ambulances.

Traffic moved, making room for the emergency vehicles to pass.

Forester shifted into Drive and took advantage of the cleared road, making a casual getaway.

She wiped silent tears from her cheeks as they left her only means of rescue behind. "Where are you taking me?" she asked.

Quaint shops and clueless pedestrians passed on historic sidewalks beyond her window.

"Somewhere you can't ruin my life." He stole a look in her direction, head shaking in disgust. "All because some punk kid saw something he shouldn't have, and you couldn't let it go."

"Gage is a good kid," Hayley snapped. "He's alone and scared in this world, and he saw you kill a woman. Of course, he ran. What was he supposed to do?"

"He was supposed to mind his own damn business. And so were you!"

Hayley jumped at his sudden yell, the malice in his tone turning her blood to ice. Any chance she'd hoped to have at reasoning with her abductor was gone. He was clearly on a mission to silence her and nothing more.

He didn't even seem guilty or ashamed. Only outraged that he'd been caught committing murder.

"Why'd you do it?" she asked. *If I'm going to die*, she reasoned, *I might as well understand why.* "Why kill Kate? Was it because her plans for a homeless shelter and community center interfered with your plans to build parks and condos? Did you even consider trying to compromise before you bludgeoned and shot her?"

He pulled his attention from the road to stare at her for a long beat, eyes hard, expression feral. "She would've cost me tens of millions with that roach trap. People don't want to raise their kids beside a homeless shelter, or walk their little doodle dogs past park benches with junkies passed out on them. I tried to buy her out. I'm not the bad guy here. She refused to take my offer, and it was well over what she'd paid for her properties. She had something against other people getting rich. As if she was the only one in this town who deserved nice things. She was a greedy, selfish—"

Suddenly the sirens that had been small in the distance grew insistent and loud, interrupting Forester's tirade and pulling his attention to the rearview mirror. "Besides, this isn't all on me. Topper owes me. I couldn't reason with her, so he was supposed to."

Hayley twisted in her seat, craning for a look at the police cruisers racing into view behind them. Cars and trucks slowed and moved out of their way.

She dared a breath of hope.

Forester hit his turn signal and took the next right toward Old Downtown. The cruisers raced past, continuing toward the highway.

Forrester chuckled. "Those aren't for us. No need to worry."

She swallowed a lump of bile, worried again for Finn.

"I'm guessing your detective had a little trouble catching my friend," Forester said. "There's no shame in that. My friend is very good," he clarified. "Not your detective. If he was any good, you wouldn't be here with me, and those adorable boys you're obsessed with wouldn't be living their last day."

Hayley's stomach lurched at his words. She considered punching his face, wondering if the results would be anything other than him knocking her out in retaliation. "Your friend?" she snapped instead. "You mean the gunman who shot into a crowd? Probably the same one who performed that drive-by at the Everetts' house and blew up the warehouse."

Forrester shrugged. "Ever heard the expression 'you've got to do what you've got to do'?"

She curled her hands into fists on her lap. "People were shot today. Maybe killed. All so you could build some bougie condos? Get away with another murder? What is wrong with you?"

"Nothing I can't fix," he said.

She dragged her gaze over the familiar buildings of the waterfront. Broken and dilapidated. Uninhabited and unsafe. Tagged and spray-painted by lost souls and street artists. Like Gage.

Memories of the explosion that had nearly killed her and Finn crashed through her mind.

The hissing stick of explosives from a nearby de-molition site that sent them into the water. Her body shuddered in response. Their survival had been miraculous, but now she was back on the same block. Alone with a madman.

Signs with the Lighthouse, Inc. logo flapped and fluttered in the growing wind. The relent-less sun was blocked by gray clouds of a brew-ing storm.

"All of this trash and rubble will soon be gone," he said, slowing outside a building surrounded by a chain-link fence. "I'm making sure of it. One building at a time." He parked and climbed out, then pointed his handgun through the open win-dow at Hayley. "Come on. I've got somewhere to be."

She eased onto her feet, scanning the vacant streets, and holding on to his last few words. If he didn't plan to kill her immediately, she'd soon be left alone. And she could be incredibly resource-ful. She wouldn't have survived her childhood otherwise.

The building behind the fence was tall and newer than most in the area. "Are the boys in there?" she asked.

"One way to find out," Forrester said, rounding the hood. He grabbed her by the arm and jerked, causing her to stumble.

Then he towed her onto the sidewalk and through an unlocked gate. No Trespassing signs warned that unauthorized visitors would be prosecuted. Other signage announced the property's scheduled demolition. Goose bumps tightened her skin as she read the date.

Tomorrow morning.

"The good news is you'll only be spending one night here," Forester said, tugging her along more quickly as they approached the entryway. "The whole place will be dust tomorrow, along with everything in it."

Her eyes strained for focus as she stepped inside. The loss of sunlight left her temporarily without sight. The space was silent. No indication they weren't alone. Were the boys really there? Or had she been duped? Believed the lie, and gone willfully to her death?

Forester led her down a hallway as her vision cleared. Then he paused outside a sturdy-looking interior door. He pulled a key from his pocket and freed a padlock from a heavy chain. He swung the barrier open to reveal a dark set of steps to the basement. "In you go."

Before she could protest or make a plan to run, the sound of his cocking gun clicked beside her ear.

"You don't want the kid to see another woman murdered, do you?"

She took a step into the darkness, and Forester gave her a heavy shove. Hayley screamed as she fell forward, clutching the handrail and pressing her body to the wall for stability. Her feet fumbled down several steps to a landing, before she crashed onto her hands and knees with a thud.

The door slammed shut behind her, and the rattle of chains being secured forced a sob from her throat. Suffocating heat covered her like a blanket. Sweat broke instantly above her lip and across her brow. There were a few more steps to navigate before she reached the sublevel and whatever awaited her down there.

Soft shuffling sounds sent her onto her feet, back pressed to the wall. "Who's there?"

A pinhole of light appeared, and the space became faintly visible. The room was lined with empty shelving. Maybe previously used for storage. A small window near an exposed-beam ceiling had been painted black and lined with bars.

"Hayley?" Gage's voice reached to her. The sound was thin and weak.

"Gage!" She rushed in the direction of the sound, down the final steps and around an overturned table near the light. Two filthy figures were huddled on the ground. "Parker." She gathered the boys into her arms and held them tight.

Gage winced and hissed.

She released them with a jolt of fear. "What's wrong?"

"He's hurt," Parker said. "He tried to get us out of here, but he fell."

"Fell?"

Parker pointed to the window high above.

"I think my arm's broken," Gage said. "This is all my fault. I shouldn't have been down here that night. I should've told you what I saw the next day."

Hayley squinted at his arm, cradled to his torso, scraped and bruised. "It's okay," she assured him. "Everyone understands why you ran and why you hid. No one blames you. No one's mad. I'm just so glad you're okay. We're going to get out of here, take you to a hospital and go home with the coolest cast you've ever seen. Okay?"

Gage nodded, but neither he nor Parker looked as if they believed her.

She refreshed her smile. "The good news is that the police are looking for you. They'll be looking for me now too."

"What about me?" Parker asked, his small voice ripping a fresh hole in Hayley's heart.

"They know the two of you are together," she said, stroking a hand over his hair. "We've all been very worried."

"I shouldn't have taken him," Gage said. "I knew he was scared, and I thought I could help. The Michaelsons were bad people. The next family might've been worse."

"No." She set a palm against his cheek. "The Michaelsons are the exception, not the rule. I'm so sorry no one realized sooner. Most foster families are wonderful and kind. Thanks to you guys, no children will ever be placed in that family's care again. I think that makes you heroes."

Parker beamed.

Gage snorted. "What kind of hero gets a woman and a little boy killed? Did you see the signs outside?"

Hayley nodded at Gage. "We can't wait around to be rescued. We're going to have to find a way out by ourselves." She scanned the boys in the little shaft of light.

Had they eaten since being brought here? Had they been given any water? Gage grimaced with each little movement, clearly in terrible pain.

"What were you doing when you fell?" she asked him. "What was your plan for escape?"

"I thought I could break the glass behind those bars and call for help, but I slipped and fell."

"What were you going to break the glass with?"

He lifted his uninjured arm to reveal bruised and bloody knuckles. "It's glass block under the paint. It's not breaking."

Parker burrowed closer to Gage, fitting himself against the older boy's side and winding thin arms around his torso.

"It's okay," Gage whispered. "I'm right here, and I've got you."

Hayley rose and walked the room's perimeter, evaluating the situation and attempting to clear her head. Her eyes returned to the pinhole of light, the result of a small hole in the exterior wall.

"We were staying at the art studio where my dad taught classes," Gage said. "We were going to be okay. I don't know how they found us."

"I was thirsty," Parker said. "It was my fault. I asked to go to the store again."

"It's not your fault, buddy," Gage soothed.

"He's right," Hayley said. "The only person at fault for this is the man who brought us here." She approached the shelves at the far wall, reaching a hand overhead and searching for something she could use as a weapon if needed.

"He caught us before we made it back to the studio," Gage said. "We tried to run, but—" His heartbroken expression said Parker was too small to outrun a grown man, and too big for Gage to carry.

She nodded. "You haven't done anything wrong. Neither of you. Right now, we have to think about how to get out of here. We can sort the rest later."

"The window is the only way," Gage said. "The door's bolted and chained."

"But the wall is weak," she said, pointing to the pinhole of light. "That brick is already crumbling. Any idea where we can find something to make that hole bigger?" she asked. "Maybe big enough for us to climb out?"

Parker's eyes widened. "That would have to be a lot bigger."

Gage pushed onto his feet with a sharp intake of air. He offered his hand to Parker, pulling him up beside him. Then he limped across the space to her side, left arm cradled across his middle. Apparently, he'd hurt his leg or ankle too. "Let's help Hayley get us out of here."

A few minutes later, they'd found an old piece of rebar, a few large nails and the broken handle of a tool Hayley couldn't name. She'd hoped for a forgotten sledgehammer, but she was willing to make do with anything that would save the lives of these boys.

"All right," she said. "Let's see what we can do about that escape."

Together, they attacked the bricks near the light, working steadily for what felt like an eternity in the heat, until the light outside began to dim. Distant sounds of thunder rumbled in the sky.

The boys stopped to rest, both saying they felt dizzy and weak.

Gage curled into a ball and heaved.

Parker cried.

Hayley offered soothing words and sat with them until they fell asleep. Then she got back to work. Tomorrow, the building was coming down. Today was all they had left and it was nearing an end.

Brick by busted brick, she had to get them out of there.

Chapter Twenty-One

Finn paced his small office inside the Marshal's Bluff police station, a cell phone pressed to his ear. Beyond the open door, his team sifted through reports from witnesses at the press-conference shooting. Thankfully there hadn't been any fatalities and only a handful of minor injuries. Unfortunately, no one had noticed Hayley leaving, but she'd been gone when he returned.

He never should've left her alone.

A soft knock sounded and Dean appeared. He waved from the threshold. "Any luck?"

Finn rubbed a heavy palm against his forehead then anchored the hand against the back of his neck. It'd been hours since the most recent shooting, and none of the resulting leads had panned out. The gunman had yet to be identified, and Hayley had become vapor. "I'm on hold with Tech Services," he said. "Someone called the tip line after we aired that piece on the news about Hayley's disappearance. The caller claimed to have been eating at an outdoor café when a dark sedan stopped at the light on the corner in the shopping district. A woman fitting Hayley's description was in the passenger seat. The caller didn't get a look at the driver and couldn't say whether or not the woman appeared upset or injured, but it's the only somewhat solid lead we've got. Tech Services used the time and location to pull a partial plate from the car. They're running the number now." He motioned Dean inside. "What about you? Anything new?"

"Maybe," Dean said, stepping into the office and leaning against the wall beside the door. "I visited the country club where the Everetts and Forester are members."

"Yeah?" Finn asked. He'd been meaning to get to the country club for days but hadn't managed. "What'd you learn?"

"According to the bartender I spoke with, the Everetts were friends with Forester until suddenly they weren't."

Finn stilled. "Keep going."

Dean shrugged. "She didn't know why, only that there's a weekly poker tournament held after hours at the club. It's an invitation-only situation and only the wealthiest are invited. Lots of money exchanges hands, and big business deals are made, but no one talks about it on the record."

Finn sighed. "But the bartender knew and shared the details with you."

"She knew because she gets paid in tips to

work the events," Dean said. "She shared because rumor has it I'm charming."

Finn sighed. "Go on."

Dean grinned. "Guess who lost a lot of money to Conrad Forester last month?"

"Tell me it was Kate Everett's husband."

Dean nodded. "I don't have specifics or proof, but that was the story making the rounds at the end of the night."

"Okay." Finn's mind raced with fresh theories. "So Everett owed Forrester. Any idea how much?"

"No, but they allegedly agreed to call it even if Everett got his wife to change the location of her community-center project." Dean's eyebrows raised and he crossed his arms over his chest, looking rightfully proud.

"Detective Beaumont?" The voice of the tech-services representative rang in his ear.

He'd temporarily forgotten about the phone in his hand. "Yeah, I'm here."

"Plates on that sedan match a vehicle registered to Conrad Forester. Would you like the home address and phone number on file?"

"Text it," Finn said, already headed into the hall to collect his team.

Finn navigated the streets of Old Downtown, his heart in his throat and a storm rolling in off the coast. Forester hadn't been at his home or office, but Mr. Everett had started talking the moment Finn and Dean showed up at his door. He confessed his debt to Forester and explained that Kate had refused to change her dream over a game of poker.

Finn was willing to bet Forester hadn't liked that answer.

Now Dean was riding shotgun in Finn's borrowed SUV, the team close behind.

Forester owned enough properties along the waterfront to keep them all busy past nightfall, but it was the perfect place to hide two kids and a woman, so they wouldn't stop until they'd searched every square foot.

"So Everett owes Forester a gambling debt he can't pay up," Dean said, verbally sorting the facts. "At first he can't pay, because his wife controls the business and the money. Then Forester kills the wife, or has her killed, to stop the project, but Everett still doesn't control the business."

"He told me a board of trustees was handling things now," Finn said. "I'm unclear about his access or control of the money."

Lightning flashed as he parked the SUV on the street where it had all began. Three other vehicles followed suit, and his teammates filed onto the sidewalk. One side of the street contained the warehouse remains. Across the broken asphalt, yellow crime-scene tape denoted the location of Kate's murder. All around, signs with the Lighthouse, Inc. logo were pelted with falling rain.

Finn's phone dinged, and he paused to check the screen.

"News?" Dean asked, unfastening his safety belt.

"The lab," Finn said, scanning the message. "Bullet casings found after the press-conference shooting match those pulled from my truck after the drive-by and the one in Kate's body."

The same weapon had been used in all three crime scenes.

"And the case just gets stronger," Dean said.

Finn released a labored sigh. "Against Lance Stevens. We probably have enough to arrest him for the shootings and murder, but we'll need to prove Forester's connection to him and those crimes."

"So first we'll find Hayley," Dean said, opening his door against the increasing wind. "I have a feeling she's all we'll need to arrest him for abduction. And as soon as you do your cop thing and offer Stevens a deal, I'm sure he'll roll on Forester for hiring him as the gunman."

Lightning flashed in the sky, and Finn stepped into the storm. He'd bring Hayley home safely, whatever the cost.

HAYLEY WHIMPERED AS thunder rolled and she worked her bloody fingers over broken bricks, painstakingly tearing them free. Her hands were filthy and swollen from the work. Her arms and chest were covered in dust and dirt from the aged mortar and crumbling masonry. Tears streamed over her red-hot cheeks, and icy fear coiled in her gut. Her voice was nearly gone from continuous and desperate cries for help.

The boys rested on the floor, dehydrated and exhausted. Gage's pain had increased by the minute as he'd beaten the rebar against the wall, each whack reverberating through his thin frame and jostling his broken arm.

She was making progress on her own, but it was too slow to expect an escape before dawn. Even if she worked all night. The hole was large enough to get her foot through, but nothing more.

She swallowed a scream of rage at the unfairness of it all and reached again for the rebar. Her sweaty, blood-slicked hands slipped as she swung, tearing the skin of her palms and raising fire in her veins. "Dammit!"

Outside the foot-size hole, rain soaked the ground, creating mini rivers and mudslides that slopped over the brick wall and onto the basement floor. The rain would prevent any passersby close enough to hear her screams. If not, the thunder would surely cover the feeble sound.

She swung her weapon harder, funneling all the hate and fear inside her into each new swing. Every jarring thud wrenched a fresh sob from her chest until she couldn't lift the metal or her arms.

"Ms. Hayley?" Parker asked, wobbling onto his feet, fear in his wide brown eyes.

She wiped her face and forced her mind into caregiver mode. Their situation was dire, but Parker was only eight, and he needed her protection.

Before she could find the words to speak, a great, rolling groan spread through the structure above them. The wall she'd been assaulting began to shift, and the bricks began to fall. Dirt dropped onto their heads from the exposed ceiling beams and joists.

Gage pressed onto his feet with a sharp wince of pain. "What's happening?"

Hayley's heart seized in horrific realization as she watched broken bits of brick and mortar spill from the wall. Her failed attempt to save them would be the death of them instead.

She'd intentionally damaged a load-bearing wall.

"The building is unstable," she said, as calmly as she could manage.

Gage nodded in grim understanding. "What do we do?"

Parker peered through the growing hole. "Boost me up! I can fit!"

Hayley dragged her gaze from Parker to the opening as thunder boomed and lightning struck.

Sending Parker alone into the most dangerous area of town, into the storm and darkness, wasn't an answer she'd ever choose. But her choices had been erased.

Gage stepped into the space at her side. "Help," he instructed. "I can't lift him on my own. Parker, keep running until you find someone to tell we're down here. Then ask to call 911. Watch out for the man who brought us here. Look for his car. Be careful."

Parker raised a thumb, his attention fixed on the small opening in the wall. "Got it," he said. "I'm a hero."

"That's right," Gage said. "You're a hero. And, hey, don't come back here without an adult, understand? No matter what happens. Even if this building makes a lot of noise. Stay focused. Okay?"

Hayley swallowed a rock of emotion as she processed Gage's words of protection. If the building fell, Parker couldn't come back alone. Couldn't try to save them. Couldn't be hurt or worse by the unstable ruins. Whatever else happened, Parker would survive.

She helped Gage hoist the little boy into the storm.

Chapter Twenty-Two

Hayley swung the rebar at the shelving on the walls, dismantling it with every bone-rattling blow. "Gage, take these," she said, kicking boards and sections of fallen framework across the floor in the teen's direction. "Wedge them in the opening. Use them to support the wall."

A few busted shelves wouldn't stop a building from collapsing, but she could at least try to buy them some time. Give the miracle they desperately needed a chance to happen.

Gage had already been abducted and injured on her watch. She couldn't sit idly by and wait for them both to be crushed to death.

His face contorted in pain as he tried to place the boards between broken bricks.

"Let me help," she said, abandoning the demolition to assist in the new project. "Go ahead and rest. I've got this."

Gage stepped away, breathing heavily and pressing his broken arm to his torso.

Hayley stayed on task, working the boards into

place between rows of still-sturdy bricks. The gap had grown exponentially with each ugly groan of the building, and a new realization hit with the next boom of thunder. "I think you can fit through this."

"What?" Gage returned to her side with a frown.

"Look!"

He squinted at the hole she'd braced, and a low cuss rolled off his tongue. "Sorry."

"Darling, I'm going to agree," she said. "Here." Gusts of cool, wet air blew into the basement as she laced her fingers together and formed a stir-rup for his foot. "I'll give you a boost."

"What about you?" he asked, unmoving. "There's no one to boost you out if I leave. You'll still be stuck down here."

"I'll figure it out," she said. "Don't worry about me. You need to go look for help."

"I won't leave you."

The battering wind picked up, and the building moaned. Dirt fell in tufts from the space above their heads. Time was running out.

She needed to get Gage as far away as possible. Fast.

"I can climb out," she said. "I still have two good arms and legs. You're limping." She crouched and wiggled her joined hands. "Come on. Hurry."

Gage scanned her face, distrusting.

"Let's go," she urged. "The quicker you get out there, the sooner I can too."

Reluctantly, he set a foot onto her hands, and a tear rolled over his cheek. "You'd better make it out. I'm trusting you," he whispered.

She nodded, then she shoved him into the night.

FINN AND DEAN crossed the first floor of the third empty building they'd painstakingly cleared. There were dozens more and not enough law enforcement in the county to search them all in a short amount of time. "Maybe we need to arrange search parties," Finn said.

"We're not even sure they're in Old Downtown," Dean countered. "Lighthouse, Inc. owns a lot of properties in this area."

"We'd know sooner if we had more boots on the ground."

"Help!" The word seemed to echo in the storm.

Finn stilled, senses on high alert. "Did you hear that?" He focused on the sound, praying it would come again.

Dean raised his flashlight beam toward the open door ahead. "What?"

"It came from outside," Finn said, rushing through the building and onto the sidewalk.

In the distance, a small figure ran along a parallel street. "Help!"

"Hey!" Finn barked, projecting his most authoritative tone and hoping he would be heard.

The boy stopped and turned, then launched in their direction, arms waving. "Help! Help! Help!"

"Parker?" Finn met him in the intersection, pulling him into his arms. "Where did you come from? Are Hayley and Gage with you?"

Parker nodded. "They're in the basement. Gage is hurt."

"Okay, buddy." Finn said. "This is my brother Dean and he's going to get you out of the rain." Finn turned to pass Parker into Dean's arms.

"No! We have to help them!" Parker cried. "The building is getting blown up tomorrow. They didn't think I saw the signs, but I did, and I can read. I'm a very good reader."

Finn's chest constricted and his gaze whipped from building to building. "Which one?"

Parker scanned the street, wiping water from his terror-filled eyes. "We made a hole in the wall, and it started to fall apart."

"Which building?" Finn repeated, more harshly than intended, earning a stern look from Dean.

Dean pried the child from his arms. "Get your team out here," he told Finn. "We've got to be close."

Finn dialed his team and relayed the information while Dean ducked under a nearby awning with Parker.

Finn followed.

"You're okay," Dean said gently. "We're going to keep you safe and help the others. Can you show us where you were?"

Parker wound narrow arms around Dean's neck and whimpered. "I don't know."

"Do you remember which way you ran?"

Parker shook his head.

"What can you remember?" Finn asked, careful not to upset the kid further. "You said there were signs?"

"And a fence," Parker said.

"That's good," Dean encouraged. "Anything else?"

Parker buried his face against Dean's neck.

Finn patted the boy's back. "You did great, buddy. We'll take it from here, and you can get dry." He waved a hand at his teammates as they filtered out of nearby buildings, converged, then rushed to his aid.

Dean passed Parker into another set of hands.

"We need ambulances and the search-and-rescue team down here," Finn instructed. "Have him checked out and kept under guard." He nodded at Parker. "Don't let him out of your sight. We also need a list of buildings set for demolition in the morning. We're looking for one with a fence."

The group split up, and Finn caught his brother's eye. "SUV."

They both broke into a sprint for the vehicle they'd left behind. Within seconds, they were onboard and in motion.

Finn pressed the gas pedal with purpose, hydroplaning over the flooding roads.

"There are a few buildings behind fences at the end of the next block," Dean said. "I saw them the day of the warehouse explosion. I was looking for construction locations that might have explosives on-site."

Finn adjusted his wipers and heat vents, attempting to clear his view. Sheets of rain washed over the windshield, and storm clouds had turned dusk to night.

He leaned forward, peering over his steering wheel and straining for visibility. A moment later, he slowed, confusion mixing with hope. "I think I see someone out there." He veered to the road's flooded edge, sending a mini tidal wave across the sidewalk.

A narrow figure weaved in their direction, cradling one arm, head bent low against the wind and rain.

The Beaumonts jumped out and ran in the figure's direction.

"Gage?" Finn called. Could his luck truly be so good? To find not one, but both missing boys, in the middle of this storm?

The teen raised his head, stopping several feet away. "Finn!" he cried. "Help!" He swung an arm to point in the opposite direction. "Hayley's still inside, and the building's coming down!"

"We know," Finn said, erasing the final steps between them and projecting his voice against the wind. "Parker's with my team. He told us about the demolition tomorrow."

"No!" Gage turned back, eyes wild. "We broke a load-bearing wall and—"

Finn's ears rang as he raised his eyes to the silhouettes of distant structures.

And in the next breath, a building began to fall.

HAYLEY DRAGGED THE remnants of a broken shelving unit to the collapsing wall and climbed on to test its strength. Overhead, the building's complaints grew more fervent with every powerful gust of wind. She stretched onto tiptoe, reaching through the hole in search of purchase. There wasn't anyone left to offer her a boost. No one to grab her hands and pull her up. She'd demanded that Gage leave her and find Parker, then bring help.

She pressed the toe of one shoe into a crevice between bricks and thrust her torso outside with a harsh shove. The busted shelving crashed onto the floor, leaving her half inside and half out. The ground was slippery and soft from the storm. Each wiggle and stretch toward freedom threatened to land her back where she'd started.

If she died, two young boys would carry a lifetime of guilt with them for leaving her behind, and she would not allow that to happen.

Slowly, she got to her knees then pushed onto her feet.

She pulled in a shaky breath, stunned and elated to know she'd won. She'd gotten the boys to safety, and she'd beaten Forester at his twisted game.

A horrendous cracking sound filled the night and set her in motion toward the chain-link fence. She ran faster than she'd thought possible as the building came down behind her.

Hunks of busted bricks bounced and rolled over the sopping ground, crashing against her feet and legs. She stumbled and fell. Her body screamed with pain, and her forehead collided with the walkway. Then the world went dark…

Hayley. Her name echoed in her ears, sounding foreign, fuzzy. Her eyes reopened, mind aware of what she'd been through.

Rain had soaked and added weight to her clothes. Lightning flashed in the sky above.

"Hayley!"

She rolled onto her back, head pounding and heart racing as the remains of the building she'd escaped from came into view. Half of the massive structure was gone, revealing the insides, like a giant, ghastly dollhouse.

Emergency sirens warbled in the distance, and the glow of searchlights danced over the rubble around her. She'd survived, and she was being rescued.

"There she is!" a male voice called. "Beaumont! I see her!"

Hayley twisted on the ground, seeking the man behind the name. She pushed up, onto skinned knees, then to her feet. Searching.

"Hayley," Finn said, striding through the storm like her personal hero. He moved faster and with purpose as their eyes met, erasing the distance between them until she was in his arms.

SIX MONTHS LATER, the summer heat had gone, but Hayley's nights were just as hot, and her days were filled with warmth and light. Today was no different.

Conrad Forester was in jail for conspiracy to commit murder, multiple counts of attempted murder and abduction, extortion, plus a whole host of other crimes. Most of which he'd readily admitted to in the hopes of a plea bargain. But a loose-lipped gunman and a rock-solid case by Finn and the Marshal's Bluff PD had put him away for life instead.

Katherine Everett's community-center project was well underway, and her husband was fully involved in making it everything she'd hoped.

Hayley had been promoted to a position for the routine reevaluation of foster families. And the job came with less overtime. All in all, it had been a pretty terrific six months.

She smiled as Finn parked the truck outside his parents' home and glanced over his shoulder at the boys in the extended cab.

"You guys ready?" he asked.

"Yeah!" Parker called.

Gage rolled his eyes.

Hayley turned and smiled at the pair.

If anyone had told her last summer that she'd be married with two children before the holidays, she'd have told them they had the wrong woman. If they'd told her the children would be eight and fourteen years old, she'd have assumed they were off their rockers. But adopting Gage and Parker was the best, smartest, most wonderful thing she'd ever done.

Marrying the love of her life a few months prior was a possible tie.

Finn climbed out, then opened the rear door and grinned. "I can't wait to see everyone's face when they hear the news."

A mass of Beaumonts spilled onto the porch before Hayley made it to the steps. Gage trailed a short distance behind, carrying a neatly wrapped box.

"Grandma!" Parker said, running to Mrs. Beaumont's arms.

She kissed his head and tousled his hair with a smile. "What's this about exciting news?"

Austin, Dean and Lincoln moved to stand beside their dad.

Nicole, Dean's fiancée, and Scarlet, Austin's new wife, closed in on Hayley.

Josi brought up the rear. "Please tell me there's going to be a baby."

Hayley turned a bright smile on Finn. "Not yet."

He pulled Gage against his side. "We'd like to get this one into college first."

"So what's the news?" Austin asked. "It's freezing, and Mom said you wanted us all outside."

Hayley traded knowing looks with her family. "We aren't having a baby, but our family is growing."

Gage raised the box in his hands, and Parker whipped off the lid.

"We got a puppy!" Parker yelled, buzzing with the same excitement he'd had since Finn and Hayley had taken the boys to select their new pet.

"He's a hound dog," Gage said proudly. "He howls. It's hilarious."

Hayley wound an arm around his back, forming a chain with Gage and Finn, while the others oohed and aahed over Parker and the puppy.

"His name is Sir Barks-a-lot," Parker announced.

"I'm not calling him that," Lincoln said, swinging Parker under one arm like a football.

Josi cuddled the pup to her chest. "I think it's cute."

"I think it's cold," Austin complained, dragging Scarlet in for a hug. "Bring that little furball inside. Parker can come too."

"Hey!" Parker laughed.

The group filed into Mrs. Beaumont's kitchen, but Hayley and Finn stayed behind.

Gage shook his head and laughed, but shut the door in his wake…leaving them to do the thing they spent an awful lot of time doing these days.

Kissing and savoring the moments.

* * * * *

Don't miss the stories in this mini series!

BEAUMONT BROTHERS JUSTICE

MILLS & BOON

Shadow Survivors
Julie Miller

MILLS & BOON

Julie Miller is an award-winning *USA TODAY* bestselling author of breathtaking romantic suspense—with a National Readers' Choice Award and a Daphne du Maurier Award, among other prizes. She has also earned an *RT Book Reviews Career Achievement Award*. For a complete list of her books, monthly newsletter and more, go to juliemiller.org.

Visit the Author Profile page
at millsandboon.com.au.

DEDICATION

For Daisy and Teddy—our two doodlebugs. Both blind in one eye. A black Poodle mix, a white Poodle mix. An introvert and an extrovert. One who will never sit in your lap to be petted but who will never turn her nose up at a treat. And the other who can't get enough personal attention and who will take a tummy rub over a treat any day. One who enjoys her solitude, and one who panics when he's left alone. One who was returned to the shelter twice before finding his forever home with us, and the other who was never wanted at all until she was rescued from a horrible situation. You two are so good for each other, and you're good for us. You have to be a special dog to be a Miller dog. Mama loves you both.

CAST OF CHARACTERS

Jessica "Jessie" Bennington—She survived tragedy and has built herself a new life rescuing and training dogs at K-9 Ranch. Her faithful service dog, Shadow, is her constant companion and helps with her panic attacks. Her dogs give her a purpose; the local silver fox deputy gives her friendship. Can she move past her fears to embrace an unexpected family? And protect them from the evil hunting them down?

Deputy Garrett Caldwell—The widower and retired army sniper has poured himself into his career with the Jackson County Sheriff's Department. Now entering his fifties, he's realizing all the things missing from his life—a family, a strong woman by his side, love. He'll content himself with his friendship with Jessie if that's the only way he can be with her. But he wants so much more—and he'll put his life on the line to protect their future.

Shadow—This German shepherd mix is the grand old man of the ranch. The smartest and most versatile of all Jessie's dogs.

Nate and Abby—An Amber Alert has been issued for the children.

Kai Olivera—The skull tattooed on his bald head isn't the scariest thing about him.

Conor Wildman—KCPD detective.

Chapter One

Shadow growled.

Tensing, Jessica Bennington looked over at her German shepherd mix with the graying muzzle, who had just risen from his sunny spot in the grass and gone on alert.

Now what? The dogs at her K-9 Ranch rescue and training center had raised a ruckus late last night, too. They had all been locked up in their kennels, the barn, or the house, so she hadn't been worried about one of them getting into trouble. She'd thrown a jacket on over her pajamas and slipped into a pair of sneakers, grabbed a flashlight and Shadow, and gone out to investigate. But by the time she'd checked each and every one of them, the hubbub had died down. One must have seen a fox or a raccoon and barked, then the others would have joined in because no self-respecting dog wanted to be left out of sounding the alarm. Other than a few extroverts who seized the opportunity to get some petting, they'd immediately settled for the night. But since her own K-9 partner hadn't alerted to anything unusual, Jessica had dismissed any threat, walked back to the house, and had fallen into bed.

But Shadow was alerting this morning. His ears flicked toward the sound that only a dog could hear, his dark eyes riveted to movement in the distance that only a dog could see.

She hated that growl. It was the sound of danger. A threat. Sometimes, even death. It was the sound of salvation and sacrifice.

It was the sound of the nightmare she'd lived with for twelve long years.

She instinctively splayed her fingers over her belly and the scars beneath her jeans. There was nothing to protect there anymore. There never would be.

Barely aware of the younger dog she'd been working with taking his cue from Shadow and turning toward the perceived threat, Jessica felt her blood pressure spike. Both dogs faced the pines and pin oaks that formed a windbreak and offered some much-needed privacy around the small acreage outside of Kansas City, Missouri. She couldn't afford to be paralyzed by the memories that assailed her. She had to push them aside. She had to let Shadow do what she'd trained him to do. She could overcome. She could survive this moment, just like she had so many others.

Jessica forced out a calming breath and stepped up beside the rescue dog that had been her protector, emotional support, and most loyal companion these past ten years. "What is it, boy?"

She sensed the tension vibrating through Shadow but knew he wouldn't charge off to investigate unless she gave him the command to do so. Shadow's black-and-tan coat was longer than a pure-blooded shepherd, thanks to the indefinite parentage of running with a pack until he'd been taken to a shelter in Kansas City and Jessica had picked him to be her first rescue. But that shaggy coat had been a comfort on more than one occasion in the ten years she'd had him. It would be now, too. She slid her fingers from her stomach into the thick fur atop his head, absorbing his heat, finding strength in knowing he was as devoted to her as she was to him.

She would never again be alone and helpless and unable to save the ones she loved.

Not with Shadow by her side.

Jessica finally heard the deep bark of one of her patrol dogs in the distance and relaxed a fraction. Her dogs were doing their jobs. That loud woof was Rex, a big, furry galoot of laziness and curiosity. He was more noise than fight—just the way she'd trained the gentle giant to behave. He wasn't much of a people dog, but he did enjoy roaming the six acres of her Shadow Protectors Ranch. A natural herder and caretaker, the Anatolian had adopted her three goats, a barn cat, and an abandoned litter of possums over the years. Had he found some other critter he wanted to take home to his stall in the barn? While Rex had yet to choose a person he liked well enough to bond with, he made a great deterrent to trespassers who wandered onto her land.

That's when she heard Toby's excited bark joining the chorus. Toby was the opposite of Rex in terms of personality. The black Lab wanted to be friends with everyone, hence he was no kind of guard dog at all. But he was a great noisemaker and loved to be in on the action. Toby and Rex had definitely discovered something near her property line to the west.

Mollie Crane, the client she'd been working with, sidled up beside Jessica, tucking her short dark-brown hair behind her ears. "Is something wrong?"

The younger woman she was helping was one breath away from a panic attack. The man she'd said she needed protection from had really done a number on her. Her fingers brushed against Jessica's elbow instead of reaching for Magnus, the dark faced Belgian Malinois who was training to be her service dog. "Is someone out there? Is it that grumpy old man who works for you? Or his grandson who cleans out the kennels? I'm not sure I like him. He's *too* friendly. Can someone be too friendly? I like his grandfather better. He's not very chatty, but at least he doesn't force me into a conversation or try to flirt with me."

Jessica squeezed her hand over Mollie's fingers to calm her. "Easy, Mollie. Take a breath." She breathed deeply, once, twice, with the woman, who was twenty years her junior. It was easier to control her own fears when she had her dogs or someone else to worry about. "Shadow's on alert because he hears and smells something atypical in his world. The dogs all know Mr. Hauck and his grandson, Soren. This is something different."

"An intruder? Could someone have followed me out here from the city? Wouldn't we have heard them pulling up the driveway?" She was one thought away from hyperventilating. Mollie's fingers were still clenched around Jessica's elbow as she looked down at her dog. "Why isn't Magnus barking? Is it because he's deaf in one ear? Does he not hear the threat? He's not going to be able to protect me, is he?"

Jessica glanced down at the Belgian Malinois who'd washed out of the Army's K-9 Corps because of chronic ear infections and hearing loss. "He's aware. Believe me, he sees more with those eyes than you or I ever will. But he's still in training. We'll get him where you need him to be. Don't worry. For now, let him be a comfort to you—something to focus on besides your fear." She tried to pull away. "I really need to go. If they've trapped a skunk, or there is someone—"

"Okay, um, Magnus?" Mollie picked up the Malinois's leash off the dry grass that hadn't had enough spring rain yet to turn green.

"Not like that." Jessica spared a moment to help her client. "You're the boss. He wants to please you. If you're *not* the boss, he's going to please himself." Jessica demonstrated. "Shadow, sit." She raised her hand. "Down." The shepherd's black nose stayed in the air, even as he eased his creaky joints to the ground. "Stay," she added, although he'd already obeyed her visual cues. She nodded to Mollie. "Now, you tell Magnus."

Mollie dutifully raised her hand. "Magnus. Sit." The young, muscular dog tipped his nose up to her and plopped his haunches on the ground. "He did it!" Mollie's success transformed her wary expression into a shy smile. "Good boy." She scratched the dog around his limp ear. "Now what?"

Although Jessica had spent a fortune to fence in the entire acreage to keep her dogs off the gravel roads and nearby state highway, she knew that a human being could either climb the fence or cut through it if they were agile enough and determined to trespass. "Mollie, I need to go." She needed to check out the hullabaloo as much as Shadow wanted to. "Take Magnus back to the barn and do some bonding with him. You've both had a good training session this morning and need a break."

Mollie's hands fisted around the leash. "By myself?"

"Sweetie, he chose you that first day you came to the ranch. Remember? He came right up to you and sat on your foot? He wants you

to give him a chance to be the dog you need."
Jessica shrugged, anxious to get to her dogs
to make sure they were safe, but equally worried about jeopardizing Mollie's training. Although she earned good money training dogs
for several paying clients, she had an affinity
for women like Mollie, who *needed* a companion to help her feel safe. Mollie lived on
a small budget, working as a waitress at a
diner in Kansas City. But because of Jessica's
own background with violence, she charged
Mollie only a fraction of her regular fee. She
would have given the young woman the dog
and trained them for free, but she'd discovered
she was as much a therapist as a trainer. Jessica understood that Mollie needed to make
her own way in the world. She needed to
build the confidence that had been stripped
away from her by her past, and Jessica would
do whatever was necessary to help. "Play a
game with Magnus," she advised. "Get on the
ground with him and pet him. There are treats
and toys in the last cabinet out in the barn."
She reached into the pocket of her jeans and
pulled out her ring of work keys. She held up
a small padlock key. "Here. This will unlock
the cabinet."

"Okay. I can do this, right?" Mollie fisted her hand around the keys.

Jessica softened her tone and squeezed the other woman's fist. "Yes, you can. Love Magnus. Earn his trust. Provide his food, leadership, entertainment and comfort, and he will be your best friend—the most loyal friend you will ever have. Answering the specific commands you need will come later." She gave the other woman's shoulder one more squeeze before pulling away. "Please. I need to see what's going on. I need to make sure none of my protectors are getting themselves into trouble."

Mollie nodded, accepting the mission Jessica had given her. Using a hand signal to get the tan dog's attention focused on her, she spoke in a surprisingly firm voice. "Magnus, heel." Then she tugged on the leash and the dog fell into step beside her.

"Just like that. Good job. You'll be safe in the barn."

Shadow remained at her feet, but his nose and ears indicated he was anxious to check out the disturbance, too. Could the ex-husband Mollie was so afraid of have found her here, eight miles outside the KC city limits? Jessica released her dog from his stay command. "Shadow, seek."

Needing no more encouragement, he took off at a loping run, and Jessica jogged to keep pace with him. She slowed as they reached the trees. Although the oaks were just beginning to bud and posed no obstacle, the evergreens had full, heavy branches she had to push her way through. She worried when Shadow dashed beyond her sight. "Shadow?" The barking tripled as the dog joined Rex and Toby.

Jessica pushed aside the last branch, stopped in her tracks and cursed on a deep sigh. "This isn't good."

Chapter Two

A protective anger pushed aside Jessica's fear and she hurried her stride to approach the trio of dogs barking at the white-haired neighbor swinging the barrel of her shotgun from one dog to the next from her side of the fence. "Miss Eloise? Good morning."

"Don't *good morning* me. Your mutts are a terror, Jessica Bennington! An absolute terror." Eloise Gardner had once been a tall woman. But now she was stooped with age and frail enough that she panted from the exertion of holding up the heavy gun and walking the quarter mile from her house to the fence. She nodded toward the broken railing that butted up against Jessica's chain-link fence. "Look what they did to my fence."

The log fence was little more than faded wood and chipped white paint after years of weather and neglect. The top rail looked as though it had rotted through and splintered in half beneath the weight of someone leaning against it or stepping onto it. Or maybe it had finally surrendered under its own weight to age and decay.

Keeping her demeanor calm so the dogs would obey her, Jessica called them to her side. "Rex! Toby! Shadow! Come." The three dogs lined up beside her, and with a set of nonverbal commands, they sat and lay down. Jessica kept her arm out at a 45-degree angle from her body to make them stay put. Trying not to panic that the shotgun was pointed in her direction now, as well, Jessica drummed up a smile and a civil tone. "Is that gun really necessary? What seems to be the problem?"

The skinny old woman hiked the butt of the gun onto her hip, but kept it trained on the dogs and Jessica in a distinctly unneighborly fashion. "Your dogs are wild beasts and need to be put down. Not only did a pack of them break down my fence, but one of my chickens is dead. My best layer. Never had problems like this when your grandparents owned the place."

"I'm sorry about your chicken." She kept her tone calm, as if she was talking to a nervous dog. "My fence is still intact," she pointed out.

"My dogs didn't get onto your property. They didn't break your fence. And they didn't kill your chicken. Maybe a fox or coyote got inside your chicken coop."

"Don't you argue with me. Doris is dead. I already called Deputy Caldwell."

Jessica's nostrils flared with a sigh of relief, but for their own safety, she refused to relax or release the dogs from their stay position. "Good. Deputy Caldwell knows my dogs. He'll straighten this out." Garrett Caldwell was a captain in the Jackson County Sheriff's Office, in charge of the patrol division. He was not only in charge of local law enforcement in the county outside of the K C city limits, but he was practically a neighbor, living just off 40 Highway in the nearby town of Lone Jack. He was tough but fair, and the widower had become a friend. "He'll listen to the facts, assess the evidence. You'll get the answers you need, and my dogs will be safe."

Eloise glanced over her shoulder at the sound of a large vehicle crunching over gravel in the distance. "I expect that'll be him." She wheezed with the effort to keep the gun from pointing to the ground as she faced Jessica again. "You're in trouble now, missy."

Missy? Jessica wanted to laugh. She'd buried a husband and a child and felt as if she'd already lived the best part of her life. But she swallowed the dark humor as she watched the older woman wiggling her nose to work her glasses back up into place without letting go of the shotgun. Eloise Gardner was an octogenarian living a hard, lonely existence, trying to take care of things as best she could without the help, resources, or energy to fully manage on her own. "Miss Eloise, are you all right? Did you take your heart medication this morning?"

"Of course, I did." Eloise touched her agespotted forehead as if trying to think. "I don't know. I'm not sure."

"Would you let me walk you back to your house?" Jessica offered. "We could check your pill box. I'd be happy to fix you a cup of tea and sit with you for a while." She glanced down at her faithful German shepherd mix. "I'd have to bring Shadow with me, but I promise, the other dogs will stay here."

"I…" For a moment, she looked as though she wanted to say yes to Jessica's offer. "No… Isla's coming today. I gave her money for groceries." Suddenly, Eloise pulled her shoulders back with as much energy as her stooped posture allowed, raising the shotgun once more.

"I don't want any of your dogs on my property. And who's fixing the latch on my chicken coop?"

"Miss Eloise?" A deep voice called out.

Jessica watched the tall man in his khaki uniform quietly striding up behind her neighbor. Garrett Caldwell stood a couple inches over six feet, and the protective vest he wore underneath his uniform made his sturdy chest and shoulders seem impossibly broad and imposing.

And then she saw Eloise Gardner swing around and point her shotgun straight at the deputy. "Garrett!"

Her warning proved unnecessary. In one swift, smooth movement, Garrett knocked the barrel of the shotgun aside, tugged it from her hands, and reached out to steady the old woman's arm to keep her from falling. Eloise yelped in surprise and clung to his forearm as he stepped behind her and braced her against his chest. All the while, he held the gun out with one strong arm and kept hold of Eloise until she stopped swaying.

The old woman's breathing fell back into a more normal rhythm, and Garrett released her and stepped back. "You all right, Miss Eloise?" Although she still seemed a little surprised by how quickly she'd been disarmed, she nodded. Then he turned his sharp green eyes across the fence to Jessica. "You okay?"

Jessica nodded, despite the lingering frissons of alarm that hummed through her veins. "Thank you, Deputy."

He touched the brim of his departmental ball cap, then concentrated on the white-haired lady beside him. "I'm not comfortable with you pointing a gun at me or anyone else when I haven't checked it out for myself." Garrett's tone held all the authority of his position, yet was surprisingly gentle with the frightened, angry, and possibly confused woman.

"It's not loaded. I just wanted to scare her. I don't feel safe around her dogs."

"All the same." He opened the shotgun, verified there were no rounds inside, then tucked the disabled weapon in the crook of his arm. "I want to make sure everyone is safe. Including you. This twelve-gauge seems a little too big for you to handle properly."

"It was my Hal's gun." Eloise sounded wistful at the mention of her late husband. "He took down an elk with it."

And she'd pointed that blunderbuss at her dogs? And her? And Garrett?

"I'm sure he did, ma'am. Now, what seems to be the problem?"

Eloise clutched Garrett's muscled forearm that was decorated with a faded black tattoo from his time in the military. "I want you to arrest this woman for siccing her dogs on my chickens."

Now that the imminent threat had been neutralized, he launched into investigator mode. "One of Jessie's dogs went after your chickens?"

"No," Jessica protested.

"Yes." The older woman's breathing was a little ragged. She pressed a gnarled hand against her heart. "During the night. Of course, I didn't hear it, but one of those mutts chewed through the latch on my coop and the hens got out. This morning, there were hardly any eggs when I went to gather them, so I know something upset them. I found Doris dead by the side of the highway. She was my best layer." Even though she was shorter by a few inches, the white-haired woman managed to look down her nose at Jessica. "Your dogs chased her right out into the road."

"My dogs haven't left my property," Jessica insisted. Then she dropped her voice to a whisper she hoped only Garrett could hear. "Although, they did go off about two o'clock this morning. I never saw anything. Maybe she had an intruder, and that's what they heard."

His lips barely moved as he answered in an equally hushed tone. "I think she needs to relax and put her feet up for a bit. She looks pale and sounds winded."

"I asked if she took her medications this morning. She couldn't remember."

"She's upset about her damn chicken."

"Not. My. Dogs."

Garrett arched a brow over one moss-colored eye, silently asking her to give up the argument. Then he smiled at the older woman and spoke in his full, deeply pitched voice. "Are the rest of your chickens okay, ma'am?"

After several moments, Eloise nodded. "They were all inside the fence this morning, but the latch is broken. Someone braced it shut with a rock."

"Well, my dogs didn't do that."

"Jessie." Garrett's eyes narrowed, asking her to be the more magnanimous complainant here. Once she nodded, he turned back to the older woman. "Miss Eloise, you go back to your house. I'll meet you there in a few minutes to take your statement and return the gun. I'll look around to make sure everything is secure."

"Thank you." Once the white-haired woman had taken a few steps toward her house, Garrett crossed to the fence. After a quick inspection of the broken railing, he braced one hand on a sturdier post and swung his legs up over both fences onto her property.

The moment he dropped down onto the grass, Shadow raised his head and growled. Rex yawned, growing bored with staying in one place. Toby's tail was wagging hard enough to kick up a cloud of dirt and dry grass on the ground behind him, but even the friendly Lab who'd greeted Garrett on more than one occasion eyed Jessica's hand and maintained his stay position.

Garrett froze in place, and Eloise hurried back to the fence in a huff. "You see, Deputy? Those dogs are a threat to all of us."

"No, they're not." Jessica was tired of defending herself and the work she was doing here. She latched on to Garrett's gaze and willed him to side with her. "These are three of my best students. None of them are smarter than Shadow. They know the property lines, and that they aren't to cross them without me. They guard *my* land. They don't invade hers.

They're all well-fed and have plenty of stimulation. They don't need to be stealing chickens for breakfast or chasing them for entertainment."

Garrett nodded toward Shadow. "If these dogs are so well trained, why is that one growling at me?"

"Because you're holding that gun. You're half a foot taller than me and you look like a threat." She glanced at her outstretched hand, still holding her dogs in place. "But he won't go after you unless I give the command."

"The fence is broken, Jessie." Making the concession to Shadow's watchful eye, Garrett laid Eloise's open shotgun on the ground behind him. He visibly relaxed his posture, although he didn't move any closer. "Your smaller dogs might not be able to get out. But one of these three could."

"Are you going to call them off?" Eloise prodded, seeming more energized now that backup had arrived.

"Are you going to accuse my dogs of something they didn't do?"

"Jessie." Garrett exhaled a weary breath, drawing her attention to the silver-studded beard stubble shading his jaw. Standing closer, she realized the lines beside his mouth were etched more deeply than the last time she'd seen him.

"Garrett?" Something locked up deep inside her fluttered with concern. Maybe the same impulse that had her worried about Eloise's health. Garrett looked exhausted. Had he worked the night shift? Had he even slept? Who looked out for the strong boss man when he had a rough night? Apparently, it wasn't a job he did for himself. "Are you all right?"

He let out his breath on a slow, weary exhale, but didn't answer. Whatever fatigue she'd detected didn't stop him from smiling at her neighbor and speaking in a tone that commanded authority, even as his words offered compassion and reassurance. "Miss Eloise, go back to the house and fix yourself a cup of tea or a shot of whiskey to calm your nerves. I'll be over in a few minutes to return your shotgun and take a closer look at what happened."

"All right. I could do with a few minutes to myself." The older woman smiled. "With Doris's demise, I guess I'll be making fried chicken for dinner. Deputy, if you'd like to join me. Isla will be here. She'd love to see you." The older woman pushed her glasses up on the bridge of her nose and winked.

"Your granddaughter?" Jessica thought she detected a ruddy hue to Garrett's carved cheekbones and held back a smirk at his embarrassment. "She's a mite young for me, ma'am."

"Nonsense. She's thirty. Just broke up with her latest boyfriend. I told her he was no good. Out drinking nearly every night. Probably doing drugs."

"Isla or the boyfriend?"

Eloise bristled at the question. "I'm just telling you she's available."

"I appreciate you thinking of me, ma'am. But I'm not interested. I'm just here to do my job."

Eloise propped her hands on her hips. "You've been widowed for ten years, Garrett Caldwell. It's time you got laid again."

There was definitely a blush now. Jessica curled her lips between her teeth to hide her grin at Eloise's blatant matchmaking attempt. Just because the man had lost his wife to cancer a decade earlier didn't mean he hadn't dated or been with a woman since then. Garrett Caldwell was a catch. If you had a thing for silver foxes with a sense of humor and muscles to spare. She doubted if he needed

Eloise Gardner's or anyone's help if he wanted to get laid.

Of course, Jessica hadn't slept with a man since losing Jonathan twelve years ago. Being abstinent for that long, she was practically a dinosaur, or at least an old maid. Dogs, friends, and more often than not, loneliness were her companions. But it was a choice she'd made. Whatever decisions Garrett had made about his love life, it wasn't her business. Nor was it Eloise Gardner's.

But Garrett had the situation well in hand. He pointed to the chicken coop and house beyond. "Go home, Eloise. And don't you be aiming a gun at your neighbor or her dogs again, you hear me?"

"Yes, sir." She turned and headed back to her house, her steps much lighter than a woman in her eighties ought to be. "Oh, I like a man who gets bossy and says what he means. Just like my Hal used to..."

Once the older woman was out of earshot, Garrett cursed a single word, then faced Jessica again. "I wouldn't put it past Miss Eloise to wring the neck of that chicken herself and call my office as an excuse to get me out here. She's lonesome, her granddaughter's horny, and quite frankly, I feel safer on this side of the property line than I do on hers. Now, please call off your dogs, so we can talk."

"You poor man." Jessica barely masked her grin as she released the dogs. Toby and Rex scampered away to find their next adventure, but Shadow thrust his head into her hand, demanding pats, and remained by her side. "Terrorized by a lonely eighty-five-year-old woman with arthritis and heart issues. Need me to rescue you?"

He scrubbed his palm over the stubble of his jaw, and she was struck once again by how tired he looked. Okay. Not in the mood for teasing.

"I'm sorry, Garrett," she apologized. "Clearly, you're here on business. Thank you for alleviating the threat and not forcing me to lock up my dogs. Looks like it's already been a long morning for you. May I offer you a cup of coffee?"

"It's been a long twenty-four hours," he admitted. "I've already had too much coffee. Besides—" he grinned, and she pretended she didn't find this boyish, charming side of Garrett Caldwell as attractive as she did his scruffy workaholic look "—I've got a caramel macchiato for you out in my truck."

So, they *were* doing the teasing thing, after all. Jessica smiled. Apparently, he'd stopped at the coffee shop in town. Occasionally, she'd met him there when their schedules allowed, and he knew her weakness. "Are you trying to bribe me?"

"If I have to. I'm asking for your help."

"Oh." The seriousness of his tone ended the friendly banter they usually shared before it ever got started. "Did you or one of your team pick up another stray? Is the shelter full?" She'd helped the sheriff's department several times in the past, rounding up strays and housing them for a few days until she found a safe shelter where they could be housed in Kansas City or one of the nearby small towns—if she didn't have the time or space to take on a new project herself. "I've got a client here right now I need to finish with, but I can drive into Lone Jack after that if you need me."

"I've got human problems this time."

Jessica tilted her gaze up to Garrett's, analyzing what had stamped his handsome features with such fatigue. The mask of charm he'd used with Eloise had vanished. "Did you sleep at all last night? Are you working a case?"

Instead of answering her questions, he asked her one. "Are you pressing charges against Eloise? She did threaten you with a gun—even if it wasn't loaded."

"No. I know she's had a hard time of it since her husband died. I knew her daughter, Misty—Isla's mother—from spending summers here with Gran and Papa. But I haven't seen her once in the three years since I moved here and started transforming the property from a working farm into a rescue operation and training center."

"Yeah, Misty followed a man to Montana— or maybe it was Wyoming. Eloise doesn't talk about her. I don't think that was an amicable parting." Garrett shrugged. "Isla's no help. She can't keep a job or a man. And I know for a fact that Isla's ex-husband, and at least one of the men I've seen her hanging with at the bar in town, have rap sheets. Drugs. Drunk and Disorderlies. Burglary and theft."

"Wow." Jessica hadn't realized just how dangerous some of the people in Eloise Gardner's world could be. "No wonder her reaction was to call you and protect herself with a gun. Do you think either of those men, or even Isla, are a threat to her? I know she has some money from her husband's life insurance. She has the spirit of a cantankerous old woman, but she's fragile."

"I know. It worries me, too." Garrett tugged off his ball cap and combed his fingers through the salt-and-pepper spikes of his short hair, leaving a rumpled mess in their wake. Jessica curled her fingers into her palms, surprised by the urge to smooth it back into place. She and Garrett were friends, nothing more. Occasional coworkers who shared a love for caffeine and canines. A widow and a widower who were perfectly content to live out their days without the stress and complications of forging a new relationship. "I was half hoping she was fending off Isla's boyfriend with her shotgun instead of you. I need something to explain the weird things happening around here."

"Weird?" Jessica's hand instinctively moved to Shadow's warm fur. "What do you mean?"

Garrett settled his cap back on top of his head. "The reason I got here so quickly was because I was checking out a vandalism call at the Russells' summer cabin. Someone cut a screen and broke a window. Rifled through the medicine cabinet. Looks like they might have stolen a couple of small items. Didn't touch the TV, though. Probably couldn't get it out through the window."

Jessica drifted half a step closer to Garrett, her body subconsciously responding to the concern she felt for him, even though her brain wouldn't allow her to touch him. "On the other side of the Gardner farm? You think that's related to the dead chicken and broken fence?"

"I don't know. But I don't like a mystery. Too many little incidents like this start adding up, and they become something big. *Something big* is the call I don't want to answer."

Had he been working these *little incidents* all night? She wasn't naive enough to think she'd left serious crime behind her in Kansas City. But Garrett's suspicions made her nervous that something more dangerous than a frightened old woman and a spate of vandalism might be lurking in the hills, forests and farmland around her. "What do you think is going on?"

"Could be vagrants looking for food or a place to sleep. The weather is warming up and we've had a few hitchhikers out on the highway trying to leave the city. Could be bored teenagers entertaining themselves by causing trouble." He shook his head, clearly frustrated by his lack of answers. "My gut tells me it's something bigger. Maybe these petty crimes are a distraction to keep me and my officers busy with calls, so we don't see a bigger threat happening. Someone could be casing the area to plan a bigger score, or they're setting up a drug trafficking route, or they're clearing a path to move stolen goods in or out of Kansas City." He pulled off his cap again and scrubbed his fingers through his short hair. "I just pray there's not something I'm missing because I've lost a few hours of sleep."

This time Jessica did reach for him. She wound her fingers around his wrist and pulled his hand from his hair, stilling the rough outlet for his frustration. His muscles tensed beneath her touch, and she quickly pulled away from the heat of his skin that singed her fingertips. But she didn't back away from her support. "Garrett, you've been with the sheriff's department for twenty-some years. You're captain of your own division." Even without the badge on his chest and the extra bars on his collar, the man exuded wisdom and experience—and the ability to get the job done. "You'll figure it out."

"I don't want anyone taking advantage of that old woman out here by herself. Or you." He glanced back at Mrs. Gardner's place, where he'd parked his truck. "In fact,

I brought the coffee as an excuse to get you to sit down and talk to me about Soren Hauck. He and a buddy of his skipped a couple of days of school this week."

"You don't have to bribe me to have a conversation." Jessica considered the teenager who worked for her two evenings a week and on Saturdays. She'd convinced him to pull his long reddish-brown hair back into a ponytail for safety reasons, but wished he'd trade his fancy high-top athletic shoes for a pair of solid work boots. But if he didn't mind getting them dirty, she couldn't really complain. "I don't know if I can tell you anything. I haven't had any issue with Soren not showing up for work. He's good with my dogs. But he's only part-time. I don't see him every day like I do his grandfather." Hugo Hauck had once farmed the land on the other side of Jessica's property. But now that his son—Soren's father—had taken over, the retired farmer had hired on as her part-time handyman, milking her female goat for her each morning and keeping the facilities running smoothly. "Hugo has worked for me since almost the beginning. He's the one who asked if I could take his grandson on part-time when he turned sixteen. Soren got his own car and needs gas money. Plus, whatever else teenage boys need."

Garrett nodded, probably expecting an answer like that. "I wish I could get Miss Eloise to take as much interest in Hugo Hauck as she does in me."

Jessica couldn't help the chuckle that escaped. "Matchmaking, Deputy Caldwell?"

"Trying to get her to focus on any other man besides me. Just because I'm single, it doesn't mean I'm available."

Not available? The most interesting man she'd met since her own husband had died was off the market? Jessica silently cursed the flash of disappointment she felt at his pronouncement. Garrett Caldwell was seasoned like a fine wine. He was fit and masculine, unafraid to take charge and be the boss. She'd learned to be strong and independent since her husband's murder twelve years earlier. And while she was compassionate and patient with clients and neighbors, she didn't suffer fools or cheats or charmers who had no substance to back up their clever words. Garrett Caldwell was all about substance. She might be attracted to a man who could go toe to toe with her, but that didn't mean she wanted to lay claim to one. She needed a friend more than she needed a lover. The county needed a deputy and protector more than she needed a mate. Still, that lonesome kernel of feminine longing that wished for the life she'd lost asked, "Are you seeing someone?"

Garrett held her gaze for several moments. But just when her lips parted to question the intensity of that stare, he answered. "No. But when I do get involved with a woman, it won't be Isla Gardner."

Why did that sound like a promise? And why did all that unabashed male intensity focused on her make her breath stutter in her chest? Resolutely shaking off the little frissons of interest that made her uncomfortable with the personal turn to their conversation, Jessica brushed a strand of hair off her face and tucked it into the base of her ponytail at the back of her head. "Get things settled with Miss Eloise, while I finish up with my client." She thumbed over her shoulder as she backed toward the trees. "I'll meet you on my front porch in about twenty minutes."

He touched the brim of his cap and turned to the fence to pick up the gun. "It's a date."

His words made her realize that touching him and laughing with him and thinking about his sex life had blurred the line of friendship she wanted to keep between them. She needed to get back to her comfort zone. "Not a date, Garrett. We're two friends of a certain age who like to share a cup of morning coffee."

"A certain age?" He grunted at the terminology. "How old do you think I am?"

"Old enough to turn Miss Eloise's head, apparently," she teased. Because friends teased each other.

"You're only four years younger than me, Jessie. So, you watch who you're calling old," he taunted right back. "I think I've got a lot of good years left, even if you don't."

"You sure know how to flatter a girl."

Something snapped inside her head, and the present blurred into the past.

"You sure know how to flatter a girl." Jessica pouted and tugged her hand from her husband's. "I'm eight months pregnant with the seed you planted there, big fella. Saying goodbye to me and my 'big baby belly' makes me sound like a beached whale."

John stopped in the foyer and turned, leaning in to press his lips against that pout. He kissed the tension from her mouth and kept kissing her until her fingers were curling into the lapels of his suit and she was stretching up on her toes to drink in the love and passion of his plundering lips.

When he ended the kiss and she sank back onto her heels, they were both slightly breathless. "What I meant to say was goodbye, my love. Have a good day at work. And..." He knelt in front of her, gently cradling her distended belly and pressing a kiss to the visible tremors they could see at the front of her dress where the baby was kicking. "Goodbye to the strong boy my lovely wife is carrying so beautifully for us."

Jessica cradled the back of John's head and smiled in utter contentment as he crooned love words to the infant she carried. "Much better, Counselor."

John was smiling as he picked up his briefcase and reached for the front door. "Remember to stay off your feet as much as you can today. You're in the office all day, right?" When she nodded, he pressed one last kiss to her lips. "I'll pick up some lunch for us when I'm done with this morning's hearings. Noon work for you?"

"Sounds perfect." He pulled the door open, and Jessica followed to catch it. "I'll see you..."

John had stopped. "What are you...?"

He shoved her back inside at the same time she saw the rumpled, wild-eyed man pointing a gun at John's head.

"You took everything from me! You lousy divorce lawyer!"

The explosion of the gunshot jolted through her.

Zeus heard the commotion and charged from the kitchen, barking a vicious warning.

Something warm and sticky splattered on her face. John crumpled to the porch.

Then the wild-eyed man's eyes met hers.

Run.

"Jessie!"

Strong hands clasped her shoulders and she startled, shaking off the unfamiliar touch.

"Easy. I've got you." A man's face swam in front of hers, and she put up her hands to ward him off. Until his green eyes came into focus, and she read the concern there.

John's eyes were blue.

The wild eyes were brown.

"Garrett?" She patted him on the chest, obliquely wondering why it was so hard. She breathed in deeply, silently cursing the cruel tricks her mind could play on her, even after all this time. "I'm okay." She took another breath, then another, pulling herself squarely

back into the present. Then she felt a warm
paw pressing against her thigh, and she collapsed to the ground to wrap her arms around
Shadow's neck and bury her nose in his fur.
"I'm okay. Mama's okay. You haven't had
to do that for a while, have you, boy. Good
Shadow."

"Good boy." Garrett went down on one
knee in front of her, running his hand along
Shadow's back, comforting the dog when Jessica wouldn't let him comfort her. "Where'd
you go? I said your name three times."

"Sorry."

"Don't apologize." Garrett pulled back as
she embraced her dog. "The flashbacks suck,
don't they?"

"I haven't had one in a long time. But they're
still there, every now and then." She forced her
nose out of Shadow's fur and looked at Garrett. "You have post-traumatic stress, too?"

"I wasn't a choirboy in the Army." His face
creased with a wry smile that never reached
his eyes. "A good ol' country boy like me who
grew up hunting? I was a sniper."

Jessica's stomach clenched, imagining the
violence he must have dealt with fighting a
war. "I'm sorry, Garrett. You must have seen

some awful things. Done some things you aren't even allowed to talk about."

"It was a while ago. I've talked to a therapist. The military is getting better about helping their soldiers cope with what we have to deal with." He threaded his fingers into Shadow's fur again, and the dog lay down, now panting contentedly between them. "What about you?"

"Talk to a therapist?" She nodded. "She was the one who recommended I get a dog ten years ago. So, I wouldn't be alone on the nights I couldn't sleep, when the memories tried to take over."

"Shadow's your lifeline," Garrett speculated.

She smiled at her beloved companion. "I didn't initially train him to put his paw on me to wake me up or pull me back to the present. But he was a natural. Dogs are so empathetic. They pick up on emotions—happiness, excitement, anger, distress."

"And your success with Shadow inspired you to start K-9 Ranch—to rescue dogs and help others who need a friend."

Jessica could feel her heart rate slowing down, the nightmare receding and her thoughts clearing. Part of her recovery was due to Shadow's warmth and support, but she suspected part of her ability to breathe more easily was due to Garrett's calm, deep-pitched voice and the quiet conversation they were sharing. "Gave me a purpose. A reason to stop grieving around the clock and get up in the morning."

"Do you know what set it off this time?" he asked.

Uh-uh. Now that she had the nightmare under control, she wasn't dredging it up again. How did she explain the perfect storm of Eloise's gun, the feelings for Garrett she refused to acknowledge, and the innocent phrase that had been some of the last words she'd spoken to her husband, anyway? Jessica pushed to her feet. "You'd better go. I don't want Eloise on my front step like Almira Gulch with a basket trying to take Toto away from Dorothy."

Garrett straightened as well, his shoulders blocking the morning sun, he was standing so close. "Are you all right? Should I call someone?"

"There's no one to call." Shadow stood beside her, leaning against her leg so that she could continue to stroke the warmth of his head "I have everything I need right here."

"You can call *me*. Anytime."

"You're not on duty 24/7."

He reached down to scratch around Shadow's ears, but angled his gaze up to hers. "No. But I am your friend 24/7. Call whenever you need me."

Jessica covered his hand where it rested on Shadow's shoulder. "Only if you promise to do the same. Like when you pull an all-nighter and need a break from interviewing victims and suspects, and analyzing crime scenes." She quickly stepped away the moment she felt her body's desire to move *toward* him. "I need to get back to my client, Mollie. Right now, she's afraid of everything and everybody. Including the dog she wants to adopt."

Garrett inhaled a deep breath, his posture and tone shifting into deputy mode. "Afraid? Anything I need to know about?"

Like he needed to take one more burden onto his broad shoulders this morning. Besides, she truly hadn't seen any evidence of a threat to Mollie beyond the woman's own skittish behavior. Jessica shrugged. "She drives out from Kansas City. Divorced from an abusive ex. As far as I know, she dumped him and she's trying to move on with her life."

"Does her situation trigger you?"

"No. My husband was never violent with me. John was a good man."

"She have a restraining order out on him?"

Jessica nodded. "Mollie showed me his picture. But I've never seen him in person. If I find out anything that's concerning, I'll let you know. Otherwise, I want her to trust in me. And in Magnus."

"The deaf dog?"

She was much more comfortable talking about work. "Only in one ear. He makes up for it with the other. And killer eyesight. I'm teaching them to rely on hand signals more than verbal commands. But it's a process."

Garrett crossed back to the fence to retrieve the empty shotgun. "Maybe I will run prints on this fence and the chicken coop, see if I can get a match to the break-in at the Russells' cabin. Just to rule out a trespasser who might be following your client. Let me know if whoever is scaring her shows up out here. Lock yourself and Mollie in the house with the dogs if you see her ex. Stay away from the windows and call me."

"I will."

He glanced back across the fence. "Wish me luck. If Isla is there already, I may be calling for backup."

Jessica appreciated that he could make her laugh, especially after her mini meltdown. She suspected the man could handle himself in any situation. But he was too much of a gentleman to be downright cruel to her needy neighbor. "Good luck. Figure out your mystery. Then bring me my caramelly coffee, and we'll talk more about Soren."

He paused with one hand on the fence's top railing. "You're sure you're okay?"

"I will be."

He touched the brim of his cap, then vaulted over the fence again.

Jessica watched him stride away. The man had a nice ass to go along with those broad shoulders. And he always got her coffee order right when he stopped by the ranch.

She could see why the Gardner ladies had the hots for him.

And why she had to keep her guard up around his take-charge strength and surprisingly gentle compassion. She couldn't do a relationship again. Not even with a good man like Garrett. She'd had love. She'd been growing her family. She'd planned a future. And every last bit of it had been violently taken from her.

She was a survivor.

She could live her life. Be useful. Find joy and a purpose with her dogs.

But she wasn't strong enough to love and lose again.

Chapter Three

"Come on, Shadow." Jessica patted the rangy dog's flank and headed through the trees back to the house.

She needed to think about why the flashback had hit her in the middle of her conversation with Garrett. She'd been doing so well for such a long time that it was disconcerting to find out how her mind could unexpectedly and painfully snap her back to the past. She was supposed to be fine on her own. She *was* fine on her own. She had coping skills that should have defused the waking nightmare long before it sucked her in. Instead, she'd been blindsided by the memories, and now she felt raw and vulnerable.

And worse, Garrett, a man she called her friend and whom she admired, had seen her lose it.

She needed to clear her head and focus on

something else, so that she could look at the situation objectively and come up with a plan to identify the trigger and neutralize its effect on her. She thought she'd gotten past the sight of a gun triggering her PTSD, and certainly, once Garrett confirmed the shotgun wasn't loaded, she hadn't viewed Eloise as a threat. An annoyance, maybe—someone she worried about—but not a threat. And, of course, she'd uttered the same phrase to Garrett that she had to John all those years ago, just before his client's ex had ended his life. There had to be something more working on her. Was there something pricking at her subconscious? Some detail in her life that her eyes missed, but her mind was subtly aware of? Was there something about her world she wasn't able to control? It had been a few years since she'd had regular sessions with her therapist. Maybe it was time to give her a call to do a follow-up wellness check, just to make sure she wasn't regressing.

With that much of a plan in mind, she crossed the driveway that led up to the house. Walking past the kennels and training corral, Jessica petted the dogs who ran up to her, looking for Mollie and Magnus. "Mollie?"

Soren was at school—at least he should

be—and Hugo would have already shooed the goats out into their pasture and was probably running errands since she didn't see his truck parked in its usual spot beside the barn. Maybe she should offer Hugo's services to Eloise. See if her neighbors could distract each other long enough to get them out of Garrett's hair and create a peaceful coexistence for her, as well. She'd offer to pay him to repair Eloise's fence and chicken coop.

"Jessica?" The dark-haired woman hurried out of the barn. Magnus jogged along beside her, a faded red KONG wedged squarely in his jaw. Good. Mollie had taken her advice and had been playing with her dog. "I didn't know whether to come and find you or wait until you got back."

"Why?" Worried that the young woman's flushed cheeks meant something more than running around in the fresh air with her dog, she reached out and squeezed Mollie's hand. "Is something wrong?"

Mollie tugged her into step beside her. "I think you've had a break-in."

"What?" Three properties in a row that had all had some kind of trespasser? What was going on around here? "Show me."

Jessica moved ahead of Mollie into the

cooler air of the barn. Other than the goats, who stayed inside each night, and a box secluded in a stall where an Australian shepherd stray had given birth to a litter of mixed-breed puppies a few weeks ago, the barn was used for storage and a sheltered training facility when the weather outside wasn't ideal. Under her direction, Hugo and his grandson had enclosed two of the stalls and added a concrete floor to secure Hugo's tools and have a place to store the donations of food and supplies she often received.

The Australian shepherd raised her head when the women walked past with Shadow and Magnus. "Hey, mama. You okay?" Some of the straw in their stall had been squashed, though that could just have been Hugo taking in fresh food and water for the dog. A quick check showed they were all safe. The pups were either nursing or sleeping. "Good girl."

Walking to the far end of the barn, Jessica could see the damage that had been done. The door to the first storage room was shut tight, with the padlock secured through the latch. But the door to the second storage room stood slightly ajar. The padlock was still secured through its steel loop. But the hinge that secured the latch to the doorframe was bent and hanging by a single screw, and there were gouges in the wood around the lock, as if someone had taken a rock or hammer to it when they couldn't get the padlock open.

"It was like this when you came in?" Jessica asked.

"Not exactly," Mollie answered. "I unlocked this room to get Magnus's toy." She touched the first door. "But as soon as he realized this was where his KONG was stored, he got excited. He jumped up and scratched at the wood. He must have jostled the frame. The latch fell off, and the door drifted open. Then I saw the mess inside."

"It looks as though someone tried to make it look like it hadn't been disturbed. But he lacked either the tools or the time to do so."

"I didn't touch anything. I know the police don't like it when you do. In case you want to report it." Mollie pointed to the barn's open archway. "I took Magnus outside to play so that he wouldn't accidentally do more damage and waited for you to take a look at it."

"Good thinking." Jessica put the dogs into a stay and told Mollie to keep hold of Magnus's leash. Then she pulled her sleeve down over her fingers and nudged the door open.

A creepy sense of violation ran its chilly

fingers down her spine as she surveyed the room. Everything was askew on one of the metal shelves inside, as if some critter had run along the back and knocked things out of place. A glass mason jar where she stored treats lay shattered on the floor. And while she was certain it had been full, most of the treats were gone. She spotted a torn bag of dog food with kibble spilling out. Old blankets that had once been neatly stacked were now piled haphazardly on the floor. There was a depression in the middle, as though the careless critter had made a nest there. And one of the blankets—probably the oldest and rattiest one of all—was missing. Who would steal a holey blanket but leave the old radio/CD player on the worktable untouched? She supposed a possum or rat could have gotten in by crawling through a gap in the siding below the barn's outer wall. It wouldn't be the first time a wild animal had helped itself to her supply of dog food. A raccoon would have the dexterity to pad its nest with the blankets, but that explanation didn't quite make sense, either.

Jessica made several quick mental notes of all that was damaged or missing before backing out. She shooed the curious dogs away from the door and reached for the cell phone in her back pocket. She bypassed calling 9-1-1 and pulled up the number of the man she knew was already working the case.

Jessica hated to dump anything more on Garrett Caldwell's plate today. But she had a feeling he'd want to know that her place had been included in his weird crime spree.

First, a busted fence abutting her land, and now a broken hinge and a ransacked storage room? Someone seemed to be making their way through all the properties south of 40 Highway, heading east out of the city. There was definitely a spate of petty crimes moving through the county. Although, unless she counted the chicken, there was no murder, assault or other violent crime. Was Garrett right? Maybe Soren and his truant friend had been messing around last night. Could all these little incidents be indicative of something sinister going on? Were they a prelude to something more threatening about to happen?

"Deputy Caldwell." Even as she felt guilty about reporting yet another incident of vandalism, Jessica warmed to the sound of his voice, and the wary trepidation she felt eased to a manageable level. He must have recognized her number or name on his phone. "Jessie?"

"Are you still coming over?"

"I'm headed to my truck now."

"Good. I have something to show you."

She heard his weary sigh. "Why don't I think that means you baked a batch of your peanut butter cookies to go with our coffee?"

"Sorry. Your mystery just expanded into my barn."

His powerful truck engine roared to life in the background. "I'm on my way."

Jessica tucked her phone back into her pocket. She wanted these break-ins solved, too, now that it had come to her K-9 Ranch. Even without Garrett's instincts and experience to suggest it, she had a feeling there was something bigger and more threatening lurking in the fringes of her world.

Twelve years ago, she hadn't known just how dangerous the world could be. Now she couldn't help but think the worst.

She wanted to believe that whatever had gotten into the storage room and made that little nest wasn't human.

But only a human would need to break the lock to get inside.

GARRETT HAD NEVER been so glad to get a phone call reporting a break-in in his whole career. Jessie's message was the excuse he needed to finally extricate himself from Eloise Gardner's machinations and enlist one of his officers to take over for him at the Gardner farm.

Eloise had indeed forgotten her heart medications that morning, so he'd sat at the kitchen table with her and watched her take the pills and check her blood pressure before jotting down notes about her morning. A quick inspection of her chicken coop revealed that nothing had chewed through anything. Yes, the gate to the yard had been forced open, and there was evidence that the chickens had scattered, then been chased back in—minus Doris, of course.

But the gate had been tied shut with a chunk of faded red yarn. Garrett knew Jessie had trained her dogs to do a number of amazing things. But not one of them had grown opposable thumbs and the ability to tie a knot.

Isla seemed to have forgotten the grocery list Eloise had given her, and when Eloise told him she'd given Isla her debit card to purchase the groceries, Garrett had immediately called to make sure she wasn't spending her grandmother's money on clothes or partying or her latest boyfriend. His instincts had proved to be sadly accurate when he heard a man's voice yelling at Isla to get off the phone and get her butt out of the car to get the cash they needed from the ATM. Not that the conversation he'd overheard was proof enough to stand up in court—maybe they were using cash for the groceries. But it was reason enough to dispatch a second officer to the bank to get a better idea of what might be going on. At least, he could get a possible ID on the shady boyfriend. Taking advantage of an elderly citizen was one of Garrett's pet peeves, and something he was always willing to investigate.

But he had a bigger case he needed to focus on right now. And he could guarantee that Officer Maya Hernandez wouldn't have to fend off Eloise's repeated attempts to get a man to stay for dinner and married off to her granddaughter.

Plus, he was worried by Jessie's news that something odd had happened at her place, too, last night.

Garrett dashed out to his truck and started the engine. He barely resisted turning on the lights and siren. He raised his hand in a quick wave to Officer Hernandez as he barreled past her down Eloise's gravel drive.

Jessie needed him. And, even if it was just the badge she needed right now, that spoke to every protective male instinct in him. That was the problem. Jessie Bennington was stubborn and independent in a way his Hayley had never been. In the years since they'd met over a call to round up a stray that had gotten trapped in a condemned building, he'd learned that Jessie was smart and funny and caring. But the moment things seemed to get too personal, she threw up walls and attitude as if she had something raw and vulnerable inside that she needed to protect.

The hell of it was that, after witnessing her panic attack this morning, he suspected she was protecting herself from something horrific. He wanted in behind those walls so that he could help keep her safe from whatever that horror might be.

Garrett understood that she didn't want to be taken care of. His late wife, Hayley, had been sick with cancer on and off for so long that it had become second nature to be more caretaker and companion than equal partner or certainly lover. It had been his honor and duty to leave the Army and be there for the woman who had owned his heart since they'd been high school sweethearts. But it had also been emotionally exhausting. He'd grieved, thrown himself into his work, first on the department's special teams unit, and then as a senior deputy. Eventually he'd been ready to move on, had given dating a few tries, and run into more Isla Gardners than anyone he'd actually consider diving into a long-term relationship with.

Then Jessica Bennington inherited her grandparents' farm and had become part of his world.

Jessie had shown him how attractive a different kind of woman could be. Mature sensibilities. Strong. Driven. Funny. Sexy without even trying with that long gorgeous silvery-blond hair and trim figure. He wanted to mean something to her. She might not need or want a caretaker, but she could certainly use a partner, couldn't she? Yet, waiting for her to reach the same decision he had already reached required the patience of a saint. Garrett liked to think of himself as one of the good guys, but he was no saint.

Whether or not she ever decided to give him a shot, or clung tightly to her friends-only rule, he'd worry about her anyway. He knew a little about her past—her husband had been killed in a home invasion, and she'd been wounded. Certainly, that was trauma enough to stick with anyone. But he hadn't witnessed her have a flashback before. The sheer terror in her pale features had made him want to wrap her up in his arms and carry her far away from whatever nightmare had seized her.

If whatever she wanted him to see on her property had triggered even an nth of the fear he'd witnessed this morning, he was going to go alpha male on somebody's ass. And probably pay the price when Jessie told him to back off and do his job—that she didn't need or want a protector to rescue her.

Caring about Jessie Bennington was an exercise in patience and frustration.

Deep breaths, Caldwell. He mentally calmed himself the same way he had before making a kill shot or taking down a perp like he had during his years as a sniper. Tamping down his emotions and slipping on the mantle of Deputy Garrett Caldwell, he slowed his truck and rolled up to Jessie's house without spitting up too much gravel.

Jessie waved to him from the barn, and he climbed down from his truck and strode toward her and the woman with curly dark hair standing beside her. The younger woman had a white-knuckled grip around the leash hooked up to the Belgian Malinois sitting beside her.

Garrett shortened his stride and slowed his pace. Jessie's client must have a thing about men in uniform—or men, period. He recognized the nervous look of an abused woman and wondered who had put that wariness in her eyes. She was another rescue project of Jessie's, no doubt. He did what he could to help ease the young woman's anxiety by moving closer to Jessie and taking off his cap to make a polite introduction. He scrubbed his fingers through his spiky hair, suspecting he was making more of a mess rather than straightening his appearance. "Jessie." She nodded in greeting. "You've had a break-in here, too?"

"Mollie discovered it. She volunteered to stay in case you have any questions for her." That had been a big ask, judging by the woman's reluctance to make eye contact with him. "This is Garrett Caldwell. Mollie Crane," she introduced. "He's a friend as well as a captain in the sheriff's department. You can trust him. I do."

Friend. Trust.

He was grateful for Jessie's words and vowed to make sure he lived up to that faith in him. Anything else between them could come later—if she ever gave him the chance.

Garrett extended his hand. "Ms. Crane. Nice to meet you. Sorry it's under these circumstances."

Slowly, the woman brought her hand up to lightly grasp his. "Nice to meet you, Deputy Caldwell."

Garrett smiled and quickly released her hand. "You want to show me what you found?"

"Magnus. Heel." Mollie tugged the flop-eared dog to his feet and led them into the barn. Garrett couldn't help but notice that she kept one hand on the dog's short fur, just like he'd often seen Jessie reach for Shadow. The dog was an anchor. A comfort. Something to focus on besides whatever trauma she was dealing with inside her head.

What Mollie Crane lacked in confidence, she more than made up for with impeccable manners and an eye for detail. Thirty minutes later, she and Magnus were driving back to Kansas City, and Garrett had a thorough report from the two women, detailing the mess in the storage room and the suspected items that were missing, including a blanket, kibble, and some dog treats.

Not exactly a million-dollar crime spree. But something weird was going on in his part of Jackson County.

By the time Garrett had snapped a few pictures with his phone, Hugo Hauck had returned, and between the three of them, they got the storage area cleaned up and had reattached the hinge, so that the door would close. While they worked, Garrett asked Hugo a few casual questions about Soren. The old man praised his grandson for his affinity in working with the dogs, but he also complained that the teen had made some new friends, and Hugo caught them drinking beer out in one of the pastures one night. He even went so far as to say that he'd smelled pot on the boy's clothing, and that his parents had laid down the law about taking away his car and other privileges if he went any further down that road.

Garrett wanted to talk to Soren himself, get a feeling if the disciplinary consequences had been enough to scare him away from his experimental behavior—or if he and his friends had simply gone underground and gotten sneakier about their vices. Maybe by breaking into a deserted cabin to party? Or engaging in other criminal mischief while under the influence of drugs or alcohol?

It was after twelve by the time Hugo left to go home and Garrett walked Jessie back to her house. Shadow ambled up the porch steps ahead of them and curled up on the cushions of the teakwood bench near the front door.

"I'm afraid your coffee is another casualty of this morning's events. It's ice-cold by now," he apologized. He stopped on the sidewalk as Jessie climbed the front steps, ostensibly because he needed to get back to the office to type up his reports and check in on his staff—but also because he enjoyed watching Jessie's backside in the worn, fitted jeans that hugged her curves. He was due one good thing today, wasn't he? He'd had a hell of a long shift since reporting for duty yesterday morning and working through the night. He wasn't being pervy about it. Just taking note of something that gave him pleasure, and then he'd be on his way. "I need to get preliminary reports written up on all these incidents. Maybe I'll find a thread that connects them. Then, hopefully, I can take off early and get a decent night's sleep tonight." Possibly feeling ignored that he'd mentioned shut-eye instead of a meal, his stomach grumbled loudly enough that Shadow raised his head at the noise. He chuckled as he patted his flat belly. "And possibly eat."

"Possibly?" Jessie turned on the porch with

an inscrutable grin on her face. She crossed her arms and studied him for several moments before she spoke. "Do you have plans for lunch?"

"You doing okay?" He frowned at the unexpected invitation. Was she worried about staying alone at the ranch after her break-in? "Need me to stay?"

She came down two steps to meet him at eye level. "Are *you* doing okay? When was the last time you ate or slept?"

"I grabbed a Danish when I got our coffee."

Garrett wasn't exactly sure what career she had before investing her time and money into K-9 Ranch, but he suspected it was something like corporate raider or drill sergeant, based on the stern look she gave him. "When was the last time you ate anything that had vitamins and nutrients in it?"

"I'm not one of your dogs. You don't have to feed me or pat me on the head. I'm a grown man and can take care of myself."

"Well, you're doing a piss-poor job of it this morning from the look of things. You haven't shaved." She reached out and brushed a fingertip across his jaw, and he nearly flinched as every nerve impulse in his body seemed to wake up and rush to that single point of contact. "Not that the scruffy look doesn't work on you. But I know you take pride in looking professional. You're surviving on caffeine and sugar. And the lines beside your eyes are etched more deeply when you're tired like this. I've got plenty of leftovers I can heat up, or I can fix you soup and a sandwich."

Ignoring his body's disappointment at how abrupt her touch had been, he eyed her skeptically. He was attracted to her, yes, but he cared about her well-being even more. "Does this have anything to do with what happened earlier this morning?"

"You mean my little freak-out?"

He liked that she didn't play dumb by pretending he was talking about anything other than that panic attack she'd had. "Are you trying to show me that nothing's wrong? That you're strong enough to take care of everyone else, from Mollie to Miss Eloise to me?" He zeroed in on those dove gray eyes. "When you should be taking care of yourself?"

Her chin came up, even as she hugged her arms around herself again. Yep, this woman wore invisible armor the same way he strapped on his flak vest every morning. "I'll admit that staying busy provides a distraction for me. But to quote a certain deputy—I'm *your* friend, too. 24/7. Feeding you lunch on a busy day is something friends do for each other. Besides, if you don't take care of yourself, you won't be any good to anybody. And we need you."

"We?"

"Jackson County. Your officers and staff. The Russells. Miss Eloise." Her arms shifted and tightened. "Me."

Hearing her admit that she needed him, even so reluctantly, sparked a tiny candle of hope inside him. Some of the fatigue in him eased at the idea of spending time doing something that didn't require his badge and his gun for a while. And there was a definite appeal to spending that time with Jessie. "All right. A friendly lunch sounds nice. Talking about something other than work for thirty or forty minutes sounds even nicer." A breeze picked up a wavy tendril of hair that had fallen over her cheek, and he fought the urge to catch it between his fingers and smooth it back behind her ear. When she smiled at his response, she lit up like sunshine and vibrated with an energy that touched something hard and remote inside him and reminded certain parts of his anatomy that he was far from being over the hill. "Let me call in to my staff that I'm off the clock for thirty minutes or so, then I'll come inside and wash up."

"Let yourself in when you're ready. I'll be in the kitchen getting things heated up."

Heated up? Yep. The parts were definitely working. She was talking food, and his hormones kicked in as if she was coming on to him.

Before he could embarrass himself, or her, with the interest stirring behind his zipper, Garrett tapped the radio strapped to his shoulder and called in a Code 7, indicating he was taking a break from service to eat. He got a quick status report from his office manager, made note of a couple of items to follow up on and more tasks that he could delegate to officers on staff. Talking business generally dampened any sex drive and put him in the right frame of mind to share lunch with Jessie without spooking her.

"Jessie?" Shadow greeted him at the door when he stepped inside, seeming much happier to see him now than when he'd been holding Eloise's shotgun.

"Back here. Lock the door behind you, please."

"Will do." Garrett removed his hat and hung it on a peg on the hall tree beside the stairs that led to the rooms on the second floor. Respecting her need for security, he turned the dead bolt in the front door before following Shadow through the front hallway that ran all the way back to the kitchen. He hung back in the archway of her homey gray and white kitchen, which was filled with both antiques and modern stainless steel appliances. He watched her set out bowls and pull a foil-wrapped loaf of something out of the oven. The enticing smells of whatever she was heating in the microwave made his stomach grumble again.

Jessie laughed and nodded toward the refrigerator. "There's sun tea in there. Or you can pour yourself a glass of milk or grab a bottle of water."

"May I get you a drink?"

"Tea, please. Hey, would you refill Shadow's water bowl? Last night, he left my room for a late-night snack, and I guess he knocked his feeding stand over in the dark." She smiled over at the long-haired shepherd mix who was walking in circles to find just the right spot to lie down on what Garrett suspected was one of several beds around the house. "Just toss that wet towel in the laundry room. Then sit and relax."

Jessie sliced corn bread and ladled up bowls of stew while Garrett completed his assignments. He felt himself relaxing at the normalcy of working together to complete domestic tasks. He'd been gone a lot in the early days of his marriage with training and deployments, while Hayley had run the house and taught kindergarten. But once he'd chaptered out of the Army to be with Haley those last two years, one of his favorite things was simply spending time with her—doing small jobs like these around the house while she supervised. Or sharing the work when she was strong enough to help. This felt a little like that, only different because Jessie was less fragile, and certainly more bossy than Haley had been. This felt almost date-like because they were spending some quality time together that had nothing to do with work. She trusted him enough to invite him into her space, to let him get acquainted with her routine. This time meant everything to him because he knew better than to take any moment for granted when it came to being with someone he cared about.

He reached for the faucet on the sink and his shoulder accidentally brushed against hers. When Jessie scuttled away from the unexpected contact, Garrett frowned and pur-posely moved some space between them.

That subtle revelation of discomfort be-neath Jessie's welcoming facade erased his pensive smile and reminded him that this was neither a date nor domestic bliss, and that she seemed almost desperate to keep him at arm's length even though she was the one who'd in-vited him here. He circled around the kitchen island instead of taking the shorter route to Shadow's bed and feeding stand and set the water bowl on its rack.

He waited while she carried their plates to the antique oak farm table, keeping the width of one of the ladder back chairs be-tween them. "Maybe while we're eating, you could explain a little bit about your flashback this morning."

She swung her gaze up to his. "Garrett—"

"I don't want to be the thing that triggers you. Whether it's the gun or my size or my gender, I want to know so I can avoid mak-ing things worse for you."

She reached across the chair to touch his forearm, her fingers sliding against the eagle inked there. So, she wasn't averse to touching him. But she wanted to control how it hap-pened. Her skin warmed his, and his nerve endings woke with eager possibilities again. Still holding his gaze with a wry smile, she pressed her fingertips into the muscle there. "You don't make things worse for me. And I'd never want you to stop being the man you are." With one final squeeze, she released him and pulled out the chair opposite his. "To be honest, I'm not sure what set me off this morning. Probably a combination of things. Or something subconscious that I'm not aware of. If you don't mind, I wouldn't mind talking it through with someone."

"I don't mind." He pushed in her chair for her before taking his seat.

A few minutes later, he was digging into a bowl of fragrant, hearty beef stew and a slice of corn bread slathered in butter and honey. He let her eat a healthy portion of her meal before he pushed her to share some of her story with him. "I know you've been a victim of violence. You told me your husband was shot and killed."

"Wow. When I said I wanted to talk, you jumped right to the heart of the matter."

"We can talk about the weather or the prospects for Royals baseball this year, if you prefer."

"No." Jessie set her spoon on her plate and

pushed the rest of her lunch away. "John was killed by the ex-husband of one of his clients. Lee Palmer didn't like the divorce settlement John negotiated. I think he blamed John for the whole divorce going through. When John saw what was happening, he pushed me away, right before Palmer shot him in the head."

Garrett made a mental note to look up Lee Palmer and make sure the man was sitting on death row for murdering an officer of the court. He kept his voice gentle, trying not to sound like a county deputy pushing for answers. "Did something about Miss Eloise or this rash of petty crimes trigger a flashback?"

"I don't think so. I mean, I wasn't thrilled that she was pointing a gun at us." Her gaze drifted over to the bed where Shadow was snoring. "Palmer killed our dog that day, too."

Garrett polished off the last of his corn bread, waiting for her to continue.

"Zeus, our dog at the time, went after that guy with a vengeance after Palmer shot John. He attacked him and held him at bay long enough so I could get away." He hated the clinical way she was reciting the facts, and suspected that was yet another way she coped with the trauma of that day. "I locked myself in the bathroom, called 9-1-1—although neighbors had also reported the shooting and the police were already on their way. That bastard shot him. Zeus gave his life so that I could live."

"That explains your need to rescue all of these dogs. They're like your children. You raise them well. You train them to do what your Zeus did if necessary. Make sure they all have good homes and a purpose. It's a noble way to honor his sacrifice." He leaned back against his chair, keeping the hand that had curled into a fist at her story hidden beneath the table. "Eloise pointed a gun at your dogs."

"I didn't panic when Eloise had the gun."

"You panicked when *I* had it. Shadow growled at me. *I* was a bigger threat."

She shook her head. Then she pushed to her feet and carried their plates and bowls to the sink, obviously needing a break from the heavy topic. "You always carry a gun. I'm not sure that's it, either."

As much as he wanted to believe she wasn't afraid of him, even subconsciously, he had to make sure. "What did the shooter look like?"

"Nothing like you. Shorter. Younger. Beer belly. Desperately needed a shower." He could see her dredge up the memory. She grasped the edge of the sink and squeezed her eyes shut against it. "Wild brown eyes."

Garrett beat back the urge to go to her, to take her in his arms and offer comfort. But she'd asked for a sounding board, someone to talk to, someone to help her figure this out. He was the guy who solved mysteries. That's who she needed right now. And he'd be damned if he'd be anything else but exactly what she needed.

"He was a man." Garrett suggested another possibility. "Any man threatening you could be a trigger."

"No." She came back and sat in the chair right beside him. "The guns don't help. The dogs protecting me could be part of it. But I think…my emotions…" Her eyes lost their focus. "In my head, I was losing everything that mattered all over again."

"What mattered? You lost your husband to violence. Zeus."

She pulled her hands from the tabletop and splayed her fingers over her stomach, as if she was caressing something precious. "I was eight months pregnant when I was shot. I lost the baby, our little boy. He was my last link to John, and… The damage was too severe. The surgeon removed my uterus, tubes, and ovaries. I lost the ability to ever have children."

He bit back his curse at the injustice of this

woman being denied the child she clearly had wanted. "I don't remind you of a baby, do I?"

Her gaze snapped up to his. "Of course not."

"Do I look like your husband?" He wasn't doing a very good job of keeping the edge out of his tone. He understood violence and loss. He'd taken lives and buried loved ones. The injustice of all Jessie had suffered ate away his ability to be the impartial sounding board she'd asked for.

"John had dark hair, too. But he had more of a runner's build. Wore a suit and tie to work. You're...beefy. More..." She shook her head. "Not really."

"What was different this morning?" he pressed. "What mattered that you thought you were going to lose?"

Jessie considered his question, studied him intently. He thought he saw a glimmer of understanding darken her eyes. Then shock quickly took its place. Oh, hell. The resolve that was guarded and cautious and willing to wait for this woman crumbled into dust as he processed all she wasn't saying.

Eloise had pointed the gun at *him*, too.

"Me? Did you think you were going to lose *me*?"

She never answered because Shadow's feeding stand slammed into the end of the cabinet. "What the…?" A muffled whimpering noise and clear thumping against the cabinet pushed Jessie to her feet. Garrett followed her to the dog's bed near the back door to discover Shadow lying on his side with his legs stretched out and twitching as if he was trying to swim. "Is he having a dream? Shadow!" Jessie dropped to her knees, her hands hovering above her beloved pet as if she wasn't sure how or if she should touch him. "What's wrong?"

Garrett knelt beside her and took in the dog's drooling and small, but rapid, head movements. "Looks like he's having a seizure." Jessie placed her hand gently on the dog's flank. The fact that he didn't startle and wake to her touch confirmed his suspicion. "Has he seized before?"

"No. Is this what happened last night? I don't understand."

He'd had enough training as a medic to start asking questions. "Who's your vet?"

"Hazel Cooper-Burke."

"In KC?"

Jessie nodded without looking up. She was trying to pet the dog, but he kept jerking beneath her hands. "He's hot to the touch. I don't know what to do."

Garrett clasped her by the shoulders and pulled her to her feet. "Call Dr. Coop." Now that she'd been given a task, she nodded and pulled her phone from her jeans. Meanwhile, Garrett scooped up the shaking dog and carried him out to his truck, bed and all. Jessie grabbed her purse and followed right on his heels. "Jedediah Burke's wife?" he clarified. "I know Sergeant Burke through the KCPD K-9 unit." He nodded toward the crew cab's back door handle and Jessie pulled it open. He gently laid the large dog on the seat and scooted him over to make room for a passenger. "Get in the back. She's in a new building after that bomb took out the old one. I know where I'm going."

"I will. Thanks, Hazel. We're on our way." Jessie ended the call and juggled the items in her hands to put them away. "She says to bring him right in. It could last anywhere from thirty seconds to five minutes. It's been more than thirty seconds, hasn't it? I'm supposed to time it. She asked if he had a head injury? If he'd been hit by a car? Has he eaten anything he shouldn't? Caffeine? Chocolate? He's been with me all morning. I don't know what—"

Garrett tagged her behind the neck to stop her panicking and help her focus. His palm fit perfectly against the nape of her neck. He tunneled his fingers beneath the base of her ponytail and loosened some of the silky waves of hair, willing her to catch her breath. "Get in the back and buckle up. Comfort him. I'll get you there as fast as I can."

Jessie's gaze locked on to his. She wound her fingers around his wrist and squeezed her understanding. "Thank you for being here with me."

He leaned in and pressed a kiss to her forehead. "Nowhere else I'd rather be. Get in."

Once he closed the door behind her, Garrett climbed in behind the wheel, turned on the lights and siren, and raced toward the highway.

Chapter Four

"Idiopathic epilepsy?" Jessica stroked her fingers through Shadow's fur while Dr. Hazel Cooper-Burke finished a routine examination on the dog on the metal exam table between them. "What's that?"

Shadow lay there like the Sphinx, his head up, his tongue out and gently panting, his demeanor as relaxed as any other visit to the vet's office these past ten years. Other than a few pokes of a needle, he liked the staff here and knew there would be a treat for him at the end of the visit. His present behavior seemed so normal that Jessica found it heartbreaking to think how out of it he'd been at the house almost an hour earlier. Despite Garrett leaning against the wall behind her and Hazel being a good friend, she was reluctant to break contact with the dog who meant so much to her.

Dr. Cooper-Burke finished her exam and ruffled the fur around Shadow's ears and muzzle. "Good boy." Shadow ate up the attention before demolishing the treat Hazel rewarded him with. "Basically, it means we don't know what's causing it. With Shadow's age, we know it's not genetic epilepsy—he would have shown the symptoms long before now. I see no signs of a head injury or heat stroke. It could be a brain tumor. Something in his diet. It could be aging and cognitive decline."

Jessica frowned, frustrated that the vet couldn't give her a definitive answer. "Shadow's as smart and alert as he ever was. And nothing has changed in his diet, although, it's possible he could have gotten into something he shouldn't."

Garrett pushed away from the wall and came to stand beside her. "You think someone poisoned him?"

Jessica glanced up, sharing her explanation with both friends. "Not everyone is a fan of my dogs. Even though it's private property, I'm certified, and it's a completely licensed and vetted business."

"I'm guessing if it was intentional poisoning, he'd have vomiting or diarrhea. And he seems perfectly fine now. Plus, you might have other dogs showing symptoms." Hazel reached across Shadow's back to squeeze her hand. "Jessica, it could be as simple and heart-breaking as an end-of-life thing. A dog his size and age…"

"Shadow's dying?" The question came out almost a sob, although she already felt cried out after the fast drive into the city to the vet clinic. She immediately felt Garrett's hand at her back, its warmth seeping into her skin and short-circuiting the impulse to break down again. "There's nothing you can do?"

Hazel hastened to reassure her. "Eleven years old for a dog his size is pretty advanced. And I'm guessing life wasn't kind to him before you took him in. Look at all the gray in his muzzle. Sadly, it's the natural progression of things."

"I know." Understanding the situation logically didn't feel like much of a balm to her psyche. She pressed against Garrett's hand, reining in any pending sense of loss and kept it together so that she could understand all the necessary facts. "What does this mean for Shadow? What should I expect?"

"I can treat the symptoms. Idiopathic epilepsy isn't going to kill him, and he doesn't feel any pain while he's seizing. But it's a neurological disorder that can come with aging. It's all about his quality of life now. As long as he'll take the diazepam pill with a bite of cheese or a dog treat when he starts to seize, we'll go that route. If swallowing becomes an issue, the seizures become frequent or last longer than a few minutes, we'll switch to a larger dose through a suppository." She turned away to get the prescription bottle her vet tech had set on the counter and handed it to Jessica. "You're okay giving him the pill?"

"Of course. I have other dogs who get medications."

Hazel smiled. "I never worry about a Jess Bennington dog because I know you'll take good care of him. Let's follow up to see how things are going in another month, okay? He may not have a seizure between now and then, but if he does, give him the pill and be sure to time the length of it, then give me a call."

"I will."

"Any questions?"

Jessica leaned over to kiss the top of Shadow's head. "If this is an end-of-life thing, how long does Shadow have?"

"He's in good health, otherwise. Possibly a year. Maybe a little more or less."

Jessica wasn't quite ready to process what that meant. Shadow had brought her out of the depths of her grief and anger. He'd given her someone to love, something to trust without fail. He'd inspired the idea of K-9 Ranch, given this new version of her life a purpose. She couldn't picture what life without him would look like. But he'd given her so much over the years, she also knew she'd do whatever was necessary to make his remaining time as rich and comfortable as possible.

"Thanks, Hazel." She tucked the prescription into her shoulder bag and helped Shadow down. Then she circled around the table to hug her friend, silently thanking her for her care and kindness to both her and her patient. When she pulled away, she glanced up at Garrett. "I'm ready to go whenever you are."

He settled his hand on the small of her back again and guided her out the door. He paused to shake hands with the vet. "Thanks, Dr. Coop. Say hi to Burke for me."

"I will."

He held on to the veterinarian's hand and glanced toward the front entrance. "It's getting dark outside. Is Burke coming to pick you up? Or do you want me to wait and walk you out?"

Hazel shook the bangs of her short pixie cut hair. "Careful, Jessica. I think this one is as overprotective as my Burke is. When you've had a day as tough as this one has been, let him do his thing and take care of you. You can be strong again tomorrow."

It was on the tip of Jessica's tongue to correct her friend's perception of her relationship with Garrett. But Hazel's advice sounded pretty good right now. And she couldn't deny how much worse this life-changing news would have been without Garrett at her side. "He has been awfully good to me today."

"I suspected as much." Hazel traded one more hug before pulling away and looking up at Garrett. "Take care of my friend, okay? This is going to be tough for her."

"I'll do my best."

She scooted them toward the front door. "I'll lock up behind you. I'll be fine. Burke and Gunny both should be here in a few minutes."

At the mention of Hazel's husband and his K-9 partner, Garrett nodded and led Jessica out to the parking lot.

She was exhausted from the tension that had been vibrating through her from the moment she realized something was wrong with

Shadow. Since the dog was feeling fine now, he wanted to sit up in the back seat and stick his nose out the window of Garrett's truck. She settled into the front passenger seat, tipped her head back against the headrest, and closed her eyes. The moment he climbed in and started the engine, she rolled her head toward him and studied his rugged profile and indomitable strength. That strength had gotten her through today, just as Hazel had said, and she was grateful. "What am I going to do without Shadow? He's my...everything. I can't lose him."

He turned those handsome green eyes to her. "You're not going to find out today. Let me get you two home. We'll drive through someplace and get dinner so you don't have to cook."

When he pulled out of the parking lot, she turned her head back to look out the window. The streetlights were coming on and rush hour traffic was beginning to thin out as they drove out of the city. Hazel had stayed late after closing for her. Too many people had done too much for her today. She needed to be more self-sufficient than this. "I'm not hungry."

"Taking care of a friend goes both ways,

Jessie. You have to eat something. You need to keep your strength up so you can take care of Shadow. He'll worry about you if you don't."

The dog would worry? *Smooth, Caldwell.* She almost smiled, but that required more energy than she had at the moment. And what she *should* do wasn't the same as what she wanted. So, she took Hazel's advice to heart. "Will you stay with me for a while? I mean, eat dinner with me?"

"I have to go inside your place, anyway. Left my hat there. Clever of me, wasn't it? Made sure I had a reason to come by and see you again, whether you invited me or not?"

She knew there was a teasing response to that goofy reasoning, but she didn't seem able to do lighthearted right now. "Never mind. You've already done so much for me today, and that's after pulling an all-nighter. You need to sleep."

Garrett grumbled something in his throat, and the glimpse of humor he'd tried to cajole her with disappeared. "I'm coming to your house for dinner, Jessie. And I'm staying as long as you need me."

"As my friend." She needed to remind herself of the distinction. That she was strong and whole—well, whole enough—and didn't need a man to take care of her. But it had been a blessing to have this one around today.

"As whatever you need."

GARRETT WRAPPED UP the cheeseburger Jessie had barely touched and stuck it in the fridge in case she was hungry later. If nothing else, she could give the meat to Shadow. He had a feeling that dog was going to be spoiled rotten now that she knew he was nearing the end of his life.

He gathered up the rest of the trash from the burger joint where they'd stopped and put it in the trash can under the sink while Jessie loaded their plates into the dishwasher. At least, she'd polished off her fries and a couple of his, along with most of a chocolate milkshake. It wasn't the healthiest of meals, but it was better than trying to go to sleep with a stomach that was empty and a head that was full of worry.

Jessie had a little more color in her face than she'd had earlier. But her movements seemed strained and sluggish, as if she was sleepwalking and simply going through the motions of cleaning up after a late dinner. Not for the first time that night, she wandered over to the edge of the counter to glance down at

Shadow lying in his bed. The dog appeared to be as tired as his mistress, but he still raised his head and looked up at her. "It's all right, boy." She reached down to scratch around his ears. "I haven't forgotten. We'll go in a few minutes."

"Go? Go where?" he asked.

"Nightly rounds around the kennels. Make sure the dogs are all okay before we turn in." She propped her elbows on the counter and rested her chin in her hand, still watching Shadow as he settled back down in his bed. "Everything about him feels so normal, like he's the same old Shadow I've always known."

Garrett moved to the edge of the counter beside her and rested his elbows on the granite top. "You need him, don't you."

She nodded, and once more Garrett was struck by the urge to touch the long tendril of silvery-gold hair that hung against her cheek and brush it gently behind her ear. "He's more than a pet. More than a protector. He was my sanity when I couldn't move past losing John and the baby. My security blanket. He rescued me more than I ever rescued him."

No, what he really wanted to do was release her hair from its ponytail and comb his fingers through its long, wavy length—find out if it was as silky and voluminous as it looked once it was freed from its restraints. But he schooled his hormonal impulses and settled for butting his shoulder gently against hers. "He's a lucky dog."

She nudged his shoulder right back. "I'm a lucky mama."

He considered what she'd told him earlier about all she had lost—not just her husband and pet, but the chance to be a mother. No wonder she was gun-shy about starting a new relationship. He and Hayley had never had kids. First, he'd been gone, and then, no matter how hard they tried, they hadn't been able to get the timing right. Then she'd been sick, and there'd been no time at all. Not having kids was one of his biggest regrets. As a soldier and officer of the law, he might not be the best bet because of the inherent dangers of his job. But Hayley would have made a great mother. She was so patient and energetic with her students, and she'd taught them so much.

He glanced down at Jessie. She'd have made a wonderful mother, too. She'd be a strong role model for any daughter, a caring example for any son, and a staunch supporter for any cause or activity they might be interested in. He supposed that was why Shadow being diagnosed with idiopathic epilepsy was such a blow to her. Her dogs were her children. She raised them, took care of them, trained them, loved them. Then she sent her dogs out into the world to help others. Today she probably felt a lot like she was losing her child all over again.

Garrett reached over and pulled Jessie's hand from her chin. He splayed his larger hand against hers, then laced their fingers together—drawing her attention up to him and forging a tender connection. "I know you're exhausted. Why don't you head on up to bed, and I'll check the kennels for you before I go."

"*You're* the one who must be exhausted. The dogs are my responsibility. Besides, it will give Shadow one more time outside to do his business tonight."

He wasn't surprised that she was trying to reset the boundaries between them. But she shouldn't be surprised that he was going to fight to maintain the new closeness that had sprung up between them today. "Then let me grab my jacket from my truck and I'll come with you."

"Garrett—"

"Humor me." When she straightened up and tried to pull away, he tightened his grip and cradled her hand between both of his. "You had a shotgun pointed at you this morning. You had a PTSD episode. You shared some disturbing details about your husband's murder and got bad news about Shadow. Dr. Coop was right. I feel a little overprotective where you're concerned. I'm not going to apologize for wanting to make sure nothing else happens to you."

She did surprise him by reaching up and laying her free hand against his stubbled jaw. Such a sweet, gentle touch. And his body was crazy to absorb as many of those casual caresses as she wanted to give out. "Thank you. I'd appreciate the company. I don't particularly want to run into one of your vandals by myself out there."

Nodding at her agreement, he pulled away and went out to his truck to pull on his uniform jacket. The calendar might say it was spring, but the night air was cool and overcast. The long-range forecast called for rain and warmer temperatures that would green things up. But until the warm front came through, it felt more like autumn than spring.

Although Jessie had some outdoor lighting at the kennels and barn, he grabbed the flashlight from his glove compartment and met her and Shadow around the side of the house. At the reminder of the mini crime spree, he felt better safe than sorry about making sure they had a secure path. The dog trotted on ahead, following where his nose was taking him, yet often looking back to make sure Jessie was still in sight as they walked the length of the outbuilding that housed her rescue dogs. Garrett refilled some water bowls with a hose while she greeted each dog by name and petted them through the fencing as well as checking to make sure each latch was secure.

"You keep them all locked up at night?" he asked, rolling up the long water hose and hanging it at the end of the building.

"Except for Rex and Toby. They're trained to guard the property, and I don't worry about them running off. Although Rex likes to bunk down with the goats in the barn, instead of using his doghouse." Just then, Toby trotted out of his own doghouse and jogged up to them, his whole butt wagging with excitement at the late-night visit. "And Mr. Personality here bunks wherever it suits him. Sometimes, his doghouse. Sometimes, the front porch. Sometimes, in the barn with his big buddy. Who's my good Toby?" She petted the black Lab around his face and ears. Then, when Garrett patted his chest, the energetic dog rose up on his hind legs and braced his front paws against him so that Garrett had full access to rubbing his flanks and tummy. "I think he likes you."

"We had a hunting dog like Toby growing up. Ace was more subdued, though." He pushed the dog down and Toby trotted back to his doghouse, where he picked up a rawhide chew and lay down to enjoy his treat.

"Where'd you get that, boy?" Jessie asked, frowning. "Did you find that treat in the barn?" She turned her attention to the well-maintained red structure. "There was a shattered treat jar in the storage room. I wonder if he got in there once the door was busted open. Or if whoever broke in tossed him a treat to distract him."

Garrett heard the suspicion in her tone, but he had already turned his light toward a sign he found even more worrisome. "How many clients do you usually have out here during the day?"

"Two or three. Unless I'm having a group training session. Then it can be up to ten or twelve." She walked up behind where he had knelt to study the curving driveway and parking area. "Why?"

Shadow came up beside him and dipped his

nose to the tire track Garrett was inspecting. "What do you think, buddy? Does this look off to you?"

Shadow sat back on his haunches and raised his dark eyes to him. Garrett interpreted that as a tacit agreement to his suspicions.

"Garrett?"

He stood and pointed out what he was seeing with his flashlight. Several rows of tire tracks were imbedded in the dirt and gravel leading from the main drive to the barn. The tracks crisscrossed each other to the extent it would be hard to determine the exact course of the vehicles that had left them. But he counted at least five different tread marks, including a distinctive asymmetrical tread usually used by souped-up sports cars or off-roaders. Not something the meek Mollie Crane on a budget or an old farm truck would use. He pulled out his phone and snapped pictures of each distinctive tread. "You had company out here while we were in KC."

Jessie crossed her arms beside him. "I forgot to text Soren and let him know I was gone. He probably stopped by for his shift to feed the dogs. They're all in their kennels, and the goats are in their stall, so someone took care of them. I'll text him in the morning to confirm."

He visually followed the dusty tracks. "If this was Soren, he didn't come alone. These extra tracks weren't here when we went inside for lunch."

"I canceled my afternoon appointments before we left Hazel's office. Do you think whoever broke into the storage room came back for something else?" He could see her visibly shivering in the cool air. "Sometimes, people get lost and turn around in the driveway." She shook her head, dismissing the possible explanation, even as she said it. "But not this many vehicles in one day. And there's room to turn around by the house. They wouldn't come this far onto the property unless they were coming to see me. Or my dogs." She turned back to the kennels. "Do you think the dogs are okay?"

Garrett caught her by the elbow before she could charge back to the kennels. "You've already checked every last one of your charges for yourself. They're fine. Here. I don't know if you're spooked or you're cold. But this will help." He shrugged out of his sheriff's department jacket and wrapped it around her shoulders. "Better?"

"Probably a little of both," she admitted, offering him a weary smile as she shoved her arms into the sleeves and overlapped the front beneath her chin. "You are a furnace, my friend. Thank you."

"You're welcome." Once he was certain she wasn't on the verge of panic over her dogs again, he shined his flashlight up at the device anchored above the barn door. "Is that a security camera?"

She nodded. "I've got one that points down toward the kennels and the training yard, and one at the front gate so I can tell when company is coming."

Cameras were a good thing. Cameras might finally give him the answers he needed. "Do they record? Or are they real-time monitors?"

"They back up the live feed for twenty-four hours at a time on my computer unless I make a copy." She burrowed her fingers into Shadow's fur beside her. "I can go up to the house and pull up the feed. See if I recognize any of the vehicles."

"Mind if I come with you?" The dust had settled in these tracks, indicating whoever had made them was long gone. He could conduct a more thorough search of the grounds, but his gut was telling him he wouldn't find anything.

"Of course, not." She fell into step beside him as they headed back to the house. "You don't need to check the perimeter or follow those tracks to see where they lead?"

"No. Whatever happened out here is over and done. I'll get one of my officers to drive out and look around. Let's get you in the house."

The hairs at the nape of his neck were sticking straight out with a subconscious alert that something was very, very wrong here. He was still waiting for the big event he suspected all these little criminal hiccups were leading up to. His years as a sniper, learning the patience to lie in wait until his target appeared—and all his years of experience with the sheriff's department—kept telling him that something was about to hit the fan big-time. And the fact that several of them were centered around Jessie didn't sit well with him. He needed to stay sharp and figure out what was going on before Jessie or anyone else got hurt.

Several minutes later, they were sipping on fresh cups of decaf coffee—Jessie's doctored up with cream and sugar—and sitting in front of the computer in her office. They'd fast-forwarded through the daylight hours, getting glimpses of Mollie Crane's small car and Hugo's truck, and Garrett's heavy-duty departmental pickup. The images had gotten darker as night set in, and slightly distorted by the light above the camera.

"There's Soren." She stopped the scrolling images and pointed to the screen. The teenager was climbing out of the passenger side of a car. "I recognize his ponytail. Toby runs up to meet him. He recognizes him, so no one sounds an alarm. But that's not Soren's car."

Garrett braced his elbows on his knees and leaned forward to study the grainy image. "Can you print me a copy of that?"

"Sure."

The printer whirred in the background while Garrett squinted at the screen. "Do you recognize the driver?"

"No. Soren's late, too. He's supposed to come at five o'clock, but the sun would still be up then." She still huddled inside his jacket, apparently unable to shake the chill from outside. She took another sip of her hot drink and cradled it between her fingers. It would be so easy to drape his arm around her shoulders and share some of his body heat, or even pick her up and set her on his lap in the same chair and wrap her up against his thighs and chest. More body heat meant a warmer Jessie.

More body heat meant trouble.

"Ready to see more?" Jessie's question startled him from the decadent spiral of his thoughts.

Man, he was tired. He shoved his fingers through his hair. He couldn't even drum up the willpower to keep his lusty thoughts about Jessie buried inside where they couldn't distract him with false hope. "Yeah. I'll run that picture by Hugo, see if he recognizes his grandson's friend."

"Garrett?" He flinched as her warm hand settled on his knee. "Are you okay? We can do this tomorrow. You need your rest."

Garrett covered her hand with his before she could pull it away. Damn those gentle touches of hers. They stirred up his senses and sneaked beneath his skin, giving him a glimpse of how good a relationship between them could be. If only she felt the same connection he did. Correction, if only she'd allow herself to feel the connection they shared.

"There has to be more on this recording. I want to finish it up."

"And find answers to your mystery?"

He squeezed her hand beneath his. "Yeah.

It's hard to relax when there are loose ends bugging me like this."

He was more pleased than he should have been when she left her hand clasped in his and set down her coffee to continue scrolling through the recording.

"Stop." Garrett was the one who finally broke the connection when a dark Dodge Charger drove onto the screen. "Who's that?"

"Look at the bling on that," she pointed out unnecessarily. "No teenager can afford that car." Without asking, she was already printing out a picture of the sports car. "I have no idea who that is. Can you make out the license plate?"

He pinched the bridge of his nose and rubbed his eyes. They burned with fatigue, but if he blinked enough, they would clear, and he could study the images more closely.

"A partial. He left the souped-up tire tracks." The glare from the headlights obscured the vehicle identification and passengers inside, and when they made a U-turn and sped away, they kicked up enough dust and gravel to see only a glimpse of the generic Missouri license plate. "Hopefully, it's enough to run." He pulled out his phone and called the sheriff's station. "Caldwell here. I need you to run a partial plate for me on a Dodge Charger. Black or dark blue. Over-the-top trim and underglow lights." The officer covering the night shift took down the info. "I know it's not much. Find out what you can and get back to me. I want a BOLO out on the car. If it shows up anywhere between Kansas City and Lone Jack, I want to know about it."

"Yes, sir."

Jessie slowly scrolled the images forward while Garrett ended the call, then rewound them to the beginning of the clip. "What do they want?"

"Nothing good." Any clear view of the driver was obscured by the headlights, although he was of slighter stature than the guy who got out on the passenger side. The baggy jeans and loose jacket made Garrett think the guy was carrying a weapon. And there was no way to get a description of his face. Even with darkness falling, he wore dark glasses and a cap pulled low over his forehead. "Can you make out any identifying marks on his hat or jacket?"

She shook her head. "A sports logo, maybe. The picture on his hat could be barbells? It's not like when Soren and his friend stopped by. This guy gets out of his car, and Toby and the other dogs raise a ruckus. The moment Rex runs out of the barn to check out who's there, both men get back in and drive away."

He reached down to scratch Shadow around his ears. The dog had settled below the desk at Jessie's feet. "Thank God for your dogs. Or we probably would have had another incident."

"You think these are the same guys who broke into the Russells' cabin and terrorized Miss Eloise's chickens?"

"These guys don't look like vandals to me. And they're clearly not good ol' country boys. There's too much money in their clothes and car."

"Illegal money?"

He couldn't prove it just by studying a grainy image, but his years of experience told him the answer was yes. "Probably drugs or moving stolen goods. Or something to do with your dogs."

"Like dog fighting? I have one pit bull rescue out there, but she's not even a year old." He watched the color drain from her cheeks. "Do you think they were here to steal bait dogs?"

"We don't know anything yet." He squeezed her knee as he pushed himself upright and stretched the kinks in his back and shoulders. "Let's not go there."

She glanced over and caught him yawning behind his hand. "I'll zoom in as much as I can and print a picture for you."

"Would you copy the whole thing to a flash drive for me? I'd like to go over it again tomorrow when my eyes are fresh." He smirked. No sense hiding the truth. "Better yet, I'll have one of my officers whose eyes are twenty years younger than mine take a look at it."

"Garrett, you need to go to bed."

"Pot calling the kettle black, Ms. Bennington. You've been on a long, emotional roller-coaster ride today." He checked his watch. "Good grief. It's two in the morning."

"I don't think I'll be sleeping much tonight." She mimicked his yawn while she waited for the image to print and dug a flash drive out of her desk. "Shadow seems so normal now. Like that seizure never even happened." She inserted the data stick to copy the video file. "But now I know there's this time bomb inside his head, and it could go off at any time."

Garrett pushed to his feet and returned his chair to the kitchen table. "Dr. Cooper-Burke said it could be weeks or months before he seizes again."

"Or it could be days." Her soft gray eyes were watery with unshed tears as she followed him to the kitchen and handed over the evidence he'd requested. He was surprised at how right it felt for her to walk past his outstretched hand and line her body up against his. She curled her fingers into the front of his wrinkled uniform shirt and rested her forehead at the juncture of his neck and shoulder. "I can't lose him, Garrett."

"Honey, you're exhausted." He dropped the photos and flash drive on the table behind her and wrapped his arms around her. He wished he'd taken off his flak vest so he could feel her curves and heat pressed against him. But he wasn't about to push her away to do so. "Why don't you take him upstairs and get ready for bed. You can watch over him until you fall asleep."

She felt the barrier of protective armor between them, too, because she lightly rapped against his vest. "This isn't very conducive to cuddling, Deputy," she teased.

Garrett tightened his arms more securely around her. "Don't worry. I can still keep you warm."

"And keep the demons away?"

He pressed a kiss to her forehead. "I'll try."

Her fingers found the edge of his vest and curled beneath it. "What if Shadow has a seizure in the middle of the night? What if I'm asleep and can't help him?"

"This is going to be your new normal for a while. You'll figure it all out." When she steadied her emotions with a deep breath, he made an offer. "Would you feel better if I stayed? Kept an eye on things while you sleep?"

Strands of her silky hair caught in his beard stubble as she shook her head. "You can't stay awake two nights in a row."

"I'm not going to leave if you need me. I'm a light sleeper. If I hear something, I'll wake up." She pulled back, considering his suggestion for several seconds. When he saw the polite dismissal forming on her lips, he argued his case. "I know you've got guest rooms upstairs, or the couch is fine. I'll sleep better, too, if I'm here. That way I'll know you're safe, that you don't have any trespassers, and the horrible things I can imagine happening during the ten minutes it would take me to get to you won't keep me awake."

She reached up and threaded her fingers through the messy spikes of his hair and tried to smooth them into place. More gentle touches. This woman was so damn addictive. "Then the practical thing would be for you to stay with me tonight. That way, we can both get a good night's sleep."

"I can work with that." She pulled away entirely and wrapped his jacket more tightly around her, in lieu of his arms. He'd take that swap, knowing his jacket was going to retain some of that faint lilac scent that clung to her skin. Soap or lotion, he imagined. "Go on up and get ready for bed. I'm going to walk around the house and check things out one more time."

She motioned for Shadow to come to her side. "I'll set out a new toothbrush for you in the main bathroom upstairs. Need anything else?"

"I'm good."

"Good night, Garrett."

"Good night."

By the time he returned after securing the entire house, inside and out, and after one more call to the C shift to drive by Jessie's ranch a couple of times through the remainder of the night, he crept back upstairs to find her asleep on top of her bed, with Shadow stretched out beside her. Although she'd left a lamp on for him in the guest room across the hall, Garrett lingered a moment in her doorway, taking in the sweetly homey sight.

She'd conked out in her clothes, her hand resting on the dog's shoulder. She'd hung his jacket over the back of a chair where she'd tossed her insulated vest and kicked off her lace-up boots. But she still wore her long-sleeved T-shirt, socks, and jeans. She'd brushed her hair out in silver and gold waves that flared over the pillowcase behind her, and he felt his weary body stirring with the desire to bury his nose in those glorious waves and claim this brave, battered by life—but refusing to be beaten—woman for his own.

Needing to move away from that dream before he did anything to ruin the gentle tension that had been simmering between them all day, Garrett quickly brushed his teeth and took care of business. He stripped down to his T-shirt and pants before coming back to her doorway for one last reassurance that she was safe.

Jessie had rolled over, and in the dim light from across the hall he watched her eyes blink open into slits, then close again. "That's not sleeping," she murmured drowsily. "That's hovering in the doorway and staying awake." She stretched out her hand without raising it off the bed. "If the guest room is too far away for you to relax, stay with me."

The tension inside him settled at her invitation. "You're sure?"

"I have a feeling you won't sleep if you don't have eyes on me." She paused to cover her adorably big yawn. "This isn't a seduction, Garrett. Nothing's going to happen. There's a dog in bed with us."

"I'd like to hold you," he confessed.

"I'm okay with that." Her eyes opened fully to meet his gaze. "I'm having a hard time shaking the chill of the night outside. Or maybe it's all in my head. But I could use the body heat."

Body heat. Garrett bit back a groan. But out loud he said, "Happy to be of help."

He went back to the guest room to turn off the light and grab his gun and holster. When he returned, she'd dozed off again. He set his weapon within reach on the bedside table, then climbed in beside her.

But she wasn't as asleep as he thought. The moment his head hit the pillow, she scooted closer and snuggled into him, one arm folded between them, the other resting across his waist. She nestled her cheek against his shoulder and buried her nose at the base of his neck. He slipped his arm behind her back and held her loosely against his side. But she pulled her top leg over his thighs and slipped her toes down between his knees, wrapping herself around him as if she was using him for a body pillow. "An absolute furnace." She buried her lips and nose against his neck. "Mmm…you smell good."

"I smell like a forty-eight-hour shift and too much time in dusty barns, vet's offices, and at crime scenes."

"Mmm-hmm."

"Jessie?" This time, there was no answer. She was more asleep than awake now, and they were snuggled up as close as two people still wearing most of their clothes could get. Who knew this prickly, independent woman was such a cuddler? It was another glimpse of vulnerability he'd do his damnedest to protect. He indulged his senses by tangling his fingers through her silky hair and bringing it to his nose to breathe in her flowery scent. Then he pressed a kiss to her forehead. "Sleep, hon. I've got you." He reached across her to rest one hand on her precious Shadow. "I've got you both."

This was the closeness and contentment that was missing from his life. Sure, he wanted to find out what kind of passion was locked up behind Jessie's protective walls. He wanted to kiss her until she couldn't think of any man but him and feel her body come to life beneath his. But he wanted this, too. He needed this.

With the woman he was falling hard and fast for secure in his arms, Garrett finally surrendered to his body's bone-numbing fatigue and fell into a deep sleep.

Chapter Five

Garrett woke up feeling surprisingly refreshed, even after only a few hours of sleep. But the schedule that had been ingrained in him years ago by the military and law enforcement meant he was an early riser. Most mornings he did some kind of workout. On others, he drank his coffee and read his newspaper or reports that needed his attention.

This morning, he wanted nothing more than to linger in bed with the woman still tucked up against his side, breathing evenly in restful sleep. But an eager panting from across the bed made him suspect his morning had already been planned for him.

The moment he began to stir, Shadow raised his head from his spot on the other side of Jessie. The two males acknowledged each other. And, by mutual agreement, neither of them made a sound as Garrett extricated himself from the cheek resting on his chest and the arm curled around his waist. Shadow quietly jumped down while Garrett pulled his jacket from the chair and tucked it around Jessie since they'd slept on top of the covers. He put on his shoes, hit the john, and went downstairs with Shadow following closely on his heels.

Several minutes later, the dog was happily munching on his breakfast and Garrett was carrying two steaming mugs of coffee back up to Jessie's bedroom. He found her squinting against the sunlight that peeked around the curtains at the window. "You awake?"

Jessie stretched out the kinks in her limbs. But when she breathed in deeply, her eyes popped wide-open. "Is that coffee?"

Garrett chuckled at her hopeful response. "Yes. I thought I'd spoil you a little this morning. Helped myself, too."

"That's fine." She propped the pillows against the headboard and sat up, her cheeks pink with the anticipation flowing through her. Garrett set their mugs on the bedside table and perched on the edge of the bed facing her. Her soft smile was prettier than any sunrise. And her eyes, rested and no longer red with tears, reminded him of the moon on a cold, clear night.

When Garrett reached out to brush her hair off her cheek and tuck it behind her ear, she mimicked the caress. She combed her fingers through his hair in a hopeless attempt to tame the unruly spikes. Another smile. "It never cooperates, does it."

Her gentle touches nourished a hungry spot in his soul that, being a widowed workaholic, had gone without for too many years. "That's one reason I keep it short."

She drew her fingers down to trace his jaw and he dropped his gaze from her eyes to her soft pink lips. Her bottom lip was curved and plump, and the upper was narrow and arched. The asymmetry of her mouth was as intriguing and beautiful as the rest of her. When she scraped her palm across two days' worth of beard stubble, her nostrils flared. And when her fingertips tugged slightly against him, he closed the distance between them and covered her mouth with his.

He lost himself in the feeling of Jessie's lips surrendering beneath his. He leisurely took his fill of her little grasps and nibbles, of her angling her mouth first one way, then another as she got acquainted with his kiss. With his pulse revving up and his desire spinning out of control, he stroked his tongue along the seam of her lips, and she parted for him. Garrett delved in to fully taste her for the first time. Her tongue was still minty from brushing her teeth the night before. Although her responses were gentle, there was no shyness to the rasp of her tongue sliding against his or the tips of her fingers clinging to his face and neck.

At the tiny whimper from her throat, he captured either side of her jaw between his hands and tunneled his fingers into her hair. He tilted her head back against the basket of his hands and leaned in to claim the passion freeing itself from the tight confines of her guarded personality. No nubile, desperate young woman like Isla Gardner could hold a candle to the measured release of Jessie Bennington's passion. The cautious beginning of this embrace only made the gift of opening up and sharing herself with him that much more precious. What she demanded, he gave. What he asked for, she returned to him tenfold.

About the time Garrett became aware of the pressure swelling behind his zipper, he had the idea that patience might be a better course for this newfound closeness than laying her down on the bed and stabbing his palms against the tight points of her breasts that poked to attention through the cotton of her shirt. And about the time that thought made him ease back from her beautiful mouth, Jessie slipped her fingers between their lips and abruptly pushed him away.

"That was a nice *good morning*." His tone was embarrassingly breathless as he smiled his thanks and pleasure. "I could wake up like this every day."

Oh, hell. This was more than her coming to her senses before he could. That was panic in her eyes. Her pink, kiss-swollen lips spoke of shared passion, but her pale skin and eyes, which seemed to focus everywhere around the room except on him, sent a message of uncertainty and maybe even regret.

He rested his hand on her knee. "Jessie?" She jerked her leg away from him and hugged her knees up to her chest. Maybe she didn't understand what she'd done for him last night, that he wasn't expecting anything more from her right now. "That's the best I've slept in a long time. My body seemed to naturally relax, knowing you were here with me. I could touch you, and I didn't worry or wonder about anything. I felt…safe…with you beside me."

Her nod said she understood, maybe even felt the same way. But her words said something else. "Shadow needs to go outside." She patted the bed beside her, as if she'd just now realized the two of them were alone. "Where's Shadow?"

"He's fine. He got through the night without any issues. I already put him out. He's downstairs eating breakfast now."

"I need to check—"

"No, you don't. We've already walked the perimeter to make sure there are no new tire tracks, and I've talked with my staff. No sightings of a car matching the description of the one you caught on camera—and not enough of a plate number to positively identify the car's owner. You can talk to me for five minutes," he gently chided. "How did you sleep? Are you feeling stronger this morning?" He picked up her mug and handed it to her. "Drink your coffee before it gets cold."

"Fine. Yes." She looked down into the milky brown depths of the coffee. "Did you put cream and sugar in it?"

"Yes." That's right, he paid attention. He knew how ridiculously sweet she liked her coffee.

She set the mug back down without tasting the drink and stood to pace back and forth between the bed and the door. "You shouldn't have kissed me like that."

Garrett stayed where he was, hoping a calm voice and less intimidating silhouette would help her calm herself. "Why not? You seemed to enjoy it. I know I did."

"Of course, I did. I wouldn't have kissed you back if I felt pressured or I didn't like it. But I—"

"You shouldn't have plastered your body against mine all night and made me believe you like me." He caught her hand when she moved past him again. "We needed to hold each other last night. I'm okay with that. That kiss was just the punctuation to the need we shared."

"Garrett—"

"I know you feel the chemistry between us, too."

"No. No chemistry. We're friends. Period." She pulled her hand away and spoke firmly, as if saying it out loud made it so. At least she was making eye contact now. "Last night, I was vulnerable. I haven't been held like that for twelve years, and I needed you. Your strength. Your warmth. Just…solid you to hold on to. You helped me through a tough day, and I'm grateful. But that doesn't mean we're an item now. Just because you spent the night—"

"—in the same bed—"

"—doesn't mean we're dating. You don't even like me that way."

Garrett sprang to his feet. "The hell I don't. You think I sleep with every friend who's having a rough go of things? What do you think that kiss was about? I bring you that fancy coffee I can't stand three or four mornings a week just so I can sit on the front porch and spend time with you. I stayed with you yesterday well beyond my body's limits and the duties of my office because you needed me, and I was worried about you." She tipped her head back to hold his gaze but didn't retreat. "I. Like. You. A lot."

"Garrett—"

"I guess I don't know how you feel about me. I thought I did, but maybe I was wrong. I believed you were keeping me at arm's length to protect yourself, because you were still grieving for your husband, or you felt guilty about caring for another man, or you just don't want to risk getting hurt." Bingo. He felt her flinch like a punch to the gut. He blew out his anger and breathed in sadness, mourning the loss of what could be between them. "But don't tell me how *I* feel. I know exactly what my emotions are. How much I'm attracted to you, how I love to see your smile. How you make me laugh, how much I admire you for all you've accomplished. How much I want to kiss your beautiful mouth again. I can keep my distance for now if that's what you want. If that's what it takes for you to get comfortable with me being in your life. But make no mistake, I *am* in your life. And until you tell me you don't feel anything at all for me, I'm not going anywhere. I will never be dishonest with you. I was hoping you could do the same for me."

"Garrett, I can't… You want honesty? I lost *everything* once. And it broke me. It has taken me twelve years and a therapy dog to get to where I am now. I can't do that again." She reached out but didn't touch him. "You deserve a woman who can give you her heart and her body and a family and forever. As much as a part of me might want to be that woman—I'm not. I'm damaged goods. And I don't just mean I can't give you children."

"You're not…" But he didn't finish the argument. If that was what she believed, then he wasn't going to change her mind by arguing with her. Instead, he plowed his fingers through his hair and tried to let her know that he understood how hard it was to find and trust a new relationship later in life, especially after surviving a tragedy the way she had. "After Haley, I wasn't sure I could love again, either. My heart felt all used up. Then I met you, chasing down that stupid stray dog, and I wanted to try." She had to understand this wasn't a fling for him, that nothing he felt for her was casual. "I still want to try."

Confusion was stamped on her face as she hugged herself tightly. He wanted to take her in his arms and shield her from the stress she was obviously feeling. But he didn't. She didn't want him to, and he would respect that.

"I don't want to give you false hope. I care about you too much to want to be the woman who hurts you." Her words were painfully sincere.

"What if you're the woman who makes me happy? Hell, Jessie, I'm a patient man. But you've got to give us a chance."

She shook her head. "You're easy to love, Garrett. But that also means you *won't* be easy to lose."

Now he did reach for her. He needed the connection. He feathered his fingers into her loose waves and brushed her hair behind her ear. "You're not going to lose me."

"You wear a gun and a badge, Garrett. You

deal with violence on some level every day of your life. I'm not sure I can live with that."

Now the flashback this morning made sense. Eloise had trained her gun on *him*. Whether or not she realized it, Jessie had reacted because on some level, she already cared for him—and she'd thought she was going to lose him.

"I can't give up my job, Jess."

"I would never ask you to."

"I've got another fifteen years before they force me to retire. It'll end up being more of a desk job by then. But I love doing what I do."

"And you're good at it." She laid her hand over his where it rested against the side of her neck. "I'm not asking you to wait for me to be whole again. I may never be. I'm telling you to move on."

"No." Not an option for him. He was going to fight for them even if she couldn't. "Jessie—honey—you are stronger than you know. Look at all the people you help. Look at the animals you've helped. You run a successful business—and don't think I don't know that some of it's charitable work. Look at how far you've come. On your own."

She let go and moved away to count off perceived shortcomings on her fingers. "Flashbacks? Bawling when my dog gets sick? Screwing up the best kiss I've had in years?"

At least they were on the same page with the physical connection they shared. "You didn't screw up a damn thing. And Shadow is more than your dog. I'd be worried if you didn't lose it a little bit."

"If that's how I reacted to his diagnosis, how do you think I'm going to react if something happens to you?"

Garrett inhaled deeply. She couldn't see what was so clear to him. "You might cry. You might use a friend's shoulder to lean on. But then you'd suck it up and get on with living. You're like me in that respect. You get the job done. Because you have to. It may not be pretty. It may not be easy. But you do it. And hopefully, there's someone kind and caring and supportive around to help you do it."

Her eyes looked hopeful, although he could tell she was trying to come up with another argument to chase him out of her life. Thank goodness he wasn't some impatient young buck who moved on to the next pretty thing when the woman he really wanted proved to be a challenge. Convincing Jessie to take a chance on loving him might not be easy, but she was so worth the fight.

But he had to table the fight for now. His phone rang and her cell dinged with a text on the nightstand just a few seconds later.

He pulled his phone from his pocket and read the number. "Sorry. This is work." He crossed to the relative privacy of the guest room across the hall. "Deputy Caldwell." His morning went from bad to worse as he listened to his officer share the details about a countywide search for two missing children.

By the time he'd hung up, Jessie stood in the doorway, holding up her phone. "I got an Amber Alert." The public notice she'd received would have been brief and to the point. "Two children?"

"Yeah. Runaways from Kansas City." Garrett suited up while he talked, tucking in his black T-shirt and strapping his protective vest over his chest. Then he pulled on his uniform shirt and buttoned it as he returned to her bedroom to retrieve his belt, gun, and badge. "The whole county is on notice. No clue where they went. The father didn't report them missing until this morning."

"How long have they been missing?" Jessie followed, sounding stronger and looking less pale now that the conversation was centered on something other than him and her and the relationship she wasn't ready for. "Does your office know what happened?"

"They haven't shown up at school for three days. They alerted the father."

"Three days? And he just now reported it? Is there a mother in the picture? Did he think the children were with her?"

He shook his head. "Apparently, she died three years ago. Drug overdose. Dad has custody."

"Is there a relative? A sitter?"

He adjusted his belt at his waist and secured his holster at his hip before heading downstairs. "KCPD has checked all known connections with no luck. Official report says they got on the bus to school, but never reported to their classrooms."

"Why would they run away?"

"That's the million-dollar question. They're from a low-income neighborhood and money's tight. They're on the free meal program at school, and teachers reported that they sometimes wear clothes that they've outgrown. But they do well in their classes, and the dad is holding down a job as a delivery driver. They don't have a history of running."

"He must be out of his mind with worry." Her hands settled on her stomach and his heart wept for the baby she had lost. An incident like this was probably a nightmare trigger for her. "Do you think they were taken?"

That was every cop's worst fear. "Two children that young don't just disappear."

"I hope they're okay."

"Me, too. These are always the worst calls. Human trafficking or the death of a child? They're the hardest cases for me to handle." He grabbed his hat off the hall tree and headed to the front door. "I need to help find them."

Jessie hurried down the stairs behind him. "Do you want some breakfast before you go?"

"No."

"But I kept you up so late. You haven't even been home yet."

"I have a clean uniform at the sheriff's station. I'll shower there."

"I'm just trying to help. It's what a friend would do." She sounded a little lost. She was probably replaying every word he'd said to her and trying to figure out where she stood with him now. "I'm guessing that's not what you want from me."

He needed to get to the station to see where they stood on the search, coordinate with KCPD, and call in all available staff to help—and reassure them that even though seventy-two hours missing generally didn't bode well for the victims, they weren't giving up until they were found. The reasons why and gathering evidence as to any foul play would come later. Right now, priority one was locating the two reported runaways.

But then he remembered that as strong and tough as Jessie was on the outside, there was a vulnerable woman underneath who'd desperately needed the warmth of his body and the shelter of his arms last night. He could use a little tenderness and support right now, himself.

Garrett turned to her, snaked his hand around the back of her neck, and kissed her soundly, thoroughly, and far too quickly. He still cupped her nape gently and rested his forehead against hers. Her eyes tilted up to his, and he covered her hand resting against his chest. "I can't turn off how I feel about you, Jessie. You let me in last night, and it's hard for me to step back and pretend it never happened. But I hope you still trust me, that if you need me again, you'll call. About Shadow or Miss Eloise or late-night visitors or anything. I'll try to dial it back a notch so we can still be friends, so I can still see you and be a part of your life."

"You would do that? Even if it's only coffee on the porch in the mornings?"

"Even if it's only that. Look, I admit that I'm a workaholic. But I'm at an age where I've decided I need...want more than that." He released her to touch her hair and smooth the long waves down her back. "You're the most interesting, intriguing thing that's happened to me since Hayley died. I look forward to seeing you, discovering what we might laugh about—or argue about—next. I care about something beyond work now. I'm...*alive* again with you. I don't want to lose that."

"You are a grown, virile man. You need more than I can give you."

He shook his head. "I just need *you*. Maybe one day you'll believe it's safe to risk your heart on me. I'll keep it safe. I promise. I won't cheat. I will never lay a hand on you in anger. I'll do everything in my power to give you what you want, and more importantly, what you need." He pulled her hands from his chest and retreated a step. "But if that never happens, I want you to know that you're still safe with me. I'll still help you keep those mutts safe. I'll still be your friend."

"I don't deserve that kind of promise, Garrett."

"Yeah, you do." He lowered his head to press a quick kiss to her lips. He acknowledged the urge to claim those lips the way he had earlier, to show her exactly how good they could be together, that she was anything but *damaged goods* in his eyes. But this wasn't the right time. She wasn't ready for that. She might never be. So, he pulled away.

He put on his hat and strode out the front door. He had work to do.

GARRETT CROSSED HIS arms over his chest as he stood at the one-way mirror outside the interview room at KCPD's Fourth Precinct office. Since he was coordinating the search for the children listed as missing in this morning's Amber Alert outside the KC city limits, he'd been invited in to observe the most recent interview of the children's father, Zane Swiegert.

The guy looked understandably rough after finding out his son and daughter had disappeared. His clothes were wrinkled and stained, and he needed a shave. He'd been tearing up and his nose was running from the times he'd broken down during the interview. Although he and Hayley hadn't been blessed with children, Garrett knew he'd struggle to deal with it if someone he was responsible for—someone he loved—was harmed or taken. He thought back to yesterday when Jessie had suffered that flashback. He'd wanted to fix it for her, make whatever frightened her so go away. He was desperate to help, to protect, to take care of her. He hated feeling helpless.

Maybe Zane Swiegert felt helpless, too.

But his years in law enforcement left him feeling more suspicion than sympathy for Daddy Swiegert. The man was hiding something. Maybe it was as simple as being a lousy father and feeling guilty for losing track of his own children. Or maybe it was something more sinister.

Someone knew where those children were. Someone knew what had happened to them. Was it Swiegert?

The detectives interviewing Swiegert asked him to retrace his children's steps the morning they'd gone missing. He'd gotten them up for school and walked them out to the bus stop where they'd been picked up for school. They ate breakfast at school. Nate Swiegert was in the third grade; his younger sister, Abby, was in kindergarten. Yes, he knew the name of Nate's teacher, although he couldn't seem to come up with the name of his daughter's teacher. After school, they were supposed to walk over to a friend's apartment and stay with him until Zane got back from driving his delivery route late that night.

But none of those details were what pinged on Garrett's radar as he studied the relatively nondescript, brown-haired, blue-eyed man in his midthirties. Swiegert wore a small, bright white cast on his left hand, indicating he'd broken some fingers. Very recently. Maybe he'd punched a wall out of anger, guilt, or frustration. Or he'd been distracted and over-tired and gotten into some kind of accident— shut his hand in a car door or put it through a window. Plus, the guy was sweating. Inside an air-conditioned building on a mild spring day, he was sweating.

Swiegert seemed even hazier recounting his own movements since the last time he'd seen his son and daughter. He'd driven his route that day but didn't show up for work yester-day. He said he'd called in sick with the flu, but his supervisor never got such a call. Why didn't he pick up his children at the friend's home? Because he was sick. How did he in-jure his fingers? At work. But you didn't go to work, the detectives reminded him. Then he got angry and sobbed again. Why were the cops grilling him and not out combing the streets for Nate and Abby?

A shadow fell over Garrett, and he turned to the tall, lanky man wearing a suit and tie who stepped up beside him. "You think he's faking it?" Detective Conor Wildman looked more like an up-and-coming executive at a Fortune 500 company than a WITSEC agent turned KCPD detective. He had been the one to call Garrett in from the sheriff's office in Lee's Summit. "I know I'd be out of my mind if anything happened to my daughter or wife. But there's something else going on with this guy, if you ask me."

"The tears? The sweat?" Garrett shrugged. "I think he's in legitimate pain. Though it's not all about his kids. Either the painkillers he was given for that hand have worn off... or he's going through withdrawal."

"Then your suspicions are the same as mine. I'm guessing he was off someplace getting high when his children went missing. It took him three days to sober up and realize they were gone." Wildman handed Garrett a file folder to read. "That's Swiegert's rap sheet. Wouldn't be the first time he's used cocaine."

"Or else the drugs are how he's coping with the stress. You do a tox screen?"

"Bad PR to lean too heavily on the parent until the kids are found."

Garrett skimmed the file. Drug possession arrests. Petty crimes to support his habit. "How did that guy keep custody of his children?"

"He was clean for a while after a mandatory stint in rehab following his wife's overdose. Kept his nose clean long enough to maintain a steady job and get his kids out of the foster system."

"So, this guy is a loser who doesn't deserve those kids. But he loves them, and they love him, and he's trying as hard as he can to stay clean or at least use less. So, the State and KCPD are doing all they can to reunite them?" He handed the file back to Detective Wildman. "Why am I here to listen to his sob story? Either something happened to them three days ago, they were taken and are long gone by now, or they ran away of their own volition. In which case, they've been surviving on the streets or out in the elements. None of that is good."

"I'm not affiliated with the missing persons' case, Deputy." That piqued his interest. "I'm part of a drug task force trying to take down a major player here in KC—Kai Olivera."

Garrett nodded. "I know the name. Second-generation American gangster living the dream in the big city. Human trafficking. Drugs. Small arms smuggling. I've made traffic stops on the highway where we've intercepted a couple of his cross-country shipments. I'm sure some of our locals who like to indulge themselves have bought his product off the streets. Is Zane Swiegert a customer of his?"

"He has been on and off for a few years." Wildman turned away from the interview to face Garrett. "My intel says Swiegert is driving for him now, too. He's using his delivery job to make drops and pick up payments from Olivera's people on the streets."

This scenario just got worse and worse. "So, Daddy Dearest is a scumbag who doesn't deserve those kids when we do find them." He refused to say *if* the children were found. "Why am I here? Arrest him already, and let me get back to work."

"We think Swiegert is key to bringing down Olivera."

"He's not going to testify against his supplier and employer." Although if there was any hint that he might, it could explain the damage done to his fingers—and why he seemed more nervous about the police asking so many questions than he was worried about his kids. "You think Olivera took the kids to leverage Swiegert into keeping his mouth shut?"

"I've got an undercover operative in Olivera's organization. While Olivera isn't above recruiting underage girls into his human trafficking business, my man hasn't seen or heard of anyone as young as elementary-school-age children being lured in with the promise of drugs, family, or money."

"That's a relief. Of sorts. Still doesn't put us any closer to finding those children." Garrett knew there had to be more to this conversation than idle speculation. Conor Wildman wanted something from him. "What is this meeting really about?"

The detective glanced around before ushering Garrett out of the interview watch room and over to the empty meeting room next door. "Zane Swiegert isn't the only witness who could talk to us about Olivera's activities. My inside man has spotted Olivera and one of his lieutenants entering Zane Swiegert's apartment building on more than one occasion. While Nate and Abby were present."

Garrett swore. "The children? You want them to testify against that scumbag?"

"If Zane Swiegert thinks they have to—"

"He'd cooperate with KCPD to protect his children." Garrett shook his head. Kai Olivera might be the worst of the worst and needed to be taken down. But to ask a third grader or kindergartner to testify against him...? "That's a mighty big risk you'd be taking."

"When I say Kai Olivera is bad news, I'm being nice." Detective Wildman's flair for sarcasm was obvious. "I need someone to find those children and put them into protective custody at a safe house before we move on Olivera." Wildman pulled out a chair and sat. "A tip from the Amber Alert Hotline said two children matching Nate and Abby Swiegert's descriptions were spotted the morning they went missing getting on a public transit bus headed east out 40 Highway. Into your neck of the woods."

Public transit didn't come out as far as Lone Jack where he lived. But if they took it to the end of the line and got out, they could hike or, God forbid, hitchhike to get farther out of the city. "So KCPD is focusing their search east of the city in Jackson County."

Detective Wildman nodded. "Your jurisdiction."

Garrett pulled his ball cap from his back pocket and sat in the chair across from Wildman. "I've had a rash of break-ins and petty thefts the past three days. My money was on teenage vandals. But it could be the kids stealing supplies or finding a relatively warm spot to stay for the night."

"You looking into those?"

"I was until the Amber Alert took precedence." Maybe the string of random crimes did make sense if he put them into the right context. "Has information from the tip line gone out to the press? Would them heading east be public knowledge?"

The detective nodded. "Our information officer updates the public so they can assist with the search."

"What kind of car does Swiegert drive?"

The detective arched an eyebrow. "That's random."

"Not really."

Conor pulled up his phone and looked it up. "An old-model Ford Bronco." So not the lit-up

Dodge Charger that had shown up at Jessie's ranch yesterday evening.

"What about Olivera? Anybody in your investigation drive a shiny new Dodge Charger fitted with underglow lights?"

Conor shook his head. "But this crew gets new vehicles all the time. Part of it is because they modify them to transport their coke and pot. Once we ID one of them, that vehicle is retired and torn apart at a chop shop. And part of it is just because Olivera and his crew have got a ton of money to spend. Are you going to explain that question to me?"

Garrett scrubbed his fingers through his hair. "Just some unexplained traffic in my part of the world. We may not be the only ones looking for those kids."

"Any sign of Kai Olivera?"

"A residential security camera caught a couple of vehicles where they shouldn't be. The images weren't clear enough to make an ID." He purposely left Jessie's name out of the conversation since she valued her privacy so much. "Are you familiar with K-9 Ranch?"

"That lady who trains protection and companion dogs?" Detective Wildman nodded. "She's done some good work for victims of violent crime. Our police psychologist, Dr.

Kilpatrick, sent an officer who was struggling with PTSD to her."

"That lady is good friend of mine."

"That's where the car was sighted?"

Garrett nodded. "And you believe Swiegert is tied to Olivera?"

"I'm certain of it."

He was already on his feet and pulling out his phone to text Jessie to make sure she was okay, that there hadn't been any other unusual incidents at her place.

"Caldwell." Garrett stopped in the doorway at Detective Wildman's harsh tone. "Are we on the same page here? If you find those kids, I want to be the first person you call. Not the search team, not Family Services. I need to know they're safe and off the playing field so I can put the pressure on Swiegert and nail Olivera."

"You'll be the first call I make."

Chapter Six

Jessica looked up from the A. L. Baines fantasy novel she was reading and wondered what the dogs out in the kennels were going on about now. So much barking. She knew sometimes it was a chain reaction type of thing— one dog saw or smelled or heard something, and all the others chimed in. But after the recent break-ins and mysterious late-night visitors she'd had, she wondered if there could be something more to it.

Although, anyone who tried to break into a place with so many dogs was either stupid or seriously desperate. *Seriously desperate.* That sounded dangerous. She couldn't be amused by her dogs' doglike behavior if there was someone dangerous out there.

After slipping a bookmark between the pages, she set aside her book and woke up her laptop that she'd brought to the coffee table to pay some bills earlier. She pulled up the camera feeds outside. Nothing at the front gate. But since her phone hadn't pinged, she hadn't expected to see anything suspicious there, anyway.

She watched a couple of minutes of the camera feed from the barn. No strange cars. No Soren Hauck. No faceless strangers. But something was out there. Even with the grainy nighttime images of black and white and gray, she could make out several of her charges pawing at their gates at the front of their kennels. Rascal had his little black nose poking through the chain links, and Jasper had his big jowls pressed against his gate to get a closer look at whatever the other dogs had seen. Even her eleven-month-old pit bull, Baby, was at her gate, her whole body bouncing with every bark.

Was that…?

Jessica pulled the computer onto her lap and replayed the last few seconds. There was a ghost of movement, something darker than the rest of the shadows that darted around the corner of the kennel and disappeared into the camera's blind spot at the far end of the building. Whatever she'd seen was low to the ground, small and quick. Skunk? Raccoon?

Someone's feet? She shook her head at the fanciful reminder of the witch's feet curling up and disappearing in *The Wizard of Oz*. Her heart rate sped up a notch, but she instantly felt Shadow's head resting atop her thigh.

"I'm okay, buddy," she reassured him, and thanked him with a rub beneath his collar. "That scene in the movie always freaks me out a little bit." She tried to freeze the image, but it was just a blob of shadow among the shadows. "I don't know what that was." She sat back and watched the dogs still barking at the disturbance that seemed to have scuttled out of there, at least from this angle. "If this is going to be a thing out here, maybe I'd better invest in more cameras. I've got too many blind spots."

She was beginning to understand Garrett's frustration with an unsolved mystery. Replaying the image again, she realized that whatever had cast that shadow never appeared on screen. It was as if it had started to come around the end of the kennels, then darted back to its hidey-hole when it saw the reception of twelve dogs waiting for him. Waiting for *it*? She glanced up. Was *it* still out there? She'd locked the front and back doors, hadn't she? Jessica exhaled a deep breath, forcing herself to relax. Of course, she'd locked the doors. She kept them locked whether she was inside the house or out with the dogs, and certainly when she left the ranch. And she'd double-checked them after letting Shadow out that last time after dinner, before she'd picked up her book and laptop and curled up beneath the throw blanket on her couch.

She watched Toby bound through the camera feed and disappear after the blur of movement she'd seen. That wasn't anything much to worry about. Toby had two speeds—fast and playful, and flat on his belly to lounge or sleep. She'd seen him chase after autumn leaves floating through the air, so his pursuit of *it* wasn't necessarily cause for alarm.

But where was Rex? Apparently, whatever had stirred up the others was beneath his interest. That calmed her a little. He was the true guard dog of the ranch, and if he wasn't worried, she wouldn't be, either. Soon enough, the barking outside subsided into the quiet night air, and she saw the dogs settle down into their beds or go back to a late-night snack in their kennels.

Jessica reached over to pet Shadow, who was stretched out on the sofa beside her. She always loved the warmth that came off his body and relished the way he stretched and rolled beneath her hand so she could scratch just the right places to make him feel better, too. "Well, that was a big hullabaloo. But if you think we're okay, then I'll think that, too."

She set the laptop back on the coffee table and checked the time on her phone. She should make herself get up and go to bed, only, she had a feeling sleep would be elusive tonight. Too many fears and memories had been stirred up in the past forty-eight hours for her to trust that she wouldn't have nightmares or that Shadow wouldn't have another seizure. The only time she'd been able to truly stop the worries and feel safe was when she'd plastered herself to the heat and strength of Garrett's body last night. She had a feeling that wasn't going to happen again anytime soon. Not after her panicked reaction this morning. Too much had happened between them too fast for her brain and her trust to keep up. She knew she had feelings for him, but risking the hard-won stability in her life was a mighty big ask. He promised to be patient with her, but was that fair to Garrett? He was a mature, accomplished, sexy man. He deserved a woman who could be his equal—not one he had to *be patient with* and take care of. He'd already gone through that with his late wife and her battle with cancer. Jessica's issues were emotional, not physical, but that didn't mean she wouldn't be a burden rather than a help to him.

Before setting down her phone, Jessica glanced to see if she'd had any more texts from Garrett. He'd checked in with her mid-morning, telling her he'd showered and shaved and eaten a breakfast burrito, so she didn't have to worry about him not taking care of himself. She'd sent back a smiley face and assured him she was fine and not to worry about her. She'd worked with two clients today and put all her dogs through some kind of training exercise—as normal a day for her as she could ask for.

Around five o'clock, he'd updated her on the search for the missing children. No leads. No luck. Allegedly, they'd taken a bus east on 40 Highway until the route ended. After that, who knew? There were so many highways crossing through Kansas City, that if someone had picked up the children, they could be several states away in any direction by now. KCPD had some suspicion about the father, since he'd waited so long to report them missing.

She sensed there was something he wasn't telling her. But she assumed it was related to the investigation, and that he couldn't share information about the case. All she knew was that it was all hands on deck in the search for those runaways, and that Garrett would exhaust every skill and connection he had until they were found. When she expressed her sympathy for the father, Garrett had replied with a cryptic response about Mr. Swiegert having trouble of his own to deal with.

Jessica had answered with a brief text saying if there was any mystery to be solved, she was sure he would figure it out. The children were the priority right now, not proving whether or not the father had committed any crime, or if he should at least be reported to Family Services. He'd answered with a single thumbs-up emoji and gone silent for the rest of the evening.

It would be another late night for Garrett, and she felt guilty that she'd misled him and made him so angry this morning. Had he eaten lunch? Dinner? A true friend would fix him a sandwich or grab a to-go meal and take it to him at the sheriff's office.

So why hadn't she done that already?

Probably because she knew deep down

inside that there was something more than friendship between them. Garrett might be brave enough to embrace the possibilities, but she was not. It scared the daylights out of her to admit that she'd been falling in love with Garrett Caldwell for some time now.

Maybe she wasn't ready to give her heart to anyone. But she could do better by him than she had this morning. "Do the right thing, woman," she encouraged herself out loud. Shadow flicked his ears as if he agreed. "Bossy."

She pulled up Garrett's number and typed out a text.

Jessica: I'm sorry about this morning. In case it wasn't clear, I'm grateful for everything you did for me yesterday and last night. I'm okay now. Don't worry about me. I don't want my hang-ups to distract you from doing your job or taking care of yourself.

His answer came through almost immediately.

Garrett: Can't promise I won't worry about you.

Jessica: No. Focus on those kids. They need you more than I do.

When he didn't immediately reply, she sent another text.

Jessica: Not to sound like an old nag, but have you eaten anything since that burrito? Put your feet up for ten minutes and rested your eyes?

Garrett: No and no. But it's nice to have someone worry about me.

Jessica: I never promised I wouldn't worry about you, either. ;)

Garrett: Okay if I bring you coffee in the morning?

Jessica: I'd like that. I will consider everything you said. I can't make any promises, though.

Garrett: That gives me hope.

Another text followed moments later.

Garrett: And fair warning… I will be kissing you again. I need that connection.

Jessica: That's your idea of being patient with me?

Garrett: Did you miss the part about me saying I needed you? It's been a tough day.

How could a text convey such exhaustion and frustration? The woman she'd once been before tragedy had irrevocably changed her would have reached out to offer comfort and strength. Hell, the woman she was now wanted to do that for Garrett. She wanted to be what he needed. She wanted to be the woman he could depend on. She wanted to be enough.

Jessica: Okay. One kiss.

She smiled at his answer.

Garrett: I'll take it.

It wasn't fair, but she felt a little lighter at the idea of seeing Garrett tomorrow morning. She was even tamping down anticipation at kissing him again. Would it be one of those quick, branding kisses where he held the back of her neck and made her feel surrounded and cherished by him? Or one of those toe-curling seductions like she'd woken up to this morning, where she'd momentarily forgotten her name as well as all the reasons why she wasn't a good bet for a relationship?

Jessica started to text him good-night and wish him luck on his team's search, but Shadow suddenly hopped up on all four legs and nudged his nose through the curtains to look out over the front porch. "Now what?"

A split second later, she heard Rex's deep woof. She hadn't gotten any notification on her phone that someone had driven onto the property, but she trusted Shadow's and Rex's instincts more than she trusted computer electronics when it came to security.

She pulled up her computer screen in time to see Rex chasing Toby out of the barn. That was weird. The only time she'd seen Rex turn on his patrol buddy was when Toby had been pestering the Anatolian's adopted goats. Jessica tapped Shadow's shoulder to bring his attention back to her. "Do we need to check this out?"

The rangy German shepherd mix jumped down and made a beeline for the back door.

"Give me a minute," Jessica chided, reaching for her lace-up boots. By the time she pulled on her denim barn coat and tucked her keys, phone, and flashlight into its roomy pockets, Shadow was scratching furiously at the door.

For a split second, she wondered if she should call Garrett or even 9-1-1 to report the commotion after so many destructive incidents happening on her and other farms in the area. But if she was tired, he had to be beyond exhausted. She didn't need him to come to her rescue again. Especially if this turned out to be nothing more than a raccoon in the barn or Toby trying to play with the goats again.

Jessica locked the door behind her and texted Garrett.

Jessica: Sorry to cut this short. Dogs are going off. Don't see anything on the cameras. Checking it out.

Garrett: Wait. I'm in the city right now. I can be there in twenty minutes.

Jessica: I have a dozen dogs to back me up. I'll be fine.

She turned on her flashlight, confirmed there were no unfamiliar vehicles in her drive, and nothing big like a deer or bobcat or neighbor with a shotgun wandering too close to her facilities. No, whatever had made Rex cranky enough to scoot Toby out of the barn probably wasn't a threat to her.

But there *was* a threat.

When she heard Shadow growling, she took off at a run to reach him in the barn. Once she got inside, she flipped on the lights and tried to make sense of what she was seeing. Shadow, the old man of the ranch and undisputed leader of the pack, was crouched down in the dirt in front of Penny and her puppies' stall. Oh, no. Had a fox or coyote gotten in and gone after one of the pups? If so, why wasn't Mama Penny going crazy? And what was Rex carrying in his mouth as he trotted back to his home with the goats?

"Shadow?" Jessica slowly approached the dog, knowing when he was tense and on guard like this, it was wise not to startle him. "Shadow." She called out more forcefully. When he looked up at her, she motioned him to her side. She grabbed hold of his collar and inhaled a steadying breath, bracing herself for a predator or carnage or whatever the dogs had cornered in the barn. Flipping her flashlight to arm herself with a club if necessary, she released Shadow, slid open the stall gate, and stared right into the tines of her own pitchfork. She retreated half a step. "Oh, my."

The little boy wielding that pitchfork had blue eyes, dirty, disheveled brown hair and a fist-sized bruise at the corner of his mouth. "Leave us alone!" he warned. "We're not hurtin' anybody."

Us? She raised her hands in the universal

sign for surrender as she leaned a little to one side to spot a small, blond-haired girl in the straw, curled up beneath the missing blanket from her storage room. A bobtail Australian shepherd puppy was snugged in her arms. Penny seemed to be okay with these children in the stall with her puppies. She seemed familiar with them, knew they weren't a threat.

Jessica brought her gaze back to the boy who was so staunchly defending the little girl. "Did you break into my storage room last night?" She remembered the indentation in the straw. "Did you sleep here?"

He pulled his narrow shoulders back. "I didn't steal your blanket," he insisted, glancing down at the sleeping girl. "It's right there."

"I don't mind that you borrowed it. You're taking care of her."

"Abby's sick. I was looking for medicine." Some of the defiance leaked out of the boy's tone and posture. "She was so cold, she was shivering." He sounded scared and tired, and had clearly been smacked hard enough to leave that bruise, but the pitchfork never wavered. "I'm sorry I broke your jar. I gave the treats to your dogs so they wouldn't bark at us all the time."

"That was smart." Jessica's praise seemed

to quiet his fear a little bit. "I hope you didn't cut yourself on all that broken glass."

He gave his head a sharp shake.

"Are *you* warm enough?" she asked. The sleeves of his denim jacket didn't reach his wrists, and he wore only a thin T-shirt underneath. "I could get another blanket for you."

"I'm okay," he insisted. "I have to stay awake to protect Abby."

Jessica's heart nearly broke at this boy's staunch defense of the little girl. She suspected there was a whole lot of backstory she was missing here. But the reasons behind their rough condition and hiding out in her barn didn't matter. She needed to get that weapon out of his hands and get them both the help they needed. She just had to keep talking until she could get the boy to relax, sort of the way she'd calm a skittish dog to earn his trust. She pointed her head toward the far end of the barn, where Rex had gone. "Rex is that big dog. He doesn't like a lot of people. But the fact that he took a treat from you means you're good with dogs. He knows you're an okay guy."

"He wouldn't let me pet him."

"Nah. He's not into that. He's happier hanging out with his goat friends." She glanced down at Shadow sitting beside her. "Would you like to pet a dog?"

His blue eyes widened. "He growled at me."

"Because he was protecting me. Just like you're protecting Abby." She stroked the top of Shadow's head. "He won't hurt anyone unless I tell him to, and I would never do that."

This boy was such a thinker, evaluating his options. He looked to be about eight or nine, just a few years younger than her own child would be now if he'd survived. But he seemed old beyond his years. "I wanted to pet the puppies, but I read that you aren't supposed to handle puppies too much when they're still with their mom."

"That's right." She was starting to make some progress. He was carrying on a conversation now. "Do you like to read?" He nodded. "I've got a ton of books in my house. Would you like to see them?"

"Mrs. Furkin said I shouldn't go anywhere with a stranger."

"Who's Mrs. Furkin?" A babysitter who was missing her charges, she hoped.

"My teacher. I'm in the third grade."

He didn't get his advice from a parent? Some other family member? Jessica knew she was about to say and do a few things that most children were taught to ignore to keep them safe from a stranger. "Is Abby your sister?" He nodded. "I'm Jessie. Jessie Bennington." She wasn't quite sure why she'd used the name Garrett called her, but it seemed friendlier, easier to pronounce. "What's your name?"

He hesitated for a moment, as if debating whether or not it was safe to answer. "Nate."

No last name. But she'd work with whatever the boy gave her. Without moving any closer, she risked putting her hands down. "You're not going to poke me with that thing, are you?" He leaned the pitchfork against the wall of the stall but kept his hand on it. That was probably as much of a welcome as he was going to give her right now. Jessica inched closer. "May I check on Abby? See if she's sleeping okay?"

At least, she hoped the girl was just sleeping. Jessica's stomach clenched at the idea of the child suffering out here on the chilly spring night. She'd like to get in there to see just how ill the little girl was. She looked to be about five or six. How long had they been out in the elements like this? Did Abby need to see a doctor?

"Nate, I'm going to show you something."

Using her hands and a clear voice, she gave Shadow a series of commands. "Sit. Down. Stay." Shadow's tongue lolled out the side of his mouth and she knew he was relaxing now that the pitchfork had been set aside and she wasn't being threatened. Then she held out a hand to the boy. "Come here, Nate. See how relaxed Shadow's ears are? Curl your fingers into a fist like this." She showed him what she wanted him to do. "Now hold it close to his nose and let him sniff you. He'll realize you're Rex's friend, and that Penny isn't worried about you being around her puppies. Dogs use their noses more than anything to learn about their world. Once he's familiar with your scent, he'll let you pet him. In fact, I bet he'd really like it if you would."

Although he avoided touching her hand, Nate knelt in the straw near Shadow and let the dog sniff his fist. When the dog slurped his tongue over the boy's fingers, Nate jerked back and landed on his butt in the straw. "I thought he was gonna bite me."

Jessica smiled and petted Shadow. "No. That means he likes you."

"He does?"

"Sure. It's a puppy kiss." She curtailed her instinct to reach for Nate and help him move closer. Instead, she demonstrated how Shadow liked to be petted. "Try again. Like this." Nate almost smiled as he petted the top of Shadow's head without incident. "You may smell like the treats you handled. That's a good smell to him."

For the first time, a spark of excitement in Nate's voice made him sound like a true little boy. "Can I give him a treat?"

"You may."

Nate scrambled away to unzip his backpack and pulled out a beefy chew. To his credit, Shadow eagerly took the treat from the boy's hand and lay down to enjoy it while Nate petted him some more.

"Good boy, Shadow." She praised both the boy and the dog for handling this first meeting so well. While Nate was distracted with the dog, Jessica scooted across the straw to check on Abby. Even before she brushed aside her curly blond hair and touched the girl's skin, she could feel the heat radiating off her fragile body. The girl had a fever, and her skin was pale. She murmured her brother's name at Jessica's touch and rolled toward her, but didn't completely wake up. "How long has Abby been sick?"

"Since last night. She threw up the dog food I gave her."

Jessica thought *she* might be sick. They were eating the dog food? "When was the last time you ate? People food?"

"We tried to eat the eggs next door, but they were gross. I like 'em scrambled."

"I do, too. With some cinnamon toast and bacon. I've got all that in the house. I could make you some."

Nate remembered his charge and came over to kneel on the other side of his sister. "I'm not leaving Abby."

"I have food for her, too. What does she like to eat?"

"Cereal with marshmallows in it."

"Well, I don't have any of that. But maybe I have something else she'd like." She picked up the spotted puppy and set him back in his box with Mama Penny.

When she came back to smooth Abby's hair off her warm forehead, the little girl opened her eyes. "I like your puppies. I named that one Charlie. My best friend at school is named Charlie."

"That's a good name." She smiled down at the little girl, who seemed to be more trusting than her big brother. "My name is Jessie, and I'm here to help you. Is your tummy upset?"

Abby glanced over to her brother, then nodded. "I frowed up."

"That's okay. That's just your tummy trying to feel better."

Jessica felt she'd won them over enough to take charge a little more. She looked at Nate. "Has she had anything to drink today?"

"We drank some water from your hose. I put it in the water bottles we brought from home."

Between hose water and raw eggs, she had to wonder if the girl had picked up some kind of intestinal parasite. She mentally crossed her fingers that this was just a touch of the flu, or the manifestation of the girl's exhaustion and their sketchy diet. And as much as she wanted to ask them where *home* was, Jessica had a feeling she already knew the answer. Besides, getting these children fed and taken care of had just become priority one. "I'd like to take you both inside my house, where you can sleep in a real bed and eat some real food." She pulled out her cell phone and showed it to them. "I have a friend in the sheriff's department. He's the police outside of the city. May I call him? He could help you."

"No!" Nate slapped her hand and knocked the phone into the straw. "I don't want to go back to Kansas City. He'll hurt Abby."

"My friend Garrett won't hurt your sister."

His eyes widened with fear, and he moved between Jessie and his sister. "The bald man will."

"Who's the bald man?" Jessica shook her head and focused on priority one. The details as to why Nate was protecting Abby didn't matter right now. These children were frightened and needed food and help. "I don't know any bald man. He isn't here. My dogs wouldn't let him hurt you."

"If you make us go back, we'll run away again."

"I don't want you to go anywhere except inside my house, where I can help Abby and get you both someplace where it's warm and safe."

Abby whimpered between them. "Natey, I don't feel good. My tummy's empty."

"Can you make her better?"

"I can try." Jessica picked up her phone. "But I need to call my friend. I won't let him take you anywhere. I need his help to take care of you."

"Natey, I want to sleep in a bed. It's itchy here." Abby reached out for her brother. "Can't the dog lady help us? She's not like Daddy's friend. She's nice."

So many questions to ask about what these two had been through. But Jessica held her tongue and waited for big brother to make his decision.

"It'll be okay, Abs." Nate squeezed his little sister's hand. "Jessie knows all about dogs and medicine. She's gonna take care of you."

"Thank you." Jessica wasn't about to correct the boy's mistaken assumption about her skill set, not if it got him to cooperate with her. Abby wore a sparkly pink tracksuit, but had no coat, so Jessica tucked the ratty blanket around her small form and scooped her up into her arms.

Abby curled into Jessica's chest. "You smell like flowers."

"Can you put your arms around my neck?" With a weak nod, the little girl slipped her grubby hands around the collar of Jessica's coat. She weighed less than some of the dogs she manhandled for baths or trips to the vet.

"Nate, will you grab her book bag and bring it with us? Yours, too."

He dutifully picked up both their backpacks but hung back. "Can Shadow come with us?"

"He goes everywhere I go." Although Shadow was looking to her for his next command, she gave Nate the job instead. "Say his name, then 'Heel,' and tap your thigh. He'll fall into step beside you."

Jessica hurried out of the barn, ignoring the barking from the kenneled dogs. Behind her she heard a small voice, "Shadow. Heel. He did it!"

"Good man." She let her praise get both boy and dog moving. "Let's go."

Jessica carried Abby into the house and up the stairs to lay the girl on the bed in one of the guest rooms. Nate and Shadow trotted up the stairs right behind them. The boys stayed in the room with Abby as Jessica hurried into the main bathroom to retrieve a cool, damp washcloth and a thermometer. Nate hovered at the end of the bed, watching her every move as she tended to the girl. Abby's fever wasn't dangerously high, but she needed to cool down and get some fluids in her. And brave little Nate needed to eat.

She gave the girl a sponge bath of all her

extremities, then removed her tennis shoes and tucked her beneath the covers. "Will you sit here and hold your sister's hand while I talk to my friend? Make sure she keeps the washcloth on her forehead. We need to get her fever down."

Nate took her place sitting beside his sister on the bed while she stepped away and pulled out her phone again. When she looked at her screen, she saw several messages from Garrett.

Garrett: Jess? Still there?

Garrett: You okay?

Garrett: I'm on my way.

Garrett: Jess?

She pulled up her keyboard and started to text him.

She looked into a pair of distrustful blue eyes and decided to call Garrett instead. Nate needed to hear what she was saying and not think she might be telling her deputy friend something other than what she'd promised.

"Jess?" He answered on the first ring. "Why didn't you answer me? There's been a development in the investigation. The kids' father may have some criminal ties. I need to you stay inside and keep things locked up."

"There's been a development here, too. Before you get here, stop and get me some children's acetaminophen and lemon-lime soda."

"What? Why?"

"I found your runaways."

Chapter Seven

"They doing okay?"

Jessica felt Garrett lean against the door-frame behind her as she watched Nate and Abby sleep in the guest bedroom across the hall from her own room. Abby was curled up in a ball around the doll she'd pulled from her backpack. It was missing a hunk of red yarn from one of its yellow ponytails. But she could tell it was well loved and had been played with and cuddled often. Nate, on the other hand, was spread out like a starfish on a pile of blankets and a sleeping bag on the floor. Her ever-faithful Shadow was stretched out on the pallet beside him. A night-light beside the bed and the light she'd left on in the hallway bathroom cast the only illumination on the second floor.

"For now. He ate everything I fixed for him. Man-sized portions. He's a starving growing boy." She glanced up at the real man beside her and found him staring at the children as intently as she had. "Abby ate the applesauce and some of the toast I gave her so the acetaminophen wouldn't upset her stomach. Thank you for bringing that. Her temperature's down below three digits already."

"Glad to do it." His voice was a low whisper against her ear. "Did they tell you anything more about what they've been through?"

She shook her head. "Abby doesn't say much, and Nate is pretty guarded. I think they've been in survival mode for so long, it'll be hard to earn their trust." She rubbed her hands up and down her arms, warding off an inner chill. "I'm half afraid they're going to bolt if I stop watching them."

His hand settled at the small of her back, sharing some of his warmth and reassurance. "I think they're taking their cues from the dogs. If Shadow and the others trust you, then maybe they can, too. At least a little bit. Any trouble getting them settled down?"

"I had them both take a bath. Then I started reading *The Phantom Tollbooth* to them. All Abby cared about was the picture of the dog with a clock in his belly. She dozed off in my lap. But Nate made it through two chapters before he admitted he was sleepy."

"He's a tough kid."

"Tougher than he needs to be at his age." Garrett made a soft sound of agreement in his throat. "I wanted to give them each their own room. She wouldn't even get in bed until Nate came in. I made him a pallet on the floor. He pulled it between the door and the bed. She didn't fall into a deep sleep until he lay down beside her and held her hand. He didn't give up until Shadow came in and lay down beside him."

"I can only think of one reason why he'd want to position himself between his sister and the door," Garrett grumbled.

"To protect her?" Garrett was practically vibrating when she nudged her shoulder against his. "Let's take the conversation downstairs." When Shadow raised his head to silently ask if he needed to go with her, she smiled and made it clear he was off duty for now. "Stay here, good boy. Relax." The dog laid his head back down on Nate's outstretched arm. It was probably the pallet he was enjoying, although she didn't think either the dog or the boy minded the company and warm body beside him.

Downstairs, Garrett peeked through the

windows and checked the locks while she went to the kitchen to brew them a fresh pot of decaf coffee. He pulled out a stool at the island counter, braced his elbows on top, and scrubbed his fingers through his hair in that habit of his that indicated fatigue or frustration. Jessica's heart squeezed at the rumpled mess he left in its wake. As much as she wanted to go to him and straighten those sexy spikes of hair, she kept her fingers busy pouring their coffee. She set a steaming mug in front of him and doctored up her own drink before pulling out the stool beside him to sit.

She waited for him to sip some of the reviving brew before she voiced her own concerns. "What happened to those children? Nate said the 'bald man' wanted to hurt Abby. What scared them so badly that running away was their only option?"

"The 'bald man'?" Garrett glanced up from the drink he'd been studying. "Did they give you a name?"

"No."

"But you think they've seen him? Had contact with him?"

"Enough that they're deathly afraid of him. Were they talking about their father?"

Garrett set down his mug and pulled out his cell phone. "This is their father, Zane Swiegert."

She leaned over to look at the candid shot that had been taken through a window at a police station. Zane Swiegert looked like a taller, grown-up version of Nate with brown hair and blue eyes. But he also looked...wild.

Wild brown eyes.

Jessica squeezed her eyes shut and shook off the memory of her husband's murderer before a flashback could take hold. When she opened her eyes, she discovered that she'd latched on to Garrett's forearm, much the same way she reached for Shadow whenever she needed to anchor herself to reality.

"Jessie?" Garrett's hand closed gently over her own, warming it against the ink of his military tattoo. "What's wrong?"

She drummed up a wry smile but didn't pull away. "I'm okay. He just..." She inhaled a steadying breath. "With that unwashed, uncombed hair and the circles under his eyes, he reminds me of Lee Palmer."

"The man who killed your husband and shot you?"

She nodded. "Palmer was high on something when he came to our house that morning. Probably had to be to make sense of doing something so desperate. As if killing John and trying to kill me would get his wife or his children or his money back." She shifted her gaze from the picture up to Garrett's concerned expression. Although he'd shaved at some point during the day, she could see the dark, silver-studded stubble shading his jaw again. "Nate and Abby's father is using, isn't he. He has the same look."

"Yeah. Cocaine seems to be his drug of choice. I snapped that picture when he was in KCPD for questioning today. He sounded like he genuinely wants his kids. But there's something more going on there." After swiping the image off his phone, he leaned over to press a gentle kiss to her temple. "Sorry for dredging up bad memories. Do you need Shadow?"

"No, I need to be strong enough to face this." She squeezed his arm before pulling away. "I want to do whatever I can to help those children."

"I think you've been amazing with them tonight."

She chuckled. "I was trying to remember all the books I read when I was pregnant. They're probably out of date now. Ultimately, though, I'm winging it. I confess, too, that I'm drawing on some of my experience as a dog trainer. Gentle when I can be, firm when I need to be. I want them to know I'm the boss, but I care, and I'll be fair with them. Mostly, I'm crossing my fingers and praying I don't screw anything up."

"Well, it seems to be working."

She wrapped her fingers around her mug to keep them warm. "I know you have to call Family Services and KCPD, but can't we at least wait until morning? They've had a hard three days and Abby still has a slight fever. They need their rest."

"I'm not calling Family Services."

"You're not turning them over to their father, are you? He can't take care of himself, much less two children."

Garrett set down his mug, snagged her hand, and pulled her out into the living room. "I have to call my contact at KCPD to let them know the children have been found. But we won't notify the father yet. There are some things you and I need to discuss."

"I bet. Did you see the bruise on Nate's face? Someone hit him."

"I saw." Garrett halted, his hand suddenly tight around hers. "What about Abby?"

"I didn't see any marks on her," she reassured him. "As protective as he is of her, I can see Nate standing between her and any kind of threat. But they're both suffering from neglect. Their clothes don't fit. They aren't being fed. I'd like to do some shopping for them tomorrow." She tugged him along behind her and sat on the sofa. "Do you know who the bald man is Nate talked about?"

"I think so." Garrett settled onto the cushion beside her and pulled up another picture on his phone. This one was a mugshot of a beefy, brutal-looking man with bushy dark eyebrows and a shaved head. To cap off his arrogant, intimidating look, he had a black skull tattooed on either side of his scalp. "This is Kai Olivera. He's the reason you and the children are staying hidden here tonight instead of going back to KC. He's bad news. Drugs. Human trafficking. Illegal arms sales. He started off as a gangbanger and worked his way up to being king of his own criminal empire."

"I think I'm scared of him, too." She shuddered and looked away from the image. "How would Nate and Abby meet someone like him?" When Garrett hesitated, she pushed. "You need to tell me everything. If they're staying here and we have to protect them, I need to know what we're up against."

His rugged face softened with a smile that didn't quite reach his eyes. "I like how you say 'we.' That you see us as a team."

"You aren't going to leave us here alone, in case one of these guys shows up, are you?"

"No."

"Then, yes, we're a team."

His shoulders lifted with a deep breath, and then he got down to the business of explaining just what kind of threat Nate and Abby were facing. "Swiegert works for Olivera. Started off as a customer, now he helps him move product."

"Product? Their dad's a drug dealer, too?"

He nodded. "And he's still using, based on what I saw this afternoon. I don't know if Zane Swiegert sent his kids away to protect them from Olivera, or if they figured out for themselves that they were in a dangerous situation. I need to talk to them ASAP and find out what they know."

"They need their sleep first," Jessica insisted. "And another good meal."

"Agreed. I'm going to hang around and keep an eye on the place tonight. I'd like to talk to Nate in the morning after breakfast."

He angled himself toward her, then pulled her hands between his, chuffing them to warm them up. "I'm also going to introduce you to the detective who's running the KCPD task force to bring down Olivera. Conor Wildman. He and his team will help us protect the kids, but I want you to be familiar with their faces. You see anyone around here you don't know, you lock yourself and the kids in the house, and you call me or Conor."

"I will. I was thinking of installing some more security cameras, too."

"You're a woman after my own heart."

She turned her hands to still his massage and let them settle atop his thigh. "I thought the way to a man's heart was through his stomach," she teased.

"Not mine. I've been at this too long and have seen too much. Knowing the things I care about are well guarded and secure? That's what makes me happy." He grinned. "Although I wouldn't turn my nose up at a homemade pie."

"Duly noted." Jessica looked toward the kitchen. "I think I still have a bag of cherries I pitted and froze last summer after picking them off of Gran's trees out back."

"Wait. You bake?" He sank into the back

of the sofa and raked his fingers through his hair. "Ah, hell. How am I ever going to keep my hands off you now?"

She laughed out loud at that, appreciating that they could lighten the mood between them after sharing such a heavy discussion about druggies and dealers and task forces that were all interested in the two children sleeping upstairs.

But this was a serious discussion, and she'd asked to know everything Garrett did. "So, what happens now? How long can the children stay with me? And are we far enough away from Kansas City that there's not an imminent threat from Kai Olivera or their father?"

"Let me make my phone calls." Garrett pushed to his feet and headed for the hall tree to retrieve his hat. "Sit tight for tonight. I'll be back to interview Nate in the morning."

"You're not staying the night?" After that talk about security protocols and safeguarding things he cared about, she was surprised that he was leaving.

"Not that I didn't enjoy wearing you like a blanket last night..." Her face heated at the memory of just how needy she'd been. "But it's probably for the best, so the kids don't stumble in and find a man they only met a couple of hours ago asleep in your bed. I'd rather they build trust in you, so they have at least one adult they'll turn to before they decide running away again is their best option, rather than have me scare them off. Abby didn't say a word to me, so she might be afraid of men. Nate? He's still sizing me up. I'm not sure if he trusts the badge or not. I'm guessing he expected a cop to help them somewhere along the way, and they let him down. I'll be fine in my truck."

His reasoning made sense. Although, she believed if Nate and Abby got to know him, they'd learn he was another adult they could trust. "You don't think that will look suspicious that you're sleeping in your truck if anyone is watching the place? What if you stay in one of the other guest rooms? Or on the couch?"

He considered her invitation for a moment, then hooked his ball cap back on the hall tree, a sure sign he was staying. "The couch. That will put me between the door and you three upstairs." She nodded, feeling relieved to know he'd be there with them. "I've already called in one of my officers to keep an eye on the outside tonight. Plainclothes. I don't want to draw any attention to your place in case Swiegert or Olivera or someone else who works for him is looking for the kids out this way. Since I'm a regular visitor, my departmental truck shouldn't look too out of place."

"Should I cancel my training sessions tomorrow?" she asked. "Call Hugo and Soren and tell them to stay away?"

Garrett shook his head. "I think you should keep your routine as normal as possible. The neighbors will talk if you start making calls like that. Olivera is going to have his people out trying to find information on those kids. An abrupt change in routine or building this place up like a fortress will get the gossips' tongues wagging, That's the kind of intel Olivera will want to check out."

"Will we be safe with just you and your friend Conor? You know I don't keep any guns in the house. After John…"

"I understand. With the kids here, I don't want them to have access to firearms, either. I'll keep my rifle locked in my truck, but I'd like to keep my sidearm with me. Conor will be armed, too."

She nodded. "You had your gun last night, and I was mostly okay with it."

Garrett reached out and caught a loose

tendril of her hair. He rubbed it between his thumb and fingers before tucking it behind her ear. He feathered his fingers into the hair at her nape and cupped the side of her neck and jaw. "I'm sorry I can't do better than *mostly okay*. But I'm not going to leave you or Nate and Abby unprotected."

"I know you won't. But it's not all on your shoulders, Garrett." She looked toward the front door. "A dozen dogs on the property, remember? We'll know someone's here long before they get to the house."

"You're sure about me staying here? I would like to be close by."

"I'm sure." She wrapped her fingers around his wrist and tilted her cheek into his touch. "I'll bring down a pillow and some blankets for you."

He nodded his thanks. "Why don't you go on up to bed. I'll get my go-bag from my truck so I can change out of my uniform, then I'll lock everything up behind me. Keep Shadow upstairs with you. He'll sound the alarm if anything gets past me."

She didn't like the sound of that. "Don't get dead protecting us, okay? I wouldn't deal very well with that."

"I won't. Good night, Jessie."

She stood there, still holding on to his wrist, not moving away. "Aren't you going to kiss me good-night?" She wasn't sure if she sounded seductive or pathetic. It had been a long time since she'd felt enough for a man that the difference mattered. "You said you were going to kiss me again."

"Maybe you should kiss me, instead," he teased. But his smile quickly faded, and he pulled away at her wide-eyed response to his dare. "Sorry. I said I wouldn't push."

"No, I..." She grabbed a handful of his shirt to keep him from retreating. She willed those handsome green eyes to understand that she was trying, but that none of this flirty, intimate banter came easily for her. "You understand I'm the queen of slow movers when it comes to relationships. It has been a long time since I even wanted to try. Not since John."

"Ah, honey. I don't know what to say to that. I've cared about you for so long. I want more, but I don't want to screw anything up."

Releasing the front of his shirt, she wound her arms around his waist and hugged him. She hated that his protective vest created a barrier between them, but she found the gap between the bottom of the vest and the top of his utility belt and clung to the warmth emanating from the man underneath. His strong arms folded around her, and she nestled her forehead against the base of his throat. "I'm just glad you're here. You're warm and strong and...you ground me. You keep me out of the dark places in my head and keep me moving forward. I'm used to handling everything on my own—well, with Shadow's help. But I feel stronger when you're with me—like, I can handle whatever I have to because you're here to back me up if I need it."

"Just like Shadow. I'm your support man."

She shifted her hold on him, leaning back against his arms and framing his rugged, wonderfully tactile face between her hands, then tipped his face down to hers. "Not like Shadow. I would never kiss him on the lips."

Feeling brave, Jessica pushed up on tiptoe and pressed a sweet kiss to his mouth. His response was infinitely patient, his lips resting pliantly as she explored his mouth and learned the different textures of his beard and lips and tongue. Then he captured her bottom lip between his, to taste, to suckle. The tips of her breasts grew hard and strained against the itchy lace of her bra. Her pulse thundered in her ears and the long-forgotten weight of molten desire pooled between her legs. There was no plunging, no claiming, just a tender exploration that went on and on until she frightened herself with how much more she wanted from this man.

When she pulled away with a stuttering breath and buried her head against his neck once more, Garrett tightened his arms around her. His lips pressed against her hair. "I could live on that kiss for days." His voice was a grumbly, deep-pitched whisper. "Thank you for pushing yourself out of your comfort zone."

"Thank you for being so patient with me."

"We'll get there." He pressed another kiss to her hair and closed his hands around her shoulders and pushed her away to arm's length. "I'm beat. I need to get some sleep, too. Go on." He turned her toward the stairs and playfully swatted her butt.

She whipped around, surprised by the touch. "Too much?"

With a blush warming her face, she smiled. "My forty-six-year-old body appreciates that you like a little of what you see."

He leaned in, bracing his hands on the wall on either side of her and practically growled. "I like a lot of what I see. I liked a lot of what I felt smushed against me last night, too."

Resting her hand at the center of his chest, she tilted her eyes to his. "The feeling is mutual."

He pushed ever so gently against her hand, moving in as if he was going to kiss her again. But at the last moment, he turned his head, shoving his fingers through his rumpled hair and backing away. "Slow mover. I can respect that. It may drive me crazy, but you are totally worth the wait." He reached behind her to capture her braid and pulled it over her shoulder. He dragged his fingers along its entire length before resting it atop the swell of her breast. "I want you all-in with this relationship when it happens."

"*If* it happens."

He shook his head. "*When.* Tomorrow. A week from now. Two years down the road. You and me? We're gonna happen."

She shivered at the certainty of his promise. "Good night, Garrett. I'll see you in the morning."

She hurried up the steps to the linen closet to retrieve a pillow and cover for him. From the bottom of the stairs she heard, "*When.*"

Chapter Eight

Garrett ignored the twinge in his back from sleeping on Jessie's couch and poured his second cup of coffee, biding his time until Nate polished off his stack of silver dollar pancakes, scrambled eggs, and bacon at the kitchen counter. It was a perfectly good couch. It was almost long enough for his body, and he'd been plenty warm. But he'd been half on alert against any noises inside or outside the house; he'd been half-hard after that incredibly sweet, mind-blowing kiss Jessie had initiated; he had a fifty-year-old back, and it was the couch.

Sleep seemed to be in short supply hanging around Jessie and K-9 Ranch, but he wouldn't trade his time here for anything in the world. This feeling of chaotic domestic bliss, this sense of home, had eluded him his entire adult life. But this morning, being a part of Jessie's world, he felt like this was where he belonged.

This was what his life was supposed to be like. Although he wore his gun and badge on his belt, he was dressed down in jeans and a navy-blue T-shirt, enjoying what was, for him, a leisurely morning. And a twinge of back pain wasn't going to dampen the pleasure of sharing this morning with Jessie, Nate, and Abby one little bit.

He leaned his hips against the counter and watched Jessie help Abby up onto a stepstool beside her to show the little girl how to make pancakes on the griddle pan. Jessie had carefully braided Abby's hair back into a pigtail that matched her own. And she was being very careful about keeping little fingers away from the hot griddle and the stove's gas burners. Garrett enjoyed the view on so many levels, watching the females work side by side. Jessie's backside in a pair of worn jeans was a thing of beauty. He had yet to hear the little girl speak to anyone except her brother, but she enthusiastically emulated Jessie and drank in everything she wanted to teach her. Abby was a beautiful child, sweet and delicate—but he suspected there was a lot of tomboy and modern woman inside her wanting to get out. He couldn't think of a better role model than Jessie Bennington, who'd overcome adversity, launched her second career, and made a living rescuing and helping dogs, children, clients in need, and even the occasional lonely workaholic deputy.

Even Toby and Shadow were circling the deck outside the French doors that led out back, leaving nose prints on the glass. He couldn't blame them for wanting to be a part of breakfast at Jessie's house, too.

He'd already gotten up to meet Hugo out in the barn to help with the dogs, goats, and morning chores—and to fill him in on the situation inside the house. Not that he expected the older man with a hearing aid and arthritic fingers to put himself in the line of fire should anything go down here at the ranch. But another set of eyes keeping watch on things and reporting anything unusual couldn't hurt. He intended to have a similar conversation with Hugo's grandson when he showed up for work this evening.

"Can I have more milk?" Nate slapped his empty glass down on top of the island.

"*May* I have more milk?" Jessie corrected without missing a beat. She turned and smiled at the boy. "And a *please* would be nice at the end of that sentence."

Nate rolled his eyes and huffed out an annoyed breath. But he did what was asked of him. "May I have more milk, please?"

Garrett set his mug down and reached for the glass. "I've got it." He opened the fridge and refilled the glass, then set it on the counter. "And now you would say...?"

Nate's blue eyes met his. "Thanks."

"You're welcome." He nodded over his shoulder toward the woman at the stove. "And who made your breakfast?"

"Thanks, Jessie."

"Thank you, Jessie." Garrett added his own gratitude, showing Nate that he wasn't singling out the boy and asking him to do anything he wouldn't do himself. "Home cooking beats a microwaved burrito at the station house."

She turned and shared a pretty smile. "You're both welcome."

Nate didn't pick up the glass until Garrett released it completely. But then the boy drank half of it in a few big gulps. The milk mustache left behind on his top lip reminded Garrett that Nate Swiegert was still a little boy, despite his very grown-up efforts to protect his sister and get them both to safety.

Garrett checked his watch. Detective Wildman would be here soon, and then the busy normalcy of this morning would be erased by some serious police work and outlining the rules of protective custody for Nate and Abby.

"Are you sure we won't get into trouble if we don't go to school today?" Nate asked. He glanced at Garrett but directed the question to Jessie.

"Nope. Think of this like your spring break. Although, I did print off some math facts you can practice to keep your skills sharp. Plus, I want you to do some reading on your own. Then I'm going to give you another lesson on how to work with the dogs."

"Sweet." Nate was clearly excited about a chance to be with the dogs again.

Abby turned on her stool. "Natey, can I come look at the dogs with you?"

Jessie answered. "I want you to take it easy today, Miss Abby. Your fever may be gone this morning, but I don't want you to do too much and get sick again." She smoothed the little girl's braid behind her back, an affectionate gesture meant to ease the sting of denying her dog-time. "I want you to take a nap if you feel sleepy. Otherwise, I'd like you to show me all the letters and numbers you know how to write, and we'll practice writing your name." Jessie tapped the end of Abby's nose.

"And if you're still feeling good this afternoon, we'll go out to the barn to visit Penny and her pups. I'm sure Charlie misses you."

Abby clapped her hands in little girl excitement. She glanced back at her brother, as if checking to see if her enthusiasm was warranted, and when he nodded, she beamed a smile up at Jessie.

Jessie smiled right back, looking as light and unencumbered by the past as Garrett had ever seen her. "See all the holes in the pancake where the bubbles have popped?" Abby nodded. Jessie slipped the spatula into the girl's hand and curled her own fingers around it. "That means it's time to flip your pancakes. They're almost done."

Abby might not have spoken to anyone besides her brother, but that didn't mean she wasn't interacting with Jessie. Or Garrett. The little girl celebrated her first successful-ish pancake by scooping it onto the spatula and holding it out to him. Her smile was the best invitation Garrett could have. "Hey. You did a great job." When she continued to hold out the small, misshapen pancake, Garrett realized it was a gift. "Oh. You want me to eat it? You don't want to eat your first one?"

Apparently, eye-rolling ran in the family.

Garrett grinned and reached for the offering. "Thank you, Abby." The pancake was freshly made, and still hot to the touch, but he picked it off the spatula, rolled it up and stuffed the whole thing into his mouth. "That's really yummy." He wasn't lying when he smiled and praised her. "Good job."

Her answering smile was worth the heat that singed the roof of his mouth.

Garrett poured himself some cold milk and drank it down. As he cooled his mouth, he looked over the rim of the glass and caught Nate watching his reaction to Abby's overture of friendship—possibly to make sure he didn't say or do anything that would upset his sister. Every choice Nate made, from running away to sleeping arrangements to keeping his eye on Garrett reaffirmed his suspicions that Nate was protecting Abby from something horrendous. His blood boiled with the possibilities of what that could mean and made him more anxious to interview Nate to get the answers he and the KCPD task force needed. And, it doubled his determination to keep this little family of circumstance safe from the evil that had chased them out of Kansas City.

Needing to keep his hands busy and his demeanor calm so he wouldn't become the thing that frightened these children, Garrett opened the dishwasher and started loading the dishes, glasses, and utensils they'd used. His movements must have been a little too sharp because when he straightened to rinse out the mixing bowl and whisk Jessie had used, he found her watching him over the top of Abby's head. The look of concern stamped on her face told him he wasn't fooling anybody with his just-another-morning-on-the-ranch routine.

"You okay?" She mouthed the words.

Garrett exhaled his anger on a heavy breath and raked his fingers through his hair. She turned off the stove and pushed the griddle to the back while he went back to the dishes.

A knock at the front door made him pause. "That'll be Conor." Garrett had already warned the children that an adult should always answer the door. But when Jessie automatically headed out of the kitchen, he grabbed her by the elbow and pulled her behind him. "Just in case it's not someone we know, let me go first."

She nodded, then reached up to straighten his short hair. The caring gesture eased some of the anger that was still scalding like acid through his veins. "Once I meet your friend,

you can talk to Nate in the living room. I'll
keep Abby busy in the kitchen or upstairs."

"Thanks."

"Of course. Remember, you're the adult,
even though Nate plays like he is. Be gentle
with him. He's a little boy who's been scared
out of his mind, not a hardened criminal."

Garrett mimicked the same caress, gently
brushing a loose strand of silvery-gold hair
off her forehead. "I won't make things any
worse, I promise."

WORSE FOR NATE, NO.

Worse for Garrett...?

He was vibrating with the kind of anger he
hadn't felt since he'd seen a terrorist strap a
bomb to his own child and send him out to
greet the convoy of soldiers while Garrett and
his spotter watched and provided cover from
higher ground. He'd warned his team over
their radios about the shifting makeup of the
crowd. In a matter of seconds, the friendly
greeting had morphed into an attack. With his
teammates trapped among supposed friend-
lies who had suddenly become their enemy,
Garrett had been forced to pick off the insur-
gents in the crowd targeting the soldiers—in-

cluding the boy with the bomb—so that his team could rescue their wounded and escape.

With his hand clenched into a fist behind his back, he listened to Nate tell his story to Conor Wildman. To Conor's credit, the detective kept the conversation going with a few calmly voiced questions. But Garrett could tell by the tight clench of the detective's jaw that the boy's story was getting to him, too.

"And that's the night when the bald man and his friends hurt your father?" Conor asked.

Nate nodded. He'd already identified a picture of Kai Olivera as the *bald man*. He'd never actually been introduced to the drug dealer, so he didn't recognize his name, but called him by the apt descriptor. He'd forced his way into their apartment one night to have a *conversation* with his father. He'd also shared the creep's fascination with Abby after another visit where he'd held his sister on his lap the entire meeting.

"Dad didn't have his money." Because he'd been snorting the coke himself with his girlfriend du jour and had passed out instead of making deliveries and picking up payments from the dealers on his route. It was bad enough that Nate had witnessed his father getting high in their apartment and had had to make peanut butter and jelly sandwiches for dinner for himself and Abby. But the fact that he'd seen Olivera and two of his enforcers punishing Zane left a foul taste in Garrett's mouth. But Nate continued on matter-of-factly recounting his experience as if he was telling them about his day at school. "I hid Abby under her bed when they started fighting. I told her to stop crying and be as quiet as her doll, so no one knew she was there. But Dad stopped when they dropped the end of the sofa on his hand. My dad cried, too. Real men aren't supposed to cry."

"They do if they're hurting as much as I suspect your father was," Conor said, trying to show a little sympathy for a man who'd blown his responsibilities to his family in so many ways. Zane Swiegert was still Nate's father, and the boy probably had a lot of mixed feelings about the man. "Did you try to help him?"

Nate nodded, his gaze darting from Conor to Garrett and back. "The bald man knocked me down. He called me a little baby and said I was in the way. He told me to go back to my room and let the men settle things."

Settling things between Kai Olivera and

Zane was when the most heinous bargain of all had been made.

Olivera would cancel Zane's debt and let him live in exchange for Abby.

Garrett's nails cut crescent-shaped divots in the palm of his hand as he replayed those words over and over in his head. A sweet little girl as payment for a drug debt?

No wonder Zane Swiegert was so desperate to find his children. But was he trying to save them? Or his own skin? Either way, Kai Olivera wasn't putting another hand on Nate, and he wasn't taking Abby.

No. Never. Not gonna happen.

Not while there was still breath in Garrett's body.

He could see that Conor was having trouble dealing with the information Nate was sharing, too. He paused long enough that Nate squirmed uncomfortably in his chair. The detective held up a hand, asking Nate to be patient a few minutes longer. Conor's nostrils flared with a deep breath. "You're certain that's what the bald man said? He'd let your father live if he *gave* him your sister?"

"I locked the door to our bedroom, and I laid down on the floor. I could hear the men talking through the gap underneath my door."

"And your dad agreed to the deal?" Conor asked.

For the first time, Nate hesitated to answer. "Abby was scared. She didn't want to go with the bald man. He said he'd give Dad twenty-four hours to pay him back, one way or the other."

"Did your dad help you run away? Or did he agree to the deal?"

For the first time, Garrett saw a sheen of tears in Nate's blue eyes. But the moment he remembered his assertion that crying was a weakness, he angrily swiped the tears away. "Dad said we could never be a family again, that he didn't want us anymore. He said I had to take Abby away and keep her safe. He gave me twenty dollars he'd stashed in the freezer and said we weren't ever to come home again."

Conor closed his notebook and tucked it back inside the pocket of his suit jacket. "He gave you the responsibility of being the parent instead of doing the job himself?"

Nate's legs swung like pistons beneath his chair. He clearly was done sitting still and answering questions. "I want to go check on Abby. Okay?"

Garrett never wanted to hug a child as badly as he wanted to hold Nate. But that wasn't

what Nate needed right now. In addition to
some serious professional counseling, what
this brave boy needed right now was contact
with the one family member he could rely on.
He needed to know that his sacrifice to protect his sister hadn't been in vain. Learning
to trust another adult would come with time.
He hoped.

Garrett stood abruptly, ending the interview, allowing all three of them to catch their
breaths and ease some of the tension from the
room. "Thank you for talking to us, Nate.
You've helped a lot. We'll be able to find the
men who hurt you and your dad, and the information will help us do a better job of keeping you and Abby safe." He laid his hand on
Nate's shoulder, and though the nine-year-old
didn't jerk away, he didn't exactly warm to
Garrett's touch, either. "Although, you might
have to tell your story again someday."

"To a judge?"

Garrett nodded.

"Will you help my dad, too?"

Not high on his list of priorities, but it was
important to Nate. Garrett squeezed his shoulder before releasing him. "You and your sister
are my first priority. But if I can do anything
for your dad, I'll try. You understand that he's

broken the law? That if I see him, I'll have to arrest him?"

Nate nodded. "But the bald man will kill him if he can't find Abby."

Also true. "Yeah, bud." Garrett hooked his thumbs into his belt beside his gun and badge. "Between you, me, Jessie and Detective Wildman, we'll keep Abby safe." He glanced back to see that Conor was standing, too. "If Detective Wildman will help me, we'll do what we can to protect your dad, too."

"You bet." Conor pulled back the front of his jacket and tucked his hands into the pockets of his slacks. "Thank you for your help this morning."

Nate considered the grown men's response to his request, no doubt weighing his conflicted loyalty to his father who'd created this dangerous situation against his desire to simply be a normal kid without life-or-death concerns.

Garrett tried to give him some of the latter. "You did good, Nate. Abby and Jessie are on the back deck. If you want, you can go out with them and play with Toby. But stay where we can see you. I need to talk to Detective Wildman for a few minutes."

He ran all the way through the house to

the back door before he stopped and turned. "You're not gonna ask Abby any of these questions, are you?" Even drawn up to his full height, Nate stood two feet shorter than Garrett, but he heard the man-to-man tone in the boy's voice. "She won't talk to you. Talking about the bald man makes her cry."

"You aren't the only one protecting her now, Nate. I'll do everything in my power to keep you and your sister safe."

Nate evaluated Garrett's promise, shrugged, then pulled open the back door. "Okay." He charged across the deck to the railing overlooking the back yard. "Toby!"

The black Lab loped up the steps to accept the bacon the boy had stashed in his pocket. Then the two were chasing and wrestling across the back deck.

Conor stepped up beside Garrett. "If he's this good a witness in a courtroom deposition, Kai Olivera will go away forever."

"If Nate makes it to a courtroom." Garrett glanced at the younger man and shook his head. "This isn't just about your damn task force. He's nine years old, for God's sake. He shouldn't have to testify. He shouldn't even know about drugs and enforcers and protecting his sister from a deviant like Olivera."

"You think Olivera wants to sell her or keep her?"

"Does it matter?" Garrett shoved his fingers through his hair. He'd kept his cool for about as long as he could manage. "He doesn't get to touch her again. Ever."

"Agreed. One hundred percent. But it could decide whether I cut off his head or his private parts when I arrest him." Right. He'd forgotten that Wildman used wicked sarcasm to dispel the tension he felt.

Garrett needed something more physical. He started pacing. "That's why he waited so long to report them missing. He was giving them a head start."

"And now Olivera is probably putting the screws to him pretty hard to find his payment for the missing drugs and money."

Garrett eyed the younger man. "You need someone from your task force to pick up Swiegert and put him in protective custody."

"It's on my to-do list. But Swiegert's gone to ground since our interview yesterday. He probably realized how much trouble he's in."

"Or he's somewhere getting high again. Drowning his sorrows. Easing his pain. Forgetting he even has kids."

Conor pulled out his phone to check his

messages. "There's nothing new from any of my team. You don't think Olivera took him out already, do you?"

Garrett paced across the living room. "What's it going to do to those children if he gets killed?"

"My question is, why wouldn't he take the children and run away with them?"

He paced back to the kitchen. "An addict with only twenty dollars, a broken hand, and a lowlife like Olivera after him is a lot harder to hide than two small children."

"Take my pocket change and run?" Conor shook his head. "It's not much of a plan."

"He's not much of a father."

"Sounds like you've gotten pretty attached to those kids already," the detective speculated.

"They're important to Jessie, and that makes them important to me." He raked his fingers through his hair. That wasn't the whole truth. "Kids in danger is a real trigger for me. Goes back to my time in the Army. Innocent bystanders getting killed? Children brainwashed by a parent or elder to sacrifice themselves for the cause? I just want them to be safe and not have to worry about the kind of crap you and I take care of every day."

Conor's grim expression indicated he understood where he was coming from.

Conor punched in a number on his phone and put it up to his ear. "I'll see if I can call in reinforcements to help track down Swiegert."

"What if he's complicit in all this?" Garrett felt his blood pressure rising. "What if Swiegert doesn't give a damn about those kids, and he wants to find Abby and make the payment as badly as Olivera does? Use his daughter to get back in his boss's good graces?"

He stopped midstride and braced his hands at his waist and stared out the back door windows. Jessie was working with a small terrier mix and showing Abby the hand signals to get the dog to sit and stay. Although Abby was more about rewarding the dog with treats and exchanging pets for licks than in learning the actual skills, she was talking—to the dog. Nate had found a Frisbee and sent it flying from the edge of the deck. Toby was off like a big black bullet, chasing it down and leaping at the last moment to catch the disk squarely in his mouth. Then Jessie showed him how to call the dog to return to him. Nate's narrow shoulders puffed up when the Lab did exactly as he asked, trotting up the stairs and dropping the disk at his feet for a reward of more petting and a treat. Nate threw the disk again and Toby was off to the races.

It was a normal scene. They were having fun. They were being kids.

The inside of Garrett's stomach burned with the goodness of it all, and just how quickly these moments of happiness could be destroyed.

He sensed the distant contact and shifted his gaze to find Jessie staring back at him, frowning with questions and concern.

Garrett blinked and quickly turned away. He ran into Conor Wildman's watchful blue eyes. "You okay?" the detective asked.

"I need a minute." He didn't bother trying to gloss over his dark mood. The detective was too perceptive for that. He heard Abby squeal in delight and Jessie laughing through the back door behind him. He was jealous that they could find any happiness in all of this. And he didn't intend to spoil that for them. He pointed a commanding finger at the detective. "You got eyes on them for now?"

"I got this." He nodded toward the front door. "Go. Burn off your steam. I need you to have your head in the game. I don't want to traumatize these kids any more than you do."

Garrett slammed the door behind him and

hurried down the porch steps. His first thought was to get in his truck and drive fast to somewhere, anywhere. But the rational voice in his head reminded him that he was the protection detail. He might not be a sniper staking down a rooftop or a mountain ridge. But he was the backup he'd promised KCPD he'd provide. He was the last line of defense who would keep Jessie, Nate, and Abby, and this whole damn county safe from Swiegert, Olivera, and his crew. He wouldn't abandon his post.

He stalked past his truck and headed to the barn. The dogs raised a cacophony of alert and excited barks as he passed their kennels. Rex came around the side of the barn, identified him, then loped away to whatever corner of the property he was patrolling today.

The cooler air of the barn tempered his anger for a moment. But then the images of everything Nate had told him filled his head. He hadn't been there, but he'd fought in a war, he'd worked a SWAT team, he'd led his patrol division to every kind of call imaginable. His imagination was as vividly clear as if he'd witnessed all Nate Swiegert had for himself.

An overmuscled, tattooed thug cradling sweet, quiet Abby on his lap and not giving a damn that the little girl was crying.

Nate finding his dad passed out on the living room floor and dragging the grown man's body over to the couch.

A nine-year-old boy wearing clothes that no longer fit him staring into empty kitchen cabinets and finally making a dinner of peanut butter and jelly sandwiches for him and his five-year-old sister. Again.

A desperate, broken man sending his young children out into the world with a twenty-dollar bill, as if that alone would protect them from the evils pursuing them.

Kai Olivera smiling with a devilish expression that matched the skulls on his temples telling Zane Swiegert he could pay his debt with his little girl.

With a feral roar, Garrett swung around and punched his fist against the post beside one of the stalls.

He heard Mama Penny's yelp of surprise a second before he felt the hands closing over his forearm and pulling his arm down to his side.

"Garrett." Jessie's firm voice called him from the depths of his mind. Every muscle in his forearm was tense beneath her grip. "You're bleeding." Then one hand was cupping the side of his jaw and angling his face down to hers. He was drowning in the turbulent gray waters of her beautiful eyes tilted up to his. "You keep it together, Garrett Caldwell. Those kids don't need anyone else scaring them."

He breathed in deeply, once, twice, willing the anger to leave him. But it only morphed into a sense of helplessness. "Are they safe?"

"Yes. I left them with Detective Wildman and Shadow. You're the one I'm worried about. I could see you were upset. When you stormed out of the house—"

Upset? Hell yeah, he was upset. There were so many good people in this world who'd been denied children. Like this woman right here. Like Hayley. Like him. While Zane Swiegert had those two brave, beautiful children to call his own. His hand curled into a fist again. "Who does that? It's bad enough that he forced that boy to be the adult in the family. That he let Olivera hit him. But he'll leave him alone if he hands Abby over to him? Who sells his own child?"

"A monster. Not a man." Her steady voice calmed him. He focused on where she touched him—his face, his forearm. He couldn't even feel the pain where the skin over his knuckles had split. "What those children need right now is a good man. Nate, especially, needs to talk to and spend time with someone who shows him how a real man acts. That's you, Garrett. He needs *you*."

But all he could see was that little Afghan boy again, his father guilting him or brainwashing him or tricking him into sacrificing himself to take out a few American soldiers. The memory of how he'd had to line him up in the crosshairs of his rifle scope and pull the trigger before the boy could detonate the bomb was as vivid as the bruise on Nate's face. Using a child. Throwing away a child. "Zane Swiegert doesn't deserve to be a father."

"Maybe not. But you can't think about that right now. You have to think about the children. You have to let go of your anger and focus on what they need."

"What about what I need? What about what you need?"

"What do you mean—?"

Garrett captured Jessie's sweet face between his hands and crashed his mouth down over hers. Anger morphed into passion. Desire morphed into need. Her lips parted beneath his and he thrust his tongue inside to taste the essence of coffee and bacon and Jessie herself. When her arms came around his neck, he skimmed his hands down her back, pulling her body flush with his. But it wasn't enough. It wasn't nearly enough.

The frantic need he felt wasn't all one-sided, either, and Jessie's eagerness fueled his own. Her fingertips pawed at the nape of his neck. And then with a moan deep in her throat, she grabbed a fistful of his T-shirt in one hand while the other swept against the grain of his hair, exciting him with hundreds of tiny caresses before she palmed the back of his head and turned him to an angle that allowed her to nip at his chin, press a kiss to the corner of his mouth, then allow some mutual plundering of each other's lips again.

His blood caught fire, burning the anger from his system and leaving him aware of her lush mouth and womanly curves plastered against his harder angles. Needing more, wanting everything, he palmed her butt with both hands and lifted her into his heat. Her breasts flattened beneath his chest as he pushed her back against the post and trapped her there. He finally tore his mouth from hers and trailed his lips along her jaw until he captured her earlobe and pulled it between his teeth. She shivered against him and breathed his name.

He'd gone so long without this. So long without her. So long without love.

"Garrett." She wrapped one leg behind his knee, giving him the access to thrust himself helplessly against her heat. Her lips brushed against the throbbing pulse in his neck. "Garrett, we have to—" he claimed her mouth again and poured everything he was feeling in one last kiss "—need to stop."

"I know."

His body was going to hate him for this. But as her fingers eased their tight grip on his hair and neck, he pulled his mouth from hers, pressing one light kiss, then two, to her warm, swollen lips before he let her feet slide to the ground and he rested his forehead against hers. He was hard as a rock inside his jeans, not bad for a man his age, but he felt lighter, saner, more grounded now that he and Jessie had taken their fill of each other.

It took a little longer to even out his breathing. A few moments more before he could fully lose himself in the stormy gray eyes looking up at him.

"I'm sorry." He gently rubbed his hands up and down her arms. "I'm sorr—"

"Don't." Her fingers came up to sweep across his mouth, reminding him just how sensitized they were after that kiss on steroids. "Don't you dare apologize for losing it a little with me. After twelve years, I sometimes forget what passion feels like. How... heady it is to be needed like that."

"I didn't give you much choice."

"If I had said no, you would have stopped."

"You've got that much faith in me?"

"Yes. I know you have demons, too, Garrett. And the story Nate shared with you and Conor triggered them. But I also know you are a protector down to your core. If you weren't, you wouldn't have gotten so upset." She ran her hands across his chest and shoulders, as if smoothing out the wrinkles she might have left there. Then she leaned back and took a stab at straightening his hair. He treasured the gentle caresses as much as he did every kiss they shared. "Are you better?"

He was. He'd needed a physical outlet for his emotions, and she'd somehow known and been there for him. Such a strong woman, yet so caring and feminine. "Feeling a little raw," he confessed. "But better."

"Good." She pulled his hand from her arm and turned so she could put even more space between them. "Now let me see your injury."

She cradled his bigger hand gently between

hers to inspect how his knuckles had fared against the post. She clicked her tongue, then grabbed his wrist and tugged him into step behind her.

She paused at the first storage room door, inserted a key into the lock, and opened it. Larger than the room that had been broken into, this one had a huge stainless steel sink where she could wash the dogs. She turned on the water and pulled his hand beneath the warm stream to clean the debris out of his wound while she opened a cabinet and pulled out a first aid kit and a bottle of hydrogen peroxide. She hooked her foot around a tall stool and pulled it out from beside the sink. "Have a seat."

He turned off the water and dutifully sat in front of her while she used a clean towel to dry his skin and gently dab at the blood seeping from his split knuckles. "Did I hear you correctly? Zane Swiegert plans to use Abby to pay off his debt to Olivera?"

Garrett nodded. "Nate overheard his dad talking to Olivera. That makes him a witness. Swiegert and Olivera are going to want to shut him up so he can't talk to the cops or testify against them."

"His own father?"

"Supposedly, it was his idea for the kids to run away, but…" Garrett swore under breath. "Drugs change a man. I'm sure Swiegert didn't mean to endanger his children, but a desperate man does desperate things. And the main thing an addict is thinking about is his next fix. Not his job, not his family, not even his own health. I think they're both a threat."

He raised an eyebrow at Jessie's answering curse. "I will not lose another child, Garrett. Not to the kind of violence you're talking about. I can't."

He stilled her hand beneath his. "We won't let that happen. Between KCPD and my team, we'll keep round-the-clock watch on your house." She nodded and went back to work. "And I'm moving in until this is over. *I* am going to watch over you and the kids. I want to talk escape strategies and survival protocol with you and them, too."

"I'm okay with that." She soaked a cotton ball with the disinfectant. "Do you want to talk about it?"

"When I think about what Olivera wants to do with Abby. How he hit and belittled Nate… it takes me back to some places I don't want to go." He winced at the sting of peroxide on his open wound. The foolish mistake of punching the barn post was certainly bringing him back to reality. "My wife dying wasn't the only reason I had to leave the Army. They could have put me behind a desk or in a training camp. But I couldn't guarantee that I could take the shot anymore."

"Those flashbacks are a bitch, right?" Although he was at first taken aback by the vehemence of her words, he looked up to see a smug smile on her face. She beat back her demons every damn day. He would do the same. "Want me to train a therapy dog for you?"

He chuckled. "Nah. I've got *you*."

"I'm your therapy *woman*?"

He stopped her doctoring and reached up to tag her behind the neck to meet her eyes and make sure she understood just how serious he was about the two of them. "You said I ground you. That I'm the solid, reliable man you can depend on. I feel the same way about you. I've seen and lost too much in my life. But with you, all that becomes the past. You make me want to stay in the present and look forward, not back. I see what the future looks like when I'm with you. I see everything that's missing in my life. I want that future. I like how I feel when I'm with you. Please give me the chance to love you, Jessie. I feel like you're the reward for surviving everything I've lost."

She shook her head with a wry smile and concentrated on wrapping the self-stick tape to keep the gauze in place around his hand. "I've got too many hang-ups to be anybody's reward."

"I don't want perfect. I want perfect for me." He touched two fingers to the point of her chin and tilted her face up to his. "That's you. I want you. I need you."

"Garrett..."

"I know, I know. I'm too intense and you're a slow mover. Let's get through this mess with Olivera and Swiegert first. Make sure those children are safe and in a loving home. Then maybe I can woo you at your pace." He released her when he could feel the apprehension vibrating through her. "This may feel sudden to you, but it's not to me. I love you, Jessie Bennington. I know it in every bone of my body. I just hope that one day you'll take a chance on loving me, too."

"I want that, too, Garrett." *But...* That unspoken word echoed through the small room. She turned away to drop the soiled items into the trash. "I don't know if I can convey just how scared..."

Her voice trailed away when his phone buzzed in his pocket. As a lawman, he couldn't ignore a potential emergency. He read the number. "It's Conor." He rose to his feet. "Caldwell here."

"You need to get in here." It wasn't the five-alarm emergency of intruders on the premises, but it was an emergency nonetheless. "There's something wrong with Ms. Bennington's dog. The kids are freaking out."

Garrett hung up and grabbed Jessie's hand in his injured one. "It's Shadow. He's having a seizure."

Chapter Nine

Jessica stood in the shadows of her living room watching Garrett stretched across her couch in a T-shirt and sweatpants. His bandaged hand was thrown up and resting on the pillow above his head. He'd kicked off the blanket and his feet were propped on the armrest. She wondered if he really could compartmentalize the stress and responsibility he took so seriously and relax his mind enough to sleep. Of course, he'd been burning the candle at both ends so much recently that maybe his body was exhausted enough that it wasn't giving him any choice but to sleep.

Hugging her arms around her waist, she leaned against the archway near the foot of the stairs and studied him from the top of his mussed salt-and-pepper hair down to the masculine length of his toes. Maybe this was enough, simply reassuring herself that he was here. Knowing he could be right beside her in a heartbeat if she needed him.

She admired the flat of his stomach and the narrow vertical strip of dark hair exposed between the hem of his shirt and the waist-band of his pants. Even that was sprinkled with shards of silver hair, and she was curious to discover if all the hair on his chest was peppered like a silver fox. She'd loved John dearly, but it had been a long time since she'd felt so viscerally attracted to another man. She might not have all the lady parts she'd once had, but there were still other parts of her that stirred with unmistakable interest in all the things that made Garrett so distinctly male. Beard stubble. Firm lips. Deep voice. Broad shoulders. Muscled chest.

She was visually making her way down his sturdy thighs when one green eye blinked open.

"Jessie? You okay?"

She swung her gaze back up to his. "I can't sleep."

Both eyes were watching her now. "The kids?"

"Dead to the world."

"Shadow?"

"Fine. He responded to the pill as quickly as Hazel said he would and has been taking it easy ever since. I fear his loyalty has switched to Nate." She sighed, feeling both a little lost and happy she'd trained Shadow so well. "That dog is intuitive. He probably senses that Nate needs some unconditional love and support from a furry friend right now."

He held out his hand. "Do you want to cuddle?"

"Not exactly."

He swung his legs over the front of the sofa and sat up, looking wide-awake and a little worried now. "Talk to me."

Jessica straightened and crossed the room on silent feet. "I've been thinking about something you said today. In the barn."

"You mean when I was losing my—"

"No. After that."

"I'm sure it was pithy and life altering. What did I say?"

"You said I was your reward for surviving everything you've lost." She circled the coffee table and sat—close enough to feel his heat, but not close enough to touch. "I feel the same way. You're my reward for surviving. I'm so grateful you're part of my life. I'm grateful you're here with us now." She ducked her head, letting her loose waves fall around her face. She was uncertain until that very moment what she wanted to say to him. She tucked her hair behind her ears and raised her gaze to his again. "But I don't want gratitude to be the only thing between us."

"It's not."

"My *pace* is all about self-protection. I want to be braver than that. I want to live like you do. I want to love again. I'm falling in love with those children. And you know how I am with my dogs." He nodded, listening carefully, just one more thing that made it easy to open up to him. "You taking care of the things that are precious to me makes it awfully hard not to fall in love with you."

He reached over and tucked a wayward tendril of hair behind her ear. "I'm not doing it to impress you. Those things matter to me, too, because you matter." He arched an eyebrow. "But I am making progress with you?"

Very definitely. She stood, holding out her hand in invitation. "Come to bed with me."

"I'm comfortable with sleeping down here."

"I'm not."

Nodding his understanding of her sincerity, he pulled his gun and holster from the drawer of her coffee table and stood. Once he'd pocketed his phone, he took her hand and followed her up the stairs.

They paused to look in on the children and dog. All safe. All fast asleep.

"Is Conor or one of his men outside?" Jessica whispered.

Garrett pulled the door to, leaving an opening just wide enough for Shadow to step out if he needed to. "One of my officers, Levi Fox, is parked at the end of your driveway until his shift ends in the morning. Maya Hernandez will replace him until KCPD sends one of their unmarked cars out to take over."

She probably should be embarrassed by the state of her rumpled bed. But she'd tossed and turned, rethinking everything that had happened over the past few days and remembering the only time she'd truly relaxed was when Garrett had held her that first night here. Releasing his hand, she quickly straightened and fluffed the sheet and quilt, then sat on the edge of the bed and patted the mattress beside her. "I'm pretty rusty at this, but I want you."

He tucked his gun in the bedside table and set his phone on top. "To sleep? To hold you? Or something more?"

"Yes. All of that." Could she sound any more inexperienced, like she'd forgotten every sexual encounter she'd had? "Maybe in reverse order?"

He chuckled, and she tumbled into him as he sat on the mattress beside her. He draped his arm around her shoulders and tangled his fingers in her long hair. The man was a furnace, and she instantly felt better being held against him. "Just to be clear, we're talking about making love? Then cuddling in the happy afterglow and falling asleep?"

Jessica pulled her knees up and let them fall over his thighs as she turned to wrap her arms around his waist. "Sounds like heaven to me. If you're up for it."

"Trust me. Around you, I always seem to be up for it." He pressed a kiss to the crown of her hair. "I just want you to be sure."

She laughed and remembered how much she loved a man who could make her laugh. Jessica cupped the side of his jaw, tickling her palm against the stubble of his beard, and angled his mouth down as she stretched up to meet him. "Let's start with a kiss. We can start where we were last night and end up where we were in the barn this afternoon."

"Sounds like a plan." He laughed as he closed the distance between them and covered her mouth in a gentle kiss.

Then he fell back across the bed, dragging her with him until she was lying on top of him.

Just as she'd requested, the tender embrace soon became needy grabs and tongues melding together. Her thighs fell open on either side of his hips, giving her a clear indication that he was as into this mutual exploration as she was. His hands swept down her body, then back up, taking her shirt with it. He squeezed her bottom and pulled her up along his body until he latched on to the breast dangling above his mouth. He laved the tip with his tongue as he plumped the other in his hand.

Jessica groaned at the stinging heat that tightened her nipples into stiff beads and shot straight down between her legs. By the time he was done feasting on her other breast, she had pushed his shirt out of the way and found his own turgid male nipple to tease to attention among the crisp curls of silver and sable hair that dusted his chest. Her hair cascaded around their busy mouths and hands as she leaned over him, and it seemed to drive Garrett's urgency. He alternately tangled his fingers in the long, silky strands, murmuring words like, "Silky…soft…beauty…" before tugging just hard enough to bring her mouth back to his.

Then his arms banded around her, and he flipped them so that he was on top. He brushed her hair out in a halo around her head as she pushed his sweatpants down over his hips to reveal the erection she'd felt pressing against her. "Garrett...please."

In the next few seconds, her sleep shorts were gone and he was naked, kissing his way from her mouth down over her belly. It was her only moment of hesitation, and she grabbed his chin and turned his face up to hers. "I have scars," she gasped, her words breathy and uneven with desire for this man.

Garrett pushed himself up over her and dipped his head to reclaim her lips in a tender kiss. "So do I. Want to see them?"

"Not right now. Not really." She valiantly tried to remind him that she was forty-six, had been pregnant once, and bore the scars of both the bullet and her surgeries.

But he wasn't having any second thoughts. "Me, neither." He splayed his hand over her belly, touching it as if it was precious to him. "I mean, I care about what they mean. I care so much about you." He planted a quick kiss to her lips, then resumed his path down her body. "But seriously, Jessie. I'm a man. I've got it bad for you. And if I don't get inside you in the next few minutes, I'm going to embarrass myself and finish this off without you." His hand slid down to cup her, and she bucked against his grip. "Every inch of you is beautiful to me. Please. Let me do this."

All she could do was nod. And when he asked about protection, she kissed him again, thanking him for treating her like a normal, desirable woman. "I can't get pregnant, remember? And I haven't had sex since John died, so I'm clean."

"Me, too. Thank you for this gift."

"Thank you for making me feel safe enough to want this." He settled his hips over hers, nudging at her entrance, and the pressure building inside felt as exciting as it was unfamiliar. She wasn't some born-again spinster who'd gone too long since she'd been with a man. She understood now that she'd just been waiting for the one she wanted to be with. "Now, Garrett."

There was a little discomfort when he first pushed inside her. But with his thumb strumming her back to that wild readiness, they quickly fell into a timeless rhythm that neither age nor abstinence nor tragedy could ever completely erase. Jessica wound her legs around his hips and welcomed him with the sense that she was finally where she wanted to be. There were no acrobatics or fancy words, just a man and a woman and the love that had grown slowly and perfectly between them, finally reaching the light and blossoming into a feeling so right, she gasped with the pleasure of it.

She shattered into a million pieces and rode the shock waves as Garrett groaned with satisfaction and completed himself inside her.

Several minutes later, after bringing her a warm washcloth to clean and soothe her tender flesh, Garrett lay back and pulled her into his arms. She draped herself against him, deciding this closeness was much more enjoyable with no clothes between them. "Feeling okay, hon?"

Jessica would have laughed if she had the energy. She murmured, "Uh-hmm. You?"

"If I was any more okay, I'd be dead."

She was drifting off to a contented sleep as he covered them both and set the alarm on his phone. "I'll sneak out later before the kids wake in the morning. You can put a T-shirt back on then, too."

She kissed his chest, thanking him for his consideration. Then he closed his eyes. Embracing the knowledge that this was what happiness felt like, Jessica snuggled in and fell asleep.

SPENDING FIVE DAYS with Nate and Abby, and five nights with Garrett in her bed—not always making love, but always holding each other close—made Jessica feel like a young woman with a good life ahead of her again.

She was a little sore, a little tired, a little scared. But her life was filled with so much purpose now. She had more to look forward to than work. She basically homeschooled the children in the morning while Garrett went to work so that no one watching the house would think anything unusual about a sudden change in his schedule, while another officer either from the sheriff's office or KCPD watched over the house. She scheduled training sessions in the afternoon for her clients, while the children stayed indoors and out of sight.

And though she hadn't said the *love* word out loud, she felt it ready to burst from her heart. She felt it from Garrett, too. With each chaste kiss, every laugh, every smile. She felt it in the eager way he touched her body, and in the firm yet patiently paternal way he worked with Nate and Abby.

They had finally reported Nate and Abby being found to Family Services and, under strict orders from a judge, promised to keep their whereabouts secret until the danger had passed. The social worker who'd driven out to check on the welfare of the children had even agreed to expedite a temporary foster care placement with Jessica that wouldn't be processed through the system until they were sure Zane Swiegert couldn't track them as the custodial parent. Paperwork was also being drawn up to terminate Swiegert's parental rights. But again, nothing official was going forward as long as Nate and Abby were in protective custody.

Conor Wildman and his wife, Laura, were good people. Laura had taken the initiative and gotten some new clothes in the right sizes for Nate and Abby, and had picked up a couple of age-appropriate toys and games for them. Their daughter, Marie, was just a year younger than Abby, and when the family came over for dinner, the little girls played together and seemed to become fast friends.

Shadow hadn't had another seizure since the morning of Conor's interview with Nate, and she hadn't had another flashback since Garrett and the children had moved in.

It wasn't perfect. Abby communicated in her own way, but still wasn't talking to any adults. And Nate seemed to be waiting for the other shoe to drop. He'd gotten him and his sister away from Kansas City, but he rarely dropped his guard, except with the dogs. He reminded Jessica of the way she'd been even a couple of weeks ago. Happy but afraid. Confident but worried. Wanting to be free of the violence that haunted him, yet always expecting it would one day return. Jessica and Garrett had discussed their concerns with the social worker, and she promised to have a child psychologist lined up to talk with Nate and Abby as soon as it was safe to do so.

If she was being completely honest with herself, Jessica was still waiting for the other shoe to drop, too.

This morning Jessica was on the back deck, sipping an iced tea and watching Nate play the flying disk game with Toby out in the yard while Abby finished up her schoolwork at the table across from her. The little girl had lit up when Hugo brought over one of Penny's puppies as a reward for doing her schoolwork. With the promise that she'd return the puppy to the barn after lunch, Hugo had patted Abby's head and traded a salute with Nate before he climbed into his truck and headed home for the day.

The hair at the nape of her neck prickled to attention when Shadow growled from the deck beside her. One second, he was lounging in the relatively warm sunshine. The next, his hackles were up, and he'd jumped to his feet.

"Shadow?" Setting her drink down, she checked her watch. Nothing had pinged on the camera alert, indicating they had visitors. She skimmed the backyard and peered as much as she could into the trees lining the property. The puppy whimpered with concern as Shadow looked toward where Miss Eloise had shown up with her shotgun last week and growled again.

Today, she only hoped it was a lonely old woman with a shotgun.

Then she heard Rex's booming bark. Toby alerted to the sound like a call to battle and raced off into the trees. To her horror, she watched Nate take off right after him.

"Nate, stop!" Jessica was on her feet, hurrying down the steps with Shadow loping beside her. The little boy reluctantly stopped and came trudging toward her. She combed her fingers through his sweaty hair and brushed it off his face in a tender gesture he jerked away from. But there was fear trembling in his bottom lip, despite his defiance. "I'll check it out with the dogs. Get your sister in the house. You know what to do."

He glanced up at Abby, who cradled the puppy in her arms at the top of the steps. Her blues eyes darted between Jessica and her brother. Nate nodded and raced up the stairs to grab her hand. "I know."

Jessica waited until Nate had locked the back door behind them. Then she brushed her fingers across Shadow's head and issued the command. "Shadow, seek."

The dog raced into the trees, and she jogged after him.

But when she cleared the low-hanging evergreen branches, she pulled up short at the sight that greeted her. Not Miss Eloise complaining about her dogs and a dead chicken.

Parked just on the other side of her fence was Isla Gardner and a heavy-duty pickup pimped out with red and orange flames painted across the sides and tailgate. And yeah, there was some kind of short rifle on a rack in the back window of the truck. Isla looked a little pimped out herself with her bleached blond hair pulled up in a bouncy high ponytail, her painted fingernails bedazzled with sparkly jewels, and her white tank top pulled tight enough to look uncomfortable over her unnaturally perky breasts.

But the scariest thing about Isla was the tall, muscular man beside her, wearing a denim cut over a sleeveless white T-shirt. He had a sleeve of tats up and down his left arm and wore dark glasses that completely masked his eyes. He sported a brown crewcut, a long beard that would rival any '80s rock band guitarist, and he had a black skull tattooed on the side of his neck. More alarming yet, he had both hands on the top railing of Miss Eloise's fence as if he'd been about to leap over it onto Jessica's property.

"Jessica, hi." Isla greeted her with a friendly smile and reached for the bruiser's hand. "I'm showing my boyfriend around the place."

"Hey, Isla." She noted that while Isla held tight to her new man's hand, he didn't care enough to fold his around hers, as well. While that was a pitying observation compared to the way Garrett treated *her*, Jessica's focus was on the dangerous-looking man and the neighbor who'd never been this neighborly before. "What is it with your family and my animals?"

"Grandma told me she'd had a run-in with you and your dogs and Deputy Caldwell. Are you dating him?" she boldly asked.

Thinking of where Garrett had spent the last five nights, she'd have to say yes. But something told her to get this get-together over with as quickly as possible without raising any suspicion. "How's your grandmother doing?" she countered. "Taking her meds?"

"I guess." She eyed the big Anatolian shepherd, who was eyeing her. "Are you going to call your dogs off?"

"They're on my land, so no, I don't need to."

Rex paced back and forth along the fence line, barking an occasional woof when he got too close to the visitors on the other side. Toby trotted eagerly beside him, still carrying the Frisbee Nate had thrown in his mouth. Jessica could have easily called them over and ordered them to sit. But she liked the idea of having a couple of big dogs between her and her unexpected guests. She kept Shadow beside her, curling her fingers into his fur to keep herself from panicking.

After a glance from the man beside her, Isla giggled. "Well, I figured since we were neighbors, we could come over and visit this way."

"Not unless you want Rex to take a bite out of you. He doesn't like surprises."

Isla's smile faded and she propped her hands on her hips. "Well, that's not very neighborly. What if I came over to borrow a cup of sugar for Grandma?"

"Did you?"

Finally, the behemoth spoke. "I heard about

this place. You rescue dogs and turn them into attack dogs." Despite his size, he had a raspy, oddly pitched voice.

"Service dogs," she corrected. "Medical alert dogs, companion animals, sometimes a guard dog."

He turned his head, following Toby's bouncy movements. "What's that one got in his mouth?"

"Toby, come." The black Lab trotted up to her and sat. Jessica tapped the top of his muzzle. "Drop it."

She quickly scooped up the warped plastic disk and tucked it into the back of her jeans before petting the Lab and sending him back to trail after Rex. "It's a dog toy."

"Looks like a child's toy to me," he argued.

"Not if one of my dogs decides it's his to chew up." She squinted up at him, wishing she could see his eyes so that she could give Garrett and Conor a better description. "Who are you?"

"I'm with Isla."

Not an answer. But that wasn't any more suspicious than the tattoos and lack of eye contact.

"Kevie, don't be mean. I said I'd show you around Grandma's place and introduce you to the strange neighbor lady. Told you she prefers dogs to people."

She'd trade the *strange* insult for a little more information on the new boyfriend.

"How long have you two known each other?" Jessica asked, trying to keep her tone politely serious. With the matching tat, this guy had to be working with Kai Olivera. But did Isla know what was going on? Was she aiding and abetting a criminal or being taken advantage of?

"I met Kevie about a week ago at a bar up in Lone Jack." She walked her fingers up over his bulky shoulder. "I don't think I've hit it off with a guy as fast as I did with you."

The moment she touched her long nail to his lips, he grabbed her wrist and twisted it roughly down to her side. "I told you not to do that." When Isla rubbed her wrist as if his grip had hurt her, he tapped the end of her nose and flashed a quick smile. "Baby."

Isla smiled as though the endearment made everything better. "What can I say? He gets me."

Or he's using you. To get to me and the children.

Speaking of children... Suddenly, Kevie wanted to talk. "Hey, I've got a friend in the city. His kids have gone missing. Have you seen a little blonde girl about yea high?" He spread his thick fingers down by his thigh. Then raised it a few inches. "Or a boy about this big?"

With her worst fears confirmed—that this guy was looking for Nate and Abby for his pal, Olivera—she carefully schooled her voice into a friendly, yet casual tone. "We're kind of in the middle of nowhere here. Children don't just wander by. Unless they're farmers' kids. And I know most of the locals. They stop by the house to sell things for school fundraisers, that sort of thing. I've got one young man who works for me a couple times a week. But he'd be taller than what you're looking for."

"Show them the picture, Kev—baby," Isla suggested, finally grasping that he didn't want her blabbing his name to Jessica.

"Yeah." Kevie pulled a folded piece of paper from the back pocket of his jeans. He shook it open and handed it over the fence. It was a photocopy of a flyer with Nate's and Abby's school pictures Zane Swiegert must have made and distributed around the city. "That's them. You seen them around here?"

Jessica shook her head and handed it back. But the moment Kevie's hand came over the fence, Shadow growled and Rex gave him a warning bark.

The big man snatched his hand back, his cheeks growing ruddy with anger. "I'm not afraid of your dogs," he insisted.

"You don't have to be afraid of anything, unless you're up to something you shouldn't be."

He turned his face to the side and spit. Jessica was quite certain that was his opinion of a strong woman who challenged his authority. "You got a mouth on you, don't you?"

Again, she ignored the insult in favor of gaining more information. "They're beautiful children. How did they get lost?"

"They're not lost. The little cowards ran away." He pointed a stubby finger at her, and when Toby propped his front paws up on the fence, thinking he was about to make a new friend, the man shoved him away. "You see those kids, give me a call at the number on the back of that paper."

"Or call me," Isla offered, backing away as Kevie stalked back to his truck and climbed inside. "I can get a hold of him."

Isla barely had the door open and her foot on the running board before he stomped on the accelerator and sped away. She fell into the passenger seat and closed the door as gravel, grass, and other debris flew out behind the fishtailing truck.

Jessica quickly shielded her eyes and spun away. She felt the sting of debris hitting the back of her legs, and heard a yelp of pain. She was grateful for a good pair of jeans and thick boots to protect herself, but knew instantly one of the dogs had been hurt. She should feel guilty for checking Shadow first, but when he seemed fine enough to bark at the truck speeding away, she turned to the other two. With the threat gone, Rex was loping away. But Toby was limping.

"Toby! Here!" Grateful that he was still mobile, she gave him a quick once-over, then scratched him around the ears and urged him to follow her to the house. "Come on, boys. It's for your own safety as well as mine."

Jessica pulled her phone from her pocket and chased after the dogs who were already racing back to the house. She tapped the familiar number and put the phone to her ear, pushing past the trees and hurrying up to the deck.

Garrett answered after the first ring. "Jessie?"

"I need you."

From the sound of his breathing she could tell he was moving. "What's wrong?"

"A man was here. Kevie Something. Said he was Isla Gardner's new boyfriend, but I think he was just using her to get access to the property. He had a tattoo on his neck like the picture you showed me of Kai Olivera."

"Did he hurt you?"

"No, but..."

"But what?"

She stomped up the stairs to the deck, trying to catch her breath so she could talk. "He acted like he knew I was lying about the children. He spooked me. He drove away way too fast. Kicked up gravel. He nicked Toby."

Garrett swore. "I'm leaving the office right now. Get to the kids, then call Hernandez. She's on duty at the gate."

"Are you coming?" She pulled out her keys and unlocked the door.

"I'm on my way. Get inside the house. Lock the doors. Take Shadow and Toby with you. You can doctor him up inside."

"I got the guy's license plate."

"Give it to me." She rattled off the letters and numbers. "All right. I'll run this. See if we can get an ID. I'm guessing he's a known associate of Olivera's. Are the kids okay?"

"I'm not inside yet." Setting aside her fears and focusing on the lock, she got it open and shooed the dogs in ahead of her. "Nate? Abby?" She didn't immediately see them. "You don't think one of his friends got in while he was distracting me?"

"Not with Hernandez there." She hoped. She locked the door behind her and ran up the stairs to their bedroom. She worked outdoors and wasn't afraid of physical labor. But her lungs were about to burst with all this running. "Get eyes on the kids. I'm almost there. Call me right back if something's wrong."

The siren blared in the background before he ended the call. Jessica tucked her phone in her jeans and searched the bedroom. Closet. Under the bed. Behind the door. Shadow followed right on her heels, searching for the children. She dashed across the hall and shoved open the bathroom door. They'd strategized about places in the house where they could hide. This room had a door with a lock and an older tub made of porcelain-coated steel. But there was no Nate. No Abby. Her heart pounded inside her chest. She looked in the tub, in the cabinet under the sink.

"Where are you?" she muttered, looking under other beds and inside other closets. Oh,

God. Had someone gotten into the house and taken the children?

She could feel the snaky tendrils of a panic attack sneaking into her head. "Shadow?"

He was at her side in an instant, leaning against her leg. She listened to him panting. She focused on his warmth. She curled her fingers into his coarse long fur and believed that she was safe. "Nate? Abby?"

She realized she was also armed with a powerful weapon. A dog's nose. "Of course." Jessica raced back into the bedroom where they'd been sleeping and scooped up Nate's pillow and pallet, holding them to Shadow's nose. She hadn't specifically trained him to do search and rescue, but she hoped he'd catch on. "Shadow, seek. Find Nate."

Understanding her meaning if not her words, Shadow trotted back down the stairs and went through the living room and ended up in the kitchen. They moved past Toby, who was curled up on Shadow's bed, licking what was no doubt a cut on his leg.

When Shadow sat down in front of the pantry door, Jessica cursed. She'd run right past it looking for the children. But when she heard a puppy whimpering from the other side of the door, she knew she'd found them. "Good boy, Shadow."

She pulled open the door. "Oh, thank God." Abby was crying, holding the puppy in her arms as she hid behind her brother. Almost dizzy with relief, Jessica reached for them. "You're safe. The man is gone."

But Nate had armed himself with the fireplace poker. "We're not going back! You can't make us!"

Jessica retreated a step and Shadow tilted his head, questioning why his new friend was threatening her. "It's okay, Shadow. Good boy." While she petted the shepherd mix, she spoke softly to the kids. "It's okay, Nate. I got rid of him. Do you know another man with a tattoo on his neck like the bald man has?"

He lowered the poker a fraction. But his eyes were wide with fear. "Did he have a long, dirty brown beard?" She nodded. "He works with the bald man. He was at the apartment when they hurt Dad." He lifted the poker and thrust it at her like a broadsword. "He can't have her, either."

For once, she ignored Shadow growling beside her. "No one is giving either of you up. The lady from Family Services said you're with me for the whole month, remember?

Longer than that, if I have anything to say about it."

"If you're lying, we'll run away again. You have to at least keep Abby here."

Jessica's overtaxed heart nearly broke. "I'm not lying. I want *both* of you to stay with me."

Abby sniffed back her tears and tugged at the sleeve of her brother's shirt. "Natey, Charlie and I want out of here."

But Nate blocked her with his arm, always the protector.

Jessica reassured Shadow that she wasn't afraid and knelt in front of Nate. "Will you let Abby out? You know I won't hurt her."

All three of them startled at the sound of pounding at the door. "Jessie! It's Garrett. Let me in."

Nate relented his protective stance. He lowered the weapon as if having the other man around meant he could drop his guard a bit. "Deputy Caldwell is here?"

"I called him. He came right away when I told him about the man. He's here to help."

Abby seemed relieved to hear Garrett's voice, too. "Natey…" She slipped around her brother and ran into Jessie's arms.

"Jessie!"

She picked up the crying girl, puppy and all, and hurried to the door. "I'm coming!"

The moment she unlatched the door, Garrett pushed it open and locked it behind him. He cupped Abby's cheek and stroked Jessica's hair. "Is everyone all right?" He quickly surveyed the main floor. "Where's Nate?"

The boy came out of the pantry, still holding the poker. Garrett moved past Jessica. "Did you protect your sister the way I told you?"

Nate's eyes were glued on Garrett's. "Yes, sir. I hid us in the kitchen closet until Jessie found us."

"Good man."

"You can't give us back to our dad. The bald man will hurt her."

"That's not the plan, son." He held out his hand for the poker, and Nate reluctantly handed it over. Jessica wished Nate would let someone comfort him and allow him to be a child again, but unlike his sister, he was a touch-me-not. He seemed to appreciate and respond to Garrett's businesslike directives, though. "Jessie told me Toby got hurt. Will you help her take care of him?"

That made the boy react. "Toby got hurt?" He raced across the kitchen to kneel in front of the black Lab. "Tobes?" He probed the spot where the dog had been licking and found blood in his fur. "He's bleeding."

"Will you help Jessie doctor him up?"

The boy nodded.

Jessica carried Abby into the kitchen, drawn to Garrett's calm, strong presence, just like the children were. He petted the scruff of Charlie's neck, then held out his hands to Abby. "Will you let me hold you while Jessie helps Nate with Toby?" Instead of answering, the little girl stretched out one arm to him, keeping the other secured around her pup. Garrett easily took them both into his arms, nestling her on the hip opposite his firearm. Then he spoke to Jessica. "Go. See if you can calm him down. I've got her. I'll need some details when you're done. I've already called the incursion in to Conor. He's sending backup, and I've got Hernandez walking the property line between here and the Gardner farm. I'll have her do a wellness check on Miss Eloise, as well."

Jessica nodded but paused to pull off Garrett's official ballcap and smooth down his hair. If the cap was off, he was staying. "Thank you for coming so quickly."

He dropped a quick kiss to her forehead.

"Nobody's hurting these kids. Or you. Go." He turned away with Abby, carrying her into the living room. "Did I ever tell you the story about the puppy I had when I was little?"

"When were you little?" Abby's shy question were her first words to an adult, and Jessica fought to stem the tears that suddenly blurred her vision.

"A long time ago, sweetie. His name was Ace…"

Chapter Ten

Conor Wildman's suit collar was turned up and his jacket was drenched when Garrett opened the front door to let him into the house two nights later.

The spring rains had finally come. And while the budding trees would leaf out and the grass would turn green once it soaked up enough sun, and the farmers cheered that their crops would start growing, all Garrett could think of was that the dark, overcast sky and wall of rain gave Swiegert, Olivera, and his crew more places to hide.

The security cameras had alerted him to the detective's arrival, but it was too dark to make out who the driver was. If Officer Fox hadn't texted him to tell him Conor was pulling up to the house, Garrett would have met him at the door with his gun in his hand.

He still wore his Glock tucked into the back of his jeans. One of Olivera's men had gotten close enough to touch one of Jessie's dogs. And although Toby's injury had turned out to be no more severe than his own healing knuckles, the danger had come too close to Jessie for his comfort. So, he was armed. He was pissed. And he was deadly. The enemy wasn't getting past him on his watch.

Conor was an ally, not an enemy, though. He folded down his collar and shook the raindrops off his suit coat before stepping inside. He toed off his wet shoes on the mat beside the door and was facing Garrett by the time he'd checked as far as he could see beyond the edge of the front porch and locked the door again.

Conor's collar was unbuttoned, and his tie was missing. The man had had a long day. "We found Zane Swiegert dead. Massive overdose. Don't know if it was accidental, suicide, or murder yet. His body's at the ME's office now."

Garrett appreciated that the detective wasn't a man who minced words. But he wasn't sure how to process the news. His gut reaction was a silent cheer that there was one less lowlife he had to worry about out there in the world. But just as quickly came the thought that somebody was going to have to tell those children, who'd already lost so much, that their father was gone. Zane Swiegert might not win any father-of-the-year awards, but he was someone whom Nate and Abby had loved. And, if Nate's account was correct, he'd done what little he'd been able to in order to help them escape his deal with Kai Olivera. It also occurred to him that their yet-to-be official foster home here with Jessie could continue for real once Olivera was behind bars and the threat to them was over.

He ended up muttering a curse and scrubbing his fingers through his hair. "Those poor kids."

He tilted his head up to where they were sleeping and saw Jessie coming down the stairs. After baths and toothbrushing, she'd been reading them to sleep each night. He sat in on one session and had gotten caught up in the story himself. But mostly, his heart had been aching for that to be his real life—a quiet bedroom, two beautiful children snuggling up on either side of the woman he loved, tucking them in and kissing them good-night—Nate only after he'd fallen asleep and couldn't protest the mushy sign of affection. Then walking across the hall and falling into bed with said woman. They'd make out a little. Or talk.

Sometimes, they'd make love. But always, the night ended with Jessie clinging to him like a second skin and him falling asleep, needing her touch like he needed his next breath.

But that wasn't his life. He was a man with a gun and a badge. Danger surrounded them; Olivera wanted to steal away Abby and kill the boy who would testify against him. And though they clearly had some type of relationship, he'd yet to hear Jessie say the three words he most needed to hear. Not *I love you*. Although, she'd already hinted at her feelings for him.

Let's do this.

Or something to the effect that she was done being cautious and ready to go all in on a relationship with him. To give him not just her body, but her heart. To trust him not just during this crisis, but for the rest of their lives.

He didn't need her to give him children. He couldn't promise that he'd never get hurt on the job. He couldn't promise that someone else who felt wronged wouldn't come after him or the people he loved again.

But he could promise to love her with everything he had until the end of his days.

He could have this life.

Tonight, she wore sweats and a hoodie,

socks, and wool slippers that had lambs embroidered on them, in deference to the dampness and cooler temperature. Her hair was pulled back in a neat braid, her face was scrubbed clean, and she looked the picture of tomboyish domestic bliss he longed for.

She smiled up at Conor and shook his hand in greeting. "You look like a man who could use a hot drink. I brewed some fresh decaf."

"Actually, I'm a man who could use a beer. If you have one."

"The news is that bad, huh?" She turned into the kitchen and gestured to the table. "Have a seat and make yourself comfortable. I'll get your beer."

She popped open a bottle and set it on the place mat in front of Conor while Garrett poured them both a cup of coffee. He added cream and sugar to hers and carried them to the table, where he pulled out a chair and sat beside her.

He let her take a few sips of the hot drink to warm her up before he reached over to squeeze her hand. "Honey, Zane Swiegert OD'd. He's in the morgue."

Her fingers grew cold within his. "What about Nate and Abby? How are we going to tell them?"

He liked that she'd said *we*, and he loved that the kids' welfare was foremost in her thoughts right now. "We'll talk about it tonight." He glanced over at Conor to make sure he wasn't speaking out of turn. "We can sit them down after breakfast and tell them tomorrow."

She nodded. "Nate will be angry. Abby will cry. I wish we could get that psychologist out here to talk to them sooner rather than later."

"I know," he sympathized. "But we can't draw that kind of attention to the house. Not yet."

Conor downed a long swallow of the tangy drink and nodded. "And in more bad news, there's a chance he wasn't a willing victim. Our medical examiner will have an answer sometime tomorrow morning."

Garrett didn't like the pale cast to her skin. She was clearly upset by the news. But he wasn't surprised to see the color flood back into her cheeks again or hear her get down to business. This woman was made of steel. "Olivera? Do you think he's responsible?"

Conor nodded. "If it turns out to be murder, he's at the top of my list. Swiegert reneged on their deal. A man in Olivera's position can't maintain his power if he allows the people who work for him to cheat him out of what he considers rightfully his."

"You're talking about a little girl."

"And drugs and money." The detective leaned forward in his chair. "This isn't a man with a conscience we're talking about. I'm building a great case against him. Now my team just has to find him and make the arrest."

"And keep anyone else who can testify against him alive," Jessie added.

Conor scrubbed his hand down his stubbled jaw and sat back. "Yeah. That, too."

Garrett kept her hand snugged in his and continued the difficult conversation. "There's no sign of Olivera or his sidekick, Kevie?" None of them laughed at the juvenile nickname for a man who was undoubtedly an enforcer for Olivera.

"Kevin Coltrane." The man had done his research. "He and Kai are cousins. He runs a custom auto shop. That could explain the light-up car you caught on tape out here, and why we're having trouble pinning Olivera to any one vehicle. He and his crew keep changing them. Coltrane and Olivera grew up in the same neighborhood, and they went into the same line of business."

"Dealing drugs?" Jessie asked.

"Kai's the brain, and Kevie's the muscle." Conor took another drink and flashed her a wry smile. "Did his girlfriend really call him that?"

"'Fraid so. He didn't like it."

"I bet not. Women are property to men like that. Not people. The only reason he'd tolerate a nickname he didn't like was if he had to put up with her for some reason."

Garrett could guess the reason. "Like he was using her to get to Jessie. He gets a general location of where the kids were last seen, then he picks up a local and uses her to find out what the people around here know."

Jessie frowned. "You think he figured out that the children are here? Do we need to move them?"

Conor answered for him. "I don't think so. If they are watching the place, then any sudden change, like you and Jessie leaving, would only put them on alert."

Garrett agreed.

"I just wanted to come out and tell you about Swiegert in person. Let you two decide how to break the news to Nate and Abby."

"Thanks, Conor." Jessie stared down into her coffee, deep in thought about something.

The detective polished off his beer and stood. "I wish you were on my team for real, Caldwell. I appreciate your experience and wisdom. Your patience, too, for the most part," he teased, referring to the day Garrett had punched the barn. "I'm not worried about you running the protection detail here."

"Just keep me in the loop on anything else you find out."

"Will do."

The two men shook hands before Garrett walked Detective Wildman to the door and watched him dash out into the rain to slide inside his car. He drove off with a friendly wave and Garrett locked the door behind him.

When he turned, Jessie slid her arms around his waist and walked into his chest. He folded his arms around her and hugged her tight. "Talk to me, hon."

She rested her head against his neck where it met his shoulder. "I don't know how much more of this I can take. With John's death, it was a shock. Unexpected. It was scary and tragic, but I never suspected it was coming. This time I know Olivera is after Nate and Abby—sneaking onto my property, sending his goons to spy on us and intimidate me. I feel like death is coming, and all I can do is wait for it to arrive. Kai Olivera and his greed and vengeance are hunting us, circling closer. I know he's out there somewhere, watching, waiting to attack. But dreading that moment is wearing me down. What if I get careless or fall asleep at the wrong time? What if I don't see him until it's too late? Someone I care about is still going to be hurt or die." She shrugged and burrowed closer. "It's still going to be violent and tragic. Only I'm living with that knowledge for days on end. The stress is wearing a hole in my stomach. What if I fail those children?"

"Not going to happen."

"How do you know that?"

"Because I know you." He leaned back against her arms to frame her face between his hands. "You are strong and resourceful, and more devoted to the things you care about than anyone I've ever met." Her concerns reminded him a little bit of his time as a sniper. The waiting and watching for his target to appear was always the hardest part of an assignment. "You never knew Lee Palmer was coming to shoot your husband and you. But you know Kai Olivera is coming. Don't let that knowledge get stuck in your head and paralyze you. Use it to your advantage. Prepare. Have a plan of attack. You know the layout of this place better than anyone. You know what weapons you can improvise. And you have me."

She reached up to wind her fingers around his wrists. "I don't want you to get hurt, either. I think about that every day, too."

"I'm doing everything I can to be prepared, too," he assured her. "I'm training the kids to do the same. This time you won't be caught off guard. Try to see the hope in that. This time you'll be able to fight back."

She shook her head. "What if I'm not strong enough?"

"You, fierce Mama Dog, are stronger than you know. This is your fortress to command. You have a twelve-dog alarm system. Security cameras. Me. Heaven help Olivera if he puts his hands on you or those children."

"Miss Eloise?"

Jessica didn't like the concern she heard in Garrett's voice that evening as he answered a frantic phone call from her elderly neighbor.

She looked up from where she was setting up a dredging station to make fried chicken for dinner to meet Garrett's worried gaze. "Have you called an ambulance yet?" He interrupted whatever argument the old woman was giving. "Then you need to hang up and call 9-1-1. I think it'd be for the best. It's better to get her checked out now than to have to drive her to the emergency room later." He got up from the table where he was helping Nate with some math work and strode out of the kitchen. "No, ma'am. I'm working another job. I'm not here for your beck and call. I'll send one of my officers to your place."

"Nate. Go ahead and put away your schoolwork. Get your sister and clean up. She can help you set the table." Jessica washed her hands and grabbed a dish towel to follow Garrett into the living room.

"Is everything okay?" Nate asked solemnly, following her. He'd taken the news of his father's death better than she'd expected. There had been a few tears, but no angry outburst. But he'd been unusually subdued throughout the rest of the day. Abby, on the other hand, had been nearly inconsolable in her grief. Pretty much the only family she'd ever known, other than Nate, was gone. It had taken a visit with Penny's puppies and an exhausted nap in her arms for the little girl to be able to function again.

Jessica wouldn't lie to the boy, but she could

ease any concerns he had. "It sounds like Garrett has a call about work. He may have to go take care of someone else who needs him for a while. But he'll be back. In the meantime, Officer Fox is here with us."

"Down by the end of the driveway," Nate pointed out. "It could take forever for him to get here if we need help."

"It's not that far. You'll be okay, bud." Garrett ended the call and ruffled his fingers through Nate's hair. "Go do what Jessie asked you to. I need to talk to her for a minute."

"You'll come back, right?" Nate seemed reluctant to let Garrett go.

Garrett reached out to grip Nate's shoulder. "I'm not leaving you unprotected. Jessie can handle things here for a few minutes, and I'll be right next door. Do you remember us talking about the grandma lady who lives there?" The boy nodded. "She had…an accident at her house, and I need to go over there and make sure she's okay. I'll come back just as soon as I know she's got the help she needs. I need you to stay inside the house and do whatever Jessie tells you to do."

"Wash your hands and set the table with your sister," she reminded him.

Nate turned his sad blue eyes up to her. "You won't leave us?"

Her heart twisting at the anxious request, Jessica borrowed the surprisingly apt and lovely compliment Garrett had paid her last night. "I'm the Mama Dog around this place, aren't I? Of course, I'm staying."

It was reassurance enough for Nate. He nodded, then charged up the stairs. "Ab-by!"

"Inside voice," Garrett called after him. He stuck his finger in his ear and smirked at Jessica. "I swear that boy has no volume control."

Right. Loud, rambunctious boy. Small problem in the grand scheme of things.

"Miss Eloise had an accident?" She followed Garrett to the hall tree, where he grabbed his hat. "Is she all right?"

The night sky lit up through the windows. A loud boom of thunder rattled the panes soon after. Shadow woofed from his bed by the back door. Dr. Cooper-Burke had warned that he might be more sensitive to storms since developing his idiopathic epilepsy. Jessica felt the hair on her arms stand on end in response to the electricity in the air.

"Easy." She felt Garrett's hand on her shoulder and automatically took a calming breath. She watched his chest expand and contract beneath the protective vest he wore and took two more breaths along with him. "You afraid of storms?"

"No." She reached up to clasp his wrist, to feel his warmth and strength and know that she was okay. "Things just seem a little tense around here tonight."

"Do I need to reassure you that I'm coming back, too?"

She shook her head. "I'm not nine years old. I know duty calls. What happened to Miss Eloise?"

His face turned grim. "Actually, she was calling about Isla. Apparently, the new boyfriend assaulted her and stole the money she had in her purse."

"*Kevie* hit her? What a surprise." Jessica felt sorry for the young woman who seemed so desperate to have a man in her life that she'd settle for one who abused her. "Probably his way of breaking up with her now that he doesn't need her help to spy on the neighbors."

"I'm going to call in an officer to take over the call, but I want to head over there to make sure the premises are clear and that Kevin Coltrane isn't in the area again."

Thunder rattled the windows again as the rain poured down. "Are you sure you want to go out in this? Do you have a jacket you can put on?"

He chuckled. "Out in my truck."

"That won't do you much good. You'll get soaked."

"Hey, you survived a trip outside to batten down the kennels and close up the barn to make sure the dogs were all okay."

"That was in daylight. It's dark as pitch out there." She shivered as another bolt of lightning streaked across the sky. "Except when it does that."

He brushed his fingers over the edge of her hair and cupped the side of her jaw and neck. "I'll be fine. You'll be fine." He leaned in to claim her mouth in a quick kiss. "Besides, if I get soaked to the skin, you'll have to strip off all my clothes and dry me off with a towel."

"You're incorrigible, old man." She mimicked his hold on her face and cupped the side of his jaw to exchange another kiss. "Go. Let me know how Isla's doing, and don't let Miss Eloise set the two of you up."

He plunked his cap on top of his head and adjusted it into place. "Not gonna happen. I'm already taken."

She caught the door when he opened it, and even with the depth of the porch, she felt the cold rain splashing against her face. "What if this is some kind of ploy to get you away from the house so we're vulnerable here?"

Garrett turned at the edge of the porch and came back to her, grasping her face between his hands and tilting her gaze up to his. "You got this, Mama Dog. You've shown me that you can handle anything." He leaned in to kiss her again, quickly, but much more thoroughly. Then he was backing away. "Plus, I'll be back. Believe that. I will always come back to you."

She caught a brief flash of light as he opened the door to his truck. Then his headlights came on and he turned in her driveway to disappear into the night.

"He's coming back," she whispered. Then she felt Shadow's warm body pressed against her side. He must have sensed her anxiety all the way out here. "Right, boy?" She stroked her fingers through his dampening hair. "He's coming back really soon?"

Maybe it was the storm. Maybe his sharp ears had heard something that she could not. Maybe it was only something a dog could sense. But for the first time since she'd begun to train him, Shadow whimpered beside her.

Chapter Eleven

Jessica knew the exact moment her world changed again.

Her phone pinged in her pocket.

She pulled it out and waited for a few seconds for Officer Fox or Garrett himself to call and let her know that someone she knew had turned into her driveway.

She waited.

And waited.

Her pulse rate kicked up a notch.

No one was calling.

"Shadow?" She called the dog to her side, and he answered immediately. She scratched her fingers around his ears, thinking, thinking.

Oh, hell. Her instincts screamed at her that something was wrong. If she was a dog, she would have barked.

She whirled around to the children who were debating about where to put the silverware around the plates on the table.

"Nate! Abby!" Abby startled and dropped a fork on the floor as she grabbed them both by the hand and pulled them into the living room. "Get upstairs. Run. Lock yourself in the bathroom and get down inside the tub. Don't peek out. Don't go anywhere else."

Okay. Not helping. Calm down.

She inhaled a deep breath and bent so she was closer to their heights, even as she tugged them along to the stairs. "Nate, you are in charge of your sister. Make sure she stays quiet. Make sure she stays hidden." Before Abby's protesting whine fully formed, she gave the little girl an order, too. "You are in charge of your brother. Make sure he does everything I say."

Nate stopped and squeezed her hand. "The bald man's here, isn't he."

"Yes, Nate. I think so. We don't have much time."

"Where's Deputy Caldwell?" he asked, latching on to Abby with his other hand.

"He's coming. He's on his way."

"Can Shadow—?"

"No." She answered a little too harshly. "I need him with me."

"He'll keep you safe, Jessie," the little boy whispered.

Jessica pressed a kiss to both their foreheads whether they liked it or not and pushed them toward the stairs. "Lock yourself in the bathroom. Now."

Abby tugged on her brother's hand. "She said we have to go, Natey. It's my job to make you go. Come on."

Good girl. "Stay completely quiet so no one knows you're there. Don't come out for anyone except Garrett or me. Nate, wait." She pushed her phone into the boy's hand. "Text Garrett and tell him we need him. No talking. Just text."

"I thought you said he was coming."

"He is." She hoped. "Tell him to hurry."

She glanced through the windows beside the front door and saw a weird, rectangular light floating up her driveway. What was that? It was hard to make sense of what she was seeing through all the rain.

"Come with us." Nate tugged on her arm, begging her to hide, too.

"No, sweetie." She pulled him to her in a brief hug. "Mama Dog has to take care of business. Lock the door. Hide. Text Garrett. Go!"

The children ran up the stairs. She waited for the sound of the bathroom door closing. Locking.

She ran past the front windows and her stomach dropped down to her toes. "Oh, no. God no."

The weird lights made sense now. They were the underglow lights of the souped-up car she'd captured on her video camera that first night they'd rushed Shadow to the vet and Garrett had stayed with her. She'd bet anything that the two bulky figures she'd seen on camera were Kai Olivera and his big bruiser buddy, Kevin Coltrane.

They were here.

They were here to take Abby and kill Nate. Probably Jessica, too.

Sparing a thought for Officer Fox, she wondered if he'd been called away or if the skull cousins had disabled him somehow. Or something worse.

No time. No time.

Garrett had reminded her that she had time to prep for their arrival, time to formulate a plan of attack. She'd lost a family once before to unspeakable violence.

But she wouldn't lose this odd little family of survivors.

She ran back to the kitchen, searched for those improvised weapons Garrett had mentioned. There were two prime candidates sitting right there on top of the stove. She cranked the heat beneath the cast iron skillet where she was heating up the oil for the fried chicken.

Then she picked up the chopping knife and went back to work cutting the chicken into even smaller pieces.

GARRETT PLACED THE bag of frozen peas over the bruise swelling on Isla Gardner's cheek and called for an ambulance himself.

With both women talking at once, it was hard to make sense of all the details about what had happened. But he could get the gist of their story.

Isla had indeed been smacked around a bit. Besides the mark on her face, she had bruises that fit the span of a large man's hand around her wrist. Even though she tried to defend Kevin Coltrane, Eloise informed him that Olivera's hulking sidekick had been to the house and robbed her, as well. Most interestingly, he'd threatened to hit the octogenarian if she didn't allow him to park his stupid truck at her place.

And Isla said her boyfriend had been insistent that her grandmother call Garrett for help, that it would make *Kevie* happy if the old guy next door answered their call for help. The old guy wouldn't be as big a threat as a younger officer, so she'd agreed. And she really wanted to make *Kevie* happy so he'd come back to her. It was just a ploy to get Garrett away from the house, a plan to leave Jessie and the children unprotected. He seriously doubted Coltrane ever planned to see Isla again, and she should be thanking her lucky stars that he was getting out of her life.

Once Maya Hernandez had arrived to take the official report from the Gardner women, and the EMTs were checking Eloise's blood pressure and Isla's injuries, Garrett drove his truck along the bumpy gravel of Eloise's driveway and turned to follow the rail fence that bordered Jessie's property.

His suspicions paid off when he found the white truck decorated with flames she had described parked to make a quick getaway with its tailgate facing the fence. A quick check of the plate number on his truck's laptop confirmed that it was Kevin Coltrane's truck. He hadn't been interested in Isla Gardner at all, maybe not even in the money he'd stolen from the two women. This was about finding the children and gaining access to the house while bypassing the security camera and guard at the front gate. It might also have something to do with approaching the house from the side where no dogs would detect an intruder. Even Big Rex wouldn't be able to stop them, because he was locked up in the barn due to the storm.

A bolt of lightning lit up the area well enough for Garrett to confirm that the truck was empty.

So, where were Coltrane and Olivera?

Pulling his cap low over his forehead and snapping his jacket all the way up to the neck, Garrett opened his truck door and stepped out into the deluge. He was soaked to the skin almost immediately and gave a brief thought to the teasing remark he'd given Jessie about drying him off. But he was more focused on finding the answer to the mystery of Coltrane's truck. A broken window on a summer cabin, a broken latch on a chicken coop or storage room—those could be attributed to two runaways looking for food to eat and a warm place to sleep at night.

But a truck parked in the back acres of a woman's land she didn't even farm anymore hinted at something much more sinister.

He discovered it when he reached the back of the pickup truck. The newly replaced railing had been torn down again, and the chain links had been cut through on Jessie's side of the fence. The hair on the back of Garrett's neck pricked to attention like it had that day in Afghanistan when he'd spotted the kid with the bomb. Things were about to go really bad very, very quickly.

He pulled out his phone and called Levi Fox.

No answer.

He jogged back to his truck and called the young officer again.

No answer.

"Damn it, Fox, where are you?"

Garrett's next call was to Dispatch, warning them of a possible officer down and requesting backup at K-9 Ranch. He told them to notify Conor Wildman at KCPD, as well.

He debated for about two seconds whether to take the long drive back to the highway, then go next door and turn in the long drive up to Jessie's house—or he could take the same shortcut across her land the way he suspected Coltrane had.

He grabbed his rifle off the rack in the back of his truck cab, leaped the fence, and ran.

"DROP THE KNIFE."

With the fury of the storm subsiding to a

steady fall of rain, Jessica had no problem hearing that the house was quiet. The children had done exactly as she asked and weren't making a sound.

Stay hidden. Stay safe.

She'd also heard the shatter of breaking glass at her back door, even the lock turning as the intruder reached inside to unlock the door. Shadow barked and raced to the door, but she called him back to her side. Thankfully, he obeyed.

She was down to diced chicken bites now, and still she kept cutting.

Jessica glanced over to see a gun pointed at her. Shadow growled and snapped at the armed man, desperately fighting his basic instinct to go after the intruder. But she was too good, Shadow was too smart, and Kevin Coltrane would never know what hit him by the time they were done with him.

"I said, put down the knife, lady."

She eyed the oil shimmering, rippling in the heavy skillet. "Hello, *Kevie*."

"I don't like to be called that."

Shadow snarled and she knew he was moving closer. "Why not? Are you going to manhandle me the way you did Isla? What do you want with me?"

"The knife."

The gun barrel pressed against the side of her neck was wet with rain and felt ice cold.

Her breath hitched in her chest. Shadow's ears lay down flat on his head.

She felt her pulse beat against the cold steel of that gun.

"I ain't playin', lady."

"Okay. Okay." Not wanting to test the limits of the Olivera enforcer too hard, she dutifully set the knife down on top of the counter, right next to a pair of oven mitts. "There. I'm not armed anymore. Who brings a knife to a gunfight, anyway, right?"

Her laugh sounded as forced as it felt.

"Shut up, already."

He smacked the butt of the gun against her temple and she tumbled on top of the raw chicken on the counter, her skull throbbing and her vision spinning. The blow must have split her skin because blood was dripping into her right eye.

"You idiot. I need her conscious. I'll make her tell me where they are if they're not here."

"She wouldn't drop the knife," the big man protested. "You want her to stab me with it?"

"Find those kids. Now!"

How had she missed the second man walking in behind Kevie? Jessica pushed herself upright, feeling nauseous as a pair of skull tattoos swam through her vision. Olivera himself. Kai Olivera.

But the other man, Kevin Coltrane, was walking away, doing the boss's bidding.

No, no, no! He was leaving the kitchen. Moving closer to Nate and Abby.

The time was now or never.

"Shadow, now!" The dog lunged at the second man's outstretched hand, clamping down with enough force to break the skin and force the gun he held from his hand.

"Damn mutt! Kevin!"

A gunshot rang out and Shadow yelped. "Shadow!" She foolishly charged after Olivera as he shook himself free of the dog's bite and kicked him toward the door. The second yelp tore through her heart. "Don't you hurt my dog!"

"I got the door." *Kevie* had circled around the island. Good. Forget the kids upstairs.

The two men wrestled the snarling, whining dog out into the rain and slammed the door shut behind him. While she mourned whatever had been done to Shadow, she sent up a prayer of thanks that he'd been able to defend her.

Two weapons gone. Two to go.

She hoped Nate had gotten hold of Garrett. She'd defend those children to her last breath, but she wouldn't last long against two armed men.

With her aim severely hampered by her spinning equilibrium, she picked up the hot mitts and grabbed the skillet.

"What is wrong with you, lady? Siccing your dog on Kai?" The big man grabbed a towel off the counter and tossed it to Olivera to stanch the wounds on his hand.

When he turned back to her, she hurled the hot oil at his face.

He screamed and wiped at the oil dripping down the front of him, burning his hands and losing his gun in the process. With his skin literally burning and peeling off his cheeks, he collapsed to his knees. Jessie swung the skillet again, this time cracking its heavy weight over the top of his head. He dropped like a stone, unconscious.

Shadow barked outside and scratched at the door. She heard the other dogs answering the alarm in the distance.

One down.

She raised her improvised weapon to strike again, but Olivera had disappeared. Then

something hot and sharp and distinctly un-
sanitary sliced across her arm. Blood seeped
up and pooled across her skin. She cried out
in pain and let the pan clatter to the floor.

A heavy hand gripped her upper arm and
spun her around. "I'm tired of playing these
games." He shoved her against the island
and bent her back partway across it. Spittle
sprayed across her face as he held her own
carving knife to her throat. She felt the edge
of the blade prick her skin and knew she
was bleeding again. "The Swiegerts are here
someplace. Tell me where to find them."

"I don't know what you're talking about.
You broke into my home. I'm defending myself."

Another cut. She flinched away from the
burning pain. "You're not a dumb broad. Don't
play dumb with me."

Fine. "I won't tell you."

"Talk, lady. Nate and Abby are mine."

Her back screamed at the angle he forced
her into at the edge of the granite counter.
"They don't belong to you. Their father is
dead."

"Yeah. Because I pumped him so full of
prime product—at my own expense—that
his head damn near exploded."

Was she about to pass out? Had she heard him right? "You killed him?"

"Don't pump me for information, lady. I'm gonna cut your tongue out, and you won't be able to tell anybody anything." He pressed his forearm against her windpipe. If she didn't die of blood loss, he could strangle her to death. "Where are they?"

"I don't know."

"That's a load of crap. You got about fifteen seconds, and your boyfriend will be coming home to a dead body."

She was getting light-headed. Losing blood. Not breathing right.

She needed more time for backup to arrive. Garrett would save them. He'd promised. "They're not here."

"Where!"

Jessica saw the red laser dot spotting Kai Olivera's temple. But he did not.

"Tell me!"

Jessica turned her head and glass shattered as Olivera's brain splattered across her new kitchen cabinet.

With one last burst of strength, she shoved him off her and collapsed. She was crawling between bodies, blood and an oil slick when the door swung open again and Shadow burst in, with Garrett right behind him.

"Jessie? Jessie!"

Shadow came straight to her and licked her face. Jessica plopped back on her bottom and pulled the sopping wet dog onto her lap. "Did he shoot you, baby? Where are you hurt? You saved Mama. Good boy. Good boy."

"Jessie?" Garrett pointed the barrel of his sniper rifle at Olivera, then kicked his body away from her. "You're bleeding. How bad are you hurt?" Next, he trained the rifle on *Kevie's* prone body. When there was no reaction, he knelt beside the bearded bully and felt for a pulse. Apparently, he could still detect one because he sat back to pull out his handcuffs and locked them around the big man's wrists. Then he turned off the burner on the stove and crouched in front of her. His hand gently caressed her cheek. "Jessie, honey, you need to talk to me." He snatched a towel from the countertop and pressed it against the wound at her temple.

She winced at the pressure on the open wound, then wrapped her fingers around his wrist to stop his frantic movements. "I'm okay. Garrett, I'm okay. Probably need to see an ER. Shadow, too. But I'm okay." She found those loving green eyes narrowed with concern. Her sweet, brave, warrior man. Oh, how she loved him. She cupped his cold, wet cheek. "Get the kids. Upstairs bathroom. They were good as gold, did exactly what I asked." He hesitated. "Go. I told them not to come out for anyone but you or me. And I can't... I can't do that right now."

"Jessie, you're scaring me."

"Go. Make sure they're all right. I need to rest a minute. Shadow will stay with me. Right, boy?"

He scrubbed his hand over the dog's head. "Take good care of her, pal. I need her."

Then he was on his feet. He slipped the rifle over his shoulder and charged the stairs. "Nate! Abby!"

She heard a scramble of footsteps and shouts of "Garrett!"

When she saw them again, he carried a child in each arm and turned toward the kitchen.

"No!" she shouted, stopping him in his tracks. She glanced at the blood and death around her and knew some of it was on her. "Don't let them back here. I don't want them to see any of this."

"Jessie?" Abby called to her.

"I'm okay, baby," she answered, praying her shaky voice didn't worry the little girl. "Go with Garrett."

Lights were flashing through the windows now. Backup was here. The cavalry had arrived.

The front door closed. Jessie leaned back against the counter and closed her eyes, inhaling the pungent, normal, wonderful scent of wet dog and thanking God, the spirits of John and her baby, and any other powers that be that she was alive. Nate and Abby were alive. The threat was over.

When she opened her eyes again, Garrett was kneeling beside her. He picked her up in his arms, dog and all, and carried her out to the front porch and down the steps to the waiting ambulance. He set her on the gurney and the EMTs quickly moved to load her inside to get her out of the rain.

Abby was there, bundled in a silver reflective blanket. She climbed onto the gurney and snuggled beneath Jessie's unblemished arm to rest her head against Jessie's breast. Nate eyed her shyly, then climbed up on the other side, his hand immediately going to Shadow's head to pet him.

The EMTs were already tearing open sterile bandages and pressing them against the cuts on her arm and neck. One shined a flashlight in her face, checking for pupil reaction, then asked her to follow his finger with her eyes. "Slight concussion. She'll need some stitches."

Garrett was the last one to climb on board the crowded ambulance several minutes later. "Conor's here. He'll handle the crime scene. We can answer questions and fill out reports later. Officer Fox had his head bashed in, but he's going to make it. He's on another ambulance. I talked to Hugo. He and Soren will come over and check on all the dogs. I called Hazel Cooper-Burke. She'll meet us at the hospital to take care of Shadow." He reached back to pull the doors shut. "Let's go."

"Sir, that dog can't come—"

"That dog is part of this family," Garrett snapped. "We all go."

Surrendering to his stubborn determination to keep them all together—if not to the badge of authority he wore—the EMT passed the word up that they were ready to leave.

As the ambulance headed down her long driveway, Garrett took a seat on the other side of Abby, holding the little girl between them, reaching over to tag his hand at the

nape of Jessica's neck and feather his fingers
into her hair at the root of her braid. When
the EMTs took a break in tending to her injuries, he leaned in and captured her lips in
a sweet, lingering kiss. She cupped the side
of his jaw and held on, absorbing every bit of
love he had to give her. Garrett Caldwell was
warmth. He was strength. He was her future.

"I thought I was going to lose you." He carefully found a spot to rest his forehead against
hers.

"You're not going to lose me, Garrett," she
vowed. "Ever."

In the crowded ambulance, there was only
the two of them. She was injured. She was exhausted. But she was surrounded by love, and
she was happy. Finally. Fully. Happy.

He pulled away slightly, a shade of doubt
clouding his eyes. "What are you saying?"

"It hurts to love again, to take that risk. But
it doesn't hurt to love you."

Abby got squished between them and the
EMTs politely looked away as Jessie leaned
over to kiss the man she loved.

A small throat cleared behind her, and she
looked down into Nate's sweet blue eyes. They
were smiling—almost. "Are you two going
to be kissing every time we leave the room?"

Garrett chuckled. "Possibly. I might kiss Jessie in front of you, too. Are you okay with that?"

Nate gave the proposition some considerable thought. "Yeah. But not all the time, okay? It's kind of gross."

Garrett extended his arm and shook the boy's hand. "I can work with that."

Garrett shifted so that his arm slipped around her back and his hand rested on Nate's shoulder. He dropped a kiss to the top of Abby's head, tying them all together as a family.

The attack had come.

And she'd survived.

Again.

Only this time, with this man, there would be a happily-ever-after.

* * * * *

Keep reading for an excerpt of a new title
from the Intrigue series,
SMOKY MOUNTAINS GRAVEYARD by Lena Diaz

Chapter One

Faith Lancaster wasn't in the Smoky Mountains above Gatlinburg, Tennessee, for the gorgeous spring views, the sparkling waters of Crescent Falls or even hunting for the perfect camera shot of a black bear. Faith was here on this Tuesday morning searching for something else entirely.

A murdered woman's unmarked grave.

If she was right, then she and Asher Whitfield, her partner at the cold case company, Unfinished Business, were about to locate the remains of beautiful bartender and single mother of two, Jasmine Parks.

Five years ago, almost to the day, Jasmine had disappeared after a shift at a bar and grill named The Watering Hole, popular for its scenic views and a man-made waterfall behind it. Instead of returning home that night to her family, she'd become another sad statistic. But months of research had led Faith and Asher to this lonely mountainside, just a twenty-minute drive from the home that Jasmine had shared with her two small children, younger sister and her parents.

Faith shaded her eyes from the sun, trying to get a better look at the newest addition to the crowd of police lined up along the yellow tape, watching the techs operating the ground-penetrating radar machine. Once she realized who'd just arrived, she groaned.

"The vultures found out about our prediction and came for the show," she said.

Beside her, Asher peered over the top of his shades then pushed them higher up on his nose. "Twenty bucks says the short blonde with the microphone ducks beneath the crime scene tape before we even confirm there's a body buried here."

"You know darn well that *short blonde* is Miranda Cummings, the prime-time anchor on Gatlinburg's evening news. Toss in another twenty bucks and I'll take that bet. Only I'll give her less than two minutes."

"Less than two?" He arched a brow. "Deal. No one's that audacious with all these cops around."

No sooner had he finished speaking than the anchor ducked under the yellow tape. She tiptoed across the grass wet with morning dew, heading directly toward the group of hard hats standing by the backhoe.

Faith swore. "She's the kind of blonde who gives the rest of us a bad name. What kind of idiot wears red stilettos to traipse up an incline in soggy grass?"

"The kind who wants to look good on camera when she gets an exclusive."

"Well, that isn't happening. She's about to be arrested." She nodded at two of the uniformed officers hurrying after the reporter and her cameraman.

"Double or nothing?" Asher asked.

"That they won't arrest her?"

"Yep." He glanced down at her, an amused expression on his face.

"Now who's the idiot?" Faith shook her head. "You're on."

The police caught up to the anchorwoman and blocked her advance toward the construction crew. She immediately aimed her mic toward one of the officers while her equally bold cameraman swung his camera around.

"Are you kidding me?" Faith shook her head in disgust. "Are men really that blind and stupid? They're fawning all over her like lovesick puppies instead of doing their jobs."

Asher laughed. "They're fawning all over her because she's a hot blonde in red stilettos. You want to go double or nothing again? I can already picture my delicious steak dinner tonight, at your expense."

"I'm quitting while I'm behind. And she's not *that* attractive."

His grin widened. "If you were a man, you wouldn't say that."

She put her hands on her hips, craning her neck back to meet his gaze, not that she could see his eyes very well behind those dark shades. "You seriously find all that heavy makeup and hairspray appealing?"

"It's not her hair, or her face, that anyone's looking at." He used his hands to make an hourglass motion.

She rolled her eyes and studied the others standing behind the yellow tape like Asher and her. "Where's the police chief? Someone needs to put an end to this nonsense."

"Russo left a few minutes ago. Some kind of emergency at the waterfall on the other side of this mountain. Sounds like a tourist may have gotten too close and went for an unplanned swim."

She winced. "I hope they didn't hit any rocks going over. Maybe they got lucky and didn't get hurt, or drown." She shivered.

"You still don't know how to swim, do you?"

"Since I don't live anywhere near a beach, don't own a pool, and I'm not dumb enough to get near any of the waterfalls in these mountains, it doesn't matter." She motioned to the narrow, winding road about thirty yards away. "Our boss just pulled up, assuming he's the only one around here who can afford that black Audi R8 Spyder. Maybe he'll get the police to escort the press out of here. Goodness knows with his history of helping Gatlinburg PD, Russo's men respect him as much as they do their own chief. Maybe more."

Asher nodded his agreement. "I'm surprised Grayson's here. I thought he was visiting his little girl in Missouri. Now that she knows he's her biological father, he visits as much as he can."

"I'm guessing his wife updated him about the search. He probably felt this was too important to miss."

"You called Willow in on this already?" he asked.

"Last night. She's with the Parks family right now, doing her victim's advocate stuff. It's a good thing, too, because it would have been terrible for them to hear about this search on the news without being prepared first."

"Kudos to you, Faith. I didn't even think about calling her. Then again, I didn't expect the word to leak about what we were doing up here this morning. It's a shame everyone can't be more respectful of the family."

She eyed the line of police again, wondering which one or ones had tipped off the media. None of her coworkers would have blabbed, of that she was certain. "At least Willow can tell the family there's hope again."

"That we'll find Jasmine, sure. But all that will prove is that she didn't accidentally drive her car into a pond or a ravine. I doubt it will give them comfort to have their fears confirmed that she was murdered. And we're not even close to knowing who killed her, or how."

"The how will come at the autopsy."

"Maybe. Maybe not."

She grimaced. "You're probably right. Unless there are broken or damaged bones, we might not get a *cause* of death.

But if she's buried up here, there's no question about *manner* of death. Homicide." She returned their boss's wave.

Asher turned to watch him approach. "As to knowing who's responsible, we're not starting from scratch. We've eliminated a lot of potential suspects."

"You're kidding, right? All we've concluded is that it's unlikely that anyone we've interviewed was involved in her disappearance and alleged murder. We still have to figure out which of the three hundred, thirty-five million strangers in this country killed her. Almost eight billion if we consider that someone from another country could have been here as a tourist and did it."

He crossed his arms. "I'm sticking to my theory that it's someone local, someone who knew the area. Out-of-towners tend to stick to the hiking trails or drive through areas like Cades Cove to get pictures of wildlife. There's nothing over here to attract anyone but locals trying to get away from the tourists."

"I still think it could be a stranger who travels here enough to be comfortable. We shouldn't limit our search to Gatlinburg, or even to Sevier County."

"Tennessee's a big state. How many people does that mean we have to eliminate, Ms. Math Whiz?"

"The only reason you consider me a math whiz is because you got stuck on fractions in third grade."

"I'd say ouch. But I don't consider it an insult that I'm not a math nerd."

"Nah, you're just a nerd."

He laughed, not at all offended. She reluctantly smiled, enjoying their easy banter and the comfort of their close friendship. As handsome and charming as he was, it baffled her that he was still single. She really needed to work at setting him up with someone. He deserved a woman who'd love him and appreciate his humor and kind heart. But for the life of her, she couldn't picture anyone she knew as being the right fit for him.

"Play nice, children." Grayson stopped beside them, impeccable as always in a charcoal-gray suit that probably cost more than Faith's entire wardrobe. "What have I missed?"

Asher gestured toward Faith. "Math genius here was going to tell us how many suspects we have to investigate if we expand our search to all the males in Tennessee."

"No, I was going to tell you *if* we considered all of Tennessee, the total population is about seven million. I have no idea how many of those are male."

Grayson slid his hands in the pockets of his dress pants. "Females account for about fifty-one percent of the population. Statewide, if you focus on males, that's about three and a half million. In Sevier County, potential male suspects number around fifty thousand." He arched a dark brow. "Please tell me I'm not spending thousands of dollars every month funding this investigation only to narrow our suspect pool to fifty thousand."

They both started talking at once, trying to give him an update.

He held up his hands. "I was teasing. If I didn't trust you to work this cold case, you wouldn't be on it. Willow told me you may have figured out where our missing woman is buried. That's far more than we had at the start of this. If the case was easy to solve, someone else would have done it in the past five years and Sevier County wouldn't have asked us to take it on. Give me a rundown on what's happening. I'm guessing the German shepherd is part of a scent dog team. And the construction crew standing around is waiting for guidance on where to dig. The guy pushing what looks like a lawnmower—is that a ground penetrating radar machine?"

Faith nodded. "The shepherd is Libby. She is indeed a scent dog, a cadaver dog. Although Lisa, her handler, prefers to call her a forensic recovery canine." She pointed at various small clearings. "Lisa shoved venting rods in those areas to help release potential scent trapped under the ground to make detection easier."

"It's been five years," Grayson said. "I wouldn't expect there to be any scent at all."

"Honestly, Asher and I didn't either. But after our investigation brought us here as the most likely dump site, we contacted Lisa and she said there would absolutely be scent. One study showed cadaver dogs detecting a skeleton that had been buried over thirty years. And Lisa swears they can pick up scent fifteen feet deep."

"Impressive, and unexpected. I'm guessing those yellow flags scattered around mark where the dog indicated possible hits. There are quite a few."

"A lot of flags, yes, but Lisa said it amounts to six major groupings. As good as these types of dogs are, they can have false positives. Other decomposing animals and vegetation can interfere with their abilities. And scent is actually pulled up through the root systems of trees, which makes it more difficult to find the true source. There could be a hit in, say, three different areas. But the decomposition actually originated from only one spot. Thus, the need for the ground penetrating radar. Lisa recommended it, to limit the dig sites. Asher called around and found a company already in the area." She motioned to Asher. "Where'd you say they were?"

"A cemetery near Pigeon Forge. The GPR company is ensuring that an empty part of the graveyard doesn't have any old unmarked graves before a new mausoleum is erected. Originally, I was going to ask a local utility company to bring over their GPR equipment. But what I found online is that it's more effective if the operator has experience locating the specific type of item you're searching for. Kind of like reading an X-ray or an ultrasound. The guys from the cemetery know how to recognize potential remains because they tested their equipment on known graves first. To find the unknown, you start with the known."

"Bottom line it for me," Grayson said.

Asher motioned to the guys wearing hard hats. "As soon as the radar team tells us which of the flagged sites has the most potential, the backhoe will start digging."

"How soon do we think that will happen?"

"Everybody stay back," one of the construction workers called out as another climbed into the cab of the backhoe.

"Guess that's our answer," Faith said.

Lisa and her canine jogged over and ducked under the yellow tape to stand beside Faith. Asher held up the tape for the GPR team as they pushed their equipment out of the way. The anchorwoman and her cameraman were finally escorted behind the tape as well.

Thankfully, they were a good distance away—not for lack of trying. The blonde kept pointing in their direction, apparently arguing that she wanted to stand beside them. No doubt she wanted to interview the radar people or maybe the canine handler. But Lisa had asked the police earlier to keep people away from her dog. By default, Faith and the small group she was with were safe from the reporter's questions.

For now at least.

Their boss formally introduced himself as Grayson Prescott to the others, thanking them for the work they were doing for his company. And also on behalf of the family of the missing woman.

"How confident are you that we'll find human remains

in one of the flagged areas?" Grayson asked the lead radar operator.

"Hard to say. We didn't check all of the sites since the sediment layers in those first two areas seem so promising. They show signs of having been disturbed at some point in the past."

"Like someone digging?"

He nodded. "There's something down there that caused distinctive shaded areas on the radar. But false positives happen. It's not an exact science."

"Understood."

The backhoe started up, its loud engine ending any chance of further conversation.

The hoe slowly and surprisingly carefully for such a big piece of equipment began to scrape back the layers of earth in the first of the two areas. Ten minutes later, the men standing near the growing hole waved at the operator, telling him to stop. They spoke for a moment then loud beeps sounded as the equipment backed up and moved to another spot to begin digging.

Faith sighed in disappointment. "Guess hole number one is a bust."

"Not so fast," Asher said. "They're signaling the forensics team."

A few minutes later, one of the techs jogged over to Faith and Asher, nodding with respect at Grayson.

"We've found a human skull. That's why they stopped digging. We'll switch to hand shovels now and sifting screens to preserve any potential trace evidence and make sure we recover as many small bones as possible."

Faith pressed a hand to her chest, grief and excitement warring with each other. She'd been optimistic that their research was right. But it was sad to have it confirmed that Jasmine had indeed been murdered. She'd only been twenty-two years old. It was such a tragedy for her to have lost her life so young, and in what no doubt was a terrifying, likely painful, manner.

"You don't see any hair or clothing to help us confirm that the remains belong to a female?" she asked.

"Not yet, ma'am. An excavation like this will take hours, maybe days, because we'll have to go slowly and carefully. But as soon as the medical examiner can make a determination of gender, the chief will update you. Since the GPR hit on those two sites, we'll check the second one as well. Natural shifts underground because of rain or hard freezes could have moved some of it. We also have to consider that the body might have been dismembered and buried in more than one area."

She winced. "Okay, thanks. Thanks for everything."

He nodded. "Thank *you*, Ms. Lancaster. Mr. Whitfield. All of you at UB. Whether this is Jasmine Parks or not, it's someone who needs to be recovered and brought home to their loved ones. If you hadn't figured out an area to focus on, whoever this person is might have never been found."

He returned to the growing group of techs standing around the makeshift grave. Hand shovels were being passed around and some of the uniformed police were bringing sifting screens up the incline.

"Looks like our work here is done," one of the radar guys said. "We'll load up our equipment and head back to Pigeon Forge."

"Wait." Asher pointed to the backhoe operator, who was excitedly waving his hands at the techs. "I think you should check out all of the other groups of flags too."

Faith stared in shock at what one of the techs was holding up from the second hole.

Another human skull.